The Great Unknowable End

The Great Unknowable End

KATHRYN ORMSBEE

SIMON & SCHUSTER BFYR

NEW YORK   LONDON   TORONTO   SYDNEY   NEW DELHI

SIMON & SCHUSTER BFYR

An imprint of Simon & Schuster Children's Publishing Division
1230 Avenue of the Americas, New York, New York 10020

SIMON & SCHUSTER BFYR is a trademark of Simon & Schuster, Inc.
For information about special discounts for bulk purchases, please contact Simon & Schuster Special Sales at 1-866-506-1949 or business@simonandschuster.com.
The Simon & Schuster Speakers Bureau can bring authors to your live event.
For more information or to book an event, contact the Simon & Schuster Speakers Bureau at 1-866-248-3049 or visit our website at www.simonspeakers.com.
Jacket design by Chloë Foglia
Interior design by Hilary Zarycky
The text for this book was set in Sabon.
Manufactured in the United States of America
First Edition
2 4 6 8 10 9 7 5 3 1
Library of Congress Cataloging-in-Publication Data
Names: Ormsbee, Katie, author.
Title: The great unknowable end / Kathryn Ormsbee.
Description: First edition. | New York : Simon & Schuster Books for Young Readers, [2019] | Summary: Told in two voices, sixteen-year-old Galliard and seventeen-year-old Stella cross paths and realize they must determine their own futures as strange events occur in Slater, Kansas, and its neighboring commune in 1977.
Identifiers: LCCN 2018012699 (print) | LCCN 2018019264 (eBook) | ISBN 9781534420502 (hardcover) | ISBN 9781534420526 (eBook) |
Subjects: | CYAC: Coming of age—Fiction. | Communal living—Fiction. | Supernatural—Fiction. | Family life—Kansas—Fiction. | Kansas—History—20th century—Fiction.
Classification: LCC PZ7.O637 (eBook) | LCC PZ7.O637 Gre 2019 (print) | DDC [Fic]—dc23
LC record available at https://lccn.loc.gov/2018012699

To Susan and Lindell Ormsbee,
who have always kept me looking toward the stars

And to Rod Serling,
who fearlessly walked the middle ground between
light and shadow

Admirer as I think I am
Of stars that do not give a damn,
I cannot, now I see them, say
I missed one terribly all day.

Were all stars to disappear or die,
I should learn to look at an empty sky
And feel its total dark sublime,
Though this might take me a little time.

—W. H. AUDEN, *"The More Loving One"*

A letter from Craig Mercer, written May 17, 1975

I'm leaving.

    I'm going to Red Sun.

    Sometimes you see too much of the world to want to stay in it.

    So I'm going to Red Sun, and I don't want you to contact me.

Kansas, 1977

1

Galliard

SUNDAY, JULY 31

Mornings at Red Sun begin with prayer to the Life Force.

Bullshit, you're saying. *You don't actually believe in a* Life Force.

I'm telling you, I do.

See, the Life Force can be almost anything. To you it could be God. It could be unseen energy. It could be your girlfriend or your favorite basketball player.

To me it's stars.

Holly.

Hendrix.

Joplin.

Those are my stars.

I see them most nights, shining from the sky. They're up there, three across, and have been ever since their untimely mortal deaths. They look out for me, and I pray to them.

At Red Sun you can pray however you want. It isn't about the how or the who so much as it is about the praying itself. Though the Life Force—the energy that has bound this universe together since its inception—can be different things to different people, what matters is that prayer is a communal act. It's a group dedication that brings together the members of Red Sun. The only rule is that your prayer must ascend (or descend, depending) between the hours of six and eight o'clock in the morning. You can pray wherever you want: in your room or the gardens or out in the cornfields. I like to pray right here in Common House, with one hundred others.

This morning, I'm talking to Holly. He's the guy I go to for confidence and understanding, and I'm going to need a hell of a lot of confidence today.

It's Assignment Day.

The Council is going to tell me where to go, what to do, and who to be. Corn farmer, livestock tender, meal preparer, textile worker—they're all up for grabs. But I don't want any of those shitty positions. There is one spot open for resident artist, and it's going to be mine.

It has to be mine.

I'm begging Buddy Holly, *Let it be mine.*

"Hear me out," I pray. "This is within your jurisdiction. I know you can make it happen. If you do, I'll be set for life. If you don't, I'll disembowel myself. I'm not shitting around—I will. So do me a solid and make me resident artist, and I'll cover your songs till my dying day. Thanks, sir. Much appreciated."

I choose to say my prayers under my breath, though plenty of seven o'clock supplicants talk to their respective versions of the Life Force at conversational volume. Common House is thick with incense and consonants and vowels—prayers sent to God or gods or self or earth or no one in particular. New-

4

comers sometimes complain about the noise, but it's a soothing sound once you get used to it.

I'm really used to it.

Prayer over, I lie on my back, hands behind my head. I breathe in the sweet, tongue-coating incense. I breathe out. I breathe in, lungs expanding to full capacity. I pucker my lips and blow out in a whistle.

Here in Common House, surrounded by all these serious prayers, my tics hardly ever show up. Here I whistle intentionally, blink intentionally, move intentionally.

But then, as always, morning prayer ends, and the day begins.

My friend Phoenix is standing outside Common House, eyes trained on the rising sun. I grin, because this is a sign. Phoenix is just who I need to see; he understands what today means to me.

Phoenix was raised outside the commune. He saw everything the Outside had to offer and found it lacking. He's heard my music, and he says there's nothing that good on the Outside. He says I've got talent.

"Hey," I say, joining him where he stands.

"Big day," Phoenix replies.

I nod, and for a moment we stand in silence, watching members of Red Sun pass by.

"Look at them," he says. "Moving with purpose toward their own tasks, keeping this community strong and well. Everywhere else, it's a mad dash for nothing. People clawing at each other to get the next paycheck, next car, next model." He turns to me, his pale face lit by the sun. "You don't know how lucky you are to have been born here."

"I've got some idea." Then I say, "Better go. Got somewhere important to be."

Phoenix pats my back. "You're ready for this day."

I take this as a benediction from Buddy Holly himself.

There's a hornet in the sitting room. Who knows how he got in, but he's determined to get out through a closed window. He keeps ramming his body against the glass and letting out a pathetic buzz at every failed attempt.

It's making me fucking sad.

Right now my best friend, Archer, is in the chamber with the Council. It's only me and a girl named Bright left waiting for our assignments. My hands are clutched between my knees, and I've sunk my head real low as a sign that I do *not* want to talk. When Saff first showed us to our seats and explained the assignment procedure, I felt confident enough (thanks, Buddy). Then Bright started pestering me with questions.

"You want to be an artist? Will you be disappointed if you don't get it? Farming is good too, though, isn't it? Isn't nature beautiful? Don't you love our land? Six hundred acres, four hundred people, and nothing but love and acceptance."

Bright is new to the commune, which means she's completed the Council's preliminary education course and been approved to live in a newly constructed residential wing of Heather House. Red Sun doesn't turn many people away, and when we do it's because their energy isn't right for the community. Honestly, I don't see how Bright passed the test, because

I for one don't find her energy appealing. She is so damn curious, which a lot of the adults find "encouraging" and "endearing," but no. No, it is not.

Normally, you get your first ten-year assignment when you're sixteen, like me. Since Bright is new, though, she's going through the process with the rest of us first-timers. I hope she gets chicken duty. Not because I wish a decade of egg collecting and shit clearing upon Bright, but because the coops are as far away from Council House as they can possibly be, and once I'm resident artist I will need lots of concentration in order to compose my life-altering ballads. There will be no Bright questions allowed.

When the chamber door opens, I lift my head, and Archer steps out grinning, exultant. He can't say anything—we're not allowed to speak from the time the Council assigns us to the time we leave the building. I know he got good news, though, when he shoots me a wink. I watch him go, distracted, and it takes me a few seconds to realize Saff has said my name.

Saff is the youngest of our three-person Council. Unlike Rod and Opal, she doesn't have gray hair yet. Her hair is black, and it hangs long, past her shoulders, twisted into dreadlocks. She talks so quietly that I usually miss the second and third syllables of everything she says. It gets annoying fast.

"Come in, please, Galliard," she whispers, ushering me before her into the chamber. Then she motions to an empty wooden chair and says, "Sah-suh-sah-muh."

Not actually that. I just can't hear her, because she's gone ahead of me and her words are indistinguishable. I'm pretty sure she's asked me to take a seat, so I do.

She takes her own seat at a long table across from me. Beside her are Opal and Rod. The three of them sit before stacks of papers. Opal, founder of Red Sun, folds her hands and looks me over with a faint smile.

"Good morning, Galliard," she says.

I don't say anything. I'm supposed to keep quiet through all of this, per the Assignment Day training I went through in the spring. I'm suddenly nervous as hell, and my jaw jerks hard to the right—one of my tics.

"You are a treasure to our community," she continues. "It has been a joy and great privilege to watch you grow. Your spirit and mind contribute invaluably to us, and you've cultivated many talents that can be put to use. Our decision was therefore a difficult one."

Inside me, a hundred bells start clanging. My jaw jerks again.

The Council's decision shouldn't have been difficult. They've received my request for resident artist, a spot that was vacated in February when Gregor—a skilled potter—left the commune for Kansas City. I wrote a long essay on my request form about how my talents would benefit Red Sun.

I write my own songs. And instead of performing them on community nights at Common House, as I do now, I could perform them at the Moonglow Café, for outsiders to hear. I'll develop a following, and I'll find someone on the Outside to make a recording of my songs, and those records will sell, and I'll be played on the radio, and soon the entire United States will know about Red Sun, through my music. That's what a resident artist is supposed to do: reach as many outsiders as possible and educate them about our way of life. Because, as Rod reminds us daily, there are plenty of outsiders who don't think we live right. Some people out there, in town, would like nothing more than to kick us off our own property. They claim we worship Satan and sell their teenagers cannabis and partake in drunken orgies. It's a laugh. Outsiders don't know anything.

They *could* know more, though. They could understand our ways and see the path we're on, and they could learn this through my music. That's what I wrote the Council.

You see now? It doesn't make sense, what Opal's saying about my assignment being a difficult decision.

What's difficult about it?

"Galliard." It's Rod talking now. "We consider every assignment request with great care and attention. We don't take lightly the fact that we are determining your future for the next ten years. We hope you know that. We appreciate your enthusiasm, but we've decided on another candidate for our resident artist."

I follow the rules. I don't speak.

I scream on the inside.

And I tic again, my jaw moving forcefully to one side.

"You didn't mark a second preference," says Saff in her way-too-soft voice. "However, we've chosen an assignment we hope you will find rewarding. We're placing you in the Moonglow kitchen. You're familiar with the job through your pre-assignment and have proved to be an asset there. And you can go on working with J. J. and Archer."

"Archer is a good friend of yours, Galliard, isn't he?" asks Rod.

"Yeah."

Well. Looks like I broke the no-talking rule. Might as well break it some more.

"Sorry," I say. "Who . . . did you choose for resident artist? If it wasn't me, then who?"

This is a no-no, and I know it, and the Council does too. The only thing worse than talking during the assignment process is questioning the Council's decision. But hey, I'm mad. Who cares about rules right now?

Saff tugs on one of her dreads, then another. She's not making eye contact with me. Opal isn't smiling anymore; she's gone solemn, and she and Rod are sharing a look.

In the end, Rod actually answers my rule-breaking question.

"We've chosen Phoenix for the position. You may be aware that he has quite the skill as a painter. He shared a very impressive portfolio. We've already commissioned a half-dozen paintings depicting scenes of life at Red Sun. We mean to display and sell them at the café."

Sirens set off inside my brain, joining the screaming and bell-clanging. They wail in big, sonic spirals, and they're so loud I can barely hear what I say next.

"Phoenix, as in Phoenix from town. Showed up here two years ago Phoenix. That Phoenix?"

My friend Phoenix. The Phoenix who patted my back an hour ago. That *Phoenix?*

"To my knowledge, there is only one Phoenix in Red Sun," says Rod. "You didn't know he'd made a special reassignment petition?"

"No. I absolutely did not."

Rod and Opal share another look. I'm unbearably uncomfortable, so of course another one of my tics kicks in. I clear my throat, loud and low. Only Saff looks startled. She fidgets with another one of her dreads.

"Galliard," says Opal, standing, "you must trust our judgment on this. We appreciate your many contributions to the commune, and we're certain you will continue to enliven our spirits with your music. But we feel this assignment is best."

I clear my throat.

I'm red in the face, and my hands are dripping sweat. I need to get out, out, *out* of here. So I nod and nod, and I stand up, and the rest of the Council stands up, and we're all standing here, facing each other, and my brain screams, *I hate this*, and my heart screams, *Phoenix is a traitor*, but my lips stay closed. I don't talk again. I just clear my damn throat.

2

Stella

We pass a dead dog on our way home from Ferrell's. I wouldn't have known if Jill hadn't cried out and pressed her finger against the window, screaming for Dad to stop the car.

Dad brakes and shifts the station wagon into reverse until I see it: a border collie lying motionless on the side of the road.

Blood encircles its head, forming a crimson halo and testament to a grisly end. Despite that, the collie looks peaceful, as though it's merely lain down on its side to nap in the Sunday sun. Its eyes are closed. Its whiskers quiver in the morning breeze.

My father turns to me, where I sit in the back seat with my little sister, and says, "I don't want her seeing this."

Jill stares at me with big eyes. This is the worst thing for Dad to say, because of course now Jill *must* see this. She struggles against me with rabid energy as I tug at her shoulder and tell her to sit back, attempting to block her view. Jill is nine years old, the baby of our family, and she often acts the part.

My father gets out of the car, approaches the dog, and crouches. It remains motionless—no rise and fall of its glossy black side. Cautiously, Dad feels around the body and inspects the dark stain of blood on the asphalt. Then he shakes his head. He stands, squares his shoulders, and looks around. He's searching for a house with a car in its driveway—a house whose family isn't at church. His gaze catches above my head, on the opposite side of the street. He motions for me and Jill to stay put, and we watch from the car as our father jogs toward a green-shuttered brick ranch. Number twenty-two, says the matching green mailbox.

Twenty-Two Cedar Street.

I look at the dog again. I raise a hand to my mouth.

No, I think. *That's not possible.*

Jill is crying. She's sniffing loudly and about to wipe her nose against her shirtsleeve. I catch her arm before she can and pull it taut, shaking my head.

I draw her into a side hug, which she doesn't fight. Then I press a kiss to her thin, dirty-blond hair and say, "It's fine, Jillie. Things like this happen."

And they do; that's true. Only it's terrible timing. Jill woke this morning to find that her goldfish, Velma, had died during the night. She shook me awake and dragged me to the fishbowl in her room, where an orange, bloated body was floating atop the water.

"We're going to hold a funeral," I told her. "In the bathroom."

Her eyes narrowed. "You mean you're gonna flush her?"

(Jill is the baby, but she's not stupid.)

"It'll be a good flushing," I said. "We'll say nice things. And it's Sunday, which is the perfect time for a funeral because it's God's day, which means he's closer to Earth now than any other day of the week."

I knew this wasn't exactly in keeping with Baptist teaching—we Mercers used to be Baptists—but the words were coming out before I could stop them, and they sounded nice. In any event, they pacified Jill, and we proceeded to flush Velma with pomp and circumstance. She received kind words, a prayer, and a firm press of the commode handle. All this before Dad woke up.

I was proud of myself for handling the situation as well as any parent would. As well as my mother would have if she were alive. I was grateful, too, that Jill hadn't made a big deal about it afterward or been mopey in the car. I assumed we could move past the incident with very little to-do.

Only now here is this poor dead dog—a dog I recognize but am telling myself I do not.

My father is talking to a woman on the front doorstep of the green-shuttered house. She is clutching a terrycloth bathrobe at the stomach, and she is shaking her head. Dad points back our way, at the dog. The woman's head continues to shake. Then she shuts the door. Dad remains on the porch a moment longer before heading back to us. Once he is in the driver's seat, he does not start the engine. I see the crease of his forehead in the rearview mirror.

"Dad?" I say.

"She said she's never seen a collie around here. Far as she knows, no one on the block owns the dog."

"He must've got loose and run here from someplace else," says Jill, who has stopped her sniffling. She pushes her bare feet into the back of Dad's seat, which is something he hates but does not comment on now. He is staring ahead, through the windshield, lost in thought.

The car is silent, though not entirely. I hear something outside. It's the sound of a dog howling. Then another joins in, higher pitched, yipping frantically.

"She said her own dog's been acting off this morning," Dad tells us, somewhat vacantly. "Been nervous, hiding away. Some change in the weather, she thinks. Said maybe the collie got spooked and ran from his home; that's how he got himself hit." After a moment more of dog cries, he adds, "She's going to call animal control."

"Is that the best thing to do?" I ask.

"Well, hon, I don't know what else."

I don't know what else either. Only it seems wrong. I do not want this dog to be carried off to an unmarked grave by indifferent hands.

"We could make posters," suggests Jill. "We could put them around the neighborhood, so the family can know what happened."

My father says nothing.

I look out the window again. I don't know why. I suppose I am hoping that the dog will change its breed and its familiar, lifeless face. When I look, though, nothing has changed, and I feel I could cry harder and longer than even Jill.

"Dad?" I say. "Doesn't it—"

"I know."

"That's not possible, is it?"

"Hon, I really can't say."

"What?" asks Jill, aware that she's being left out of an adult conversation—as often happens in our three-person family. "What is it?"

Neither of us tells Jill what it is. We don't say that this dead dog looks exactly like Major, the collie that belonged to our former neighbors, the Metcalfes. Neither of us mentions that this dog brings back memories of a bad summer and of a closed-casket funeral and of Craig—our Craig. Dad just tells Jill to put her feet down, and, once she does, he starts the car and drives the remaining half mile to our house.

We Mercers keep to ourselves. We do not go to church as our neighbors do. We do not speak to our neighbors, and they do not speak to us. They whisper about us, though. I know, because I hear them every night at the Dreamlight, where I work. They whisper about how the moon drove my mother to madness and my brother joined a cult of weed-smoking hippies and how I never accompany young men to Slater football games the way normal seventeen-year-old girls ought to. They don't think I can hear them through the plexiglass of the concessions hut. They're wrong.

It wasn't always this way. Before my mother died, we attended First Baptist Church every Sunday morning and most Wednesday nights. We brought casseroles to neighborhood barbecues, and we had houseguests and parties. I had friends then—Linda and Brian and Dennis and Marci. That last summer my mother was alive, the five of us roamed Slater like wild animals. We played Marco Polo in the cornfields and spat seeds off Brian's father's pickup. On rainy days, Linda and Marci and I would play dress-up with a trunk full of Linda's mother's old costumes from her time as a professional dancer with the Kansas City Ballet. I always wore the emerald tiara, which took at least eight bobby pins to secure, and I would grant wishes to Linda and Marci with my magic wand—an old green spatula that had warped in the heat of the dishwasher.

That was life before.

This is life after:

My father works full-time as a janitor. He cleans Slater's schools, its library, and the courthouse. He also cleans Slater Creek Generating Station, the nuclear power plant outside our town that began operations two years ago.

I used to work part-time at Vine Street Salon and at Dreamlight Drive-In Theatre. Since school ended, I've been working full-time at the salon *and* part-time at the Dreamlight, which means I've begun to make a decent income. I don't intend to move out and buy my own place, though. That would defeat my purpose for staying here, which is to look after Jill.

For Jill's last birthday, I gave her the Nancy Drew book *The Sky Phantom*, because she loves mysteries. I also bought her a new pair of Keds, because she is growing too fast and Dad doesn't notice these things. He doesn't notice, either, that Jill has begun to steal my lipstick and wear it to school. I know he won't notice when she'll need a training bra. He won't notice when she comes home from school with bloodied underwear, in need of a tampon and a hug and a comfortable chat about what is happening to her body. He won't notice with Jill because he didn't notice with me.

I don't blame my father for this. He sleeps most of the

day, and he works at night when Jill and I are at home and need him most. When we can spend time together, we spend it well. On Sunday mornings—like this morning—he takes us to Ferrell's Drive-In and lets us order a malt *and* a Coney dog *and* a large order of tater tots. We eat and slurp together in the station wagon with the windows rolled down and the radio tuned to 580 AM, a local station out of Kansas City that plays the latest hits. When we are through, we wipe our grease-coated fingers on napkins, toss our trash, and drive home.

We are loners, but we're loners together.

When we arrive home, Jill races to the house and uses her latchkey rather than wait for my father to open the door.

Dad and I take our time. Usually, he makes a show of how much his belly has bloated with the food from Ferrell's. He pats it as though he's a Santa-in-training and says, "I need to lay off," and I will only smirk at him because he never does.

Today he makes no jokes. We're silent on our way to the house. We're thinking of the same thing, I know.

"Stella," he says, once we've reached the porch. "It couldn't have been him. That was over two years ago."

"Dogs come back, though, don't they? They come back to their homes."

"Two years later? That's not likely. It only looked like Major, that's all."

"I guess so."

Only I am not convinced, and I don't think my father is either.

• • •

Jill and I always watch the evening news together while eating our dinner, and Sundays are an especially big deal because that's when Cassie Mackin reports on *NBC's Sunday Night News*. Jill loves Cassie Mackin. I do too. In my opinion, she is second only to Barbara Walters.

I place our TV-dinner trays in the oven, side by side, thirty minutes before the news begins. On Sunday nights, we eat the macaroni-and-cheese dinner, which probably should not be considered a real meal. Then again, nothing premade in a tinfoil tray should be considered a real meal. I am hopeless in the kitchen, though, and Dad hardly has the time to eat, let alone cook, so it is frozen trays of macaroni, corn, and peas for the Mercer family.

Jill sets up our plastic eating stands in the den, and by the time I arrive with our meals and two full glasses of milk, we are primed and ready. I switch on the television as the *Sunday Night News* theme begins. Jill blows on a forkful of macaroni, her eyes bugged and glued to the screen.

Sometimes I wonder if Jill should be seeing and hearing everything on the news. Tonight, for instance, Cassie Mackin reports on how two more people were shot in New York City by the killer who calls himself Son of Sam. His killings have been a regular report since last summer, but every time they're mentioned I worry about how wide Jill's eyes grow and how still she becomes.

"Hey," I say, attempting to draw her attention from the screen. "They'll catch him."

Jill looks at me, affronted. "Of course they will. They'd just better hurry up."

When the news is over, we throw away our trays and return to the sofa. I sit on one side, Jill on the other. She is rereading a Nancy Drew book from the library. I am reading *The Cosmic Connection* by Carl Sagan, which is about all sorts of things, including the probability of extraterrestrial intelligence.

An hour passes, and my father comes through the den on his way to work. He kisses my head, then Jill's, and leaves for the power plant, which is first on his janitorial rounds. Then, at eight o' clock, it's my turn to leave for the Dreamlight.

"Keep the doors locked," I tell Jill, as is my nightly custom. "Call me at the hut if something's wrong."

"I know, I *know*."

"Nine o'clock." I point a warning finger. "I'll *know* if you stayed up later."

Jill nods distractedly, lost again in *The Clue of the Velvet Mask*.

I leave through the garage, wheeling my road bike out. Something is off with the chain, and it makes an insistent *tick-tick-tick* as I ride the bike out of the driveway. I'll have to figure out how to fix it later.

It's windy out—so windy that I wobble once when I mount my bike, overcorrecting for the force of the breeze. I push up to a coast, then pedal faster down Oak Street. *Tick-tick-tick-tick*. Our neighbor Mr. Metz is out mowing his lawn. I remember attending one of his cookouts when I was Jill's age. He does not wave at me. I do not wave at him.

From Oak Street, I take Elm, then turn onto Vine—Slater's main drag. I pedal away from the shops and streetlights and out to farm country. Vine turns into Eisenhower Road, which is wider and less well kept. There are potholes to avoid, and on either side of me stretches an endless green forest of cornstalks. Dreamlight Drive-In Theatre is nestled in these cornfields, a mile outside the town center.

The sun has begun to set, lowering through a hazy, plum-tinted sky. Soon, the stars will be out. In a moment like this, when it's just me and my bike and the road, I get to thinking about *That Stella*.

In my mind, I like to imagine two different lives for Stella Kay Mercer. At the start, when I was a child, they were the same road. They forked once, when my mother died, and they spread wider still the day Craig left us. One road is *This Stella*. Me. The one who works most hours of her life and who cannot even consider the possibility of college. Then there is *That Stella*. The one who will attend KU and study engineering. The one who might one day help launch a vessel into space. *That Stella* does not have to worry about her little sister or estranged brother or overworked father.

I like to tell myself that in another, parallel universe I am *That Stella*. But in this universe, the one in which I am presently conscious, I have to pay my dues as *This Stella*. I have to work my nightly shift at the Dreamlight and my daily shift at Vine Street Salon. As *This Stella*, I must contend with a finicky bike chain, a potholed road, a mighty wind blowing so hard that I have to squint against it, and even then tears spring up in my stinging eyes. When I pass the town's only billboard, I see that the months-old ad for Slater's Pizza Hut has torn away, one end tattered and whipping wildly about. Around me the cornstalks sway and bend, undulating with ripples caused by unseen pebbles.

I skid my bike to a stop, then slide a hair band off my wrist and work it into my hair, pulling back unruly strands from my face. Once my vision is clear, I start again, pushing into the wind and wondering as I do if Mr. Cavallo will cancel tonight's show. Even if he doesn't, there are bound to be complaints about the wind affecting the screen; that's the risk you run with an outdoor theatre.

There is hardly any traffic on Eisenhower on a Sunday evening, but even so, I keep my bike close to the road's edge. That is why I see it.

At first I think it's a mound of dirt or sod. Then I think perhaps it's rope or a garden hose. Then I am close enough to really see, but even then I do not believe it. I slow my bike.

Tick . . . Tick . . . Tick.

I drop one foot, easing to a stop. I look closer.

They are snakes. They are small and thin and striped in varying shades of green and black. Garters—nothing to be afraid of, under normal circumstances. I've encountered plenty over the years, in my yard.

I've never seen them like this, though. There are at least two dozen of them, and they're not doing the things I would expect from a pile of snakes. There is no writhing or slithering. They are, all of them, perfectly still. I look closer, at the snake nearest my shoe. Its head is tucked into the very center of its coiled body.

Now I see. Now I cannot *un*see. The snake's mouth hangs open, pinkish-purple, fangs exposed. Where its eye should be, there is nothing but a small, bloody crater. My vision blooms wider to reveal that they are all this way—all motionless, all dead, piled onto one another.

My stomach is telling me I need to vomit, but my throat is telling me I cannot. It's cinched up tight, allowing no breath in and no bile out. Blurry white dots swim inside my eyes.

I shake my head. I force a swallow. Then another, and another. I breathe in, fill my lungs.

Move, I instruct my legs. *Pedal on.*

My legs listen. They pedal faster than they've ever pedaled before—a frenzied *tickticktickticktick* the rest of the way to the Dreamlight.

3

Galliard

SUNDAY, JULY 31

I was six years old on the day of the Almost Apocalypse.

It was the first and only time Ruby hugged me. Normally, the commune doesn't stand for that kind of thing: We kids belong to everyone, and biological parents aren't supposed to coddle their offspring. That encourages particular familial bonds, and *particular* familial bonds create division within the *community* familial bond that unifies Red Sun. That day, though, Ruby coddled the hell out of me, holding me close to her damp shirt and clutching my hair in her fingers. I'm sure she meant to be comforting, but since she had never hugged me before, the closeness only freaked me out more. I felt suffocated in her arms, drowning in the smell of sweat and turmeric. I felt her heart beating fast against my ear, a sure sign she was terrified. And I knew that if the adults had a reason to be scared, I absolutely did.

The whole time it was happening, Ruby whispered these words in my ear, like a chant: "We were right. We were right. This is why we came."

She clutched J. J.'s hand as we sat huddled among the

other commune members, inside Common House. I remember the feeling in that place. The way you feel in the microsecond before a sneeze, when all your energy is focused and your thoughts hang suspended—that's what it was like. I *felt* the fear in the room. We were afraid, because the world was ending.

But the world didn't end. That's the *Almost* part of the Almost Apocalypse.

At three o'clock that afternoon, the commune siren went off. It was tied to an alert system that the Council had installed in their offices, meant to inform us if a nuclear attack was imminent.

When that siren went off, the Council ordered everyone to pile into Common House. We waited until a little after seven o'clock that night, at which point Opal came in and told us that we were safe and would not, in fact, be blown off the face of the earth.

Thus ended the Almost Apocalypse.

We later found out that there had never been any threat. The alarm had been the result of a technical error. The next morning, the Council brought in an electrician. They also began construction of a fallout shelter.

Here at Red Sun, we believe in signs, and the Council believed this false alarm of ours to be a warning of real danger—a call for us to prepare a better hiding place, should we be well and truly nuked. Because, had we been nuked while crammed into Common House, it wouldn't have mattered if we'd survived the blast—we'd still have been exposed to a shitload of radiation.

I wouldn't understand any of this until years later, but I

never forgot Ruby's chant: "We were right. We were right. This is why we came."

And I agree with that. She and J. J. *were* right: The US government, like all governments, is corrupt. The Outside is a scary place. Modern folks care more about the latest kitchen appliance than they do about their next-door neighbors. That's why Ruby and J. J. came to Red Sun. That's why they stayed. Even so, at the age of twelve, I came to a grim little conclusion:

My parents were right to come to Red Sun. But had the *Almost* Apocalypse been an *Actual* Apocalypse, we would've been dead with the rest of the wrong, wrong world.

There's a strong wind blowing outside when I leave Council House. Even though the sky is a perfect, cloudless blue, a damp gust knocks into me like it's bringing on a storm. An unfastened shutter slams against Sage House, like a drumbeat keeping unsteady time. In the nearby chicken coops, the birds cluck uneasily. At more of a distance, a dog is howling. I back up, shielding my eyes against the burning summer sun, to look at the weather vane atop Common House. There, a proud copper rooster is spinning from east to west, then west to north, then north to south, changing direction with every new surge of wind.

A gust whips up around me, unsettling the red dirt at my shoes, and then something smacks into my face, clinging to my cheeks with agitation. I grab at it, and my hand comes away with a crumpled white sheet of paper. Working against the hard wind, I open the paper to reveal black-ink words:

**DON'T MISS THE MOVIE SENSATION OF
THE SUMMER**

STAR WARS—EXTENDED SHOWING, BY
POPULAR DEMAND

AT THE DREAMLIGHT, SLATER'S
<u>ONE & ONLY</u> DRIVE-IN THEATRE

MOVIE TIMES AT 9 & 11:30 PM

EVERY NIGHT TILL LABOR DAY

It's an advertisement from the Outside. I guess I shouldn't be surprised it found its way in here, with winds like these. Still, a chill shoots down my spine, and I drop the flyer like it's diseased, and like that disease might infect me.

I clear my throat again and again, in low, guttural heaves. My tics haven't let up since I left the Council.

I don't want to think about the Outside right now. I don't want to think at all. That's why I head straight to work.

The Moonglow kitchen is in a lull when I arrive. It's late for lunch, early for dinner. As I walk in, Dawn, our sous-chef, sends me a wave with her paring knife. J. J. cocks his head and says, "Get started on the peppers. Then onions and beets."

No welcome. No acknowledgment that I have arrived a half hour early for my shift. No superfluous instruction.

Just how I like it.

From a nearby counter I grab the crate of green bell peppers, delivered this morning from Red Sun's gardens. I haul it to my station, grab my board and knife, and set to work. With the pepper head down, I make quick vertical strokes across its center. I'd be lying if I said I'm not mentally substituting this pepper for a certain part of Phoenix's anatomy.

My mouth tic is acting up, and I'm glad my back is to J. J. and Dawn so they can't see me rapidly stretch open my lips—a yawn that never comes. Not that they care. J. J. knows I do good work, regardless. And, as he told me on my first day on the job, that is what matters in the kitchen: quality work and communication. I do quality work, though not because I care about the culinary reputation of the Moonglow Café. I do it because I know, even if I'm currently pissed about it, that I'm lucky to have gotten a slot in the kitchen.

There are some *bad* assignments. Like working the gardens in mid-July's heat and humidity, building layers of callus on sunburn on callus on sunburn. Like cooking at Dining Hall, which is little more than a mindless conveyor belt churning out variations of a dozen recipes on a strict schedule of breakfast, lunch, and dinner, for our four hundred commune members. The Moonglow Café, on the other hand, is a *professional* kitchen. The café's diners are outsiders, mainly from Slater, though sometimes from as far as Wichita and Kansas City.

I've got a good assignment here, though I'm pretty sure it has less to do with luck and more to do with being J. J.'s son. While parental bonding isn't encouraged at Red Sun, no one denies certain biological factors. It's clear that I have J. J.'s dark, curly hair and Ruby's high cheekbones, and the Council must have also figured that if J. J. was good in the kitchen, his offspring would be too. What they didn't consider was what J. J.'s offspring might be *feeling*. Sure, I work hard enough in the kitchen, but I don't want to cook for the rest of my life. I don't want to do anything for the rest of my life save play the commune's Yamaha. It was only a dream before. Then Gregor left Red Sun at the beginning of the year, and I knew this was a sign for *me*. A sign that I could fill the Outside with my music.

As it turns out, I was wrong. It wasn't a sign. It was false hope, and I've now been sentenced to a decade of cutting and sweating in this kitchen. I won't be up for reassignment until I'm twenty-six, and at that point I might as well be dead. Real musicians—musicians who make a difference, the way my gods did—burn bright and early, way before they ever reach twenty-fucking-six.

Archer shows up with the rest of the team: Sunshine, Eduardo, Lola, and Heath. Though my enthusiastic chopping has deprived him of the usual prep work, he grabs a few remaining beets and takes his place beside me.

Unlike me, my best friend, Archer, *likes* kitchen work. For a couple of years he and I have been on prep and dishwashing—typical preassignment jobs. Now that we've been officially assigned here, we'll replace workers who've been reassigned to other jobs in Red Sun. My guess is that we'll be taking on saucier, since it's the most commonly vacated role in the kitchen. Until the commune-wide changes go into effect tomorrow, though, it's more prep work for us.

I feel Archer's eyes on me, even as he cuts.

"Watch yourself." I nod to his rapid knife strokes before returning to my own. Then I scrape a diced beet from the board and into the steel bowl between us.

Archer sets down his knife. He's staring at me like a dumb fish, and he looks especially dumb because his long red curls are bunched up under a hairnet.

"Holy shit, man," he says. "Just . . . *holy shit*. Why didn't you say something?"

He knows. Someone told him about my assignment. Bright, maybe. Or even Phoenix himself.

I grab a new beet, severing the roots in one clean cut. As I do, I stretch my lips wide. Then I speak.

"It happened this morning," I say. "When would I have said something?"

"Did he tell you beforehand, or was it . . . *BAM*. Surprise!"

Archer waves his knife in a manner that's not at all in keeping with J. J.'s kitchen safety regulations.

"I don't want to talk about it."

"Fuck that, Galliard. I'm not gonna have you sniveling over there the rest of the day. Out with it."

I tic again, opening my mouth. It's comical timing, really, like I'm letting out the silent scream I feel deep inside.

I set down my knife and say, "He didn't tell me. I knew there were some other members who'd applied, but I thought I was a shoo-in. I didn't know until Rod was going on about how they'd already commissioned paintings from Phoenix."

"Holy shit," Archer says, this time in a whisper. Then he shrugs. "You were the one who wanted to be his friend."

I glare. "What's that supposed to mean?"

"All I'm saying is I never liked the guy much. I told you the day he came here that he was a pompous ass. He's an outsider. What did you expect?"

My jaw jerks rightward. I stretch my lips apart. "Yeah, that's not helping right now."

"What *would* help? Now's the time I'd expect all-out fisticuffs, but we both know you would lose. Hard."

I slice away at my beet, uncovering its red heart with angry strokes. "I don't want to fight him. The Council made their decision. A fight's not going to change that."

I feel noble for saying this, and also kind of nauseated.

"Well, yeah, sure, but . . ." Archer hems for a moment, then says, "Phoenix knew better."

And there it is. Archer has named it: Phoenix—Red Sun outsider, friend, and role model—*knows better*. He knows I've wanted to be resident artist since way before he ever met me. He knows what it means to me. None of that stopped him, though. He did what he wanted, because he's a selfish prick.

I stop there and ask myself, *Is that fair?*

I give it some thought. I think back two years, to when I first met Phoenix. I think of a crumpled letter in a wastebasket—a memory I can't shake. I scrape the chopped beet from my cutting board. Then I decide: Yes. That's an entirely fair assessment. Phoenix is, without a doubt, a selfish prick.

"Okay," says Archer. "Here's what'll make it better: Dreamlight Season."

A chill runs through me, same as it did before, when I tossed that paper from my hand—an advertisement for the Dreamlight itself. Thanks to Archer, I know all about that Outside attraction.

No Red Sun member is allowed to leave the commune for any reason other than a medical emergency. That's a foundational rule of commune life. Every set of rules has its exception, though, and Red Sun rules are . . . no exception. What Archer calls Dreamlight Season is more formally known as Crossing.

The thinking behind Crossing goes like this: Adolescents are bound to experiment, act out, and push boundaries. That's the natural order of things. For this reason, the Council instituted Crossing—a period of bending rules. From the age of fourteen to sixteen, for three summers, the first day of June through the last day of August, Red Sun members can leave the commune and explore the outside world, provided they return by a nightly curfew. At the end of those three summers, should an adolescent wish to leave Red Sun, they're free to do so. If not, they'll settle into adult life here and work their assigned job. The point is, no one here at Red Sun is forcing us younger members to stick around. If we want to leave, we can. The only hitch is this: Once you leave, you don't come back. You've broken with Red Sun's energy, and you're on your own. The same holds true for any adults who choose to leave. There haven't been many, but there have been some—Gregor, our former resident artist, among them.

Archer is a big fan of Crossing. His first summer, he went to Slater's drive-in theatre, the Dreamlight, and watched every new release the Dreamlight showed. I can recite the full list of movies he's seen, because he would not and will not shut up about them:

The Apple Dumpling Gang
The Rocky Horror Picture Show
The Omen
Murder by Death

Jaws

The Last Tycoon

Star Wars

That's not all Archer does. He and the other crossers head into Slater and go to parties with actual outsiders our age. They explore the town and eat and drink and generally mess around. He says it's great.

I've never left the commune.

I don't feel what Archer calls "the itch"—an undeniable desire to get out and see what I've been missing. I've heard enough from Ruby and J. J. and met enough Red Sun newcomers to satisfy my curiosity. I know what I'm missing out on. But I don't miss it.

For my three summers of Crossing, I've stayed in the commune, working extra hours in the kitchen and spending nights alone at the piano or talking to Phoenix. For these three summers, I've been fine.

I guess Phoenix is responsible for a lot of that. He made me feel like the commune's favored son. I sneered at the shameless way Archer and the other crossers threw themselves at the Outside, as though it could offer them anything they hadn't already been given. I made a vow to never step outside the commune fence. Because to step outside means to admit Red Sun is missing something.

And it's not.

"Galliard. Did you hear me?"

Archer's fingers dig into my forearm, and I reel back into reality.

"Yeah, I heard you." I shrug off the grip, and my mouth tic picks up again. Perfect. The last thing I need right now.

"It's getting old, man."

"What is?"

"The holier-than-thou phase. You know you're not getting a medal for keeping yourself penned in here, right?"

"I'm not after a medal."

"Then what? Just scared?"

I open my mouth, then press my lips back together, forming a seal. I know Archer is trying to rile me up, but I don't have the fortitude to rise above it. Not now. After this morning, my fortitude is completely shot.

"I'm not scared of anything," I say.

Which is a magnificent heap of bullshit.

Sure, I'm scared.

I'm scared Phoenix has been wrong.

I'm scared the Outside might be as obscenely good as Archer and the others make it out to be.

And what scares me the most? It's the fear that after this summer, Archer won't come back from the Outside; he'll be one of the few Red Sun members who cross straight out of the commune.

"Boys!" J. J. barks from across the kitchen. "This isn't tea-time."

"Yes, sir," Archer and I say, and, thoroughly chastised, we return to our beets.

I'm thinking now not of my fears but of a piece of paper that a strange wind blew my way. That advertisement was for the Dreamlight, and now here is Archer, urging me to go to that very Dreamlight with him. I can't help wondering if this means something.

34

It might be that Janis or Jimi or Buddy is trying to send me a message.

It might be that I've been thinking of that flyer since it first hit my face.

It might be that I'm angry at the Council and Phoenix and every stupid dream I had about being resident artist.

Whatever the reason, I speak.

"I'll do it," I say, slicing with hot energy. "Tomorrow night, I'll do it."

Archer doesn't look up from his work, but he doesn't have to. I can feel the triumph radiating off his pink skin.

4

Stella

If you ask anyone in town, they will tell you it was the moon landing that ended my mother's life. If you look at the timing, you will understand why.

On July 20, 1969, at 3:18 p.m. central time, Buzz Aldrin and Neil Armstrong landed on the moon.

I was nine. My mother, brother, sister, and I were at a church potluck, to which my mother had brought a big bowl of Waldorf salad, crowned with a circle of maraschino cherries. We sat outside on folding chairs, the radio broadcast turned all the way up. My friends Linda and Dennis and I wore matching green construction-paper helmets we'd made from Sunday school art supplies.

When the landing was announced, people cheered. Some even embraced.

My mother cried.

They were not tears of excitement—little glimmers in the corners of her eyes, like the other mothers had. She sobbed. Her frame shook, and she covered her face, and two of her good friends patted her back and asked her what was the matter. Eventually, they took her aside to recover, because she was scaring Jill, who was just a toddler and very fussy.

After some minutes of soothing, my mother dried her eyes and returned to us with a smile, as though nothing was wrong in the wide, wide world.

My father was working double shifts that day, so he was not at home that evening. My mother put Jill to bed at her usual time, but I was allowed to stay up late. I sat in the den with her and Craig, and we watched the live broadcast from space.

At 9:56 p.m. central time, Neil Armstrong set foot on the moon.

Craig and I jumped up and down on the sofa. My mother did not tell us to stop. She wore a calm smile. Later I fell asleep there, on the sofa. Craig did too.

When we woke up early Monday morning, my mother was not home. We looked for her in our parents' bedroom and the kitchen. Then we looked outside and found that the car was gone. It was strange of her not to leave a note, but Craig and I assumed she was running errands. Time passed. Jill woke, and Craig and I fixed our own breakfast. My father returned home from work. Then lunchtime came, and Craig and I fixed our own lunch. It was at dinnertime, when my father woke and there was still no sign of my mother, that something first felt wrong. My father called family friends; no one had heard from my mother. After an hour more, he got into his car to go looking. He ordered us to stay at home and look after Jill. We fixed our own dinner, and we watched television, and we fell asleep.

In the morning, my father woke us. Betty Hume, our

mother's closest friend, was there. She was red in the face. Her mascara was running. She smiled at us, though, and said everything was going to be all right.

I am not sure when I actually understood what had happened. I only know that from that day on, everything shifted. Everything changed.

They found my mother's car in the empty parking lot of Slater High School.

They found her body inside the building. She'd broken a window in the library to get in. Then, according to the police, she made her way to the planetarium, where she turned on the projector. She then tied a rope around one of the exposed pipes beneath the projection booth. She hung herself under the constellations of the southern hemisphere.

You can understand, then, why people would say it was the moon landing. For my mother to kill herself in the planetarium on the night Neil Armstrong made one giant leap for mankind was too coincidental, especially after her unexplainable sobbing at the potluck. According to a client at Vine Street Salon—a loud gossip unaware of my parentage—my mother was "star-crazed."

Star-crazed. That is what people say.

But they are wrong. I know, because I read my mother's letter.

When I arrive at the Dreamlight, I am sweat-caked and sore, and my heart is hammering. Though the urge to vomit is gone, my unease remains, and a stitch cramps my side as I chain my bike to the rusty rack outside the concessions hut. My coworker Kim is already there, starting up the popper.

I take a few long gulps of night air, attempting to regulate my breathing. I don't want Kim to ask what's wrong, because, honestly, I am not sure what is wrong. I only know something is . . . *off*. Very off.

First, this morning, there was Velma the goldfish. Then there was the border collie—a dead ringer for a dog that couldn't possibly be in town. Then came the wind, as unexpected as it is relentless. And now *this*. Dozens of dead, eyeless snakes.

It's only coincidence. I know that, deep down. Weather can be strange, and animals can react strangely to it. Yes, I witnessed an inordinate number of odd occurrences today; that doesn't necessarily *mean* anything.

When I enter the hut, I am still shaken, though not enough for Kim to notice. I tie on my cheery yellow-and-white-striped apron and set about replenishing the candy display. Kim and I exchange hellos and nothing more as we settle into our nightly routine. Soon the concessions hut is busy with dozen-person lines at our two ordering windows. Our work is rhythmic—order, scoop, two pumps butter, cash, register, next.

I am a loner, but if I were to count anyone as my friend, I suppose Kim Dupree would be it. We were in the same grade at school, but we didn't hang out there. Kim and I only got to know each other at the Dreamlight, where we spend our nights packed close together in an overheated hut the size of a large closet. Kim has buzz-cut hair, dyed platinum, and several tattoos on her left arm. During the day she works at the Exchange, a record shop on Vine Street. She smokes—both kinds. I like her because she is never phony. She enjoys talking about the things I read in my Carl Sagan books, and I enjoy hearing her rave about a new band called the Ramones, which she claims is going to revolutionize the music scene. And we both pretend not to notice when the other sneaks a handful of popcorn from the popper.

Sometimes I see Dennis and Linda around here. They were my closest friends when Mom died, and we still hung out afterward, through middle school. When Craig left, though, I stopped sleeping over at Linda's and made excuses for why I couldn't meet them both for a weekend matinee. It was easier that way, with everything else I had to do: school, my jobs, and taking care of Jill. Then Linda and Dennis started to date, accompanying each other on trips to the Dreamlight. I didn't mind. It seemed only natural that I had faded from their lives.

Since the drive-in is only a mile outside Slater proper, most kids make a night of it by driving or biking out. The owner, Mr. Cavallo, has partitioned off a large patch of browned grass close to the screen, where people can set up plastic chairs and blankets. The cars line up behind the rope fence, and everything plays out the way it did in the sixties, during this place's glory days, before the national economy tanked and people here in Slater started closing stores, losing jobs, and failing to find enough money for the mortgage, let alone the movies. Based on Mr. Cavallo's mutterings, sales aren't what they ought to be. I'm pretty sure I'm working in the twilight days of the Dreamlight.

Though *Star Wars* has shaken things up some. I know of many high schoolers who've come to the showing over ten times. Even now the lot is nearly full—a summertime miracle, and an even bigger turnout than there was for *Jaws* two summers ago. Every night I am surrounded by moviegoers more eager than ever to root for the Rebel Alliance and scoot closer to their dates whenever the evil Darth Vader makes an appearance. Personally, I am tired of the film. I like the story well enough, but seven nights a week of the melodramatic, brass-heavy opening is enough to turn anyone off; most nights I tune the movie out. I've become a pro at numbing my thoughts and relying on muscle memory to get me through the night.

"Excuse me, miss. I want three cups liquid butter and just a sprinkling of popcorn."

I look up from sliding a ten-dollar bill into the cash box and find a handsome guy smirking at me from the other side of the counter. His name is Derrick Schultheis, and he was the president of my graduating class. His girlfriend, Pat, hangs on his arm. His best friend, Scott, is squinting at the menu board as though our prices might have magically changed since their visit last week. The wind is doing a number on Pat's long, stick-straight hair. Every few seconds she tosses it back from her face, like a poor attempt at a Cher impression.

"That'll be extra," I deadpan to Derrick.

"Fine by me," he says. "I once sold my soul to the devil for a large pizza."

Scott snickers. Pat shoves Derrick's arm. "You shouldn't make those kinds of jokes. They're sacrilegious."

"Got you down for a popcorn," I say. "What else?"

"*Two* popcorns," says Pat, who has assumed command of this order. She folds her arms over the counter and adds, "Three Cokes. A box of Gobstoppers."

"Coming up."

I pass Kim on my way to the chest freezer, and we exchange looks. Kim wasn't as much of a pariah as I was in school, but she certainly didn't run in the same crowd as our student government. Serving the likes of Derrick and Pat is the least savory aspect of our job—primarily because they never leave a tip in the stripped soup can we keep on the service counter.

I tip scoops of ice into three large paper cups. Then I set to work on the soda, filling each cup until the fizz reaches the brim, waiting, topping off. As I do, I listen to my customers' conversation.

". . . been such a drag. She's on that couch with a box of tissues and a bottle of Merlot and refuses to leave his side. She's convinced this is the end."

"Rudy's old, though. Isn't it kind of expected?"

Soda spills over the brim of the cup I'm filling, hits my hand. I hiss, step away from the soda fountain, and grab a napkin. Still, I don't stop listening.

"He's getting on, yeah. Great Danes live less than most dogs. Eight or so years? But he wasn't acting sick or anything before today. Then Mom found him in her bed this morning, whimpering, piss all over the sheets. Don't get me wrong, it was awful, but Dad says it's the weird weather we've been having. Rudy's just anxious about whatever storm's coming in. And he's old, so the bladder control isn't such a surprise."

I return to the window, cups lidded, and then concentrate on scooping out the two popcorns. I give no outward indication that I am hanging on every word that Derrick, Pat, and Scott are saying. I push the popcorns across the counter. Then

I grab a package of Gobstoppers and toss it into the mix, and Derrick hands over the money.

I shouldn't say anything, but curiosity is burning in my chest. It isn't as though I have anything to lose—these people already don't care about me.

"You think it's the weather, then?" I ask, as I hand Derrick the change he will pocket and not tip. "It's the weather that's making the animals act funny?"

Derrick's head jolts up. Clearly, he was not expecting someone like me to address someone like him. He fixes me with a half-confused, wholly dirty look.

"Well, yeah. What else would it be?"

"Nothing." I shrug. "What else *would* it be?"

His look gets dirtier. "Yeah, sure."

They grab their food and drinks, and as they walk away, I hear Pat laugh and say, "Freak," followed by Scott's voice: ". . . heard she and Kim get it on during the movie."

This doesn't rattle me. I heard much worse in school hallways. What rattles me is an account of another animal acting strangely.

Outside the concessions hut, the wind howls on like a rabid wolf.

The movie begins—bold yellow words on a starry sky—and Kim and I reach the end of our lines. After the rush, I only have to field the occasional stragglers, who are mostly potheads after popcorn or overeager boyfriends back to refill their dates' Coca-Colas. The hut may be hot and run-down, but I prefer my position here to Kim's, which is "sex patrol" during the movie; she and Mr. Cavallo walk the partitioned section, shining their flashlights in the eyes of any couples getting a little too physical on their grandmothers' quilts.

There are wind ripples cutting across the movie screen tonight, but the picture is clear enough, and whatever storm is rolling in remains a ways off. This isn't a showing worth canceling after all; instead it's a night for dates to hold each other close under the pretense of protection from the elements. There's no doubt that Kim is in for a busy night, and I think at first that this is why she doesn't leave the hut straightaway. I watch from my perch atop the back counter as she hacks at the clumped ice in the chest freezer. She uses the tip of the metal scoop, as though this will do much good. It is a mindless and mostly inefficient action.

"Pent-up rage?" I ask, when she stops to rest.

She glances up, shrugs, then drops the scoop into the freezer and slams it shut. Her shoulders are hitched high, like she's nervous. She draws something out of her back pocket and flaps it in my direction.

"Okay, here," she says. "I found this when I was cleaning a couple nights ago. It was on the floor, by the sink."

Instantly I know what she is holding.

I want it to be anything else, but I can think of only one envelope that belongs to me and has been missing for three days. It is my most recent correspondence from Craig—the last of his letters, sent nearly two months ago. I'd been keeping it in my back pocket to analyze during the lulls at the concessions hut. When I noticed it missing, I assumed it had fallen out during my bike ride. In a panic, I retraced my path down

Eisenhower, even digging into the cornfields, horrified by the thought not only of losing the letter but of it finding its way into someone else's hands. Now I'm finding out those hands were Kim's.

I take the letter, equal parts relieved and mortified.

"I read it." Kim isn't apologetic, more matter-of-fact. I don't know what to say, so I don't say anything.

"You and that Phoenix seem pretty close," Kim says, folding her arms. "He trying to convert you or something?"

I study Kim's face. I don't think she is trying to bait me. I think she is asking a genuine question.

She knows about my older brother, Craig. Everyone at Slater High knew about the well-rounded, artistically gifted basketball captain who had it all and then decided to leave his whole life behind and take up residence at Red Sun—Slater's very own hippie commune. What Kim does not know is that Craig has since changed his name to Phoenix, and that he and I have been writing each other letters during his two-year absence. There is no way she would know that. Not even my family knows. No one knows but me.

I could tell her about it. Kim may be the kind of person to read private letters, but she is not the kind to judge. Even so, telling Kim about Craig before telling my own father would be a kind of familial betrayal. Also, I am still stunned by the revelation that Kim Dupree found my letter and that it was not lost in a maze of cornstalks, blown out of my reach forever by hard summer winds.

"No conversion," I say. "I met him a couple years ago when he was on Crossing. He's an okay guy."

"So you're in love with him." Kim doesn't even smile.

She would be smiling if she knew what she is asking. She would be rolling on the floor laughing.

"No. I'm not."

"Sad. Because the way he writes, you'd think he was in love with you."

I am tempted again to tell her. I would like to laugh and say, *The closeness you're reading is sibling understanding, not sexual undercurrent.*

Instead I say, "We're friends."

Kim is wrestling with words on her tongue. I can tell. She is wearing the fidgety, almost cross-eyed expression everyone in this town gets when they bring up my mother or my brother.

"He a friend of Craig's?" she finally asks.

"Something like that."

"Huh. You ever hear from him?"

I consider again. I shake my head.

"That's rough, man."

"It's fine."

"I'll be honest, those guys creep me out. Manson Family vibes, you know?"

"I think they mean well, though." I note Kim's expression and add, "I'm *not* being converted."

I'm surprised by my own words. I wouldn't have said any of this two years ago, when Craig first left the family without warning, explanation, or apology. I was so angry at him then, and even angrier at the commune for taking him away. When he answered my first letter, that anger calmed, and over the many months since, it's faded to a faint stirring. I am still upset with my brother. I still think he was selfish to leave us. All the same, these letters mean he hasn't abandoned me entirely, and I have to cling to the hope that he will not now. Because recently, I made a mistake, and I haven't had a letter from Craig since.

"Live and let live, I guess." Kim pushes out of a lean and unfastens her apron. "It's all right, you befriending one of their kind. Next time they come calling here, I'm directing them to your line."

"Sure. Send them my way."

We get our fair share of Crossing kids here at the drive-in. Since Red Sun is only a quarter mile away, a little deeper into farm country, the Dreamlight is one of the closest attractions for curious commune teenagers. I've served girls and guys alike—every one of them long-haired and clothed in white linen tunics over jeans. They are big spenders, usually. I once served a girl who ordered one of every boxed candy we have. It's understandable. With only three summers to experience life on the outside, they've got to make the most of it.

Craig, now Phoenix, is beyond that stage. He had eighteen years out here, and he's chosen to live on the inside of Red Sun for the rest of his life. It seems this confinement means he will never see me in person again. Because that is the mistake I made: I asked to see him.

"Okay," says Kim. "Off to stop some baby making."

Just when she is through the hut's back door, I say, "You haven't seen any dead animals today, have you?"

"Sorry, what?" Kim bends back inside, one brow raised high. The wind is pushing the door against her, and her arm strains to hold it open.

"Nothing. I . . . came across these dead snakes on the way here. Kind of freaked me out."

Kim's face transforms with disgust. "Dead *snakes*? Fuck's sake, Stell."

"My sister's goldfish died this morning too. And we passed this dead dog. . . . I don't know, sorry. It's just been bothering me."

Kim shakes her head slowly. "Yeah, no dead animals to report. But that's messed up."

I nod. "Probably a coincidence."

"Or an omen." Kim smirks. "Maybe you should stay inside tomorrow."

I laugh so Kim doesn't think I've lost my mind. "Maybe."

She leaves for real, slamming the door behind her.

I watch her through the plexiglass. She switches on a flashlight, illuminating the blue-gray of early evening. Around her, a congregation of fireflies lights up in sporadic bursts.

Not everything is dropping dead, I remind myself. Despite the change in weather, not every creature is acting strangely. Birds still chirp. Fireflies still light up. It's only my natural repulsion at seeing several dead things in such a short span of time that has stirred up this unease. It is coincidence, and that is all.

Some people say there is no such thing as coincidence. But those are the same people who got my mother's death wrong.

August 20, 1975

Craig,

Today I'm going to tell you about the Pioneer
program. Do you know it? <u>Pioneer 10</u> launched
three years ago, and <u>Pioneer 11</u> launched a
year after. Nobody made as big a deal about
them as they did the rockets.

I don't understand why that is, because to
me, the Pioneer program is the best thing NASA
has done to date. They're probes that have
gone farther than any human has—to Jupiter
and Saturn, and now beyond. I've enclosed a
drawing of <u>Pioneer 10</u>, and the stamp I'm using
to mail this letter has an accurate rendering
of the spacecraft too. Only, of course, <u>Pioneer
10</u> is much, much, <u>much</u> smaller than Jupiter.

I want to tell you about the most
interesting part of the Pioneer missions.
(Or, at least, what I find most interesting.)
Each probe has a plaque attached to it, which
the people at NASA made <u>in case it's picked
up by aliens</u>. The plaques are made of gold-
anodized aluminum, which is good at resisting
degradation. This means that even after the
probes have sailed deep into space and we have
lost contact with them, they will continue

onward, with those plaques attached. Carl
Sagan calls it our "cosmic greeting card."

Here's what is on the plaque:
A sketch of a hydrogen atom
A map of our solar system
A pulsar map, to show where the sun is
located in our galaxy
Figures of a man and a woman,
superimposed on an image of the spacecraft, to
give aliens an idea of scale

It's all in the hopes that maybe there's
extraterrestrial life, and maybe they will
find us and have some idea of what to expect.
Isn't that something? The smartest
scientists in our country have acknowledged
that there might be aliens, and this is what
they've decided aliens most need to know. It
is a message in a bottle, cast into the sea of
space. We've sent it out in the good faith that,
should an alien civilization as advanced as
or more advanced than ours find it, they will
want to seek us out for the betterment of both
our worlds.
Only, it may be that by the time aliens
find the plaque and then find us, we will be
long gone. Not just you and me, Craig. I mean
humanity. Perhaps millions of years will

have passed, and humans will have died off—
wiped away by famine or flood or disease or,
most likely, a nuclear holocaust. It's sad to
think about: those hopeful aliens coming out
to meet us and instead finding only charred
ground and radioactive air.

I wonder sometimes what I would send out,
if I had one plaque with which to tell aliens
about myself. What would I want them to know?
My street address and how I look, or pictures
of Dad and you and Jill? What would I want
them to know about me, even after I am long
gone? What would I want to send deeper and
deeper into space, fated to travel after my
death?

I don't know, Craig. I'm thinking it
through. You might try thinking about it too.

Your sister,
Stella

5

Galliard

MONDAY, AUGUST 1

"Peace upon you, brothers and sisters. May we be renewed this first day of the new month. May light surround us and fill us and guide us. May all actions of ours be united through the abiding Life Force."

It's the first evening of the month, which means most members of Red Sun have assembled in Common House for the community meeting. We sit on the floor in straight rows, legs crossed and eyes fixed on the Council standing before us: Rod and Saff and, between them, Opal, our leader.

Opal is kind of creepy, but I like her. She founded Red Sun in 1960 along with her husband, Leander. Together with twenty other founding members, they established the guiding principles of the commune. Red Sun would set itself apart from the outside world, avoiding a life reliant upon industrialization and commercial waste. Its members would live off the land and consume as few products from the Outside as possible. It would be a place free of the selfish bonds that cause so much contention and turmoil on the Outside. There would be no divisions, no ranks, no hierarchy; even the Council members were not to be considered power holders, but rather community servants. No divisions would also mean no individual families. In Red Sun, all members would belong to one family and share their land, their resources, their everything. The Council would decide on fair assignments, each one necessary to keep the self-sustaining community operative. And the guiding principle that bound all these beliefs together would be a belief in a Life Force—a higher power, however personal or impersonal each member wished it to be—that brought the community together, merging its members' resonating, complementary energies. So Red Sun became what the wooden engraving at the entrance of Common House professes it to be: *An egalitarian family devoted to one another, the Life Force, and the land.*

Twenty members turned to two hundred, drawn from all over the Outside, as far west as San Francisco and as far north as Burlington, Vermont. Then two hundred members doubled to the four hundred we have today. Leander is no longer with us; he passed away from lung cancer when I was still a kid. Opal's been here from the very start, and she's both the head of the Council and our spiritual leader; if anyone's in tune with the Life Force, it's her. She's almost seventy, and her face is raisiny, while her eyes are clear and sharp and very light blue.

At the moment, Opal's speaking with stretched arms and open palms tilted heavenward. Her face is at peace. Her blue eyes sweep over us with the tenderness of a mother, and behind her gaze is a comfortable sort of *knowing*. It's creepy, sure, but she's easier to like than Rod, who is loud and forceful and always giving orders. Saff oversees the residential houses, kitchens, and gardens. Even though I can only hear her half the time, she's all right. Tonight her head is bowed, dark dreads draped over her face. She murmurs quietly as Opal welcomes us, offering a prayer to the Life Force to restore balance and accord within the commune.

I want to be anywhere but here.

Hey, you're saying, *this seems like a sacred moment. You should appreciate it.*

Yeah, well, you haven't had to sit through loads of these.

Community meetings are never that interesting—a disappointing realization I got when I turned thirteen and was allowed to attend my first one. Up until that point, Archer and I had theorized that these meetings were where the adults discussed pain-of-death secrets like where they grew the special cannabis stash and what kind of outsiders they let into the gates after midnight. As it turns out, all we talk about here is how the crops are doing and any upcoming events and how we're holding up in the public eye.

From what I can tell, most people in Slater don't mind us, and plenty of them love the food at the Moonglow Café. The local police have paid us some visits, though. Once because one of our Crossing youths got hit by a car. He was fine, just broke a leg, but there was a lot of squabbling about bringing him back here to be treated by our three physicians—trained on the Outside but also believers in a holistic view of the body and its relationship with the Life Force—rather than taking him to the hospital. In the end the commune won out, and the guy (his name is Cal; we aren't that close) was better in a few months. The most recent police visit was back in May, after some Slater teenager got caught with a bag of weed and insisted he'd bought it off a member of Red Sun. The police came in then and searched the whole place. They didn't find anything. They could've saved themselves the trouble if they attended our boring monthly meetings. Then they'd know Red Sun has absolutely nothing to hide. No dark secrets or hidden perversions here. Those are on the Outside.

It's chilly in Common House. Hard breezes keep sweeping through the open windows and giving me goose bumps. And under my skin there's hot, nervous energy.

I'm going out tonight. For the first time in my life, I'm going out.

Archer has promised he's going to make tonight "unforgettable," but he won't let me in on any details. He usually runs with the rest of the Crossing crowd—teenagers, younger than us, who are on their first or second summer. Archer has assumed the role of their wise leader. I guess he's earned it. Tonight, though, he assures me, it's only the two of us. I get the special treatment.

I didn't think I'd be this worked up about going Outside. It's kind of been eating at me all day—during my morning prayer to Janis Joplin and my work in the kitchen and my expert dodging of any interaction with Phoenix. It doesn't help that the weird winds from yesterday have stuck around. They've been blowing up dust and dirt, unsettling the animals, whipping up everyone's clothes and hair. Those winds, they're acting the way I feel inside, heaving one way, then the other, indecisive on what direction I'm going. The truth is, I'm well and truly worked up about the Dreamlight, and Archer can sense it, even when we're sitting, saying nothing; he keeps casting me these sidelong smirks.

Rod gets up to give a report on corn, wheat, and livestock. Of the three Council members, I like Rod least. He oversees the farming and commerce and came on after Leander died. Since he joined the Council, he's made a whole lot of changes, and even though Opal is technically the head of the Council, she's allowed Rod to do what he wants. Most people say that's because Opal got old and tired, and she's never been the same since Leander died. Plenty of those people also say that Rod transformed Red Sun into the organized, well-run collective it is today. Some of Rod's changes were unpopular, though. Like the decision to stop importation of music and literature from the Outside.

According to Rod, the crops are faring well. This summer he and his workers have scattered hair collected by our commune barber across the fields; apparently the human scent keeps away deer. It's a smart plan, I guess, but I'm having trouble hearing it over the winds blowing within me, and without.

It's as Rod is droning on about the upcoming wheat planting that I feel it growing in my chest: the throat tic. Seconds later it bursts out of me—a brief but noticeable throat clearing. Then silence. Reprieve. Then it comes again. And again.

"Fuck," I mutter, only to give way to yet another burst.

Archer casts me another sidelong look, this time sympathetic. It's the law of the land that I get my most obvious tics when I'm sitting in a crowded space. It's kind of funny, I'll admit. Mostly, though, it's humiliating. I sink my head into my hands and press a swallow down on my throat, willing the tic to let up, cut me a break for once. In this new, dark hiding hole of mine, Rod's booming voice sounds more serious than usual.

"... strange, to say the least. From what we can tell, they've been riled up by this shift in weather we've been having. But the winds are bound to die down soon, and we have no doubt our hens will resume their normal egg-laying schedule."

The crowd is whispering. I look up in time to see Harmony, a friend of Ruby's, raise her hand. Rod nods toward her, and she stands and says, "The winds *have* been bad. Unpredictable, too. It was especially difficult harvesting the pepper crop today. But, Rod, do you think it's only those winds upsetting the hens?"

"We're looking into every possibility," Rod answers her. "We've also taken out their feed for examination."

"But they only stopped laying when these winds kicked up?" asks a man two seats over from me. Clive. He works in the orchards.

"That's correct. Hence our theory. No doubt those of you who work with our goats and horses have noted that they've been unsettled as well." There's murmuring in the crowd, and people around me nod their heads. Rod smiles out at us reassuringly. "Only a change in the weather. It's not a cause for panic, I assure you."

"Bad call," Archer mutters, leaning in to me. "Never say 'panic' in a crowded room."

Rod gives the floor to Saff, who begins her report on the gardens. This summer's tomato and watermelon crops have been especially good, and she's taking her sweet time thanking each of the commune members who tilled and watered and gathered in the past months. At this rate, we'll be recognizing every single one of Red Sun's three-hundred-odd adult members for their agrarian service.

My tic won't settle, and I know it's bugging the people around me, even though they don't look my way or say anything. Everyone in this room knows who I am: Galliard, the kid who can't help it. I've been that kid since I was nine, when the tics first started up. It was Arlo, the youngest of the commune's three physicians, who diagnosed me and told Ruby and J. J. that, while there were some new medicines that might help me, they would have to see a doctor on the Outside about them. Normally, Red Sun parents stay out of medical stuff, to keep from forming bonds and all, but Opal said this case was special, so Ruby and J. J. got to make the call. They discussed sending me out, but eventually they decided against it. Ruby was afraid that leaving the commune so often would disorient me, and in the end, as Arlo told us, there's not a cure for what I have, which on the Outside is known as Tourette's syndrome.

I guess, in a way, it was nice to hear that there was a name for what I was going through. When the tics first started up, I felt out of control and alone; no one else at Red Sun jerked their jaw or cleared their throat the way I did. A *name* for those jaw jerks and throat clears meant I wasn't the only one.

A name doesn't make *having* Tourette's any easier, though.

Eventually, Saff stops thanking the world, and the meeting-that-will-never-end ends. Even as Archer and I head down the back steps of Common House, my tics won't leave me. They're sticking around until further notice, obeying an unheard command to clear my perfectly clear throat.

"So, uh, don't look now, but there's a Phoenix at your back."

Archer warns me only seconds before I hear Phoenix call out, "Galliard! Hey, Galliard, wait up!"

Not a chance. I walk faster. Archer keeps in step.

Phoenix doesn't get the message. He runs, catching up and rounding in front of us, blowing out short breaths of air.

"Can I help you with something?" I ask my former friend.

Phoenix is a big guy. He's tall, with a hard-cut jaw and harder-cut biceps. His face doesn't belong on his body, though. It's big-eyed and babyish, like a doll's. Other members of Red Sun, at a loss for a word that describes this phenomenon, call it "charming." Ever since Phoenix showed up at Red Sun two years back, he's managed to charm his way into a comfortable existence. I guess you could even say he charmed me into being his friend.

But that's over. That's done.

"Would you let me explain?" Phoenix says. "That's all I'm asking. Hear me out."

I look at Phoenix. Archer looks at me. A gust of wind heaves against us, raising the hairs on my arms. I clear my throat.

"Okay," I say. "Explain."

Phoenix's collar flaps in the wind, but he remains stalwart. "I didn't know how to tell you," he says. "I knew how much you wanted resident artist, but . . . I did too. Always have."

"Oh *yeah*. Always. Since you showed up here two years ago."

"I didn't mean *always*. I—look, I used the wrong word. Cut me some slack."

"Sure." My blood temperature is shooting sky-high, but on

the outside, I stay calm. I know it'll make Phoenix mad, and I want him to feel as furious as I do. "Of course, you're right. I should cut you some slack. Now that you have what you've *always* wanted and I have nothing, *I* should be the one cutting *you* slack."

"I was miserable in the fields. It wasn't my calling. I don't make a good farmer; I make a good artist. It's how my talents can best serve the community, and the Council saw that. They wouldn't have considered my special petition otherwise. They wouldn't have chosen me."

"They wouldn't have chosen you if you hadn't *made* a special petition."

"Come on, is that fair? Just because you told me how much you wanted resident artist, that means I can't go for it? Even if it's what's best for *me*? Anyway, the assignment is only ten years. You'll have another chance. I'm older than you, so it makes sense that I should get it first."

I can't look at him. I can't look at his stupid baby face. Instead I look beyond him. At the commune gate. Another gritty sound emerges from the base of my throat.

Then I say, "You know this is what I've wanted since I was a kid. You knew what it meant to me. And now they have me working in the kitchen. The fucking *kitchen*, Phoenix."

"Hey," says Phoenix, all soft and packed with charm. He reaches out, but what is he expecting? I'm not touching his traitor hand. "Hey, you've got a right to be angry. I know I should've told you ahead of time. Just tell me what I can do to make it better."

You can forswear painting. You can leave Red Sun and

never come back. You can drop dead. You can do a lot.

I sidestep him and keep walking. Archer hurries to join me.

"Cold move," he says, glancing back.

I don't glance. I don't want to see Phoenix. I'm not any closer to forgiving that confirmed prick than I was yesterday morning, and I've been doing an excellent job of avoiding him between then and now: closing my door in Heather House; grabbing meals from the kitchen and eating them outside, behind the tractor shed; staying on hours later than my regular shift at the Moonglow.

Don't run away from your problems, Galliard! you're shouting.

Okay, calm down. I'm not an idiot. I know this whole thing will eventually blow up. Right now, though, I can't picture a full conversation with Phoenix that doesn't involve me punching his face, and as Archer has already pointed out, there's no way I'll win that fight.

I tell myself it's not that I'm a coward; I'm playing it smart. I need time and space away from Phoenix, even if he can't get that through his thick skull. Could be I won't be seeing red in a few days. Or months. Maybe a half decade or so. Until then, I'll ice him out. It's not juvenile; it's in the interest of preserving breakable bones.

Phoenix must have given up, because I don't hear him call again, and the footsteps behind us thin out until it's only me and Archer, taking the narrow dirt path to the commune's front gate.

"Got cash?" Archer asks.

I pat the back pocket of my jeans, nod.

There's a set protocol for how Crossing is done. At the start of the summer, every eligible youth is given an allowance—money made from the proceeds of the Moonglow Café and any farm sales—to spend on the Outside however they want. I've always refused mine until this morning, when I paid a visit to Saff's office and asked if I could have this summer's allowance after all. She looked at me funny, as though she wanted to ask a long list of follow-up questions. In the end, though, she didn't. She said yes, of course, I was welcome to my allowance until the end of August, and since I hadn't ever taken advantage of it until now, she was giving me a little extra. She took a stack of green bills from a metal box and handed them to me, and since that time they've sat, folded, in my jeans pocket. I didn't bother counting them; the numbers wouldn't mean anything.

"If we play our cards right, we won't even need money tonight. Then again, you never know where the wind will take us." Archer is walking backward, facing me, hands atop his head. He's enjoying this too much, knowing what I don't. The very wind he's talking about is having its own fun, grabbing the ends of Archer's big red hair and twirling it around, sending it skyward one moment, into his eyes the next. It's working on me, too, billowing through my linen tunic, giving me fresh waves of chills.

That you? I wonder, glancing heavenward, catching sight of my gods up there, three across in the sky. That's when the wind changes direction, blowing into me like a great big push at my back.

I take this as an answer. I keep on following Archer.

We make our way past the gardens, past Dining Hall, all

the way to the Moonglow and the long metal fence that runs out from the building on both sides. To the right of the café is the front gate, one of the commune's only two exits—or entrances, depending on your perspective. The back gate is over by the farmland, and it's only for authorized vehicles.

"Charlie!" Archer calls, waving ahead to a bulky, mustached guy manning the front gate. Charlie looks over everyone who goes in and out of Red Sun, inspecting their pockets and bags for any sign of contraband upon their return. We crossers can experience the Outside, but we cannot bring any part of it back in. Those are the rules. In the past, one too many adult members asked for a crosser to sneak back their favorite drink or unapproved book. Then, when Rod joined the Council, he appointed Charlie and another guy, Rex, whose sole assignments are to take shifts checking over every Red Sun member who returns to the commune from the Outside. I've never actually spoken to Charlie, but for a big, six-foot-five gatekeeper he seems nice enough. He waves at Archer and then looks at me.

"Well, I'll be," he says. "Never thought I'd see you coming through here. Thought you were a dichard."

I can't tell if Charlie's looking at me in admiration or disappointment. Could be a little of both.

"Guess I'm not," I say, shrugging.

"Ruby and J. J. know about it?"

"No."

That's when I realize that, for all the thinking I've done about Crossing today, I never once thought to mention it to Ruby or J. J. They would care more than the other adults, sure, but it's not like I owe them an explanation. They're not recognized as having a claim on me any more than Charlie himself.

"Well." Charlie screws up his eyes. "Just be back by midnight, remember."

"Always have been," says Archer. "Not gonna turn delinquent now." He salutes Charlie and heads through the open gate.

A fresh wind blows over me, restless and forceful. I study the gate. It's chain-link metal and stands a foot taller than me. I've lived behind it my entire life. And that hasn't been a bad thing.

Maybe it's greedy to leave, or plain stupid. Maybe I'm making a mistake.

My jaw tic shows up, turning out my chin.

"Hey!" Archer calls from the other side—the Outside. "Don't get cold feet on me."

Charlie's watching me closely. He definitely looks disappointed. Though about what, I haven't a clue.

"I dunno," I call to Archer, jerking my jaw to the right. "I guess I'm thinking better of it."

"No! You're thinking *worse* of it, man. Get out here, or I'll come back in and kick your ass out."

Charlie makes a coughing sound, and I think I finally understand: It's not disappointment; it's *pity*. He doesn't think I'm going to do it. He feels bad for me, because he thinks I won't cross the line.

Bastard.

Phoenix's voice is in my head: *I'm older than you, so it makes sense that I should get it first.*

Then the wind is at my back, pushing on my spine, urging me forward.

I can cross that line. I will.

My jaw jerks.

Then I walk through the open gate, and Archer cheers.

I don't trust myself to look back. Instead I look to the sky.

My gods are still there, shining as brightly as they did on the inside of that gate. They're looking down on me with . . . what? Approval?

I guess I'll find out soon enough.

"C'mon, man!" Archer shouts. "Time's a-wasting!"

He sets off, running into the night, and this time I don't hesitate. I follow.

6

Stella

MONDAY, AUGUST 1

Vine Street Salon is the cheeriest place in Slater. If you were to take a glass of orange juice and extract its essence—pulp-free— and if you were to paint that essence all over the walls and floors and ceilings, then you would have Vine Street Salon. I don't say that just because the walls are orange (they are), but also because there is something bright and slightly tart about the place, and whenever I walk inside, I feel a little healthier. It may also be because Connie Nall, the head beautician, spritzes a round of Tangerine Dream air freshener each morning before we open.

Connie Nall is excellent at what she does. She knows it, and Slater knows it, and so do the farmers' wives who live farther afield, in parts of east Kansas even more rural than this. She overbooks herself, but it's not my place to say so. I'm only the receptionist, and Connie did me a big favor by taking me on when business at the salon was good but not good enough to warrant my part-time position. She did it, I know, because I was the Girl with No Mother.

Now, three years later, I sometimes feel I'm the one doing

Connie the favor. I am the one who answers phone calls and welcomes clients and checks the books and keeps everyone in the bustling salon well informed. I know Connie's business—its revenue and traffic and reputation—even better than she does.

There are two other beauticians at the salon, Carol and Sibyl, and they keep busy with their own specialties. Connie is the main event, though; she is always booked a month out. *More* than booked, because she is constantly squeezing in appointments behind my back. I know when she has, too, because she assumes a high-pitched titter and says, singsong, *"Stella Kaaay?"* like a drawn-out question. Then she will tell me she's agreed to do "the quickest of trims" for her good friend Marie, and it will only take two shakes. In reality it takes upward of twenty shakes, because Connie and Marie inevitably get to talking about Marie's divorce, and meanwhile Connie's officially booked one o'clock must wait a full hour past her appointed time.

It has become a real problem. Many of our clients drive more than thirty miles to see Connie. To make the trip worth their while, they stop by the other stores on Vine Street, like Mike's Hardware and Belmont Electronics, or one of the several boutiques. An hour spent waiting inside the salon—cheery though it may be—is wasted time, and these women have limited minutes to spare before they must pick up their children from school and put dinner on the table. I could tell them it will be another fifteen minutes, so they can leave the salon and peruse the store next door, but you never know with Connie. Sometimes it is fifteen minutes, and sometimes it is three, or thirty. This is why I am working on a secret project. Though it's not perfected yet, I am certain it will help.

This Monday morning, the salon is bustling, each of our three beauticians occupied with various stages of shampooing, trimming, and drying. Beneath it all is Donna Summer's hypnotic voice on the radio, singing "I Feel Love." Two clients are already waiting at the front of the shop when another opens the door, letting in the winds that have yet to die down, and walks toward me with purpose. It's Betty Hume—the woman who looked after me and Craig and Jill on the day they found my mother's body. Mrs. Hume is the head of First Baptist's hospitality community. She was also my mother's closest friend. For a long time she tried to help my family out. She brought casseroles to the house and picked up me and Craig from school and looked after us in the afternoons. She wasn't the only one, either. Many of the ladies from First Baptist were attentive during the fallout of my mother's death. But then we Mercers stopped attending church, and my father began to work longer shifts, and one night in late February he got into an argument with Mrs. Hume at the grocery store. He yelled at her and called her a gossiping harpy, and after that Mrs. Hume stopped visiting. It was then we became loners in earnest.

I still see Mrs. Hume around on occasion. Slater is a small town, so run-ins are inevitable. She comes to the salon four times a year. Today, it seems, is one of her quarterly appointments.

She looks down at me, pleasant-faced and smelling strongly of White Shoulders perfume. I wish she wouldn't look that pleasant. I wish she would frown, because I am certain that's what she does on the inside whenever she sees one of us

Mercers. I feel certain I remind her of that fight with my father and, worse than that, my mother's death.

"Hello there, Stella Kay."

I close the book I've been reading—*The Cosmic Connection*.

Mrs. Hume taps a nail on the desk. "Connie ready for me yet?"

"With another client," I say ruefully, as though this is an unprecedented event. "Can I get you a glass of water?"

"Hmm? Oh no."

Mrs. Hume's smile is weaker than it was before. She bites her lip, leaving behind a blotch of fuchsia on her front tooth. Then she takes a seat, opens her purse, and pulls out a compact mirror. It is as though she can sense something amiss on her teeth, because moments later she's spotted the issue and blotted the lipstick away with a handkerchief. Then she gets to primping her windblown hair.

As I reopen my Carl Sagan, Mrs. Hume strikes up a conversation with the woman sitting next to her. I half listen as I read a chapter entitled "Has the Earth Been Visited?" Their conversation is predictable enough; I've heard every possible variation of small talk during my years at the front desk. It begins with the weather—"windy enough to topple a person over, I declare"—and proceeds to polite politics—"good idea to have a department devoted to the crisis, though we can only hope bureaucracy won't get in the way"—and on to more personal inquiries—"Molly's in junior high this year, is that right?" It's nothing of note, which leaves me to ponder the possibilities of extraterrestrial life until something Mrs. Hume says pricks my ear.

". . . took her to the vet this morning, but he said she's in tip-top shape."

I close my thumb in the book and look up. The women don't notice my interest in the conversation, which is how I prefer it.

". . . sorry to hear that," the other woman is saying. "But that's good news, isn't it? That nothing's seriously wrong."

"I suppose. Dr. Briggs said he'd seen three other dog owners in the past day, complaining of the very same thing. His theory is that it's anxiety. *From the weather.* Can you imagine? Anxiety—my Daisy!"

"Nonsense. Terriers are a steady breed. Really, Betty, you ought to find yourself a better veterinarian. I'll give you the number of ours; he's in Wichita, mind, but I assure you, it's well worth the drive. None of this quackery about *animal anxiety.*"

Mrs. Hume releases a heavy sigh. "You know, Lisa, every new day I live is further confirmation this world is spinning out of control. So much death and suffering and catastrophe, and it's only increasing."

"I fear for our children," says Lisa, with an all-knowing head bob. "This new generation going absolutely wild, and the drugs, and this lax view on—well, you know, those Red Sun people, it's—sometimes I can't believe that place exists right here, in Slater. California, I'd expect it. *Here*, though . . ."

Mrs. Hume smiles. "I don't know. They're not aliens. They're people living their lives as best they can, same as us."

I am back to staring at my Carl Sagan, heat wicking up my face. I feel the women's gazes on me. They are thinking about

70

Craig, I am sure of it. They're thinking of my runaway brother, a prime example of this new, wild generation.

I stare hard at the text—so hard that the words blur.

"Come quickly, Lord Jesus," says Lisa. "That's all I can say."

The store bell jingles. I glance up, vision fuzzy. Another client has arrived, bringing the wind in with her.

"Good morning, Mrs. Spieth." I look over our sign-in book and come up frowning. "When was your appointment?"

"Oh, don't have one." Mrs. Spieth gives me a confidential wink under a set of long, fake lashes. "Connie said she could pop me in at ten thirty."

I cast a wary look at Connie, who has only just brought her nine o' clock back from the washing basins and of course isn't anywhere near Mrs. Hume, her ten fifteen.

I shouldn't be surprised; it's a typical day at Vine Street.

It's *This Stella's* life.

That Stella might be eagerly preparing for a fall semester of engineering courses, but *This Stella* must deal with impatient customers at Vine Street Salon, and the sooner *This Stella* finishes her secret project, the better.

I keep the project in a wicker bin under my bed. I don't hide it because I am ashamed of what's inside; I just don't want Dad or Jill to see and ask questions. It's only a project, and my projects lead either nowhere or to unremarkable somewheres. It's nothing worth bringing up at the dinner table.

I've been working on this project since the start of summer. It's more a matter of mechanics than math—my bare hands and wires and a strong desk lamp—but it's been slow going, because the kind of walkie-talkies I'm using cost money. The good thing is that I've worked out the most difficult part. Now it's a mere matter of repeating the process and bettering the aesthetic; if we're going to use this invention at the salon, it will need to look appealing.

Today, when I arrive home from Vine Street, I get straight to work. I lock my bedroom door, pull out the wicker bin, and heave it onto my desk. I flip over the hollowed platform I constructed in the garage back in June with Dad's tools and spare wood I begged off Mike at Mike's Hardware. A maze of circuitry lies before me. Only to me it isn't a maze. It's a well-mapped city, made up of freeways and side roads and important buildings, each with a purpose. These days I am in the business of connecting cities and prettying them up. It's work that requires concentration, though not so much that I wear myself out. Instead I lose myself here, drifting into a comfortable haze of quick-working fingers and the sound of Elton John's *Goodbye Yellow Brick Road* album coming from Dad's old record player. I don't even check the time until there's a knock at the door, at which point I switch off the volume and say, "Yep?"

"It starts in five minutes!"

By "it" Jill means *NBC Nightly News*.

If it is time for the news, that means it's almost five thirty, which means I'm late putting our TV dinners in the oven. I check my watch, confirm my suspicion, and say, "Darn."

"What?" calls Jill.

"Nothing." I am already tucking the wicker bin beneath my bed.

There's a rattle at the door. Jill is trying the handle, which is of course locked.

"Stella," she whines. "Why can't I come in?"

"I told you before, I'm working on something."

"Why can't I see?"

"Because you're a kid, and you don't get to see everything."

I tug the canary-yellow bed skirt down to completely conceal the bin. Even when I'm out of the room, I have to lock the door. Jill is a confirmed snoop, though she prefers the term "sleuth."

It's as I'm kneeling, hiding away the last trace of my project, that I hear a heavy, shifting sound, and then a *thwock*. I jolt up my head, certain at first that Jill has managed to pick my lock. The door is shut, though; it's my window that's open. The wind has pushed so hard against the latch that the double panes have blown apart, and the breeze is now having its way with the contents of my desk. It stirs around the papers there, scooping them up with invisible hands and flipping them this way and that.

"No," I say.

Those papers are private. They are important, even sacred. They are drawings for me and only me to see. I scramble to my feet and grab at them, one by one, until they're all in my keeping. I shove them into a safe place, half beneath the quilt on my bed. Then I turn my attention to the window and, after a struggle, latch it shut.

My effort is only effective for a half second. The moment I step away from the desk, the wind blows the panes open once more, and the stacked papers rustle nervously on my bed. I realize that there's no use for it. I need to formulate another solution.

Hastily I take the papers from my bed and return to the desk, opening its top drawer. From a reused tuna can I fish out a handful of tacks, and then, with resolve, I begin to pin the papers to the wall, arranging them carefully and securely.

The doorknob jiggles. "*Stella*. What's going *on* in there?"

"None of your business!" I shout, pushing the last of the tacks into place.

I take a step back, observing my handiwork. Two images grace the wall over my desk—hand-drawn blueprints. I had forgotten that these papers were on my desk, resting idle there for months. There is something right about this new arrangement, though. Something *fitting*. These papers are where they ought to be, invincible against the strong breeze blowing through the open window

I've only so much time to admire my work before Jill calls out, "Stell-*a*. The news is *starting*!"

I open the door wide onto Jill's consternated face. Her nose is wrinkled higher than a nose ought to go. I pay no mind, acting as though nothing is out of the ordinary.

"Come on, you goof." I poke her right cheek. "Let's go be informed citizens."

Then I shut the door, leaving the wind at my back.

Weekday nights at the Dreamlight are far less hectic than weekends. Mr. Cavallo only runs weekdays during the summer, and now that August is upon us, there are only a couple of weeks left in the line-up before school begins and local teenagers are much too busy with band practice and tryouts and homework to spend a lazy Monday evening doing their best Chewbacca impressions. For now, business remains good, even though it's our second night of hard wind and a rippling screen. Mr. Cavallo's response to the complaints is simple enough: "You pay for an outdoor movie, you pay for the *outdoor*." No one's angry enough to ask for a refund, though.

Kim and I are through serving the brunt of customers after only twenty minutes, and since the movie hasn't started and Kim has not yet been summoned for sex patrol, the two of us sit side by side, cross-legged, on the back counter. I am certain this is a health-code violation, but what Mr. Cavallo doesn't know won't hurt him.

"You should come by the Exchange," Kim tells me. "There's this new band I want you to hear. Australian. Cost a fortune to import the album. They're called Radio Birdman. Heard of 'em?"

I give Kim an incredulous look. "I hear of my bands *through you*. If not, I get my bands *judged* by you."

"I said you're allowed to dig Elton John if you must."

"I'll come by sometime. Next week at the latest."

"Great. Though, fair warning, they're of the punk variety."

It is no secret between us that I don't care for Kim's punk music. To me, every song is the same three chords again and again, shouted over by hoarse-throated boys. However, Kim does have good taste in many other respects. She introduced me to Queen, and that is no small service.

"Hello? Excuse me?"

There is someone at the window, though I can barely see

her. She cannot be older than Jill, and she is much shorter.

"Hey!" she calls again, jumping so her pigtailed head is visible over the counter. "Hey, someone! There's a problem in the girls' bathroom."

Kim cusses. I feel like cussing myself—not that I ever would. I get down from the counter and lean out the window, into the brisk wind.

"What kind of problem?" I ask the girl.

"The toilet's stopped up. Someone went major number two!"

Kim swears again, this time close at my ear. She rams her elbow into my side and says, "You heard her. Girls' bathroom, and you're a girl."

I do not point out to Kim that she, too, is a girl and equally capable of addressing this crisis. She has the unenviable task of sex patrol, while I stay comfortably inside the hut. I feel I owe this to her.

"Okay," I tell the girl. "I'll take care of it."

I slam shut my window and flip the laminated sign there to the side that reads CLOSED. Then I open the flimsy particleboard sink cabinet and take out a pair of elbow-length yellow gloves and a bottle of Clorox. We keep a plunger in the bathroom itself, though clearly no one has the decency to use it.

"Good luck," Kim tells me on my way out.

I am not hopeful.

I take my time approaching the restrooms, which luckily are not crowded. Most of the regulars know to use their own toilet before coming out here, and hold it until they get home. These facilities have not been updated since the early sixties. No matter how hot or dry it is outside, they are perpetually

76

dank, musty swamps of concrete and chipped orange tile.

As I near the door marked LADIES, the wind picks up in a sudden change of direction and blows my way. On it is a hard, definite scent, skunklike and sweet.

Marijuana.

I stop in my tracks. Mr. Cavallo has a strict policy against pot use, and most everyone knows that. No one is foolish enough to light up on the drive-in lot itself. But here, on the outskirts, near the edge of cornfield territory yet close enough to see the movie screen—every so often we get some delinquents. It is Mr. Cavallo who catches them and scares them off, though. I've never encountered them myself.

I stand immobile, uncertain, my feet pointed toward the restrooms but my head cocked toward the flat, shadowy farmland that sprawls beyond me. The concessions hut's sizzling fluorescents shed enough light for me to make out the silhouettes of two figures sitting several yards off.

I could ignore it. No one would know. Mr. Cavallo will most likely find them later, when he makes his rounds.

I am thinking of that little girl, though, who will no doubt be back at the restrooms within the hour. I don't like the thought of her smelling the pot, or possibly stumbling upon the smokers. I keep picturing that girl as Jill.

I adjust the direction of my feet. I walk, resolutely, toward the scent and the silhouettes.

As I draw closer, I clutch the bottle of Clorox tight, like it is a weapon. It could be, I suppose, if it comes down to that. I stop for a moment, unscrew the cap, and tuck it in my back pocket.

The shadows have not noticed me. One of them is leaning back, into the tall grass, and releasing a long exhalation, which winds upward in a lazy curl toward the sky above—light gray on smoky blue. I've come within a yard of them, still unnoticed. They are talking in low voices—male voices. One of them is laughing when I clear my throat, take one step nearer, and ask, "What do you think you're doing?"

7

Galliard

MONDAY, AUGUST 1

"Hey! Ow," says Archer.

I cover my mouth and cough.

"What are you doing?" the girl repeats. She's barely more than a shadow, but I can feel her extremely solid anger from where I sit.

"There are families here," she says. "Little kids. This isn't the place."

"Oh! We are ever so aware, love."

Archer is putting on this bizarre accent, his vowels mixed together. He sounds a lot like Rowan Gentry, a member of Red Sun who's originally from Manchester, England. I know he's talking that way on purpose, too, because the two of us only lit up a few seconds ago.

The girl steps closer, and like magic, my waving tic kicks into gear. My left hand sweeps across the air in a tight arc.

"Leave," she tells us. "I work here, and you're on drive-in property. Leave."

"We're here for the show, same as everyone else," says Archer. "This is our preshow treat. Which you're ruining."

"Maybe you're ruining everyone else's preshow. Ever think of that?" Then she asks, "Did you even buy tickets?"

"Of course we did. What do you take us for? But we're sitting back here specifically so we won't bother anyone. You're the one coming out to us, love."

"Why're you calling me that? What makes you think you can call me 'love'?"

I wave again. The girl whips her focus onto me.

Damn.

"What is *your* problem? You have my attention. What?"

"Nothing," I say, waving.

"You think that's funny?"

"Hey," says Archer, dropping the accent and the joint we've been sharing. "He doesn't mean anything by it."

The girl takes a step closer. "You're from the commune, aren't you?"

"Why would you think that?" asks Archer.

"Because you're wearing *those*." She points at our white linen tunics and jeans. It's standard dress for most Red Sun members. "I'm sure the police would love to hear about this. I know how fond they are of you people."

"Hey now! No need to play dirty."

Archer finally sounds kind of worried. I guess I should be worried too, only I'm hung up on my waving tic and how I've accidentally made this girl mad at me. I told Archer this was a bad idea, smoking this close to a public place; especially after that police search, we should be playing it safe. Archer wasn't having it, though. He went on about how this was my first night, and it had to be done right, and the best way to see my first movie was under the influence of locally grown weed. Though not grown in the commune, of course. Archer scored this off some town friend of his, using a good chunk of his Crossing allowance. I've smoked with him before, on the commune outskirts, near the wheat crop. Archer managed to sneak the weed past Charlie by employing a method he claimed left him shitting funny for days. Back then, I felt this constant jab of paranoia, afraid that at any moment one of the adults would come through and catch us, so I understand the appeal of smoking out here, in the open.

Or at least I did. Until now. Until the girl.

"I won't have to play dirty if you move," she's saying. "*Move*, okay? Please."

Please. Something about that word—civility tacked onto the curtness—makes me laugh. Archer rams his elbow into my side. Then he rustles, pulling something from his backpack. There's a clicking sound, and light bursts around us. Archer is shining a flashlight directly at the girl.

She doesn't shout or throw her arms in front of her eyes. She doesn't cuss; I can tell she's not the type, because she's already had plenty of reasons to cuss at us before now. She stays where she is and says, "You won't intimidate me."

I guess I'm supposed to be annoyed. A little threatened, maybe. Instead I'm fascinated, because I finally see the girl. Her nose is snub. Her eyes are dark and large, her eyebrows darker and larger. Her jaw is weak. Her lips are thick. It's not a pretty face, but it's plenty fascinating.

It's also familiar.

"All right." Archer says, getting to his feet. "It's not worth it. Come on."

I stay where I am, though, staring at the girl. Her brown, frizzy hair is shooting straight up in the wind.

"Hey," I say. "I know you."

She takes a step back, looking uncertain. "No, you don't."

I wave, my hand arcing high over my head. "No, I do. I know you. *Stella*. You're Stella Kay."

The girl's big eyes get bigger.

"Come *on*." Archer grabs hold of my arm mid-wave and, using the leverage, pulls me to my feet. My knees are stiff, popping as he drags me away from the lights of the drive-in. Away from the ghostly girl.

I do know her. It's *her*, I'm sure.

"Being a creep may not have been the best strategy," says Archer once we're on a narrow dirt path that cuts through two cornfields. His flashlight beam catches on dark green stalks and passing gnats. Around us there's a constant, low murmur of wind pressing into the crops.

I'm no longer waving. Instead, I'm blinking—rapid squeezes, open, shut, open, shut.

"I wasn't trying to creep her out."

"'I know you'? Only murderers and predators say shit like that."

"I do know her, though," I say, blinking.

"Sweet baby Jesus, Galliard, how could you possibly know her? This is your first time on the Outside."

"I *know* her."

"Okay, man, now you're creeping *me* out."

"Didn't she look familiar to you?"

"No, she did not. Granted, I was less focused on her face

82

and more worried about the threats. If she'd reported us to the police, do you know what the Council would do? What *Rod* would do? Possession of marijuana, watching a movie without paying? I bet Rod's dying for a good reason to shut down Crossing, same as he did all the imports. No way we're going to give him that."

I don't bring up how Archer was the one to suggest both the weed and the "free" seats on the edge of the field. He knows. We walk in silence, through cornstalks taller than us, and my blinking continues, minute after minute. We're not taking the route we came by, but I trust that Archer knows where he's going.

"Ruin a perfectly good evening," he mutters, as though he's been talking this whole time and is now reaching a conclusion. "Perfectly good joint, too."

"She's Phoenix's sister," I say.

Archer stops walking. He turns, shining his flashlight in my face. "Phoenix said his family was dead."

"Yeah. He told me that too."

"Then how is that his sister?"

I tic—five fast blinks in a row. "It just is."

Archer hacks out a frustrated laugh. "How do you *know*?"

"The painting. It was over my dresser in Sage House, and now it's over my desk in our new room. It used to be his, and I would stare at it all the time, because the face was strange. Phoenix said it was his sister, remember? And then later he gave it to me because he said he didn't want to be reminded of her. Remember that?"

"The painting over your desk? The funky blue one?"

"It's Phoenix's sister."

"That girl didn't look anything like your painting."

Through several blinks, I say, "Yeah, she did."

"Listen, Galliard. I've seen that god-awful picture every day for more than a year, and I didn't recognize her."

"You *saw* it," I say. "You didn't *look* at it."

"You are such an ass."

Archer starts back up. I keep pace, still ticking.

"I only mean, it's hard to forget a face like that. It's so . . . weird."

"You should go back and tell her that. Girls love to hear how weird their faces are."

I'm grateful for the cool wind on my hot skin. "What I mean is—"

"Really. Go on back. I'm sure she'll find you irresistible once she knows you've jacked off to her picture for over a year."

"I haven't—"

"Never mind. Let's focus on the real question, which is, If that's Phoenix's sister . . . well then, what the hell?"

Well then, what the hell indeed.

I could tell Archer everything. Right about now would be the time. I could tell him that Phoenix's family might be dead to *him*, but they're alive and well right here in Slater, Kansas. I could tell him I've been writing to Phoenix's sister for almost two years. But that would mean telling him everything, like how I've been lying about my identity and intercepting Phoenix's mail and defying the Council's rule that there can be no correspondence between Red Sun residents and their family mem-

84

bers on the Outside. And I can't go that far. It's too messy. He wouldn't get it.

"Maybe he was wrong," I say, before stretching my lips as wide as they will go. "Maybe she got kidnapped or ran away, and he *assumed* she was dead."

"And now she's hanging around the Dreamlight, of all places, for kicks."

"Maybe." I don't know why I'm even trying.

"Okay," says Archer. "What's more likely? That Phoenix's sister comes back from the dead *or* . . . that the same Phoenix who stole your job is the Phoenix who tells big, fat lies?"

I open my mouth in another unyawn. I don't respond. I'm kind of pissed. I'm also amused. Because how funny is it that I've broken my three-year vow and left Red Sun in order to forget Phoenix, only to find him on the Outside, too?

It's all so ironically hilarious.

Archer says, "I know what this is about."

"No, you don't."

"Come *on*. He's your hero. You've worshipped him ever since he showed up. Maybe you weren't in love with him like everyone else, but you *worshipped* him. He's a god to you, same as one of your dead musicians. And now he's fallen out of the sky."

I wait for an unyawn to pass before I say, "That's not what's going on."

"Sure, man. Keep telling yourself that."

"It's not."

It is, though. Archer's right. I always liked my life at Red Sun, but Phoenix gave me a reason to be *proud* of it. There he was, this older guy with good looks and a smooth attitude, born and raised on the Outside, saying he envied *me*. He made me feel as cool as he was, and in return I revered him almost as much as I did Janis, Jimi, and Buddy. He was like them in so many ways—a rebel and an artist, determined to shine bright.

And the best part? He convinced me that I could be like my gods too. Phoenix was the first person I played an original song for, on the Common House Yamaha. He told me my work was genius, that I was going to make something out of myself. He said there was no one on the Outside writing the kind of songs I was. And he followed through, too. He met up with me countless nights in Common House, listening to my compositions, giving me feedback, applauding, an audience of one.

Now every memory I have of those private concerts coats my stomach with acid. It'd be one thing if I didn't know the guy and he'd stolen my spot. But Phoenix knew me well. He knew my music better than anyone else in this commune. He told me I could *be* resident artist.

He didn't just steal; he *betrayed* me.

I'm not going to say that to Archer, though. I'm not going to breathe a word. In fact I'm about to reiterate one more time how mistaken he is, when Archer throws out a hand in front of me.

"Oh, whoa. Wait. Hang on, wait. Look."

All this time, we've been walking through farmland, flanked on both sides by dense rows of corn. But here the corn comes to an end. Before us, prairie sand reed spills out in rippling waves.

Red Sun is hedged in by a fence and barns and wooden

buildings. Everything there is lines and borders. Nothing sprawls there. Not like here, where the grass forms a sea, and the sea is telling me to dive in.

"Do you see them?"

I'm about to ask Archer what he means, but then I do see: a light, small and yellow as a corn kernel. It flickers on for a second, then fades to black. My vision adjusts, and as it does I see more lights, turning on and off in a scattered, syncopated rhythm.

When I was little, I learned that fireflies don't live everywhere. There are people farther north and west who have never seen a firefly in their lives.

"That's why we are very blessed at Red Sun," said Melly, our early elementary teacher. "Every summer, the fireflies come out and shine for us. Not everyone is as fortunate as we are, to live in a place where we can experience the joys of nature and want for nothing."

I believed Melly. I thought she was telling the truth. I was five—why wouldn't I? Even now, I guess I believe her; I *am* fortunate to live at Red Sun. But the thing is, when Melly told us that not everyone could see fireflies, I assumed she was talking about *everyone on the Outside*.

But this is the Outside. I'm standing on the Outside, where I've never seen this much sand reed and this many fireflies in my life. The unruly wind sweeps over the plain, pushing into the long grass with far-reaching fingers. I shiver, but it's a good kind of cold.

"I told you," says Archer, who sounds unusually reverent. "There are some almighty views out here."

87

"You weren't joking."

Because up until now, I thought he was—joking, exaggerating, *lying* about the Outside. It couldn't have been as vast and good as Archer and the other crossers made it out to be.

This is vast, though. And good. No lie.

Which means Phoenix has been the liar all along.

December 2, 1975

Stella,

I wish there was a way to read Sagan in here.
No one's censoring your letters, though, so
you can keep sending me the good things he
says and the discoveries happening. I think
it's interesting.

I've been thinking about aliens, though
maybe not in the way you do.

I've been thinking about outsiders.
People we don't understand, people who don't
understand us. People who are different,
with different beliefs and ways of looking
at the universe. I know you're intrigued by
the idea of extraterrestrial life, but isn't
it overwhelming enough thinking about plain
old terrestrial life? People who don't look
and think and act the way we do. They're all on
this planet, but I don't hear about us sending
golden plaques to each other or trying to help
each other out.

I guess what I'm getting at is, why do we
think it'd be any better with aliens from
other planets? Even if they're the nicest in
the world and _want_ to help us, do you think
we'd let them? I think we'd shoot them down. I

think we'd nuke them or run experiments. Why not? It's what we do to each other.

I'm not trying to make you feel bad or anything. But I've got a different theory: If these aliens are smart, they'll keep their spaceships far away from the human race. If they're smart and kind, maybe they'll help us out from a distance, so we'll never know it was them. I don't think they'll want to meet us, though. If they know what's best for them, they'll steer clear.

Phoenix

8

Stella

MONDAY, AUGUST 1

Until I came across the Red Sun boys, I was preoccupied with
a sufficiently long list of concerns:

My project.

My two jobs.

My sister's well-being.

My brother's radio silence.

It is, I think, the last item that accounts for my actions
tonight. I am fairly certain I wouldn't have called the boys out
on another evening, when my mind was calmer and tolerance
higher. Something about the sweet scent and low laughter and
the sheer arrogance of lighting up near such a public place—
they tipped me toward confrontation.

Then, to make matters worse, I saw their clothes.

Like all Slater residents, I know about Crossing. Red Sun is
already prime fodder for jokes at Slater High, but Crossing is
an open season of salacious remarks. Chris Kennish swore up
and down that he was going to score with three Red Sun girls
this summer. Leslie White claimed the guys were uncircum-
cised virgins and she had proof. Norm O'Brien said they were

sex-crazed hippies who took part in daily orgies and other forms of free love. A rumor circulated school hallways that the residents wore long hair because they did not believe in gender. These were unoriginal offerings I did not take part in, not only because they were unoriginal, but also because they were much too close to home.

More than two years ago, Craig left us for Red Sun. Unlike my mother, he did not give an explanation. He only wrote where he had gone and that we were not to contact him. The day before that, unbeknownst to us, he'd sold the car he had saved for and bought his junior year. Then he collected a few belongings—clothes and his best paintings—and he left.

One day Craig lived in the bedroom across from me. He drove me to school activities and shared new music with me and occasionally fixed me French toast on Saturday mornings. He was an accomplished artist and a star basketball player. He had received a small academic scholarship to attend the University of Kansas. He was going to study business. He was Craig the Strong, the Steady, the Unchanging.

The next day, he was gone.

None of us Mercers have seen Craig since. My father refused to pursue the issue. Craig was eighteen when he left. He was his own person, said my dad. He could make his own decisions.

I was too angry to do anything at first. Then, after two weeks of silent seething, I wrote my brother.

It was a bad letter. Each line bled with hurt and vitriol. I called him the most selfish person alive. I demanded he explain himself. I demanded he write back. He met one of the demands.

It took him a month, but he wrote back on five sheets of folded paper, typed. He did not explain why he left. He said he was happy, and that was enough.

I wrote him back. I was still angry, and I still blamed him. It was clear, though, that unless I wished to bike out to Red Sun and scream for Craig to show himself—something I was not near brave enough to do—this was all I had left of my brother. And I needed my brother. I really needed him. That's why I kept on writing. And, to my cautious delight, he wrote back. We began to talk about books and music and ideas—topics we hadn't discussed much before his departure. He shared thoughts I never imagined were churning in his mind, and, as months passed, I felt that at last Craig saw me as more than his little sister; he saw me as someone whose opinion mattered. Before, Craig had been my big brother—the one who yelled at my school bullies, who fixed my broken roller skates, who taught me how to tie my first pair of laced shoes. Before, Craig was the one to fix me and Jill our dinners, the one to remind Dad that I was a growing kid and needed a new pair of jeans. On the day that Marci Dougan told me she'd found a best friend to replace me, Craig held me as I wept, and he told me that Marci didn't know a good thing and, anyway, she had an obnoxious laugh.

When I first wrote to Craig, it was because I needed the Craig he was before. I needed his advice, his comfort, his expertise. Then I began to write for a different reason. I wrote because Craig had become someone new: my friend. I could tease him for growing his hair long, and he could make fun of my childhood love for Herman's Hermits. We were almost normal siblings, as we'd been before. I didn't want to lose that. That's why I never asked him again why he left us. For two whole years, I didn't write anything too dangerous or confrontational.

Then I made my mistake.

At the start of June, I wrote to tell him about my graduation. Then I told him I wanted to see him.

I have not heard from him since.

I've written two more letters, calling him a coward, telling him he as good as owes me a meeting.

He's written nothing.

I never told my father or Jill about the letters. I guess I've been selfish in my own way. If I'm honest, I wanted Craig to myself. I wanted to be an exception to his abandonment. Now, it seems, he has finally abandoned me too.

After Craig left us, my father expressly forbade me and Jill from going anywhere near the commune, including their public café. I've respected my father's wishes. I have written my brother behind his back, but I've never gone to Red Sun. What I did not expect was for Red Sun to come to me. I didn't expect to see those boys in their long white shirts, and I never, ever expected one of them to know my name.

I know you.

Stella Kay.

Even now, after taking care of the mess in the girls' bathroom, back in the heat and relative safety of the concessions hut, the words make me shiver.

There is only one explanation for why that strange, waving boy—whom I most certainly do *not* know—recognized me:

94

Craig. Craig showed him a picture or, more likely, a painting of me. Craig told him my name.

Maybe he's disowned me, I think, pulling a new tower of paper cups from their packaging and stacking them by the soda fountain, *but he hasn't forgotten me.*

Then a couple of junior high boys show up at the window, demanding two large root beers.

There is no wind on my bike ride home—not even the slightest stirring. It's the heat that alerts me to this fact, rising from the pavement and pressing down on my shoulders, utterly uninhibited. It's as though someone has flipped a giant switch, cutting off every breeze in town. After only a few minutes of biking, I've built up a sweat.

When I get home, the lamp in the den is on—an anomaly, since my father is away at work and Jill should be in bed. I'm readying a lecture for my sister when I walk into the creamy yellow glow of the room and find my father sitting in his La-Z-Boy.

"What're you doing here?" I ask, happily surprised.

"Switched a shift. I wanted a chance to talk to you alone."

Panic whirs inside me. For one irrational second, I am convinced he has found out about the letters.

"O-okay."

"Don't worry, it's nothing bad." He reflects for a moment. "Nothing I consider bad, anyway."

"Okay." I sit on the sofa, opposite him. I become aware of my scent, competing with that of the house. My frizzy brown hair smells of liquid butter and earth but not, luckily, marijuana.

"Have a good time?" he asks.

"Good for work, I guess."

"I bet you've memorized that movie."

I smile and tuck my hands between seat cushions. I appreciate the way the rough-woven fabric feels on my palms. In a low voice I say, "I've got a bad feeling about this."

My father laughs. "I told you, it's nothing bad."

I lean back and study the spin of the ceiling fan. For many years now, we've turned off the air-conditioning on summer nights and let our ceiling fans do the cooling. I often wake up hot and itchy, but the practice does make a difference in the electricity bill.

My father is clearly nervous. He keeps running his right hand over his left. He no longer wears a wedding band; he removed it three years ago. I never asked why.

"Stella."

"Hmm?"

"You didn't tell me about the fish."

I'm confused for one moment. Then I remember: *Velma.*

"Oh." I remove my hands from the cushions and fold them in my lap. "I meant to tell you. Only it happened early yesterday, and I didn't want to bother you with it."

"I—" He breaks off, frowning hard. The movement shifts his mustache, sends it bristling more than usual. "Were you afraid to tell me?"

"What? No, it's just that Jill was near hysterics, and I knew you needed the sleep. I was fine."

"Because you can tell me those things, ask for help. I'm your father."

"I know that, Dad."

He looks as though he wants to say more. I am not sure I want to hear it. I don't hold my father responsible for the extra housework and the looking after Jill. They are not things I have to do because of him; really, they're because of my mother. I work two jobs and will not attend college because of something my mother did on July 20, 1969, when I was only nine years old. I could not have known then what her death meant to my future.

My father settles into silence, but I don't think he's through talking. He would not have missed a shift to ask me about a fish named Velma. He must be working up to something more. So I wait.

"Stella." He throws my name out like an anchor.

I let it catch, and I smile reassuringly. "Dad, just say it."

"I . . ." The word comes out as a wheeze, then dissolves. "Sorry, hon. I don't exactly know how to word it, but I met someone at the plant. We've been seeing each other, and . . . well, I thought it was about time I brought her to the house to meet you girls. I wanted to ask you about it first, though. I want to know how you feel about it, and how you think Jill will take it."

"Dad," I say. "Are you talking about a girlfriend?"

"Well. Well, I don't think that's what it's called for someone my age."

"Sure it is."

"Then . . . yes, I'm talking about a girlfriend."

"She works at the plant?"

"Yes, she's in administration. A nuclear physicist."

My mouth opens wide. "*Nice*, Dad."

My father is quiet. He scratches at his chin, though I doubt very much that he has an itch.

At last he says, very soft, "You're not angry about that?"

I scratch my own chin, in need of something to do. "I . . . don't feel anything about it. Is that weird?"

"It's been eight years."

"Yeah."

I am not sure what he means by that. *It's been eight years.* I don't know if it's justification or observation, or perhaps both. Here is the fact, though, hanging heavy on the room: It has been eight years since my mother hung herself—almost two weeks since the anniversary.

"I think I'm fine with it," I say. "I think Jill will be even more fine than me."

"Yeah?"

"Yeah."

"Her name is Gayle."

"I don't dislike the name."

"And if Gayle were to come over this Saturday night—"

"I can ask off."

"Well, that's . . . that's very good to hear. Thank you."

I'm not sure what he is thanking me for. I was only honest. I do not feel anything about it. Even as I brush my teeth and comb my hair and shut myself into my bedroom, there is no great revelation of emotion. No anger, nor sadness, nor even a bittersweet pang. My father is bringing his girlfriend to the house for dinner Saturday night. It is the first girlfriend, at least that I know of, since my mother's passing. There it is. I attempt to turn the fact into something more—a tear, a shudder, a laugh. In the end, though, it remains stubbornly true to its original form: It is only a fact.

My window, impossible to close before, sits open, letting in the hot and muggy outside. I latch the panes with ease this time around and, as I do, note the newly placed drawings above my desk. They belong to *That Stella*'s life, I know, but I can at least look at them. Even now that the winds have died down, the papers feel as right tacked up there as they did before.

I turn on the ceiling fan and shift my attention to a wooden crate that I've placed on my bed. Craig made this crate his junior year, in shop, to hold pieces of his art. It is one of the few things I kept when I moved into his room last year. Craig was clearly never coming back, and sharing a bedroom with Jill was more than inconvenient. Our house is small enough as is, and it did not make sense to leave the room unused. That's why, one weekend, I went through Craig's remaining things and boxed them up. I tried not to be hurt by what I found—little things he'd left behind, like a homemade macaroni frame I'd made for him in the third grade, containing a photo of us at the neighborhood Fourth of July barbecue. I told myself that Red Sun must have had rules about the possessions you brought inside. I told myself that Craig had left behind plenty of important things, like extra pairs of shoes and his favorite winter coat. He simply didn't have room for a silly picture frame from his sister.

Then I finished boxing up what remained and stored everything in the garage.

I kept the crate, though, and the artwork inside.

There are several charcoal sketches in here—cars and trees and various storefronts on Vine. The paintings are all portraits. Of me and Jill. Of two old girlfriends. Of faces I do not recognize and assume to be Slater residents Craig charmed into sitting for him. Craig was always a charmer. He knew how to butter his questions and demands in ways that made them impossible to resist. Many times, he convinced me to do one of his chores in such a way that I felt Craig was doing *me* the favor.

"Stella," he would say, "I'm going to *let* you take out my trash. It's a top-secret mission, though. Don't tell Jill or she'll be jealous."

Though those lines stopped working on me as I got older, I witnessed Craig use them repeatedly, with much success, on teachers and friends and girls. I used to joke that his true vocational calling was not art but *con* art.

The largest portrait in the crate is of our mother, Diane Mercer, at the age of twenty-one. I've seen the photograph Craig used as his model. It was taken at our parents' wedding. The photographer snapped a shot of my mother laughing at an uproarious joke told by her maid of honor, Betty Hume. Her brown eyes are crackling with life, her face stretched in pure joy. It's an already vibrant expression, but Craig's painting transformed it into something more alive. He painted in bright blues and greens, and the face looks both nothing and everything like my mother. Anyone can see that the portrait was made of more than canvas and acrylics; it was brushed on thick with love.

Craig loved our mother so much.

More than Jill could have at such a young age. Even more than I did; I am the first to admit that.

Craig did not see what my mother did as an unknowable past, as Jill does. Or as a desperate measure, as I do. He saw it as an act of fearlessness. He told me that late one night, a month before he left.

"Maybe it ended badly," he said, "but we shouldn't remember it for how it ended. We should remember why Mom did it. What she was after."

I've revisited that conversation many times in the past two years. I have asked myself, why did *Craig* do it? What was *he* after? There are many possibilities: He was bored and after adventure. He was confused and after answers. He was angry and after solace. I have no way of knowing for certain, and for all his letters, Craig never gave me an answer. Lately, I've resigned myself to the idea that he won't contact me ever again.

Then that Red Sun boy said my name.

I place the portraits and sketches back into the crate and set it on the floor. Stretching out on my bed, I study the ceiling fan, its brown blades a blur.

"It doesn't matter," I tell the ceiling. "It doesn't."

Stella.

You're Stella Kay.

That boy knows Craig.

Craig talked about me.

I don't know why it bothers me this much. It does not matter if he refuses to see me and refuses to answer my letters. There is nothing I can do about it.

That is what I've told myself until today.

Only now I wonder how bad it would really be if I paid a visit to the Moonglow Café.

Sudden pain jolts through my eyes. I hiss and shut them, rubbing at my temples. The pain fades almost as quickly as it came on, and when I blink my eyes open again, all is well.

Except, all *isn't* well.

In that moment, I notice what I didn't notice before: There is a kind of light on the inside of my open closet door. And the light is *writing*, and the writing is *numbers*. They cut across the wood paneling in faint violet marks.

Alarmed, I clamber out of bed, and as I do, I attempt to land on an explanation. Jill might have snuck into my bedroom and written on the door with marker as I slept. That isn't possible, though. I always lock my door. Even if I hadn't, I would have noticed the numbers before now—when I opened the closet door to get dressed this morning, for instance. More than that, recent memory tells me there's been a change. There are glowing numbers on this door where there most certainly were *not* numbers a minute ago.

I stand before the door, squinting, and raise a hand to rub at the writing. I drive the flat of my fist against the wood, pressing so hard that my skin turns red with irritation. The effort does no good, though. When I am through, the numbers remain, visible as ever. Nothing has changed.

But something *has* changed. One of the numbers—the one farthest to the right—is different.

Where once the markings read *17:01:34*, they now read *17:01:33*.

I know what this is. What I do not know is how and why it

is on my closet door, or what it means. I know what to expect next; even so, I cry out when the rightmost number changes again, before my eyes. The three vanishes from sight, and a two fades into its place.

17:01:32.

It is a countdown. If it can be trusted to follow the usual pattern of countdowns, it reads seventeen days, one hour, thirty-two minutes.

I tell myself that I am dreaming. I must be. I pinch my left arm, and I pinch my right. I dig my nails into my scalp, and I spin in place—a single, tight rotation.

I don't wake, though. The countdown remains: *17:01:31.*

And I am left with one, dumbfounded question:

Seventeen days, one hour, and thirty-one minutes till what?

9

Galliard

TUESDAY, AUGUST 2

Here at Red Sun, we don't encourage the use of surnames. We call each other by our given names, most of which we gave ourselves. For example, can't-stop-asking-questions Bright used to be called Patty Hewitt. Six months ago, she shrugged off that name, and forevermore she will be Bright. Like that.

I was born in the commune—the first kid born here, actually—so I got my name from the Council. They named me Galliard, which is some kind of old French dance. This is because, when I came out of the womb, I was kicking my feet in what Ruby described as "an intentional, rhythmic pattern."

Ruby gave birth to me, but we don't call her my mother, the way people would on the Outside. Ruby is as much my mother as Opal, and any of the older women at Red Sun. And J. J. is as much my father as Rod, or any of the older men. J. J. and Ruby came here in '61, when Ruby was seven months pregnant with me. Before that, they'd lived in Cleveland, Ohio. Their names were Joe and Roseanne Lazzari. That's all I know about the Before, and that's only because, when we were fourteen, Archer sneaked a look at my record in Rod's office.

It was too weird, thinking of Ruby and J. J. as Roseanne and Joe. It was weird thinking of them being my age and living on the Outside in the distant and unknown state of Ohio. So I didn't think about it for long. What was the point? It wouldn't accomplish anything any more than it would for Archer to try to remember what life was like for him when he was little and lived in Los Angeles. Most of his memories are of Red Sun, from the time his parents moved him here at age six and onward. That's the life that counts now.

Ruby and J. J. didn't raise me. The community raised me. We raise one another. That's how it works. Kids are cared for in the nursery, Brush House, and at the age of ten they go to Sage House, where they're given a roommate and a supervisor. That's when they get a preassignment—a service to the commune while they continue their studies.

When we turn sixteen, we meet with a school official from the Outside, and our natural parents sign some papers saying it's all right for us to stop school and start work. Then we get our actual assignments. These are the roles we will play in Red Sun for the rest of our lives. Once we assume them, we become fully incorporated members of the commune, and we move to Heather House—the largest building on commune property, where the adults live, and where Archer and I moved in yesterday. It was a fifteen-minute process that entailed transporting our very few possessions to a furnished room.

So you see, there's plenty of order to life at Red Sun. It's all about structure and a day-to-day schedule. That's why, when I'm asked to report to Council House, I'm sure I'm busted. I've never been summoned before. It's completely out of the ordinary. I'm convinced that somehow, some way, the Council found out about me and Archer irresponsibly lighting up on the Outside, and from here on out, my Crossing privileges will be revoked. Now, of all times, when I actually want those privileges—*need* them, even. Maybe going Outside started as the wind at my back—a directive from my gods and a kind of "fuck you" to the Council for passing me over. Now, though, I need more. I need to know what else is out there. What the *people* are like. If they're as bad as Phoenix told me, or if that's another thing he lied about. And then there's the matter of Stella, but I'm doing a great job of not thinking about that, and I plan on keeping it up.

It's not that there was anything ominous about the way Saff told me. She caught me on my way into Heather House and said Rod wanted to see me in his office, at the start of morning prayer. She didn't look angry about it, or even disappointed. But it's possible she doesn't yet know what Rod knows. About my misconduct. About the Dreamlight and the weed and Stella Kay Mercer in the flesh. Though I wonder—does Rod know *all* that? How much should I play dumb when he calls me into his office and asks me to explain myself?

My head is so jammed with questions, at first I don't notice the men right in front of me, exiting Council House as I come up the dirt path entrance. There are two of them, one tall and bulky, one tall and thin. They're wearing uniforms—policemen from the Outside. And since I'm thinking doomsday shit as it is, my first thought is, *They've come for me. They know I've broken their Outside rules, and they're going to put me in their Outside prison.*

That doesn't happen. One of them gives me a look as though I reek of body odor, but neither says a word as we pass on the path. The winds of the past two days have finally settled down, turning the world hushed and hot, and I notice a long trickle of sweat running down the tall one's cheek. They keep heading out, quiet. I walk slow, way slower than usual. I take the stairs to the Council House door one deliberate step at a time. I try the handle, hoping it won't turn—stupid, since not a single door in Red Sun has a lock.

Galliard! you're shouting. *Quit delaying the inevitable and get on with it!* I know, I *know.*

I get to Rod's office. Though the door is open, Rod is hidden from view, sitting in a tall-backed armchair, facing away from where I stand. I get this horrible urge to shout, "Boo!" Because if he's going to revoke my Crossing privileges, I at least want to scare the shit out of the guy. And he deserves getting scared shitless regardless, what with locking down our record collection. But before I can be any stupider than usual, Rod swivels his chair, and we're facing each other.

"Galliard," he says.

"Rod," I reply.

Then I clear my throat of a familiar, unclearable fog.

"Have a seat." He motions to the folding wooden chair before me, on the opposite side of his desk. I take it. It squeaks under my weight. I try not to freak the fuck out about any of this.

"I appreciate you coming in this early—"

"What were the police doing here?"

I shouldn't be asking questions, and I definitely shouldn't

be interrupting Rod, but hey. If I'm in trouble anyway, right?

Rod looks kind of surprised. He leans forward and picks up a paperweight from his desk. It's glass, a sphere cut clean in half. He turns it over in his hand. Even though he doesn't owe me a reply, I can see him thinking, deciding if he'll give one to me anyway.

"There have been some deaths on the Outside," he says, and when my chair squeaks again at my sudden shift, he adds, "Animal deaths. Dogs, mostly. They thought our crossers might have had something to do with it."

I clear my throat, making a face. "They think we're killing animals for fun? Who do they think we are?"

Rod scratches his jaw, which is so cleanly shaven the morning sun gleams off it. Rod is always clean-shaven. I've never seen him with scruff, not once.

He says, "That is the heart of the matter, Galliard. They think we're villains. That's how it is on the Outside: No one takes responsibility; everyone looks for someone else to blame. Since they do not understand us, they fear us. Since they fear us, they blame us."

Rod isn't telling me anything I don't already know. This topic comes up a lot during commune meetings—especially when Rod is the one talking. The Outside doesn't like us. They think we should have families made of mother and father and child, and we don't. They think we should go to their public schools, and we don't. They think we should go to their churches, and we don't. So really, I shouldn't be surprised that the Outside assumes we have something to do with their animals dying.

"It's insulting," Rod's saying, "but we must always be the ones to defend ourselves against their accusations. When *they* are the guilty ones. When it is their chemicals and their mass production—you understand that, don't you, Galliard? You see the irony of it?"

Sure, I see irony, though not the kind Rod's talking about. I see a guy talking about how the Outside is bad for blaming us, and then two seconds later he's turning around, blaming *them*. It's hilarious. It makes me want to blow up in laughter right here, in front of him. Rod is a creep for saying this stuff. I told you: I like him least.

But I say, "Sure, Rod. I see it."

And Rod says, "I know you do. That's why I called you here." He scratches his smooth, pale jaw again. "Do you know why I called you in, Galliard? Any guess?"

Absolutely. It's because Archer and I smoked weed on the Outside, and also I've been carrying on a correspondence with an Outsider under false pretenses, and also I hate my assignment in the kitchen, and also if you're a mind reader, you know I kind of hate you and wish you'd lift your stupid regulations on the Back Room record collection.

My throat rumbles with another clearing.

Then I say, "No, sir. Not a clue."

"Then let me explain myself." Rod leans closer. He folds his hands over the midpoint of the table between us. I shift a little. The chair squeaks.

"Galliard," he says, "I know you're upset over not receiving our resident artist position."

Well, lo and behold, he *is* a mind reader.

"I want you to know," Rod continues, "it was, indeed, a difficult decision. The Council is well aware of your gift for music, and we do not doubt your sincere desire to help extend Red Sun's influence beyond our walls."

I wish he wouldn't say this stuff. Every sentence he completes is a fresh punch to my face. If I were qualified, I'd be resident artist. But I'm not resident artist, so what is the fucking point here?

"Galliard," says Rod. God, he's using my name a whole lot. "Have you considered that you were meant for something other than resident artist? Something better?"

I clear my throat, and I stare at him like some stupid kid who doesn't know the answer to a math problem.

"What I'm trying to say, Galliard, is that the Council thinks you have potential. So much so, we believe you will make an excellent leader."

I'm damn slow. Rod is making some grand connection, but I don't see it.

"Uh. Sure." Seems the safe thing to say.

Rod can see I'm not getting it. He scoots his folded hands closer to me. He leans in. "What I'm saying, Galliard, is that we can see you on this Council one day."

Now I get it. Man, do I get it. My chair squeaks real loud. Sound bursts from my throat—three quick clears.

Then I say, "Wow. Oh wow. Wow, that's . . . okay."

"Have you never considered the possibility?" Rod's lips are stretching outward. I think he's laughing at me.

"Honestly? No."

I could give the long answer, say I've never considered

being on the Council because ever since I was a piano-playing pip-squeak *I fucking wanted to be resident artist.* Something tells me Rod wouldn't appreciate this elaboration, though.

"Think about it," Rod tells me. "You were born here. You were raised here. You clearly love Red Sun enough to want to share its message with the Outside. You're a model resident, Galliard. You're happy here. Aren't you happy here?"

"Uh."

"More than that, you're our only youth, to date, who has chosen not to engage in Crossing. You chose instead to continue contributing to the commune. That demonstrates high moral fiber. Don't think it's gone unnoticed."

"Uh."

I feel hot all over. Sweaty under my linen collar. I give a giant throat clear.

"Now, I *know*." Rod pulls apart his hands and raises them high, like I'm shouting him down. "I know how dearly you love your music, son. I want you to think about it, though. Think, long and hard. To be a musician is a fine thing. You can create songs and words that will outlive you. But Galliard, a song is just a song. As a leader, you can effect change. You can shape minds. You can alter the course of a group's future. *This* group's future. *That* outlives you too. And that outlives you longer than songs ever will. It lives on in generation after generation. Do you see what I'm saying? Do you understand the possibility?"

I could say a lot here. A whole lot. I could argue. I could say that a song is never just a song. I could say that Hendrix's riffs make me feel *alive* down in the grit of my bones. The thing is, Rod is being nice to me. Instead of revoking my Crossing privileges, he's offering me more privilege. More possibility. And even if it isn't the possibility I want, it's *something*.

That's why I say, "I get what you're saying."

Rod looks immensely satisfied. He lowers his raised hands, grips them tight together, and bows his head. "You understand, then, why we've chosen to keep you in the kitchen. When the time comes for you to step up to a position of leadership, the members of Red Sun will want to know you're one of them. They couldn't respect you if they thought you'd been given a free pass—done little more than write songs, knew nothing of what it means to support our group with your own two hands."

"Yeah. Sure. No one respects a musician, right?" I try pushing out a laugh, but it clogs at the top of my throat before sludging out, pathetic—my very body punishing me for my betrayal of Holly, Hendrix, and Joplin. After that embarrassment, a throat clear manages to push itself out.

Rod smiles at me, even though he doesn't seem particularly happy about anything. "Starting in September, I am going to bring you into this office. Not in place of your work at the Moonglow. A supplement. You'll get to see how I work, help with some odd tasks. Little by little, you'll learn what it means to lead a community. Sound agreeable?"

"Uh, sure. Agreeable."

"I'm glad we understand each other, Galliard. I'm glad we had this talk."

"Yeah, me too. Definitely. Thanks."

I stand up, because it sure feels like Rod's asked me to

leave. As I head for the door, he says, "I hear you went out last night."

Damn.

I turn around. "Yeah, with Archer. To the movies, that's all."

"Your first time Crossing. Even though you could've gone anytime in the past two summers. Why is that, I wonder?"

"Yeah, I don't know, I guess I . . . don't know."

Rod's looking straight at me. I look back at his clean, hairless face. He knows why I crossed. I know why I crossed. And we each know that the other knows.

"Now that we've had our talk," says Rod, "I think things have changed for you. Do you think so, Galliard?" He's not actually asking me, though, because he goes on. "Crossing is for the weak among us. You're not weak, Galliard. *Leaders* aren't weak. Keep that in mind."

A different tic shows up. My jaw jolts to the right.

"Sure. I'll keep that in mind."

"For every action we take, there is a consequence. The Life Force sees to that. Weak actions—*wrong* actions . . . those result in negative consequences. Here at Red Sun, we strive only for the positive consequences. For harmony with our Life Force. Understood?"

Sure I do. I've heard the law of consequence my whole life.

My jaw twitches. I say, "Understood."

"Good."

And *that* is Rod dismissing me.

So I leave. I get out of that room before I can tic again.

10
Stella

TUESDAY, AUGUST 2

Slater is holding a town meeting this afternoon. I know all about it, because working at Vine Street Salon means knowing everything about anything in town.

This morning, the salon has been crackling with talk of the strange weather in Slater these past two days. The town meeting was not called to specially address this issue—Slater always holds a town meeting the first Tuesday of every month—but there is a consensus in the salon that the meeting's discussion should be wholly devoted to the strong winds and their effects.

The winds died down last night, and though they didn't bring in the storm everyone expected, they have blown in a different kind of disturbance. It seems that I'm not the only one who has had an encounter with a dead animal. One client recounts how a robin slammed into her window and dropped dead. Another talks about the deceased raccoon her husband found in the garbage bin. Far more common than deaths, though, is mere *odd* behavior.

"Pam's little tabby was walking along the windowsill one moment, and *fhwip!* Like that, she drops to the floor hissing, when she's never hissed before. I swear to heaven, that is God's honest truth."

Mrs. Grace Corich, who owns the dress boutique three shopfronts down, is in a flurry. Her salon cape rustles and swells as her hands move beneath it, fighting against their captivity to illustrate her every word. Not for the first time, Connie asks her to tilt her head down so she can get a proper trim in the back. Mrs. Corich complies for a few seconds, until a new thought comes to her and she straightens, fervent as ever.

"It's those hippies! It's a scheme, that's what it is. They've gotten greedy. They want this town for themselves, and they've sent out their young people—those crossers, as they call themselves—to poison our animals. They are trying to scare us from town."

"Grace. If you could—"

"Oh right, yes." Mrs. Corich bends her head and Connie snips straightaway, trying to get in as many good strokes as possible before Mrs. Corich's next thought.

"I read the paper this morning," says Connie, "and it said several vets have found no evidence of poisoning or any other cause for alarm. And if it's due to a weather disturbance, as so many are saying, Red Sun can hardly control *that*."

"That's what they'd like you to believe, isn't it?" Mrs. Corich sits straight again, and Connie backs away, scissors held high. "I'll ask you this, though, Connie: Why is it only happening here in Slater?"

Mrs. Corich is right about that, at least. There have been no reports of heavy winds or oddly behaving animals outside Slater. None of our clients from other towns have seen anything out of the ordinary in the past two days. They claim the weather's been calm and hot as an oven. Slater, and only Slater, seems to have been affected.

Sudden and swift, the image of eyeless garter snakes flashes into my memory. What was it that drove them to death? What killed them in the end? And what about the all-too-familiar collie, or Velma the goldfish? Could it be they heard or saw something in those winds that we humans could not? Then I think of those numbers, violet and glowing, written on my closet door. I shut my eyes and shake both the memories and the questions free.

When I leave the salon, I have every intention of cycling straight home. I've attended town meetings before. Our townspeople do not discuss anything I don't already hear ad nauseam in the salon. More than that, they come to fewer conclusions and courses of action than our clientele. Town meetings are a place for loud-mouthed, big-opinioned people to be heard. I suppose it's cathartic for them, but it's not very constructive for anyone else. That's what I expect from today's town meeting: more of the same.

I'm biking past town hall, with no plans of stopping, when I see it. There's a large crowd—dozens and dozens of people—gathered before town hall's columned entrance. There, above the doors but below the clock tower, superimposed upon brick, are six violet numbers separated by two colons, shining like a fluorescent sign. Only not as solid as a sign. They're more of a . . . "hologram" is the only word I can think for it. The numbers are solid enough to be read, but they hang over the bricks as though they're a projection of light.

I stop my bike and wheel it across the sidewalk to join the gawking crowd. These numbers were not here this morning; I would've seen them on the ride in. They must have appeared very recently, as suddenly as they did on . . . my closet door. I've been trying to forget since last night, trying to pretend it was all a dream. I checked this morning, though, as I got ready for work. I opened my closet, and there they were, as clear as they'd been before: numbers, violet and undeniable.

A countdown.

I study the massive projection above my head. It is very like my own closet countdown, except that each of its numbers must be at least as tall as Jill. Combined, they read out *16:08:13*.

It's the same. I am positive that if I could instantly transport myself home and check my closet, that door would bear the very same numbers. Not that I'm going to let on to anyone here that I have a secret at home. I'm scared enough as is, and more confused than ever. I am not about to risk getting mobbed by the people around me. Though I desperately want to ask, *Who else has seen this? Everyone? Only a few? Who else has seen these numbers in their own house?*

Then the projection alters. The last of the numbers changes before our eyes: Thirteen flickers into twelve, and the crowd gasps. A child shouts. Close to me I hear a man say, "God help us."

My heart turns heavy. Because this is not a shock to me, as it was to them. I knew this was a countdown. I've known since last night. And if any of these people had a countdown of their own, emblazoned on *their* closet doors, would they be surprised?

Now there is another question I want to ask—more desperate and terrible than the others: *Am I the only one?*

"They're starting!" shouts a suited man close to the town hall doors. "They're starting, everyone!"

The crowd surges, men and women pushing against me, straining toward the open doors that lead to the assembly room. I hang back, letting them flood past. I stand like a stone driven deep into the earth, my neck craned, eyes barely blinking, until the projection shifts again, and the twelve turns to an eleven. Only once the entire crowd has fit into the building do I follow, and even then I do what I have always done at these assemblies. I keep near the exit, alone and silent—here to observe.

Our mayor, Grant Branum, is already standing at the podium on the raised stage before us, looking down on bodies packed tight into rows of puce-green folding chairs. He's an older man—a retired banker—with a full head of white hair. I've seen him before at our county fair and Fourth of July parades, and I like him. He has a relaxed face, and his mouth naturally rests in a smile. Even now, as he addresses a clearly jittery audience, he's smiling through his words.

"Welcome, ladies and gentlemen, and thank you for attending our monthly public forum. I'm well aware that we congregate today under somewhat alarming circumstances. These winds have been mighty strong, and it would seem some of Slater's animals haven't taken too kindly to the change. As to the projection of numbers above this very building—a countdown, some are calling it—let me assure you that, at this very moment, I have men attempting to locate their source.

We will, as a community, find an explanation for what has occurred here, and I have no doubt we will grow into a *closer* community as a result.

"Now." Mayor Branum lifts a yellow notepad into view, scanning over its contents. "That being said, it's never been town policy to let recent events overshadow our schedule of discussion. We have an agenda for this evening, and the first topic of discussion is whether or not the signage out on Herring Street should—"

"Now, *now*!" A deep voice resounds in the hall, cutting into Mayor Branum's words.

Startled, the mayor lowers his notebook and frowns out at the audience.

"Now, *now*!" the voice repeats, and every head in the room turns toward it.

I knew who it was from the first. I would know that voice anywhere. It is John Barkley, the pastor of First Baptist—my old church. The man whose sermons I sat through every Sunday morning of my childhood.

Pastor Barkley is standing in the third row from the front, arms raised high above his head. He is dressed in a pressed suit, and his pale neck is splotchy around the collar. "Now, begging your pardon, Grant, are we to leave it at that? The people here don't want to know about signage on Herring Street. There is a spirit of distress in this congregation."

From the back, somewhere close to me, a man shouts, "Amen!" Many townspeople clap their agreement. Encouraged, Pastor Barkley goes on in his booming voice.

"Far be it from me to disrespect my local authority, but

I believe I speak for these people when I say the impetus of tonight's conversation should be the portent of doom hanging over this town."

Mayor Branum is not smiling anymore; he looks annoyed by Pastor Barkley, and a little frightened, too. He clears his throat before saying, "I hardly think we should be throwing around words like 'doom.'"

"It's the Second Coming!" shouts another voice, closer to the front. "It's the Rapture!"

There are loud murmurs around me as Mayor Branum waves his hands in a quieting gesture. "Please, *please*. As I was saying, John, I appreciate your concern for our town, but we have a set way of conducting—"

"The people need answers!" Pastor Barkley interrupts, waving for the crowd not to quiet, but speak up. "My people, let me tell you where you'll find them: in the Good Book. Not on your television screens or in fashionable new philosophy. And let me tell you: *That* is the reason the Lord is judging our town. Because we have turned our backs on him. We have abandoned him for our own selfish lifestyles. Just take the pagans on our very doorstep. How have we allowed ourselves to live comfortably side by side with the members of that so-called community? How do we sleep quietly in our beds when those God-haters live on in sin? And now the Lord has come to judge us for it. Heed his warning, my brothers and sisters. Could it be he has struck down your animals in order to save your souls? Do not be deceived: God is not mocked. We must not allow the wicked to flourish among us!"

By now, the crowd has grown loud with chatter and shouts.

Some people shake their heads, in disagreement with either Pastor Barkley's method or his message. A good many seem to be nodding along, though. I shrink back farther against the wall.

Mayor Branum, meantime, is pounding a gavel into the podium. It is only when Sheriff Allen joins him on the stage and shouts for quiet that people settle down. Then Mayor Branum speaks again, addressing the matter of a new speed limit to be posted on Herring Street. He is determined to adhere to his agenda, and I do not blame him. I suppose, in his eyes, it is the only way to maintain order—to give us some semblance of normalcy.

The trouble is, the strong winds and odd animal behavior—even deaths—are not normal. Violet numbers appearing over town hall is not normal. Pastor Barkley sits down, and there are no more rogue shouts from the crowd, but that does not mean the people are at peace. I hear them whispering, conjecturing. I hear snatches of sentences: "aren't good for the town" and "probably poisoned the water." And when Mayor Branum asks if there are any questions on the Herring Street topic, the only person to raise her hand is an elderly woman, who asks, "What are the numbers counting *toward*?" The room fills with gentle laughter, but it's nervous laughter too. We want to know the answer. *I* want an answer most of all, because that countdown is *in my bedroom*.

I leave town hall before the meeting has adjourned, less satisfied than when I walked in. Further discussion of the strange events is shut down by Mayor Branum's placating assurances that he and the town council are doing everything in their power to "look into it." No one has answers, only blame to cast around. According to Pastor Barkley, it's all to do with the sinful ways of Red Sun. It's an absurd idea, but it's appealing, too—in a very bad way. It is nice to have someone to blame. It feels good to pitch your dirt upon another person. I think, before he and I began to write, Craig was that for me.

Even on my bike ride home, Pastor Barkley's words stick on my skin, like cold and insidious leeches.

I take two Salisbury steak dinners out of the oven. Jill has already switched the television on to *NBC Nightly News*. She is in a pouty mood tonight, which she claims is owing to her friend Rachel Mayer being sick with a head cold and therefore unable to go to the park when, in Jill's words, "No one gets head colds in *August*."

When I point out that Rachel cannot help that she's on the wrong side of the slim odds of getting sick in summer, Jill explodes, "Well, where were *you*? You were a whole *thirty minutes* late!"

I could shout back that I do not owe Jill anything save dinner, and I can stay out as long as I want. But something about the town meeting and those violet numbers has sapped away my will to fight. Jill notices this, I think, because she gets very quiet during the news—even the brief update on the search for Son of Sam. When the thirty-minute report is over and we take our emptied trays to the kitchen, Jill hangs back by the oven.

"What?" I ask her.

"What *what*?"

This is usual. I press on. "What's the look for?"

"Nothing," Jill says, and then I wait for it. *Something* always comes after the *nothing*.

Only a few seconds later, as I am scrubbing my hands, she asks, "Are you mad at Dad?"

It's not what I expected. My mind is fogged with countdowns and angry townspeople. I haven't thought of Dad or his news all day.

"No, Jill. Why would you ask that?"

"Seems normal to be mad. You remember Mom. I don't. So."

"I'm not mad at him," I say, and I am happy to find I'm being honest. "I think this is good for him. I really do. I'm excited to meet her."

"Yeah," says Jill. "I guess I am too."

I tug a strand of her thin hair. "Sorry you couldn't go to the park today. Maybe I could take you instead. On Saturday, before the dinner?"

"Yeah, maybe."

It is later, as I'm lacing up my sneakers for the Dreamlight and Jill is reading her Nancy Drew on the couch, that I finally work up the courage to ask it.

"Jill."

"Huh."

"Have you noticed anything strange in your room?"

Jill drops her book, spine tenting over her chest. "What?"

"Anything strange? In your room. Maybe . . . maybe your closet."

"What the heck do you mean? Like mice or something?"

"I . . . guess."

Jill has already answered my question, though. Now I

wonder why I asked it. She would have already told me. If Jill had that same countdown on her closet door, I would be the first to know.

"You're weird," Jill supplies after a few beats of quiet consideration. Then she says, "I'm getting more freckles."

"Well, that's good." I am absentminded, focused on my left shoestring.

"No, it's *not*. Freckles are ugly. Rachel told me she knows a cure, though. You have to take a bath in tomato juice."

"Is that right."

"Yeah. So can I?"

"Can you what?"

"Have a bath of tomato juice."

I frown at Jill, finally listening. *"What?"*

"To get rid of my freckles!"

"What? No, Jill. That would take cans and cans of soup. We're not rich enough to waste food."

"But she—"

"Anyway, Rachel's misinformed. You can't get rid of freckles."

Jill makes a face. "I'll find a way."

At that, I smile. "If anyone could, it'd be you."

It's true. Jill has a lot of growing up to do, but I admire both her persistence and her brashness—what she calls being a good sleuth. I think sometimes I could learn from my little sister. Perhaps I could do with some more persistence and brashness of my own.

11

Galliard

WEDNESDAY, AUGUST 3

"Where are my greens?"

"Up in one minute, Chef."

"Should be up *now*."

I take the reprimand with a bent, repentant head. It's what you do in the kitchen: absorb the blame and do better. Before, my blame was a mere matter of poorly peeled onions or rogue seeds left on bell peppers. Now J. J. has put both Archer *and* me at the stoves, per our assignments. The new preassignments will take over my chopping and washing, and I'll start to cook.

Using tongs, I turn the green beans over in the skillet, coating them in the butter, vinegar, and garlic—all perfectly proportioned by J. J. in a recipe that's made them the Moonglow's most popular side item. During lunch and dinner hours, there's always a steady stream of green-bean orders. And now it's my job to cook them. It's just so damn fun.

I wish Archer were here. J. J.'s making big changes, and today's the first time he's put us on two entirely different shifts. I guess it makes sense, since two in-training cooks would be chaotic. Doesn't mean I'm not pissed about it, though, because the Council spun this position like Archer and I would work side by side. No such luck. I take the grunt work that Lola—the experienced saucier—assigns me, and that's that. No more cracking jokes with friends at work; I guess that's what becoming a Red Sun adult is all about.

Apparently, it's also about private conversations with Rod. About becoming a *leader*. About training to be on the Council itself. I haven't wrapped my head around that. All the stuff Rod said blindsided me so hard, my brain was a white blank afterward, and has been since. I was sure he was going to yell at me for smoking pot, only to be told he's handpicked me as some kind of successor. That he's going to train me to lead come September; *that's* why I didn't get resident artist.

Thing is, I don't buy Rod's story. The Council already as good as said Phoenix's art was more profitable than mine. *That's* why they screwed me over. And up until now, I never once got the impression Rod thought I was the stuff leaders are made of. I didn't think he liked me—*noticed* me, even. Then again, he has to mean what he said, at least a little. If he's bringing me in to Council House, he's got to mean *something* by it.

I've never pictured myself on that Council. I'd have to be some delusional ass if I did. There have only been two Council appointments since Red Sun was founded—one when Leander died and one when an elderly founding member named Miriam stepped down for health reasons. I've had no reason to think that another appointment is coming anytime soon, but maybe it's possible that Opal is thinking of taking it easy. Or . . . maybe Rod and Saff are thinking that Opal's days are numbered; it's a morbid thought, sure, but she *is* in her seventies.

Even now that I know this whole Council thing is a possibility, I still don't picture myself on a team with Rod and Saff. In fact, the thought makes me kind of nauseated, and shouldn't that be a sign? I've only seen myself as one thing: a songwriter. The Council knows that. They know, because I wrote it down in the essay I submitted. Which means Rod knows. Which makes me think this has to be a consolation prize. Or something worse. After all, there's no knowing when Opal's going to pass. I could be waiting for more than a decade, and if that's the case, Rod's logic will hold every time I apply for a reassignment. I won't get resident artist when I'm twenty-six, thirty-six, maybe even forty-six—all because I'm meant for something "better."

Smells like bullshit to me.

There's this, too: I can't shake what Rod said when I left his office. About Crossing being for the weak. About how I was changed now. About "negative consequences." It sounded like a threat. A threat against ever Crossing again. Maybe I've got it wrong, though. Maybe I really am a delusional ass.

Heat rises from the pan, drawing beads of sweat from my forehead. The bath of butter and vinegar sizzles and slowly evaporates. Today's shaping up to be a bad throat-tic day. The low, clearing sound punches its way out every couple of seconds. Somewhere else, I'd be self-conscious, worried someone's bothered. It's not that people are ever mean about it. I was only teased a few times by other kids growing up, and the last incident was addressed in a commune-wide gathering during which Opal emphasized how Red Sun had been established as an accepting place for every human. These days, I only get the occasional strange look from a Red Sun newcomer, and those soon vanish. At Red Sun, I don't have to explain myself to anyone.

I know my tics are annoying; *I'm* annoyed by them. It's not like I can stop them, though, and even if I try—as I attempted so many times when I was younger—they'll resurface with a vengeance. The tics are going to happen no matter what, but here in the kitchen, they aren't as noticeable. They turn into white noise and peripheral movement, same as everything else. My fellow workers are used to the way I move, including my rare waving tic, and they make allowances accordingly, same as I adjust around the distinct ways they move. That's one thing, at least, I like about the job.

If I were to be a Council leader, though? That would mean the public spotlight. That would mean speeches and talking to people day in and day out. What part of *that* is appealing? Once again, I think of Rod's words and get to feeling sick.

"Beans up," I shout, sliding the three requested portions onto their waiting dishes, then wiping the plate edges free of speckled oil. I pretended not to notice Mac, one of the waiters, leaning against the kitchen line, shooting eye daggers at me.

"About damn time," he says, loading up his arm with the dishes. He disappears behind the swinging door before I can respond. Not that I would. The kitchen is no place for apologies or for fights; J. J. taught me that early on.

When I get back to my station, a tall brunette woman stands in my place, coating the sauté pan with a new round of olive oil. It's Miracle, who's a few years older and usually never shares a shift with me.

"You're early," I say.

Miracle laughs. "Hardly."

I look at the large clock that hangs over the sinks: 6:05. I could've sworn it wasn't even five thirty.

"Oh."

"*Oh*," Miracle imitates, swatting my elbow. "Get out of here."

I can't untie my apron fast enough. I throw it on its peg and run out the back door.

It's hot out, no more strong gusts of wind, no nudges at my back. Instead humidity licks over my skin. The smells of the kitchen linger out here, taunting Red Sun members with food meant only for outsiders and *Wichita Eagle* food critics. I'm allowed to take a supper plate to go, but tonight I don't have much of an appetite. If I get hungry later, I'll dip into the sack of granola I keep in my bottom desk drawer.

Or maybe I'll eat on the Outside.

Maybe I'll go out again with Archer. He's off tonight too. And according to him—someone who can make sense of what the numbers on my dollar bills mean—I have an impressive allowance saved up. If I wanted, I could eat in style.

Rod shouldn't have talked to me. He shouldn't have said that stuff about Crossing. Because now I want to do it more. If that makes me weak, then too bad: I'm weak. If there are negative consequences, then I'm ready for them. Rod acted like he knew me, but he doesn't. The Council members, Ruby and J. J., *every* adult at Red Sun—they don't know what's in my head. Maybe my head is telling me to *get out*.

"Galliard! Hey!"

I haven't taken ten steps when I hear the shout at my back.

It's none other than Mac, the Impatient Waiter, on the back stoop of the Moonglow. He's waving to me as though I'm a distant ship.

"What?" I shout back.

Don't tell me someone sent back the beans. That they were overcooked. That there was a hair. A roach leg. A toenail.

"Oh, hey." Mac looks like he didn't expect to catch my attention. Now it's my turn to be the impatient asshole.

"I'm off my shift," I say, throwing up my hands in a gesture that screams, *Seriously?*

"Yeah, yeah, I know. It's just, uh, there's a girl in here. Asking about some guy named Craig? Then she says wait, he goes by Phoenix now. *Then* she says she's his sister. And *then* she says she's not going away until she sees him."

Like that, my skin is on fire.

Stella Kay Mercer.

Here, at Red Sun.

Her weird, weird face stares into my mind's eye, painted in cold shades of blue.

Holy shit.

I blink forcefully—a tic.

Janis Joplin, give me strength.

Outwardly, I am unmoved. I keep my shoulders raised in the *why the hell is that any of my business?* stance.

"And?"

"I don't know, man. I thought you could talk her down. You know, since you and Phoenix are close."

Ladies and gentlemen, the joke of the century. Applause. Laughter. Ha, ha, ha.

I consider my options. I can tell Mac:

a) Fuck off. I don't owe him anything, especially after that attitude back in the kitchen.

b) Yeah, sure, I'll see what I can do.

I'm tempted by option A. If Stella Kay Mercer is on a manhunt for her brother, then that's technically Phoenix's problem, and his alone. Visitors aren't supposed to come calling at Red Sun for long-lost relatives. If word of this gets around, Phoenix will probably get brought in to the Council to explain himself. So the obvious choice is A.

But then there's the small matter of my conscience.

Even if this is technically Phoenix's problem, it is entirely my fault. Because I'm the one who's been writing the letters. I'm the one who knows Stella Kay Mercer, even if she doesn't think she knows me. I'm the reason she's here, because two months ago she asked to meet with Phoenix in person, and I freaked the hell out. It's on me to explain.

And it's something more than that too.

I want to see Stella Kay Mercer, unpainted, in the daylight. I want to talk to her face-to-face as me, Galliard. And I want to ask if her brother has always been a colossal prick.

So option B is the clear winner.

"Yeah, sure, I'll see what I can do."

I say it in a small-breathed way to remind Mac I *don't* owe him anything. My eyes squeeze shut, then open as I follow him back in.

We cross through the kitchen and out the swinging door that leads to the dining area. Here the walls are rough-hewn wood and brick, decorated in soothing photographs of the commune. The happy buzz of diners fills the room. We're at about three-fifths capacity, teetering on the edge of the dinner rush. There are a few spots left at the bar, and one of them is taken by none other than Stella Kay Mercer.

She looks different than she did at the drive-in—defined, more made of flesh. Her eyes hook on me from across the room and don't let go as I approach. Anger rolls off her body like waves, crashing over me. But I feel something else, too, in the undercurrent: She's scared. I see it in the tense way she's perched her feet on the bar-stool railing, in the uncertainty that clouds her face right before I reach her, in the way she says, "You're not Craig."

I blink a few times. Then I say, "Yeah, I'm aware."

"I came here to speak to Craig. Or . . . *Phoenix*, if that's what he's calling himself. I know he's here, so don't try telling me you don't know who I'm talking about."

"I know exactly who you're talking about."

I'm sounding way more arrogant than I mean to, and Stella is not amused. A fresh wave of her anger breaks against me. Her hands clench into fists.

"I'm not leaving until I see him."

"Then you'll be waiting forever. Phoenix doesn't work here, so there's no chance you'll bump into him. And in case you weren't aware, outsiders aren't allowed to barge in and demand to see members."

"He's my brother."

"And?"

"He's my *family*. I should be able to see him."

"Why? You haven't asked to see him for two years."

I grimace, blinking hard. What the hell am I doing? I'm

defending Phoenix. I'm accusing Stella, when I should be apologizing to her. I should be telling her the whole truth.

Of course now, of all times, my mouth tic decides to pay a visit. I stretch my lips wide for a yawn that will never come.

"What are you . . . ?"

Stella doesn't finish the question, and I can see it play out in her too-wide eyes. There's confusion first. Then annoyance. Then understanding. Her face goes soft with something I absolutely do not want to see: sympathy. Then she stops looking *at* me and looks *over* me, scanning the room.

"Maybe I should talk to someone else."

I hate how nice she suddenly sounds. I step to the side, blocking her search, forcing her focus back on me.

"If you're going to talk to anyone, it's me. I'm Phoenix's friend."

The joke of the century isn't as funny told a second time around. Something inside me snaps, then aches.

Stella doesn't look surprised by my claim, only thoughtful. "That's how you knew who I was, right? Did he tell you about me? Does he have paintings of us?"

The sympathy's gone. The way she's talking now makes me way too uncomfortable, like I've walked in on her changing. The questions she's asking are tender. Vulnerable. I don't have the right to answer them.

For reasons unknown, I decide to blurt out the worst answer possible.

"He doesn't care about any of you anymore. He disowned you. He said you're dead to him."

I watch in some sort of sick, fascinated horror as her light skin pales even more and tears gather in her eyes. A sharp sound bursts from her throat—something close to my most common tic. She grips the counter and steps down from the bar stool.

"Fine," she whispers. "Fine."

She heads for the door, this quivering blur of red sundress and frizzy brown hair.

And I've never felt so wholly worthless in my entire life.

It was instinct that pushed out the spiteful words, and it's my better instinct that now launches me after Stella. I catch the heavy glass door as it's slamming shut and hurl myself down the porch stairs, pumping my legs to catch up with her, realizing simultaneously that Stella is really fast and that this is only the second time I've been past Red Sun borders.

"Stella Kay!" I catch up with her in the parking lot. She's stopped and thrown a hand over her face, but I can see the tears streaming down her cheeks, dripping off her chin.

Rod's voice is in my head: *Weak actions—wrong actions . . . those result in negative consequences.*

Damn if the law of consequences isn't real.

"I'm sorry," I pant. "Christ, I'm an asshole. I'm sorry."

She drags her hands down her cheeks, catching tears. "Nobody even calls me that."

"What?"

"Nobody calls me Stella Kay. It's just Stella."

"Oh." Then my mouth opens—the yawn tic.

"And why are you sorry? If it's true, why are *you* sorry? I wanted to know. You told me. No need to apologize."

She makes another clumsy swipe at her cheek. There are

streaks of black mascara and blue eye shadow across her face.

I need to tell her a whole lot. I *do* need to apologize, and I *haven't* told her the truth. I haven't told her the half of it.

"I only wanted to see him," she says. "But clearly he doesn't want to see me."

"That's not true. I mean . . . I don't know if it's true or not. From everything he's told me—"

"What's he told you? What's he said about us?"

Shit. I can't say a single damn thing right. My lips spread apart, but this time it's a tic, and no words come out.

Stella's not waiting for an answer, though. She's squints past me, toward the café and asks, "Are you even allowed out here?"

"It's Crossing."

"Oh right. Of course."

Her tears are drying. She heaves in a long sniff and clutches at her elbows like she's cold, even though it's plenty hot. Out of nowhere, I get this scary urge to hug her. Instead I jerk my head to the side.

Not the time! I shout to my body. But my nerves and muscles, coconspirators, jerk my head again. Since when has my body ever cared about good timing?

Stella's staring at me. "Forget about it. I don't know why I came here. I don't know what I was expecting."

She's already turned to leave when I say, "It's not contagious."

Stella spins back around. "Excuse me?"

"It's not a disease you can catch. If that's why you're leaving."

Her weird face gets weirder, contorting. "I know it's not contagious. I know what Tourette's is."

"Okay." My jaw jerks. "Fine."

"No." Stella steps forward, closing the distance between us. "Not *fine*. Just because I don't belong to your hippie town doesn't mean I'm a callous xenophobe. Is that what they teach you in there?"

I've never heard the word "xenophobe" before. I've got a pretty good guess as to what it means, though.

I say, "I don't think that."

"Maybe I want to leave because it was stupid of me to come in the first place. Because I've made a fool of myself in front of—" She waves toward the café, but she also seems to be waving at me.

"Look," I say. "He can't see you right now. I mean, *can't*. He's . . . he's doing a silent workshop."

Stella frowns. "What?"

Damn.

Damn, damn, *damn*. I'm lying, and I can't stop. The words slide off my tongue like oil.

"It's where a member goes into self-imposed isolation— prays and eats and lives alone. It's supposed to be a period of renewal that brings us closer to the Life Force. Everyone does it at some point. Phoenix is doing one now, and it's important not to interrupt him. He can't be disturbed until the silence is over."

Her frown intensifies. "And how long is that?"

"In a week."

My jaw twitches to the right. I'm flushed from the lying, and I wonder if she can tell. Silent workshops are a real thing. That much is true. But it's the *only* thing I've said that's true. I don't know why I keep speaking before I think. I was supposed to tell Stella the truth, and now all I've done is slather more lies on top.

All I can think is that I need more time. Somehow I've got to buy more time.

This is *Stella*, my correspondence partner of two years. This is a girl who's lived her whole life on the Outside, like Phoenix did, but come to a different conclusion. Rather than follow Phoenix to Red Sun, she's stayed on the Outside, and there's a part of me—a big part—that wants to know what Stella knows. I want to pick her brain in a way I couldn't through our letters. I want to see with her what not even Archer can show me, what *no one* can show me, save someone who's grown up in Slater, Kansas. If I tell her the whole truth now, I won't get that chance.

Stella folds her arms. She toes the parking-lot gravel, coating her sneaker in a dull gray powder. At some point, this head jerking will stop. When I'm not thinking about it. When she isn't looking.

"You can come back then," I say. "In a week, when it's over. I don't know if he'll want to see you, but at least we can ask. Maybe he will."

Stella looks up. "Is that an *actual* maybe, or not? Because I'm not going to work myself up if he's just going to ignore me again."

Again. I should tell her I'm the one to blame for that. I'm the one to blame for all of this.

My jaw jerks as I say, "It's an actual maybe."

I can't say that Phoenix trashed the first letter she sent him, two summers ago. Or that I found it and read it and called him out. I can't tell her that after Phoenix disowned Stella, told me he had no family, I kept the letter. That I couldn't stand to think she'd never get an answer. That I wrote to her only meaning to write once, to make her feel better. That since then it's spiraled into something out of my control. Something that makes me feel all wrong, like I'm a criminal.

Wrong actions have negative consequences.

I don't want to face them yet. Surely the Life Force—Holly and Hendrix and Joplin, in their infinite mercy—can understand. I feel sure now that they were the ones who sent that Dreamlight flyer my way, and they were the ones to push me out of Red Sun's gate. If my gods wanted to tell me something, they'd use the weather, wouldn't they? That makes sense. And I can't shake the feeling that they haven't finished talking.

"I'll have to think about it," says Stella. "Maybe . . . maybe I'll come back."

"Okay."

"And if I do, you'll be here? You can find Phoenix for me?"

Another thing I can't say: I'm not currently acknowledging Phoenix's existence. I'm miserable as my jaw jerks for the umpteenth time.

"My shift here is different every day," I say. "If you ask for me, though—ask for Galliard—someone can probably track me down. Or, I don't know, maybe I'll be at the drive-in again. If that's someplace you go a lot."

Stella raises one of her thick brows. It now looks less like her makeup has run and more like her face was on the receiving end of a small explosion. I smile a little and say, "I'll be there *without* the weed."

"Mm-hmm." She smiles a little back. "Well, thanks for that. I guess . . . I'll see you around. Maybe."

"Is that an actual maybe?" I call after her.

She doesn't answer. She's slipping into a chrome jungle of parked cars, and I'm left wondering if I've made a promise I can't keep.

12

Stella

The numbers have not left my closet door.

The countdown continues, and on Saturday morning, when I get out of the shower, it reads *12:17:15*.

Twelve days until some unknown end.

The same countdown remains on Slater's town hall. I see it, along with a perpetually milling crowd, on my daily bike rides to and from the salon. The people of Slater are very stirred up about it. Town officials have exhausted all means of investigation, including sending men up with ladders to ascertain the physical nature of the countdown clock. Their only determination is that it is simply light. A projection from nowhere.

Throughout the week, I've waited for reports of other townspeople who have found the same strange numbers in their homes. Only there have been none. No accounts in our newspaper, no word in the salon or at the Dreamlight, where all anyone can talk about is town hall. And I think it highly unlikely that every single resident of Slater is as secretive as I am.

I've attempted to gauge my father, same as I did Jill. Unlike her, I'm not sure he would tell me first thing if he discovered flashing numbers in his closet; I get my secretive side from Dad. However, what I thought was a sly way of bringing up the topic last night, before he left for work, resulted in nothing more than a confused remark from my father about mothballs.

Since then I have made a decision. I won't tell anyone about my situation until I know what the numbers *mean*. Daily, I think through explanations, each one as untenable as the next, though I do not let myself think long of the one ringing loudest in my mind:

It could be aliens.

I do not believe in the supernatural. I believe in reason. And in the face of something as unreasonable as the numbers on my closet door, perhaps extraterrestrial intelligence is a reasonable explanation. I think Carl Sagan would agree with me. Only it might be that I've been reading too much Carl Sagan. Because there are other scientific explanations. Medical ones. I might have a brain tumor. I might be hallucinating. I like to consider those explanations even less than I do the possibility of aliens; if these are hallucinations, and they are this vivid and consistent, it must mean I'm not long for the world.

Anyway, I have other things to worry about. My father doesn't know about my visit to Red Sun. There is no need for him to find out. It was such a brash thing to do. Brash, like Jill in sleuth mode. Each morning, after I wake and before I move from bed, I wrestle with indecision, punching and accepting blows. I can never settle on which is worse: to return to the commune, hoping a stranger will keep his word, or to forgo what might be my only chance to make contact with Craig.

I decide on one course of action, but then uncertainty creeps in again, and between work at the salon and the drive-in and ensuring Jill eats dinner every night, I do not have time to clear the haze for good.

Now Saturday has arrived, and though I've taken off work at both the salon and the Dreamlight, I am occupied with the task of helping my father prepare the house for his . . . *girl-friend*. Dad was right before: That title doesn't fit. I cannot invent any good substitutes, though. "Could-be stepmother" or "Dad's serious paramour" simply won't do. It is an awkward title for an awkward situation, and I suppose it can't be helped. Even so, I am looking forward to meeting my father's mystery date, Gayle Nelson, who he says has requested that we call her "Gayle," not "Miss Nelson." I am eager to see how she looks and how she behaves around my father. It is more than that, though: I am curious about what kind of woman was hired to help run a nuclear power plant.

I set the table with the black stoneware we reserve only for birthdays and holidays. Tonight's dinner is a special occasion, even though the meal itself is takeout lasagna from Salvatore's on Vine. As I place the silverware—knife and spoon on right, fork on left—I coach myself on how to subtly bring up the subject at the table. Nothing to make Gayle feel uncomfortable— *How did you afford a college education? Why nuclear physics? Who on earth encouraged you to do that?*—but nothing so vague that Gayle could misconstrue it, such as a general inquiry as to what she does at the plant. Though I am curious about those details too.

I've never had warm feelings toward Slater Creek Nuclear

Operating Corporation. Despite my father's numerous reassur-
ances and my own awareness that he isn't being exposed to
unhealthy levels of radiation, I cannot shake an instinctual
fear that the plant is doing him some kind of harm. I much
preferred it when he just worked his shifts at town buildings. But then Craig left, and that was the summer the plant
began operations. More families moved to Slater. New, finely
dressed students appeared in my classes. I heard of some anti-
nuclear protests in Kansas City, and it was well known that the
members of Red Sun were not happy with the development,
especially as the plant was constructed less than a mile from
commune limits. Overall, though, Slater welcomed the development. We were reassured that nuclear energy was perfectly
safe, and no one could deny the sorely needed boon of new
business brought to our town.

Personally, I've had no reason to think well of the place
until now, as it brings Gayle Nelson into my life. She is a
woman with a doctoral degree and a good career, and I want
to know the *why*. I want to know the *how*. It's strange, but
how I see her as my father's girlfriend and potential member of
this family means relatively little compared to how I see her as
her. And I suppose that's a good thing.

I've folded the last of the napkins and am slipping it under
my own knife and spoon when there is a knock at the door.

"She's here!" Jill yells, bounding down the hall. "Stella, get
the door!"

"Calm down, you goof," I say, poking Jill's nose. She is
wearing her only sundress—lavender cotton with a fringed
hem.

I lean into the swinging door that leads from our dining room to the kitchen. My father is blaring the radio and following my instructions for preparing a garden salad. I know he would prefer to be the one to greet Gayle and usher her into our home.

But I change my mind. I'm too eager, and too selfish. I want my first impression and initial survey to take place without my father in the room. So I do not shout over the radio to alert him. I swing back out of the kitchen and hurry down the hall, Jill on my heels. I open the door.

Gayle Nelson is a full foot taller than I am, and she isn't even wearing heels. She is broad-shouldered and dressed in a wrap dress patterned with squash-colored hexagons. Her skin is warm and beige. Her toenails—visible through threaded sandals—are painted a bright goldenrod to match her finger-nails. Her lipstick is plum, and she is plump and smells of a spicy perfume I do not recognize. She is lovely, and for a moment I forget what I am supposed to say.

She speaks first. She does not say "Hello" or "You must be Stella," as I am expecting. She has been looking to the sky, and when her gaze settles on me, she says, "There's a storm rolling in. The forecaster lied to us."

Her words are hoarse—I'm guessing she is a smoker—but her tone is friendly. Confidential, even. Perhaps it's the way she says "the forecaster lied to *us*," as though we are in this together. I decide that I like her.

I do not reply to her comment on the weather. I say, "I'm Stella. Dad is in the kitchen."

"Is he?" Gayle's laugh is hoarse, same as her words. "He told me he doesn't cook. I thought he'd order out."

"We got Salvatore's," Jill says from behind me.

"Oh!" Gayle peers past me to get a look at Jill. "Well, excellent. I love Italian."

As Gayle crosses the threshold, I glance outside at dark looming clouds rolling in from the east, over the neighbors' rooftops.

I love the way Gayle talks. Everything she says is a little comical so that, if you wanted, you could laugh at any moment and not feel awkward. I cannot put my thumb on what it is that makes me feel that way—whether it is the smoky roughness of her voice or the way she says my name enough to make me feel known, though not talked down to. I think it must be something beyond that, some combination of her voice and cadence and physicality. I would like to see an equation for it, written out. I'd like to solve it and adapt the answer to fit my own life.

I see why Dad likes her. She is pretty and confident and kind, too. She is, however, very different from my mother—or at least my memory of my mother. Diane Mercer was small and quiet. I don't remember her ever beginning conversations, or extracting answers, or filling the room the way Gayle does. In my memory she is soft, blurry on the edges, an ethereal thing. Gayle seems denser, more defined than other people. She has a way of ensuring that everyone at the table feels part of the conversation. During the salad course, the topics range from how she met my father—in a hallway where Gayle, naturally, struck up a conversation—to Jill's favorite subject at school—social studies—to my work at the drive-in. Then she brings up the fact that the first woman priest was ordained in the Episcopal church a few months back. (Gayle is Episcopal, but church is one thing she *doesn't* ask about, thank goodness.)

It is inevitable that, sooner than later, the conversation lands on the town hall countdown. My father is convinced that it is an elaborate marketing ploy, no doubt arranged by some big company in Kansas City. In the end he and Gayle agree that it's nothing to worry about—no doubt for Jill's benefit. I see uncertainty on my father's face, though. Gayle is too new an acquaintance to read, though she seems to be a person who's near impossible to worry. I stay quiet throughout the discussion, afraid that if I open my mouth I'll let loose my secret about the closet door. I jump at the chance to clear away the salad dishes.

We've just begun on our squares of lasagna and oven-warmed freezer rolls when Jill says, without warning, "Everyone in New York is scared."

My gaze slices to her. Dad, too, is staring at Jill, a half-eaten, now-forgotten roll in his hand.

Only Gayle is unfazed. She shifts her shoulders toward Jill and asks, "Why is that?"

"You *know*. Because of that man. He keeps killing people."

"Jill," I say, finally capable of speech. "That's not appropriate."

"It's okay," says Gayle. "It's a scary business, and all over the news."

"Perhaps Jill shouldn't be watching the news right now," Dad says to me.

Jill gawks. "Don't you want your kids to be informed? It's just the *news*. Why is everyone mad at me?"

"No one's mad at you," Gayle says, reassuring. "It's only . . . that's rather heavy material for someone your age."

Jill forks at her lasagna. She doesn't say anything. I don't either. I feel as though I have been unfairly chastised. As Jill says, it's just the news. I would like to tell my father that, were he around more, *he* could monitor what Jill watches on television.

"They're going to catch him." Gayle's every word is heavy with confidence, and she's drawn Jill's eyes to hers, as though by magnetic force. "I think he wants to be caught. I think he's similar to boys who steal from a convenience store and then come back the next day to hang around. Because they want to be acknowledged. They're arrogant."

It seems Gayle has transferred her confidence to Jill in that magnetic gaze, because Jill speaks again.

"They were talking about the letters he wrote to the police. About more murders he's going to do."

Dad shakes his head, still looking at me. "I had no idea you were seeing that, Jill."

"It's not Stella's fault!" Jill near shouts. "Anyway, I'm almost ten. I'm old enough."

"They'll catch him," says Gayle. "In fact, maybe *that's* what our mysterious countdown's about. Counting down to the capture of Son of Sam."

"It'd better be sooner than that." Jill's words trip out, uneven.

"It's more than a thousand miles from here to New York, Jillie," I tell her. "He's not going to get to you."

"I don't think he is!" Jill snaps in her most babyish voice. "I'm not stupid. And I'm not scared."

My father is clearly ready for this conversation to be over. With authority he says, "Nothing to be afraid of. No big bad murderers come to Slater, Kansas."

That is when the lights flicker. A crash of thunder shakes the house, and I wonder why I did not notice that it is sheeting rain outside.

Then the lights go out entirely.

There is a scream in the darkness—Jill's. My father swears, which is a strange sound almost more terrifying than the darkness itself. I get out of my chair, fumbling in the dark toward where Jill sits. When I find her shoulder, she screams again and swats me away.

"It's okay," I tell her. "Jillie, it's okay. It's only a storm."

Though even I am not entirely convinced by my words. I know it must be an ordinary power outage, but my mind is filled with images that have played repeatedly on the news: police searching a roped-off crime scene, bloodstained headrests. My skin prickles all over, and my wrists feel weak, almost elastic. I touch Jill's shoulder again, and this time she turns in to me and wraps her arms around my middle. I don't think she's crying, though her breath is coming in and out in rapid bursts.

There's a scratching sound and, suddenly, light appears. Gayle is holding a lighter, and her face is thrown in sharp relief against the blackness.

"Good Lord," she says. "My heart's hammering."

"Mind if I borrow that?" Dad asks, leaning across the table, palm open.

"Certainly not."

Gayle clicks off the lighter, casting us back into darkness, and Jill's grip tightens on my waist. The next light we see, Dad is carrying it away to the hallway.

"There's a crank lantern in the garage," he calls to us. "Circuit breaker's there too. I can check to be sure it's the storm, not a blown fuse."

"Dad, no!" Jill shrieks. "Don't go out there. Don't go out there alone!"

It's difficult to make out my father's expression, but I'm fairly sure he's smiling. "I'll be fine, hon. Don't you worry—I can take on any madmen hiding out there."

"Hang on, Dad," I say.

"What, *both* of you?" He's laughing now. "I swear to God, Son of Sam is not in our garage."

"It's not *that*. I don't want you leaving us in the dark."

I gently push out of Jill's grip and fumble through the shadows to the sideboard. I open the leftmost drawer and feel blindly inside. My fingers light on cold, cylindrical wax—two taper candles we use for Christmas dinners.

"Here." I walk the candles toward Dad. "Light these. Then you can go be brave."

He does. Gayle, meantime, has taken my place at the sideboard and located the candlesticks. My eyes are adjusting to the dark. I can make out shades of purple and gray, the silhouettes of solid objects in the room—chairs, table, curtains. Gayle and I fit the candles into their cheap ceramic stands and bring them back to the table. Jill has gone very quiet and pulled her knees in to her chest. When I get close to her, I realize she's chewing on a piece of lasagna.

"I think that's the best thing to do," Gayle tells her.

"What?"

"Keep eating!" Gayle forks an extra-large piece of lasagna and raises it to her mouth in the winking candlelight. She makes a show of enjoying herself, saying, "Mm-mm-mmm!"

Jill begins giggling, until another round of thunder rattles through the house and her giggles turn into a shrill squeak.

"Here," I say, an idea coming to me. "I'll be right back."

I take one of the candles and carefully make my way into the kitchen. There, next to a cutting board covered in tomato juice and seeds, is the portable radio. I turn it to 580 AM, the local station. I reason that if the storm is very bad—so bad it's affecting Kansas City, too—there will be an alert of some kind. There isn't any special bulletin, though, only the smooth-jazz hour with Reggie Holt. I keep the music on. The plaintive ramblings of the saxophone are actually soothing, and I bring the radio to the dining room in hopes that it will calm Jill, too.

"Dad's taking too long," she says. "We should check on him."

"He's fine. Probably just rummaging around."

There is another boom of thunder. They keep getting louder. The rain is slamming hard against the windows and the roof, and I feel suddenly heavy, pressed down upon by an unseen force that's boxing itself around our house.

"No one forecast this?" I ask Gayle, hoping she won't think I'm as nervous as Jill.

"Not even a summer shower." Gayle smiles, looking out the large dining-room window.

I can tell she likes the storm. I think I do too. Even though it's an inconvenience, and a little frightening, it is also unexpected. It is real and loud and powerful, and it has changed our plans. That's what I like about it, I think.

The front door opens, and moments later harsh, bright light fills the room. Dad has found the crank lantern. Even in his big hand it looks weighty.

"Well!" he says. "We can finish our supper as the Addams Family."

Gayle begins humming the *Addams Family* theme song and snaps her fingers at the appropriate times. Dad and I join her. Jill looks on, brow furrowed, as though we are the children and she is the adult. She's too young to remember that show.

We finish supper while the storm grows worse. The rain pounds so hard against the roof I begin to sneak glances upward, certain I will see water stains forming, expecting at any moment to hear little *drip-drip*s and *ping-ping*s around the room. There are none. The rain rages on, and the thunder shakes us from our eating every half minute or so. We move on to dessert—homemade cannoli from Salvatore's, delivered to our plates fresh from a brown paper bag. This is a real treat, after many years' worth of TV dinners. I savor each bite, relishing the crack of the fried dough under my teeth and the burst of cold, sweet ricotta on my tongue.

The crank lantern goes out, and Dad says he won't bother to restart it until we're ready to clear the table. We sit there in the candlelight, savoring our cannoli and only starting slightly every time the thunder makes an appearance. We've moved on from the unsavory topic of killers to talk of baseball. My father is a big Kansas City Royals fan, while Gayle roots for the Chicago

White Sox. They're sparring cheerily enough over statistics and predictions for the World Series, and I am content to sit here, watching them. I am happy, I realize. Surprisingly happy. I don't even once wish the power would come back on or the storm would let up, and when we've cleared the table and moved the light into the kitchen, where we wash dishes and revive the chorus of *The Addams Family*, I am happier still.

This is something different. This is something new in our house, after eight years. Gayle is here, and that does not make us any less the usual loners, but perhaps she would be all right being a loner together with us. Perhaps she could join our small band.

The storm hasn't let up when we are through with washing. There are still no notifications on the radio, no warnings of flash floods or storm damage. Even so, Dad says Gayle shouldn't attempt to drive home in this kind of weather, and Jill and I agree. Gayle says she'd be happy to sleep on the couch; I insist she take my room. It is only somewhat uncomfortable, navigating this. I know my father would offer his room, but that is too strange a thing to do in front of me and Jill. I understand: The task of hospitality falls to me.

I retrieve our only fresh sheet set—what used to be Craig's sheets—from the linen closet. Gayle says that if she is taking over my bedroom, she should at least help me strip and make the bed. She teaches me a trick she calls "angel wings"—folding triangles of sheet at the end of the bed, then tucking them snug between the mattress and box spring. After I fluff the pillows and spread the quilt, I notice Gayle standing by, candle raised, staring at my desk—or, really, at the wall above my desk.

I'd forgotten. The papers that the wind blew around days ago—they're tacked there, in plain sight. Sudden paralysis keeps me in place, staring at Gayle as she stares at my work. It's not as though I bring strangers into my room, and the drawings only face inward, toward my bed, away from the hallway. I didn't think Dad would ever notice them, and Jill would know better than to ask. Now, watching Gayle, I feel uncovered. It is a serious sensation, and I don't like it, so I say, as flippantly as I can, "Oh, those are stupid."

Gayle turns to me. "Are you interested in space?"

I shrug. "Who isn't?"

"No," says Gayle. "Sorry. I mean, are you interested in rockets?"

She draws nearer my desk and taps the largest of my works—ten sheets of graph paper aligned five across, in two rows. There are sketches on the paper, and equations, too. They are plans I created more than six months ago and have been erasing and adding to ever since.

I stay where I am, at the head of my bed. "I guess so. Like I said, it's stupid. They're only sketches. For fun."

Gayle taps another of the papers—a pencil-drawn sketch of a shuttle. "This is missing something, you know. The NASA logo."

She turns to me again, and she is smiling so big and wide that I laugh with nervous energy.

"Hardly." There is feeling back in my feet, and I walk to where she stands. "I know they're working on their design, probably doing lots of tests as we speak. I just thought it'd be fun to guess at it, you know? Figure out what it'd take to reenter the atmosphere the same way you leave it. I like to imagine how it will look."

Gayle shakes her head slightly. "This is more than guesswork, Stella. These equations, you worked them out yourself?"

"I know they're off," I say quickly. "I was approximating. From things I've read."

"Things you've read?"

"Well. For a small public library, ours is pretty well stocked. And I bought some books when we went to Wichita in January."

Gayle says nothing to that, only shifts her gaze across the wall and, after moments more of studying, points to another collection of papers arranged in three rows, three across—a perfect boxed containment of plans.

"What's this?"

I am blushing hard. It is strange, because I think I wanted Gayle to ask me that question. Only now I don't want to answer.

Sensing my discomfort, she says, "I'm sorry." She removes her finger from the wall. "I'm prying. Heaven knows you didn't expect some snooping lady in your bedroom."

She is ready to leave it, to walk away and start a new conversation. It's in that moment that I find my courage and spit out, "It's an escape pod."

Gayle presses her lips tight. She is waiting for me to go on.

"Have you seen the movie *Marooned*?" I ask.

Gayle frowns in thought. She nods slowly, then faster. "Gregory Peck is in that one, isn't he? Came out ten or so years ago? Right around the moon landing."

"That's it. I was Jill's age then, and I snuck into the theatre to see that one with my friend Dennis. Well . . . I mean, we're not friends anymore. Not that that matters." I am still blushing, and I am certain Gayle notices, even in the candlelight. "Anyway, the movie scared me. I know it was meant to be suspense, but it was more than that. It was a horror story, watching those astronauts trapped in a little bit of tin, rotating Earth, unable to come back down. And the scene where the one astronaut cuts loose, and his oxygen goes out, it . . ." I am speaking very fast, and I know it is too much. I should stop. I have never told anyone this. Gayle is listening and nodding, though, and she looks understanding in the flickering light—something beyond human, a patron saint come down to listen to my innermost confessions. So I continue to confess. "I was crying at the end. I couldn't stop. I think I scared Dennis. My mother had . . . had passed a few months earlier, and Dennis thought it had to do with that. Maybe it did, but I don't think so. It was just—I kept imagining what it would be like, trapped in space with no way home. I had nightmares for a while, and then I mostly forgot it. But then *Apollo 13* happened, and it got me to thinking of *Marooned* again and everything that can go wrong in space, and I thought, *shouldn't rockets have better lifeboats?* That's when I decided I would come up with the perfect escape pod. A way to get home, with thrusters and the proper shielding and an extra store of oxygen. Though I know now it's stupid. I know NASA has good reasons behind their designs, with plenty of precautions in place. And there are regulations concerning size and weight and money spent, I know that. So it's stupid. Just this dumb thing I came up with."

"You thought of that when you were nine?"

I am so startled by the question, I laugh again and say, "No. I mean, I drew a lot of plans when I was that age. I didn't work out the math until freshman year."

Gayle's expression does not change. "You were fourteen. When you drew that."

"Yes." I am wondering now what possessed me to put up the drawings. Had I left them alone on my desk, I wouldn't be enduring this inquisition. It's all the fault of those horrible winds.

Gayle doesn't notice my discomfort, though maybe that's because I do too good a job at hiding it. Oblivious, she asks, "How old were you when you made the shuttle designs?"

"That was this year," I say. "Like I said, though, those things wouldn't fly. They're only bare-bones ideas, you know."

"Yes," says Gayle. "I know."

As she holds the candle closer to the drawings, I get an urge to blow out the flame. I purse my lips.

"This is upper-level math, Stella. Past high school calculus."

"Well, my teacher wasn't the best," I say, unsure of what I am trying to explain. "I did a lot of studying on my own."

Gayle is silent. That serious, uncovered feeling is back on me.

"You know what's funny?" I say. "I only saw that movie once, but I remember it really well. Even better than movies I saw last year. The only women in it are the astronauts' wives. And even back then, I remember getting so angry about that. The wives were *awful*. I don't mean they were bad people, or anything, it was that . . . There's this scene when the engineers tell them there's been a problem, and one of the wives tells the other one, 'The best thing is to let the men do their jobs and keep our emotions to ourselves.' Something like that." I am laughing again. "Isn't that ridiculous? I thought that even when I was nine."

Gayle is looking at my sketches when she says, "Ridiculous."

I want to ask every impertinent question I have been biting back. Why did she get the degree she did? How is she a nuclear physicist? What is that like, a woman among so many men? I feel certain if I asked them, she would understand. She would answer.

I cannot ask, though. Gayle has grown quiet, and she seems almost . . . *angry*. I decide this should be over. My father is probably wondering what's become of us. I should leave the room and get ready for bed, before we use up the last of our candles.

"Anyway," I say, "I'll leave you to—"

"Sorry. Sorry, hang on." Gayle's eyes are swimming. Too much candlelight, I suppose. "Stella, hang on. Your father tells me you're not going to college. Is that right?"

I say, "I can't leave Jill. And we need the money."

"I see."

She looks so displeased that I have to say something more.

"I know what you're thinking. I'd like to go to college, and I mean to. Just later on, when Jill's older. People go to college later in life. That's what I'll do."

I don't know where this is coming from. It is the first time I've thought it, and certainly the first time I've said it. I *don't* mean to go to college later. By the time Jill is my age, my life will have moved on, and college won't be an option. What I want is for *Jill* to go to college, to get an opportunity I will not have. I know that. What I don't know is why I was compelled to lie to Gayle in order to make her think better of me.

Though my lie seems to have changed things. Gayle's face clears, the anger no longer there. She smiles, which makes me realize she hasn't been smiling all this time, and she says, "I understand."

"Hey! Hey, you two!"

My father appears at the doorway, holding the crank lantern aloft. He reminds me of a mythical character—a guide with magic in his blood, straight from the pages of the Lord of the Rings. Jill is by his side, dressed in a flowing white nightgown, hair pulled out of its braided pigtails, long and crimped.

"You have to see this." Dad is so excited he's short on breath. He waves us into the den, where he yanks up the blinds from the window there. Raindrops are crowded densely upon the glass. Beyond them are sky and the short, weedy expanse of our front yard.

"What?" I ask, as Gayle and I approach the window. "What's—"

A flash of light knocks the words out of me. Another flash follows, and another.

Veins.

That is what I think as I watch them pulse against the sky, bright pink and branched out in jagged lines. They are the veins of something larger than us, and something powerful. Something unfeeling and impersonal. And yet . . . something wonderful. I cannot take my eyes off the sky. I have never seen lightning like this—pink and relentless. I have never heard thunder like this—booming outside, but within me too, down to my bones. I cannot stop looking and listening. None of us can. We stand still and watch in wonder, as the pink light illuminates our faces.

13

Galliard

SATURDAY, AUGUST 6

My gods died young.

Janis and Jimi were each twenty-seven, and Buddy was only twenty-two. Can you imagine? All that talent and life, snuffed out by an overdose, asphyxiation, a plane crash. It isn't fair. It isn't right. That talent and life have to go somewhere. I think they went to the stars.

I don't believe in ghosts. It's not that I think those three are still around, or that they're actually living in the sky. And I don't mean any disrespect to their memories or their living relations. I guess it's more what they represent. I pray to Buddy for confidence and understanding, which is something he had in spades. I pray to Janis for bravery and strength. And I pray to Jimi for discipline and cool. Sometimes they fail me, but most days they've got my back. And these days I'm starting to think they might be the very wind at my back.

Even now, when it looks like I'm stuck in J. J.'s kitchen for life with no hope of playing my music full-time, I've got hope. You have to keep playing, right? You've got to have talent, but you've also got to persevere. My gods sure did.

There's one piano on Red Sun property, and it's located in Common House. I go there to play when I'm not on shift—late morning some days, early evening on others. Ruby gave me my first lesson when I was five. She taught me how to curve my hands over the keyboard as though I was holding on to fragile bubbles. She taught me sharps and flats and the circle of fifths, and I worked my way up from "Hot Cross Buns" to Rachmaninoff's Prelude in G Minor over the course of eleven years. Until I was nine, Ruby could place requests for new sheet music to be brought in from the Outside. Then Rod came on the Council, and things changed. Members were no longer allowed to request importations; the Council would decide on everything, from fabrics to soap to linens. The biggest change was that there would be no more additions to the Back Room collection.

In the Back Room, there's a record player, an LP collection, and a small library of books, all from the Outside. Members are allowed to visit with a pass from the Council. Leander, Opal's husband, believed humans work best when their souls are well-nourished or something, and that both music and writing are the best food for the soul. But when Rod assumed authority, he claimed to have noticed a "disturbing trend" in the commune. More workers seemed restless while performing their tasks, he said, and more youths were leaving Red Sun. So he introduced the cutoff: no more music and no more books— nothing created after 1970. Technically, the whole Council implemented the rule, but everyone knew it was Rod's idea.

I try not to think about what I've missed in the past seven years. Instead I listen to what we do have, which includes the Beatles and the Byrds and the Rolling Stones; Simon and Garfunkel, the Beach Boys, James Brown; and, of course, my gods. My weekly listening sessions always include a line-up of "Manic Depression" followed by "Kozmic Blues" followed by "Words of Love." To top it off, at the close of each session I listen to Elvis Presley's "It's Now or Never." Because Elvis is the King, and to end on anything else would be sacrilege.

I listen to the music the same way I end my morning prayers—lying down, eyes closed. In the Back Room, wrapped up in the music, the beat *thump-thump*ing through my skeleton, I feel all right. The week's aggravations don't reach me there. I melt into the music. Buddy, Janis, and Jimi usher my spirit to the sky, and for an hour I exist outside myself, carried along by chord progressions and the tap of cymbals. And then the hour ends, and Saff knocks on the door and tells me to hand in my pass.

I started writing my own songs when I was thirteen. I don't know if they're any good; I only know they're mine. I mostly sing about life on the commune. I sing love songs too, though they're based on the love songs I've heard, not personal experience. In case you're curious, I'm not popular with the ladies. In a commune of four hundred people, your options are already limited, and after what happened with this girl named Cynthia, I've gone into a kind of lockdown. You take what you can get, and if you don't get anything? Well, you can write a song about that too.

Here's the thing: Music is a kind of magic. When I'm lying down in the Back Room, and even when I'm playing chords and singing lyrics, a calmness washes over me the same as it does during my morning prayers. When I'm wrapped up in the music, my tics can't find me. They fade to nothing, and all that's left is melody. No jaw jerks, no throat clears, no self-conscious thoughts. Just me and the notes and the magic in between.

Lately, I've been in need of that magic, and so today, at the Yamaha, I'm mixing some Liszt with some Stevie Wonder with some original composition. I pound at the keys with more force than necessary.

I haven't spoken to Phoenix, and Phoenix hasn't spoken to me. He's stopped trying to make nice and realized that we're only going to talk again when I deign to speak to him; back-stabbers don't get to set the terms of reconciliation.

Trouble is, I don't want to be reconciled. I'm still mad as hell at Phoenix, and matters definitely aren't any better now that some of his paintings have started to show up on display at the Moonglow, replacing old photographs of the commune. Next to each painting is a paper listing the title and price; the Council is selling each work for a hundred dollars. I guess canvases sell better than songs.

The trouble about the trouble is, I *have* to make nice with Phoenix, and soon. Stella Mercer is depending on it. If she shows up here on Wednesday with those big, sad eyes, asking about her brother, I will lose it. I will break down and tell her everything and invite her to run me through with J. J.'s sharpest chef's knife, because I deserve it.

So I have to talk to Phoenix. I have to play it nice, even though he has ruined my life, because I myself have quite possibly ruined Stella Mercer's life.

Hence the pounding on keys with undue force.

I try to make the music louder than my thoughts. Maybe, I think, the chords can drown out the memories of all the nights Phoenix sat across from me at this piano and told me I had a unique musical talent.

"Gonna break that thing, man."

I've been so lost in my bad feelings and a corresponding run of octaves that I haven't noticed Archer standing a few feet off.

"Goddamn it," I say, skidding back on the piano bench. I begin to blink—quick, relentless flutters.

Archer snickers. "Aw, poor brooding artist, alone with his craft." He places his hand on his forehead in faux distress. "No one understands my tortured soul."

I mean, it's absolutely true. No one does.

"What time is it?" I ask.

"Past time. The guys are gonna leave without us unless we get a move on."

Still blinking hard, I stack the sheet music and stow it in the bench. Archer is watching my every move.

"You ready for this?" he asks. "Cause I don't think you are."

"Yeah, me neither." I look over at what Archer is wearing. It's not the usual Red Sun tunic, but a purple T-shirt that reads KANSAS CITY ROYALS. He looks like an outsider.

I point to my own stark white tunic and ask, "Am I going to stand out?"

Archer shrugs. "We'd stand out anyway. Everyone knows we're from the commune. Follow my lead and you'll be fine."

Archer and I have gone out once since the drive-in, on

Thursday night. We biked to what Archer called the "main drag"—a long street of shops and restaurants. We walked around and eventually bought some deli sandwiches, and I had my first try of something called pastrami. It was good, but not better than anything we cook at the Moonglow. I'd heard Archer talk enough about Slater to know what to expect. It's not like I haven't read about stores and roads, and I've seen cars before. But things are different in person. Larger and way more solid, moving in ways I didn't exactly expect. It was an all right visit, I guess. I've got nothing to compare it to. According to Archer, though, I still haven't had a *real* introduction to the Outside.

That real introduction comes tonight.

Archer and the other crossers have been invited to an outsider party. Archer says he's been to plenty of these, and they turn out okay so long as you don't drink everything you're handed. I plan on following his advice. I want to be alert and aware tonight, because tonight I'm meeting actual *people* from the Outside. It's the next step. A chance to see if what they've told us here in Red Sun is true. If the people out there are selfish backstabbers, out of tune with the Life Force. If Phoenix was right about something, *anything*.

Not for the first time, I think about what Rod told me in his office—that Crossing is for the weak. That weak actions are *wrong* actions, and they deserve punishment from the Life Force. Yet here I am, Crossing not only because I think my Life Force approves, but because I think it's telling me to. Janis, Jimi, and Buddy were risk takers, innovators, *rebels*. Maybe Rod would call their actions wrong too. All I know is that if my Crossing bothers Rod, tough. I'm not near close to forgiving him for passing me over for resident artist, whatever his reasoning. Because songs aren't just songs. And what I've been playing on this Yamaha? It's who I am.

"Hey, hey! Put a drink in this man's hand!"

The party's underground. Or, to be totally accurate, it's in someone's basement. Archer says this is the usual. The guy who's hosting—someone by the name of Evan or Ethan, I can't remember—has parents who regularly go out of town on the weekend, making his place *the* place to party. Only he insists everyone stay in the basement so that no irreparable damage is done to his mom's china collection. Based on what I've seen tonight, that's a valid concern.

The place is packed. There have to be at least sixty people here, all around my age. Girls are sitting in guys' laps, and plastic cups are in everyone's hands, and the air is thick with cigarette smoke. Everywhere around me, people are talking and laughing. I've already seen six different couples making out. Bowls of chips and plates of brownies are passed around the room, from hand to hand. At one end of the basement, a half-dozen people are bent over rows of red, blue, yellow, and green circles, their arms and legs jumbled together.

"It's Twister," shouts the same guy who's insisting someone put a drink in my hand. "Never seen it before, flower child?"

I don't know if I'm supposed to be offended by this guy, so I just edge away and slip back into the crowd. Slipping out of notice entirely is a tougher task. Archer lied to me about clothes; none of the other crossers are in the Red Sun tunic, which leaves me looking like a colossal idiot. Dressed this way, my very person seems to be screaming, *Ask me about life on the inside!*

"Are you all virgins?" asks a giggling girl in a paisley wrap, before being shushed and carted away by her girlfriends.

"You heard of disco in there?" asks another girl, who's hanging upside down over a couch arm, her pupils as large as moons.

I don't answer any of them, but they don't stop asking. My heart's beating fast, and my blinking tic is in full force, and my skin is suddenly way too small for my body. To make matters worse, I haven't seen Archer for the past five minutes.

Then there's a heavy weight on my shoulder. A hulking guy with a buzz cut and rancid breath is hauling me into a corner. He rams me against the wall.

"Okay, don't fuck around with me, man," he snarls, spittle flying from his lips onto mine. "I know you've got it in that hippie paradise of yours. No way you fruits can be that naturally happy. So c'mon, tell me: How do I get hooked up with the stuff?"

Drugs. He's talking about drugs.

But what does he want from *me*? I can't think of a single possible answer that's going to make this guy happy.

I'm quiet too long, blinking fast, and this guy is beyond normal levels of intoxication. He grabs my tunic and wrenches it in his fist.

"I SAID DON'T FUCK WITH ME, MAN."

"Christ almighty, Brian, lay off him."

The girl sounds so bored, I don't think she can possibly

be directing her words at us. But as it turns out, my assailant reacts. He wrenches his head around, affording me a view of a dark-eyed, deep-tanned girl with a buzz cut to match his—only hers is bleach white. She's puffing half-heartedly at a cigarette, and she looks as bored as she sounds.

"Stay out of it, Kim." Brian's words slur, the consonants sloshing around.

"I said lay off him," Kim says in as disinterested a voice as before. "Go lie down, huh? You don't look good."

For whatever reason, the girl's droning seems to be working on Brian. He glances between me and her, torn. Then he lets go of my tunic, though not before ramming me once more into the wall. He points a finger in my face, looks ready to say something. In the end, nothing gets said. He lurches away, and the last I see of him, he's stumbling up the basement stairs.

I let out my first full breath in minutes and smooth down my tunic.

"All right there?" The buzz-cut girl comes in closer. She puffs out a cloud of smoke, and I try not to cough. Fighting that urge seems to set off another one, because my waving tic sets in.

Kim watches the first of my waves. Then another. On the third, she seems to get it. Only I don't see the usual pity that shows on most people's faces when they get it. She keeps on smoking, unperturbed.

"Thanks," I say.

Kim shrugs. "Yeah, Brian's wanted in my pants since junior year. At this point he's a well-trained puppy. But hey, that happens again, you got to shove back, okay? And don't come to any more parties dressed like that." She disdainfully waves a hand over my whole body. "Good as walking around with a 'kick me' sign taped to your ass."

"Yeah, I gathered that."

Kim raises a brow. "This your first time out?"

"Good as."

"And how're you liking it?"

I feel fine being honest with this girl, so I say, "Right now? Hating it."

She laughs at that, surprising me. She doubles over and cackles hoarsely.

"Oh God," she says, straightening. "Good for you." She gets lost in a round of coughing, then says, "I'm Kim, by the way."

"Galliard."

"Mm-hmm. And you find nothing about tonight to be likable, Galahad?"

I wave. "It's Galliard."

"Yeah, okay."

"Well." I look around the room, as though searching for some heaven-sent blessing that will change my bad opinion. Then a new song starts to play on the speakers, and I realize something. "I'd like the music, if I could hear it. I mean . . . I'd like listening to what's popular now. I haven't heard anything new since 1970."

There's an actual expression on Kim's face, and I'm pretty sure it's surprise.

"*What?*" she asks. "Nothing since *1970*. Man, that's the craziest thing I've ever heard about your cult. And believe me, I've heard a *lot* of crazy shit."

I don't know what I'm supposed to say to that, so I just kind of shrug. Then I wave again.

"Uh-uh," says Kim. "Uh-*uh*. That's not cool. I tell you what, next time you come Crossing into town, you stop by my work, okay? The Exchange, on Vine Street. Your buddies will know it. You come by any day between nine o'clock and three, and I will give you an *education*. You dig me?"

"Um. Yeah, I dig you."

"All right."

Then she's gone, sucked back into the crowd. I'm actually disappointed. She's the one outsider I've met tonight that I haven't wanted to flip off. I was kind of hoping she'd stick around.

Now that I'm thinking about music, I try harder to concentrate on what's playing. I inch closer to one of the speakers, from which a man is singing something about playing funky music.

"Groovin' beat, man, huh?" shouts a bare-chested guy who's camped out beside the speaker and pumping his fist in the air in time with the bass line.

I nod, offering no other musical critique. I'm scanning the crowd for Archer and coming up empty. It's not easy, given that he's a whole foot shorter than me. I push into the crowd again, away from the speaker and toward a quieter corner of the room where a long-haired girl is playing guitar, and a boy beside her slaps his knees, singing, "'Suicide is painless . . . it brings so many changes.'"

Holy shit, I need to get out of here.

Voices crowd in on me from every side, none of them friendly.

"... what I'm *saying*. Jackie swears to God that's why she was gone in April. She got it done at some clinic in Kansas City."

"... motivation do I have to drive?"

"... it's a dump there, I warned him."

"... failed out his first semester, so the rooming is back to square one."

It's too much. It's too close. It's pushing my bones to the snapping point, threatening imminent implosion.

I've got to get out of here, whether it's with Archer or not.

I push against bodies, rougher than necessary. All I can think of is surfacing from here and dragging down gulps of fresh air. I make my way to the stairs, and I rise and rise until I reach the foyer and the front door and—suddenly the wind is knocked out of me. I'm reeling back toward the staircase, and I barely manage to grab the basement door's handle and right myself.

"I dunno what you think you're doing, hanging with Kim, but you steer clear, man. Y'hear me?"

It's Brian again. My favorite guy.

Janis, Jimi, and Buddy above—show me mercy in my hour of need.

"Sure thing," I say, putting as much distance between myself and Brian as possible. Which is unfortunate, as he's blocking the front door. "Sure thing. I don't want to fight."

"Yeah, you don't, because I would DESTROY YOU."

Yep. No one's arguing with you there, Brian.

But for some reason my mouth opens wide.

"What?" Brian demands.

With difficulty, I drag my lips shut. It doesn't help. The tic shoots into different muscles, different nerves. I blink hard, and my chin jerks to the right.

"What the hell?" says Brian.

I can't get the tics to let up. They've never been this bad—this rapid and violent. I'm blinking every second on the second. My jaw won't stop jerking.

"Seriously, man," says Brian. "What the hell is your problem?"

I want this to end. And thanks to Brian's most recent movement, I've got a clear shot at the front door. It's as I'm about to make my move that everything goes black.

The blaring music cuts out. There's a second of still, silent darkness. Then screams from the basement. The sound of glass breaking. Confused shouting. A voice on the stairs shouts, "Calm *down*, people. It's a blown fuse!" No one seems to be listening. Everyone down there is either too drunk or stoned to hear reason. As for Archer and the rest of the crossers, I've given up on them. If this is how they usually spend their summer nights, they've got to be used to this kind of thing. Me, though? I'm leaving.

My eyes now adjusted to the new dark, I shove past Brian and throw open the door. I'm running when I leave, and at first I don't understand why it is that I'm suddenly cold and dripping.

It's raining. Raining *hard*. In only a few seconds, I'm drenched through, my tunic clinging to my body like little more than paper. It's enough to make me stop and look up.

The party was so loud it drowned out the sounds of rain

and thunder. Now all that sound crashes down on me. There are a million raindrops smacking into the pavement, full force. Lightning slices across the sky.

"Holy *shit*. Did you see that?"

"What's going on?"

More people have joined me on the lawn, confirming that I'm not hallucinating. The lightning really is *pink*. There's too much of it, and its bolts are too long, uncoiled rope thrown across the sky.

I've never seen a storm like this, and a stupid part of me wants to explain it away by saying this is how storms are on the Outside. But that makes no sense, and even if it did, the stunned reactions from the partygoers would be enough to tell me this isn't normal.

Something's wrong.

I search the sky for any sign of stars, but everything is clouded over. My gods are in hiding.

14

Stella

SUNDAY, AUGUST 7

When I wake Sunday morning, the storm is over—no more thunder or strange lightning—but the rain is still coming down hard, slanted with wind. The ceiling fan in the den is whirring, which means the electricity must have come back on sometime in the night. I'm surprised to find Dad awake and in the kitchen, drinking a cup of coffee. He tells me that Gayle left an hour ago. She attends Saint Stephen's Episcopal, the church where we held my mother's funeral.

Jill appears soon after me, woken by our voices and determined not to be left out of our conversation. She demands we go to Ferrell's, despite the rain. It is tradition, after all.

The route to Ferrell's requires us to pass by our old church, First Baptist. Jill is the first to notice the steeple. Tower and belfry remain, but the spire is gone, and in its place is a jagged, black hollow.

"My God," whispers my father, slowing the car and straining toward the windshield to better see. "It's been struck by lightning."

"Does that mean God's angry?" asks Jill.

"Who knows, Jillie," says Dad. "Though I'm sure Pastor Barkley will make the most of it."

There are many reasons why we Mercers stopped going to church, but Pastor Barkley is the biggest one. After my mother's death, he refused to hold the funeral at First Baptist. He claimed he could not commend my mother's soul to God, because to take one's own life is to despair, and despair is the one unforgivable sin. Many of the congregants disagreed. Mrs. Hume was in an absolute rage about it and even shouted in Pastor Barkley's face during a church financial meeting. In the end, my father's Sunday school class and most of the women's committee helped us plan and pay for the funeral at Saint Stephen's.

We arrive at Ferrell's, and we order our malts, tater tots, and Coney dogs. Station 98.5 is playing "You Made Me Believe in Magic" by the Bay City Rollers. When the song fades into the hourly news, Dad turns up the volume. The local reporter comments on traffic and a marathon being held in downtown Kansas City. The weather report mentions rain, but not the strong storms from last night. I take this to mean that Kansas City did not experience any of the pink lightning we did in Slater.

The reporter goes on to mention the Son of Sam situation in New York, and Jill turns rigid beside me until the report ends and Stevie Wonder's "Sir Duke" fades in. Then life returns to her limbs, and she begins wiggling back and forth to the beat, waving her plastic malt spoon and singing "'They can feel it all ooover.'"

"Those chops!" shouts Dad.

I am less impressed and more bemused by how Jill can move seamlessly from a state of petrification to silliness. It's clear the news of the New York killings is affecting her. Perhaps it's that it is a real-life manifestation of her favorite mysteries—a mystery that cannot be solved by Nancy Drew or Frank and Joe Hardy over the course of twenty-five chapters. Whatever the reason, I can only hope the police catch the killer soon and that the news will move on to less traumatizing topics, like the energy crisis and new political scandals.

I worry about Jill. When I was her age, I was not consuming mystery books and asking questions about murders. I was obsessed with rocket launches and my new bike. Then again, when I was nine, I had not lost a mother and a brother. I had not been fed eight years' worth of subpar dinners by my older sister. I had not sat at a table with my father's girlfriend and tried hard to make do with the new situation. So it could be that Jill's behavior is perfectly normal for the kind of nine-year-old Jill is. I only wish she didn't have to be that kind of nine-year-old.

She cannot help that she is far younger than me and Dad. She cannot help the reality that he and I talk about things above her head and behind her back—like now, when we get home. After Jill's disappeared to her bedroom, Dad pulls me into the kitchen and asks what I thought of Gayle.

It's a difficult question to answer. Had he asked me right after last night's dinner, I would have replied with unreserved approval. Things have changed since my conversation with Gayle in the bedroom, though. I don't know why I told her the things I did. I've never shared them with anyone—my memory of *Marooned* and what those sketches and equations mean to me and that I would even consider college in my future. It must have been the familiar way she spoke. She made me feel more comfortable than I should have. Then she made me feel wrong for not attending college, even when there clearly is no other option. For a moment she made me forget the distinction between *This Stella* and *That Stella,* and I'm upset with her for that.

Last night I thought I liked her so much. This morning, after the thunder and lightning and cannoli, I am thinking better of it. My mind is clearer, and I decide Gayle Nelson is a decent woman, and I do not mind her dating my father, but she is much too prying, and I need to be on my guard the next time she comes over.

"She's fine," I tell Dad. "I like her just fine."

Usually, I find the sound of rain to be soothing. Tonight it keeps me up. Something about the way it hits my windowpane is uneven—too loud at times, so soft at others. Then the thunder starts back up, and the lightning, too, pink as it was last night. Every minute, it flickers against the windowpanes, filling my bedroom with rose-colored light.

Though I cannot make out the drawings over my desk, I stare in their direction. When I created those blueprints, I was filled with feverish inspiration, and with hope. Those blueprints are precious to me, the most personal of my projects. Now I feel as though they have betrayed me. Perhaps I should blame the wind that blew them up, forcing me to tack them in plain sight. At least the wicker bin wasn't out, because I can only imagine the questions Gayle would have asked had she seen the walkie-talkies. And at least she didn't see the back of my closet door.

I've kept the door closed since Gayle's overnight stay, but now, in the dark of my room, curiosity burns inside me. After minutes in silence, I cannot stand it any longer. I get out of bed and, with jittery force, fling the door open.

The numbers are still there, projected across the wood panels. I stare at the violet markings: *11:01:39.*

I believe in coincidences. I do. But the fact of the matter is, there is a glowing countdown in my bedroom, which matches exactly the countdown over Slater's town hall. Those are strange facts, and they cannot be denied.

I suppose I should be frightened. I'm not, though. I'm something else. "Excited" can't be the right word, but it is close. As I think on it more, there in the dark, I come to a realization: I am feeling now the same as I did when I drew those shuttle designs. I feel inspiration, mixed with hope. I feel . . . *freedom.*

If the worst is true, and these numbers are counting down to the end of the world, that means all futures for myself are equally unlikely. And if I look at that a certain way—well then, all my futures are equally *likely.* If there is an apocalypse around the corner, it doesn't matter which version of myself I choose to be. If the end is coming, I might as well live as *That Stella* in the here and now.

I find myself imagining what Craig would think of Gayle Nelson. What would he make of her? Would he approve of this new trajectory for us Mercers? I wish I could ask him, even if it would be too much of a personal question. I wish I could ask him *every* kind of personal question, face-to-face. Then I tell myself, this isn't something *That Stella* would wish; it's something she would *do*.

A fresh flash of lightning fills the room, casting a rosy hue on all I see. I take this as confirmation of the decision I'm making. I take it to mean that my future, however short, will be *rosy* from here on out. I will make it so.

I will meet Craig before this countdown ends. On Wednesday I will go back to Red Sun, as the boy named Galliard instructed. I will see my brother.

It's what *That Stella* would do.

The rain does not clear. It pours down all Monday and straight through Tuesday. The storming lets up during the day but returns every night, with more of the bizarre pink lightning. We receive several cancellations at the salon—women who call in to say that their drives are flooded and they cannot get out to Vine Street. The Dreamlight is shut due to the inclement weather, so I spend my nights at home with Jill. We eat dinner together, and we play games of dominoes, Connect Four, and—Jill's favorite—the *Happy Days* board game. Mostly, though, we keep reading. She finishes two Hardy Boys and a book called *The Witch's Buttons*. I finish *The Cosmic Connection* and begin *Riddles in Mathematics: A Book of Paradoxes*, which contains more than two hundred brain teasers. I check them off one by one, using the lightest of ticks with my pencil since, unlike the Carl Sagan, it's a library book.

On Wednesday the rain calms to a drizzle. It is enough to keep the drive-in closed, though not enough to prevent me biking out to Red Sun. Jill doesn't know the Dreamlight's weather policy, though, and a couple of hours after dinner, I leave like I'm going to work as always, biking toward the western town limits.

I steer down Eisenhower, around dips and crevices filled to brimming with rainwater, as even more rain patters on the hood of my jacket. The bottoms of my jeans wick up water splashed from the road, despite my careful biking.

I'm not questioning the decision I made last night. I will be *That Stella*. Even so, I'm realizing that a transformation from *This Stella* to *That* may take time. I know *That Stella* wouldn't panic about this meeting with Craig, but I am. As I swing my bike into the parking lot of the Moonglow Café, I try to block from my mind why I am here and who I am attempting to contact. Those thoughts turn me weak-legged, and I need to be strong for this. I need to be prepared, because undoubtedly Craig is. I wonder if, at this very moment, he's expecting my arrival. What he can't expect is this: a brand-new version of me.

The café's hostess—a tall girl in a white linen sundress—is familiar. She was here last week and witnessed me when I was much less in control of my wits and demanding to see my brother. Her face falls the moment she sees me walk in.

"*You*," she says, leaving no doubt as to her poor opinion of me.

She continues to look me over with disdain as I request to speak to a boy with the first name Galliard and a last name I do not know.

"Sorry," she tells me. "It isn't my job to do personal favors. I seat paying customers; I don't run messages back and forth."

I cannot say I blame her. I'm insistent, though, because that's the kind of girl *That Stella* is.

"It'll take you ten seconds." I motion to the restaurant's few diners (business here has clearly been affected by the weather too). "You've got plenty of time on your hands."

She casts me a dirty look, but she tells me fine, she will see if Galliard is in the kitchen. Meantime I can wait outside.

Satisfied, I walk out to the café's front porch and sit with my back to its wood-paneled wall. I blink in surprise when I realize the drizzling has stopped and the sun has emerged from the clouds, just in time to set. It draws down deep against the horizon, rotating onward to shed its light on other continents, other cities, and other seventeen-year-old girls. I watch it, and I wait.

Dusk rolls in. Crickets strike up their songs. From a distant tree I hear a whip-poor-will—a brief trill, ceaseless and repetitive, ending each time on a high-pitched burst. I've lost track of time, thinking of nothing but Craig's last letter to me, when I hear the whine of a screen door. I turn, and since I am sure this will be just another set of patrons leaving the restaurant, I have already turned back around when I realize that it is, in fact, Galliard. I make to stand. He waves me down.

"I'll join you." He sits beside me, then says, "I wasn't sure you'd come."

"I told you I would."

"It was a 'maybe.'" His gaze shifts over me. "You're wet."

I look over my damp jacket and bell-bottoms. "I biked here."

"Sorry."

"No need to be, unless you're the one who's controlling this weather."

"I'm a whole lot of things, but weather god isn't one of them."

I find myself smiling. Then, shocked, I find myself wanting to flirt. Why not? That's precisely what *That Stella* would do.

"What kind of things are you, then?" I ask. "Are you the one in charge of human sacrifices? Or the drugs?"

He laughs. It is a warm, rounded sound, and overloud. "Is that what you think we do in here?"

"In *there*, you mean." I tip my thumb over my shoulder, toward the café. "We're not in the commune here."

Galliard's brow contracts. Then he blinks, quickly and intensely—a tic, I think. "Guess not."

"Do they let you smoke in there?"

"No. Contrary to popular belief, we don't grow the weed. My friend Archer knows someone on the Outside."

"Do you like it?"

"What, pot?"

"Yes."

He blinks. "I mean, it's probably the best thing about the Outside."

"That's depressing."

"Well, the Outside is depressing."

I frown at him. He keeps blinking in quick bursts.

"If you waste your time, then yeah, the real world is sure to be awful."

"I'm not—"

"What exactly do you do for Crossing?" I say. "If it's depressing, you're not doing it right."

"I don't know. I've only been out a few times."

I look Galliard over. The café's porch lights illuminate his face. It is deeply tanned, and there is a bit of stubble under his lower lip. Dark, curly hair comes down to his shoulders. His eyebrows are thick and dark, and a permanent crease runs across his forehead.

I say, "You don't look that young."

He blinks forcefully. "Thank you very much."

"I only mean, doesn't Crossing stop when you're sixteen?"

"It's my last summer. I didn't want to go out before."

I don't understand him, but I find I want to. "What changed your mind?"

"It just changed."

"But now you wish it hadn't, because the real world is depressing?"

"Something like that. Anyway, about your brother—"

"Wait." I really do interrupt. I really do stop him right as he's about to tell me about Craig. I don't feel ready to move on yet. I cannot make sense of this boy across from me.

"I'm trying to understand," I say. "Because I don't see how the Outside could possibly be more depressing than your life in there. If you had a proper education about the real world, you might like it."

Galliard blinks. "Stop calling it that."

"What?"

"The *real world*. Like Red Sun is a fake world."

"Well," I say. "Isn't it?"

"How do you figure that?"

"Because you're scared to be outside of it."

"I'm not scared."

He produces a deep, throaty sound that makes my head snap toward him. Then I realize the sound is a tic, and I immediately feel bad for looking.

"And you're planning on staying in the commune the rest of your life?" I don't know why I keep asking questions. I cannot quit.

"Okay," says Galliard. "What's so good about the *real world*? Do *you* like it? Are *you* happy?"

I consider the question, surprised to be on the receiving end of one for a change. In the end I say, "Relatively happy. Happiness is always relative, I think."

"Okay. Then what's your secret?"

I laugh—a solitary "bah!" "Are you asking me the secret to happiness?"

"I'm asking for recommendations. What do *you* say I should do on the Outside?"

"I'd have to think about it," I say. "Make you a list."

"Or you could show me."

"Excuse me?"

I keep getting distracted by the humming sound Galliard is making. I am upset at myself for getting distracted, and I am further distracted by getting upset.

"You could show me in person," he says again.

I am convinced I've heard him wrong. To confirm this I say, "You're not asking me to show you around Slater."

"Sure. If you're going to be judgmental, I think that's only fair. And I'm not on shift tonight."

I squint at his face in the bad light. He makes the humming sound again. He jerks his head to one side. I continue to squint.

"Just messing around." He sounds uncomfortable now. "Anyway, about your brother . . ."

"Did he agree to see me?"

I attempt to act unaffected, as though the answer to this question means nothing to me. I do a poor job. It doesn't matter anyway, because Galliard knows the truth. He witnessed my breakdown a week ago.

He clears his throat and looks away, toward the parking lot. Then he squeezes his hands together, over his knees.

"No, actually. He, uh . . . he decided to extend the silence. He'll be doing it another week."

Everything within me—heart and mind and throat—seems to descend a full inch in disappointment.

"Oh." I shake my head. "No one can interrupt him?"

"I mean, I *could*. I think it'd upset him pretty bad, though, and that's not the mood you want him in when I ask him about you, is it?"

"I guess not. No. You're right—he should be in the best mood possible."

"Which, if we're lucky, he will be after the silence. He'll be refreshed and renewed and in unison with the Life Force. That's the best time to ask."

"In another week."

"Yeah."

I shake my head. "I don't know how he can do that. How any of you can."

Only I'm not sure that is completely true. Though I cannot

imagine sitting in silence by myself for two weeks, we Mercers do a good job of sitting in silence together, and we've been doing that for nearly a decade.

"All right," I say, getting up. It's a hard task, as my bones feel heavier. "Thank you anyway. Guess I'll be back here in a week."

Galliard continues to look out at the parking lot. "Yeah," he says, after a long silence, as though he has only just heard me. "He . . . seems to mean a lot to you."

"He's family," I say on instinct. Thinking longer, remembering two years of letters, I add, "He knows me, and I know him back. There aren't a lot of people like that in my life."

"Yeah. Yeah, mine either." Galliard doesn't move. He doesn't break his stare from the lot.

I begin to back away toward the bike rack. Then I stop. I watch Galliard some more. I know he must feel my gaze on him, though he doesn't acknowledge it.

"When does Crossing end?" I ask.

"Three weeks."

"And then you stay in the commune. Forever."

"That's about the size of it."

I stare at him some more. At last he looks at me.

Then I know what I am going to do. The words coming from my mouth feel like an inevitability.

"I have the night off too. You can hang with me, if you want."

I say it because of the way he looks in the dusk light. I say it because my father has been spending time with someone outside the Mercer family, and maybe I should too. I say it because it's the end of summer, and there is a literal countdown ticking, and a skittish feeling inside tells me I'm hurtling toward something dark and final, and I should do something I never would in winter, spring, or fall.

I say it as *That Stella*—the one with a rosy future.

Now he is the unbelieving one. He's blinking rapidly. "Wait, really?"

"Do you have a bike?"

"Sure. That is, *we* have bikes I can use."

"Then we can bike together. Do you have to get permission first?"

"Uh, no. They trust us as long as we get back by curfew. Crossing is about *trust*."

Galliard laughs, though I can't see what he finds funny about what he's said. He looks at me a while longer, assessing, blinking. Then he says, "Okay, give me a few minutes."

He goes back into the café. I look at my watch. It is fifteen past eight.

"It's for Craig," I say into the dark. "I need to make sure Galliard is actually going to talk to him for me. Maybe he'll tell me things Craig would never tell me about himself. About his life in there."

I don't say out loud that I am genuinely curious about Galliard, this boy who has lived on the inside of the commune his whole life and, until recently, didn't even want to take a glimpse of the world outside. I'm not sure I can blame him; Slater isn't much of an outside world to glimpse. It is no Kansas City or Chicago. Still, if he thinks the Outside is *depressing*, then something needs to be done, and it would seem I have assigned myself that task. For Craig, my brother.

Galliard reappears, though not where I'm expecting. He calls my name at the commune fence, many yards from the porch. I walk out to meet him. The grass is soft and drenched, and my feet squish deep into earth.

"Where did you come from?" I ask, noting his silver mountain bike. I wonder what kind of biking they do in there, on that land. Do they ride in circles around the corn? The idea makes me laugh, and the sound trickles out as I reach him. I attempt to cover it with a cough.

"The gate." Galliard points back at a tall, hulking man standing guard. "It's the official way out. And I couldn't exactly haul this thing through the restaurant."

"Oh, right."

"Where are we heading?"

"Have you eaten supper yet?"

"No." He grimaces, clearing his throat. "I've been kind of avoiding Dining Hall. For personal reasons."

I nod as though I understand any of this. "Let me get my bike."

I do, and we mount in the parking lot. I lead the way out toward Slater's lights. Though the rain has stopped, the air is damp, and as I speed along the asphalt, casting a glance back to be sure Galliard is keeping up, the wind picks up my hair and sweeps chills over my body. There is a charge in this air, and a charge inside me, and I have an unshakable feeling that this charge is about to spark against another and burst into some great unknowable thing.

It may only be the change of weather toying with my mind.

I know only one thing for certain:

That Stella has officially taken over.

15

Galliard

WEDNESDAY, AUGUST 10

*What a tangled web we weave . . . something, something else . . .
deceive.*

I don't remember the exact wording anymore, but Melly,
Red Sun's elementary teacher, taught me that. She made our
classroom write it three dozen times in our notebooks and
taught us that lying was a terrible thing, because it disrupted
unity and understanding in our community.

Now, as Stella and I bike to town, the incomplete rhyme
won't quit rattling around in my head.

Because damn it if I'm not caught up in a tangled web.

I didn't mean for any of this to happen. Saturday night, the
crossers and I pedaled back to Red Sun, soaked bone-deep and
determined to return by our midnight curfew. Pink lightning
tore up the sky around us, and Archer kept shouting, "Yeah,
man! *Yeah!*" Like it was this great, beautiful thing.

Me? I wasn't so sure. I'd been assuming that my gods
were talking to me through the weather. They'd used those
winds to blow me toward the Dreamlight; that was clear.
Hendrix, Holly, and Joplin—they were risk takers. Explorers.

Innovators. They wanted me to be like them. They *wanted* me to go out and see the Outside for myself. Meet the people. Figure it out.

If that was true, though, then what was I supposed to make of pink lightning? How was I supposed to act with the three of them hidden away behind storm clouds? On that bike ride back, I heard Rod's voice in my head, saying, *Negative consequences for weak actions.* I considered that maybe that was what it was: a bad storm, in response to my bad behavior. Maybe Rod was right.

That night felt violent and dangerous, as though we were biking up to the edge of a chasm and at any moment would fly over the edge. Once I was finally back, safe and dry in my bed at Heather House, I sent a prayer to Holly, figuring he'd be most forgiving if I'd done wrong.

"Phoenix was right about something," I whispered in the dark, over Archer's snores. "Outsiders are the worst. They're stupid and selfish and cruel. He was right about that, at least."

Then I made promises. I said I'd stay in the commune, if that's what I was meant to do. I'd work in J. J.'s kitchen, and I'd become the leader the Council supposedly wanted me to be. I'd even make up with Phoenix and come clean with his sister.

Pink lightning does a lot for a guy's resolve.

Only, in Sunday's morning light, everything seemed a little less dire. Rain was coming down, but in a normal way, and there was no pink lightning to be seen. The promises I'd made in a heat of panic didn't feel so . . . *pressing* anymore. I decided not to seek out Phoenix after all, and I haven't since. It's become habit now, keeping my head down when I see him in Dining Hall, changing my path so it doesn't cross his.

I guess I was telling myself that Stella's "maybe" meant "no." That she wouldn't come back, and I wouldn't have to be brave. I was deluding myself. And now here I am, biking with Phoenix's sister to some unknown destination, after I myself asked her to show me around.

What's wrong with you, Galliard? you're asking. *Do you not learn from mistakes? Do you* want *to sabotage your own life?*

I wish I knew.

But there's this, too: I *want* to be biking with Stella Kay Mercer on the Outside. Because maybe Rod isn't right; maybe he's dead wrong. One thing's for sure: The Red Sun Council doesn't know me. If they did, they'd know that nothing compares to my music, not even leading the whole commune. They're the ones who didn't give me resident artist. They're the ones who stuck me with ten long years of working in J. J.'s kitchen. It's not my fault that I want to see if maybe there's something better for me. Something on the Outside.

I only wish I didn't have so little time to find that out.

I purposefully stayed inside Red Sun for almost three whole summers, stupidly thinking that I was made for better things and a bright, shiny future.

Now? That future's gone, and I only have three weeks to figure out if there's a future outside the commune walls.

As I follow Stella's lead over asphalt and past cornfields, I pray to my gods.

I'm thinking I misinterpreted the lightning. Maybe it wasn't a punishment. Maybe it's a test. You want me to try this out on my own, without you. That's why I'm doing this one more time. And if you're okay with that? Buddy, give me confidence. Janis, give me strength. And, Jimi, please, please *give me cool.*

Even though it's not raining anymore, water has puddled all over the street, and it sloshes under my tires. Stella shouts something from up ahead, but I can't make out the words. Soon after, she veers right onto a side street, and I follow. There's a sign ahead, lit up in greens and yellows. In big, loopy script the neon spells the word FERRELL'S. Under that, in smaller letters, DRIVE-IN. A large flashing arrow points below, to a restaurant. The building itself is small—nothing more than a box with a large, lit window and a single door. The attraction seems to be the giant metal canopy that encircles the building and the dozen slots fitted beneath it, each big enough to accommodate a car.

"It's a different kind of drive-in," says Stella as we skid to a stop.

She dismounts and wheels her bike to the building. An attendant appears at the big window, and Stella waves me over.

"Come on," she says. "See what the real world has to offer."

I wheel my bike to where she stands, hands on hips, looking at the menu marquee.

"I highly recommend the chocolate malt," she tells me. "As for the food, you can't go wrong with anything. You ever had a burger?"

I consider lying, to save face. In the end I shake my head. "We don't eat those."

"You don't eat meat?"

"Sure. We eat eggs. Sometimes chicken. We don't eat . . . burgers."

"Well, this is only my opinion, but, Galliard, I think you need a burger."

"Okay."

She's watching me. I clear my throat—not a tic this time—and concentrate on the menu options. The truth is, I'm lost. I don't know what the hell the words "tater tot" and "slushie" and "Coney" mean.

"Hey." Stella's voice is soft, and closer than I expected. She barely touches my elbow. "I can order for you."

"If you want," I say, like I'm granting her a favor.

She heads up to the window. The attendant takes down her order and tells us it will be up in five minutes or so. Then Stella places something on the counter between them, and I realize it's money.

"Oh hey, wait, I can pay." I reach into my jeans pocket, but it's too late. The attendant's already taken the money, transaction complete.

Stella smiles at me. "Don't worry about it. My treat."

She waves at the space around us. There are only two cars here; I guess the rain has kept people away. Nearer to us are a half-dozen metal tables and benches.

"Where do you want to eat?" Stella asks. "We could pretend to be a car and sit in a space. I recommend a table, though."

I choose the table farthest from the building and closest to the flashing neon arrow.

As we're sitting, I start to tic. This one is a blink-and-throat-clearing combo.

Cool, Jimi. Grant me cool.

"Did Craig ever tell you he wrote me?" Stella asks.

Please. Give me cool.

"Uh," I say. "Phoenix, you mean?"

A look crosses Stella's face. Like I've twisted her arm until it hurts. "Right. Phoenix. I don't know if he ever mentioned that he and I have been writing letters back and forth. You don't have to worry; he's not sharing commune secrets or anything. I guess your leaders would censor his letters if they thought he was. He never talks about his life in there. We discuss bigger things."

"Bigger things?" I blink forcefully.

I feel like such a fraud right now. I know all about the bigger things: Carl Sagan, space, scientific theories. I've read every single one of them.

"Yeah. Science and art and what we think about life in general. I write him about books I'm reading, and he and I talk about them. It's a bunch of nothing, really."

I could tell her now. I should. It's the perfect segue, handed to me on a platter. I don't want to tell her like *this*, though, while I'm ticking and she's pretending she doesn't notice but clearly does.

"All right! Two burgers, two fries, two malts."

My conscience is spared by our bubble gum–chewing attendant, who has reached our table via roller skates and slides our trays before us with practiced ease. Then she's off, and Stella's expression has changed to one of excitement.

"This is it," she says. "Your first burger."

"Uh-huh." I look at the small, grease-stained box before me.

"Don't think too hard. Just pick it up and eat."

Stella takes her own burger out of its box. Using both hands, she raises it to her mouth and bites in.

"I don't need a demonstration," I tell her.

"Okay, fine. Then eat it."

Sound bursts from my throat—three *hrm*s in quick succession. When that's over, I take a first bite, then a second. And it's good. The flavor hits my tongue and coats my mouth, and it's like nothing I've had in the commune, where usual meals consist of salads and beans and the occasional fried egg. This is something more. It takes over my senses and leaves me with only one thought: I have to eat more of it. I devour the burger, without stopping to try a fry or some of the malt. Stella's staring at me again, but I don't mind, because she's smiling.

"See?" she says when I'm through. "See what you've been missing?"

I look at the empty box. "That was good."

She points at the remaining food on my tray. "You might want to get started on the malt before it melts."

We don't talk for the next few minutes. We just eat, and Stella casts me the occasional grin. Like she knew how this would affect me. When we finish, I tell her about the deli Archer took me to, and she scrunches her nose in disapproval.

"I mean, Frank's is okay," she says, "but it definitely shouldn't have been your first experience. That's the kind of food you get on a workday, when you're more concerned about nourishment than fun."

"Do you go there a lot?" I ask.

"Every once in a while. I work across the street, at the salon. Most days I pack a lunch. If I forget, though, I'll grab a sandwich. They're not bad. The Reuben, especially."

I have no idea what a Reuben is. Over the past few days, I've realized that I have no idea what a *lot* of things are. They're small things, but they're everywhere, all over the Outside. And suddenly that lack of knowing seems to be pressing in, suffocating me. How am I supposed to keep up with all of it? How does *anyone*?

I'm about to ask for a definition of "Reuben"—fill in this one tiny speck in a gaping hole of ignorance—when Stella's expression changes. She's looking past me, at first confused and then pleased.

I hear a shout at my back. "*Stell*, what the *hell* are you doing here?"

I turn to see a tall, tan girl with a white-haired buzz cut walking toward us. It's Kim, the one decent person from Saturday night's party. When she catches sight of me, she snorts loudly.

"Well, if it isn't Sir Galahad."

She slides in next to me at the table and, without hesitation, takes a handful of my fries and shoves them in her mouth. Stella is looking between the two of us, surprised.

"How do you know each other?"

"We met at Evan's party Saturday night," Kim says through a mouthful of fries. "You know, the first night of spooky lightning."

"Oh." Stella seems at a loss for words.

"Anyway, came by here to give Janet her apron." Kim leans over to lace up one of her black boots. "Left it at my place last time she was over. But *you* haven't answered my question: What're *you* doing here?"

"I'm—I'm showing Galliard around. He said he hasn't liked what he's seen of the Outside."

"Yeah, I don't blame him." Kim sits up and faces me, her expression serious. "Don't let those fuckers get to you, okay? They're a bunch of meatheads. Or airheads. Either way, no functioning brain matter in there."

Stella's looking between us again, her big eyes bigger. "Why? What happened?"

"Nothing," I say, and funnily enough, my jaw-jerking tic starts up right then. Talk about comedic timing.

"I heard Brian giving him shit about the Tourette's," says Kim. "You know, about what you'd expect from a guy with the IQ of a ferret."

Stella stares some more. She's got to be remembering what I said earlier, about the Outside being depressing. Now she's got to be thinking of me as some wounded, whining child.

"Kim's right," she says. "They're idiots, Galliard."

"Yeah, Stella makes a point of staying away from *all* of them. She hides at home and reads her science fiction."

Stella gives Kim a look. "It's science. Not fiction."

"Yeah, okay. Sure. So where are you taking him next on this grand tour?"

Stella fiddles with her malt straw. "I haven't decided. This was the only place I had in mind."

"Wow. Okay." Kim jabs my arm, and my jaw jerks. "You know Stell's not the person to be showing you around, right? She's basically a recluse."

Stella flinches. "Hey, he just had his first burger."

"Not saying that's bad." Kim raises her hands and addresses me again. "A party, a burger . . . you been to the Dreamlight yet?"

On instinct I look to Stella. She's smiling a little. I smile a little back.

"Yeah," I say. "I've been there."

I don't mention that I never actually saw the movie.

"You're telling me you've been to all these places, but not the Exchange?" Kim shakes her head. "Whatever. Suit yourself, man."

"No," I say quickly. "I want to check it out. Music's the one thing I like about the Outside."

Stella opens her mouth wide. "The *one* thing?"

"And burgers," I add. "And the malt. And the fries."

The sand reed and fireflies, too, only I'd feel like an ass saying that.

Kim is snickering. "Oh my God. You cannot be real." She juts a thumb out and says, "How about we do a brief listening session now? Give you the full drive-in experience. Sans backseat sex."

Kim is already up and moving, so I don't have time to think out the sex comment. Stella grabs both our trays and pitches the trash in a nearby bin, and we follow Kim to her car. She's parked it in a drive-in slot that runs up against an open field and, beyond it, a flat expanse of corn. For the first time in days the clouds have parted, and the stars are visible. A faint sliver of moon shines down.

Kim pats the hood of her bright green car and says, "You know anything about automobiles, Galliard?"

I shake my head, which ends in my jaw jerking rightward.

"Well, this is a '71 AMC Gremlin. And it's a piece of shit, but I love it. It's why I work long hours. My point: Don't put your feet on my dash."

"Wasn't planning on it," I say, but Kim's already in the driver's seat.

"Come on," she yells through her open window. "I don't have all night."

I glance to Stella for guidance. She looks kind of amused, though maybe a little worried, too. Or maybe that's just her eyes; it's difficult to tell when they're as big as hers.

I open the passenger-side door and slide into the seat as Kim shouts, "Watch your feet! Watch 'em!"

On the floorboard are a dozen small plastic boxes, scattered so as to make planting my feet impossible. I decide to stay absolutely safe by sticking my shoes out the open door, sitting sideways.

"You getting in?" I ask Stella.

She shakes her head, pointing behind me, and I turn to see that this AMC Gremlin has only two seats—no room for Stella. She doesn't seem to mind, though. She moves in front of the car, to the concrete ridge where the drive-in ends and farmland begins, and she sits there, chin in hands, looking out into the dark.

"All right," says Kim. "1970, huh? You haven't heard a thing after '70?"

"Right."

"My God," Kim mutters, shaking her head and looking through a cardboard box in her lap, which contains even more of those plastic boxes—cassettes, I think they're called; Archer has mentioned them before. "Okay, but you know Bowie, right? He was around before then."

I look blankly at her.

"Shit, man, you don't know *Bowie*?"

"I guess we don't have any of their LPs."

"*His* LPs," Kim corrects. "It's one person, David Bowie."

She pulls out a plastic box with the image of a redheaded man on the front, rainbow-colored lightning bolt painted across his face. The words *Aladdin Sane* are printed beneath his bare collarbone.

"You've at least got to hear some Bowie." She takes out a smaller plastic object from the box—the actual cassette, I guess. Then she fits it into a slot in the car dash and turns up a knob. The music blasts out, mid-song.

Over a driving electric guitar, a man—this Bowie—sings about catching a trick on Sunset and Vine. Kim nods along, looking very serious. As I listen, I notice a thick, folded paper among the cassettes on the floorboard. I pick it up and turn it right side to make out the text:

OKLAHOMA

KANSAS

Beneath the words is a drawing of a happy family of four

riding in a red convertible along a country road. At the bottom is the scrawled message, *Happy Motoring!*

Kim turns down the music and says, "You look like you've never seen a map."

I shake my head. "We learned geography in school. But they didn't show us a map of Kansas."

Kim snorts. "It's not that interesting, man. Though you should ask Stella about Hutchinson. God, she won't shut up about that place. The way she talks, you'd think it was fucking NYC."

"Hutchinson?"

"Mm-hmm."

A lit cigarette hangs in Kim's mouth; I've been so entranced by the map I didn't even see her light up. She lets out of a puff of smoke in my direction, and I can't help it—I cough.

Kim turns the music up. She flicks her cigarette against the open window and says, "If it bothers you, you don't have to stay in the car."

I don't want it to bother me. For some reason, I don't want to disappoint Kim. But the stench of the cigarette brings back my bad memories from Saturday night, and my jaw jerks, and I clear my unclearable throat.

"Sorry," I mumble, feeling flushed and ashamed. "I'm not used to smoke."

Kim shrugs, which seems to be her favorite thing other than snorting. I get out of the car and breathe in fresher air. Then I walk over to where Stella sits. Her head's tilted to the sky, her eyes closed.

"Can I sit here?" I ask.

Her eyes flutter open, big and dark. She really does have the weirdest face.

"Not a fan of Bowie?" she asks.

"No, he's fine." I sit, though not too close. My chin is still jerking. "It was the smoke."

Stella glances back at the car. "Oh yeah. She kind of breathes the stuff. I forget that sometimes. She's not allowed to on the job."

"What job?"

"The Dreamlight. We work together every night. I mean, we went to school together, but the Dreamlight is how I know her."

"Oh."

"Or do you figure I know everyone in Slater?"

"Kind of seems everyone here knows everyone."

She shoots out a breathy sort of laugh. "I'm not everyone."

"Kim says you're a recluse."

"I guess that's true. If you can live with two other people and go out every day for your job and still qualify as a recluse."

"You live with your parents?"

We might not use that term in the commune, but the idea of kids living with just two adults while they're growing up has always fascinated me.

"My mom's dead," says Stella. "It's my dad and my little sister. And it was Craig, too. Until he left."

Damn. Just when I hadn't felt a guilty twinge for a full minute.

My jaw keeps jerking. I clear my damn throat.

"I have this memory," Stella says. "It was a few years

203

before Craig left, the '72 Summer Olympics. Jill was tiny, and I was twelve, and the two of us were obsessed with the games. Craig scavenged Slater for boxes—big refrigerator ones—and he formed them into a podium in the backyard. He made medals for us out of paper clips and foil, and we played these made-up three-person games with his basketball and the badminton net. He did that. *All* of that. For us. Every night, for a week. Dad was our audience sometimes, but Craig was the mastermind. He made it special, for the family." She pauses, looking thoughtful, her brow creasing. "It's strange, because right after that was an awful time. There was the hostage situation, and the massacre, and it was all over the news. I felt so much older after that, like the spell of the whole summer was broken. But before the horrible things, there were our backyard games, and it's my favorite memory of us, together."

I can't be having this conversation. I can't. I open my mouth, my only thought that I have to change the subject.

Stella beats me to it, though, with a question. "Do you know who your parents are? I heard you don't believe in them."

I almost collapse onto the concrete from relief.

"We don't," I say, "but I know who they are. I work for J. J. in the kitchen. And Ruby taught me piano."

"You play piano?"

"Yeah."

"Is that strange? Knowing who they are?"

"I mean . . . I don't know what would be strange about it. They are who they are."

"I guess if you grow up that way . . ." Stella looks to the sky again. She points. "Clouds are coming back in. It might storm again."

I look, and sure enough, a whole bunch of gray clouds are rolling quickly toward us, swallowing up the stars.

"Covering the gods." I say it softly, without thinking.

Don't be negative consequences, I think. *Just be clouds.*

Stella's quiet a long time, and I think she hasn't heard until she asks, "What do you believe in there, exactly? You worship Zeus or something?"

I smirk, shake my head. I could lie again, but I've already lied so much. For once it would be nice to be honest. Even if she thinks I'm crazy. Even if she never looks at me the same way again. I want to tell Stella something to her face that is true.

So I do. I tell her about the Life Force and Buddy Holly and Jimi Hendrix and Janis Joplin. I point them out in the sky—lined up three in a row—before the clouds eat them up. Then I tell her about the Back Room and about my favorite records, and how I finish each listening session with "It's Now or Never." For some reason, she giggles at that last part, and she keeps catching herself and then giggling again, catching herself and giggling some more.

"What?" I ask, a little annoyed.

"It's funny, picturing you alone, listening to *Elvis*. My mom loved him. Maybe that's why it's funny."

"Because I remind you of your mom?"

"Maybe," says Stella. She's stopped giggling.

"Elvis is a great musician," I say, as my blinking tic shows up.

205

"Well. He's a great *performer*. Music-wise, I'd say he's mediocre."

Indignation curls inside me. I turn a hard gaze to the field.

"Hey." Stella touches my elbow in that barely there way. "I didn't mean to offend you."

"It's your opinion," I say, blinking. "In my opinion, he's the best."

"When he dies, does he go up there to join the others?"

I shake my head. "When Elvis dies, I don't want to be around. I hope I'm dead by then."

"Wow. You really must like him."

We're quiet a while longer, and then Stella starts to giggle again.

"Sorry," she says. "Sorry. But you know Orion has been around for a while, right? His belt buckle was up there before Buddy Holly ever died."

I glare harder at the darkened cornfields, blinking rapidly. "Yeah, I know."

I'm mad at Stella. I shouldn't have told her anything, because now she's making fun of it. She's treating me like I don't know what stars are actually made of.

But then . . . I don't have a right to be mad at her. She's the one who has a right to be mad at me. And she would be, if she knew the truth. My eyelids move without ceasing—open and shut, open and shut. My tics have a really sick sense of timing.

"Hey." She touches my elbow again, sounding really apologetic, which makes me feel even shittier. "Hey, sorry. I didn't mean to upset you."

"It's fine."

"No, really. I know what it's like to love things other people think are stupid. Things you know they'd laugh in your face about if you told them everything. I shouldn't have laughed at you."

I look at her this time. "It's fine," I say, and I mean it.

"I have a question for you, though," says Stella. "It's not making fun, I promise. I'm only curious. Jimi and Janis and Buddy—they're your gods. But . . . they lived on the Outside, right? They made their music *out here*."

"Yeah?" I say, not seeing Stella's point.

"Well, isn't that hard to reconcile?"

I frown. "No. It's not hard at all. They gave their all to the Outside, but what did they get out of it? The Outside killed them too soon. Think about how much better things would've been if they could've had a Red Sun to keep them safe and foster their growth. In Red Sun they could have lived longer, done even greater things. Red Sun would have understood them. It would have . . ."

I trail off, because I'm telling Stella something I've believed for years, without question. Only now, just now, I'm realizing something: I don't know if I believe it anymore. Would my gods really have been better off within the commune's walls? What if they'd been told that *they* weren't resident-artist material? What if Janis had been ordered to ten years out in the fields, or Jimi had been assigned to cook a decade's worth of green beans?

Where would my gods have been then? What kind of music would they have made?

I never finish my sentence. I fall silent, and from Kim's car

David Bowie keeps singing, this time over the rattling keys of a honky-tonk piano. A breeze pushes on our backs and rustles through the cornstalks.

"You want to know something interesting?" Stella asks. "Something you might not have heard about on the inside?"

"Sure," I say, nonchalant, as though I didn't bike out with her hoping for a moment exactly like this.

"All right. So, NASA's big project right now is the Voyager missions. They've made two probes, and they're sending them into space in the next few weeks. It has to be around now, because there's a favorable alignment of the outer planets. And they're sending these probes out to pick up data and take pictures of the planets. Maybe even beyond the planets. They're going to go farther than anything we've ever sent out before. Though maybe not as far as your gods." Stella smiles a bit here. "That's pretty great, right? That we can make something that will fly *that far*? Farther than any of us could ever go."

Stella's eyes are wet and shining, and her voice grows thinner the longer she talks. She waves her hands, animating each of her points. And I get it. This is Stella's thing. The thing she's written Craig/Phoenix/me about for two years. It's the thing other people would laugh about. That's why she's telling me. She's trying to even the playing field, make me feel better.

"No people?" I ask. "Just probes?"

"They haven't found a way to support people in space that long. Anyway, it's a one-way journey. Those probes aren't coming back. Who would sign up for that?"

"I dunno. I might."

Stella turns to me with her whole body. "Seriously?"

"I dunno," I repeat. "It might be worth it. To be the first human to ever see the planets, in person?"

"It would be so lonely, though."

"Says the recluse."

"I told you, I live with my family. That's different. I can't imagine leaving them behind."

"I'd miss people, sure," I say. "But . . . once, J. J. told me something. It was when I first started working in the kitchen. He said I was lucky to have a job at the commune, because they understand me. They make allowances, you know? But he said I couldn't make it on the Outside. With my tics. He said people out here wouldn't understand, wouldn't even give me a job, and it was fate that I was born at Red Sun."

I've never told anyone this, though my memory's replayed it plenty of times. Mentioning my tics has caused them to show up again, and I open my mouth for its long unyawn. I don't want to know how Stella's reacting, so I drop my head and study the concrete. An ant passes by, and then another.

"Your dad told you that?" Stella's whispering. "He said you couldn't make it?"

I unyawn again, and my jaw jerks to the right. "Out here, yeah. And I think he's right. People don't seem to be that understanding."

We're quiet for a while, and my tics continue, and I know Stella's feeling sorry for me, and I feel the shittiest I've felt all night. I try to shake it up.

"Did your parents like space too? Is that why they named you Stella?"

"Oh." Stella huffs out this tiny laugh. "No, actually. It's a town—Stella, Missouri. It's not even a town, more of a road. It's where my mom grew up. Then she met my dad, and they got married. She wanted to get out of there as fast as possible."

"But she named you after it."

"I guess she liked *something* about it."

We get quiet again, and then Stella says, "I'm sorry about what happened at the party. People can be awful. A lot of them grow out of it, though."

"Sure," I say, my jaw twitching, my eyes blinking fast.

"For what it's worth, I think you *could* make it out here. Considering you lived your whole life in that commune, I'd say you're pretty well-adjusted. All you need is some orientation."

"I don't know . . . what's the point, though? I mean, isn't it better to be alone than in bad company?"

Stella's smiling at me like I've told a joke. "That's something Craig would say. I mean . . . Phoenix."

My body ices over. I've said too much. I've gone too far. I can't slip up again, or Stella might find it less than funny. I rack my brain, trying to think of every personal thing I've written her under the name of Phoenix. Not details about my personal *life*, but personal *things*—thoughts and opinions and reactions to her books, adages and philosophies and every meaty topic we've ever touched upon by mail. There is no way I can remember it all. But then, there's no way she would suspect me.

Suspect me. Like a criminal. Like a liar and an impersonator.

Buddy Holly, help me. I am well and truly fucked.

I clear my throat with all the force inside me.

There's a sudden spattering sound around us. It's raining, and while we're shielded under the drive-in awning, the rain-drops splatter an inch from our feet, on the edge of the concrete.

It takes me a second to notice. Or maybe I notice right away and simply can't figure it out.

Because the rain hitting the concrete isn't clear.

It's blood red.

16

Stella

WEDNESDAY, AUGUST 10

Kim drives through the downpour, toward Red Sun.

"Shit, shit, shit," she says—one long, sibilant string. "I don't even know if it's going to wash off. Stell, can you tell? Is it eating away at the car? Is it staining the paint, can you see?"

I find this funny, though not the kind of funny I would ever laugh about. It's only that Kim seems more fixated on the state of her car than the fact that we are driving through blood rain.

Though . . . I cannot be sure it is blood, and I cannot tell if it is doing permanent damage to Kim's Gremlin. All I can do is stare, mesmerized, as bright red liquid runs down the hatchback window. The car is a two-seater, so I sit on the rear floorboard, jammed next to Galliard's bicycle. We could barely close the hatchback with just the one bike, so Kim begged her Ferrell's friend, Janet, for some utility rope to secure my bike to the roof rack. Now I am thinking we should have strapped both bicycles topside. A pedal is rammed against my back, and since there's no room for me to readjust, I can only wince through the pain.

"Sure you want to be let out in this?" Kim asks Galliard,

even though she already asked him three minutes ago, when he first requested to be driven back to Red Sun. Now we are pulling into the Moonglow Café's empty parking lot.

"It's almost curfew," Galliard tells Kim. "I've got to get in there."

"Sure, okay, but don't you think staying alive is more important than beating curfew?"

"It'll be fine. It's not like it's acid."

"Blood," says Kim. "It's blood."

"No, it's not." Galliard sounds impatient, and I am annoyed that I cannot make out his face from the back seat. I only catch angles of his chin and cheeks in the rearview mirror.

I am about to tell him he should stay in the car, and we should wait it out. I do not get the chance. Without warning, he throws open the passenger door and steps into the rain. Kim doesn't scream at him. Neither of us does; I think we're too stunned. We both watch in hushed suspense as Galliard straightens to full height. He turns his face to the sky and opens his mouth. This, at last, solicits a response from us.

"The fuck, man!" Kim shouts, as I simultaneously yell, "Don't!"

Galliard closes up his mouth. He pauses, assessing, then speaks. "It's just water. Water that's red."

"Or it's *arsenic*," I say. "Or some tasteless toxin. You wouldn't know the difference."

"It's water." He moves around back and opens the hatchback.

Kim shrieks. "No sir! No *sir*! Don't drip that fucking freaky rain in here."

213

"It's water," Galliard growls, reaching in and hauling out his bike. I help, shoving at the front wheel.

"My baby," Kim mutters, shuddering as Galliard brings the bike down in a less-than-gentle descent. "My poor baby."

I start to laugh. I can't help myself; this is what *That Stella* would do. I laugh at the strangeness of it all, the sheer absurdity. I laugh at Galliard's bravery and that feeling of freedom trembling inside me. Yes, the rain is red. Why shouldn't it be?

Galliard doesn't question my behavior. He grins as he slams shut the hatchback window and then, through the glass, he asks, "Next Wednesday?"

"*Yes,*" I say in between giggles. "Now get inside before you melt."

He throws a wide wave into the air, and I cannot tell if it is intentional or one of his tics. He wheels his bike to the commune gate, toward a wall of darkness. Then he is gone, and then so are my laughs.

Kim pats the passenger seat and says, "Get up here. I'll drive you home."

I climb over the gearshift, and Kim doesn't wait for me to fasten my seat belt before speeding out onto Eisenhower.

"That commune, man," she says. "Gives me the creeps. He does too, a little. Sorry."

"Why 'sorry'?"

"Don't you like him? Why were you hanging out?"

"It's . . . complicated."

"But he's not that Phoenix guy you're writing?"

"No."

"Damn, Mercer. You're starting your own Red Sun harem."

"We weren't on a date."

That sounds wrong coming from my mouth—fake.

"Okay, okay," says Kim. "Say no more."

I like this about Kim. She might read private letters, but she knows when to let things alone. Tonight, I think some of that disinterest is due to the fact that we are facing a more pressing concern: blood rain.

Kim turns up the radio. There is no special broadcast on 580 AM, no mention of our predicament by Kansas City DJ Jim Goddard. "Hotel California" plays serenely on. I shut my eyes, losing myself in the minor melody. This red rain is wrong—*bad*, even—but it doesn't scare me any more than the pink lightning did. It's one more apocalyptic happening, which means one more excuse to live my life as I want to, as *That Stella*.

Then, as Kim turns onto my street, the rain stops. It simply stops—the tapping on the car hood, the crimson rivulets running down the windows. The wipers screech against a dry windshield. Everything is calm.

Kim puts the car into park outside my house. She leans over the wheel, head cocked toward the sky.

"That all you got up there?" she shouts.

"*Hey.*" I knock my elbow against hers. "Don't encourage it."

I'm not afraid of the rain, but I'd rather not get soaked on my way to the front door.

"C'mon!" Kim keeps shouting. "Isn't this the part where the earth opens up and swallows us whole?"

I wonder. I hope that part doesn't happen quite yet. I'd like a little more time to live as this version of myself. I'd like as much time as the countdown on my closet door has to offer.

Kim settles back in her seat, shaking her head. She jams in the cigarette lighter, then points to the glove compartment. "Cancer stick."

If I were a closer friend, I would lecture her. I would tell her that cigarettes are bad for her health and that—unlike our parents—she has no excuse to light up, because she *knows* how toxic they are. I would tell her that secondhand smoke hurts my head. I am not Kim's close friend, though. I'm no one's close friend. So I open the glove compartment, find Kim's pack of Kool Super Lights, and tip out a cigarette. She grabs it, lights it, and then takes a long, deep inhale.

"Jeez," she says on the exhale. "Fuck this."

She cranks down her window an inch and adds, "Seriously, what's happening here?"

"I have no idea," I say. *But I think I like it,* I want to continue. *I think it's beautiful.*

Kim flicks her cigarette against the window's edge. Golden-orange bits of ash explode into the night, then scatter. She takes another inhale, and I crank down my own window, in need of fresh air.

"You get it, though, right?" Kim says. "The winds, the lightning, the storms. The animals acting weird? The goddamn *countdown* over town hall. And now this: fucking blood rain. That'll finally bring out the news crews."

The countdown. I could tell Kim about my own countdown. I could, but I don't, and for the same reason I didn't tell her about Craig: It's a little too private to say out loud.

"What do you think it is?" I don't know when I began whispering.

"Uh. The apocalypse, obviously. Man, the preachers must be eating this up. The end of days! The last judgment! The four horsemen! They'll have a field day on Sunday. If we make it that long."

"There has to be an actual reason, though. Some logical explanation that connects all those things. Maybe it's something to do with chemicals, or . . . or . . ." I try hard *not* to think of extraterrestrial life. Instead my thoughts bring me to Gayle Nelson, of all people. "What if something happened at the plant? Something they're not telling us?"

"At Slater Creek? Oh, no doubt. I'm with the hippies on that one: Humans shouldn't be screwing around with nuclear anything."

I frown. "Well, we wouldn't have a lot of scientific advances if—"

"Whoa. *Whoa.* You don't need to go there. I'm just saying, I feel kind of accepting of the whole thing. We humans fucked it up. I guess we've had it coming."

"But . . ." I search for the words. "From what we can tell, it's only happening in *Slater*."

Kim shrugs. "Why not? I'd say Slater deserves to be wiped off the face of the earth about the same as any other town."

I smile. "You don't mean that."

"I dunno. Guess not."

I look out at my house. For the first time, I realize the den light is on.

"Oh no."

"Hmm?"

I crank my window up. "My sister's awake, and she never stays up past her bedtime. She must be freaking out."

"Huh. Well, probably a good idea to head in anyway. Don't know when the death rain is gonna start up again."

I throw open the door. "Sorry," I say. "And thanks for everything. I'll see you around, okay?"

"Yeah. Catch you on the flip side. Or, like, the *other* side. You know."

I run for the house, processing Kim's attempt at a joke a little too late. The front door is locked, and I am digging around for my key when the door swings open and I find myself inches from a red-faced Jill.

"Stella!"

"Hey," I say, stooping to hug her. She wraps me in a tight embrace. "Hey, it's okay. You're fine; we're fine."

"They caught him," she whispers in my ear.

At first I do not understand. I am expecting her to ask about the rain. My next thought—completely absurd—is that she's talking about Galliard; she is telling me that Galliard was caught for breaking curfew at the commune. Then the absurdity clears. I hear the radio playing in the den, and the newscaster's words take on meaning.

". . . police headquarters in Lower Manhattan, Mayor Beame addressed his constituents, saying, 'The people of the City of New York can rest easy tonight because police have captured a man they believe to be the Son of Sam.'"

"The murderer," Jill says, removing any doubt. "They caught him."

218

Jill leads me into the den, where she has set up a burrow of sorts on the couch—blankets and pillows piled high, the radio nestled among them.

"You're not mad at me, are you?" she whispers, crawling into her hiding place. "I couldn't fall asleep, so I brought the radio into my room. And then they made the news report, and I *really* couldn't sleep"

"I'm not mad." My voice sounds very far from me. "I should've been home earlier. Anyway, I . . ." I watch Jill, who has stopped paying attention to me. She sits with the radio propped on her knees, listening intently as the newscaster continues to repeat the same half dozen facts in varied ways.

"Jill," I say. "Did you . . . see the rain?"

She looks at me, uncomprehending. "What do you mean, *see* the rain? I *heard* it, if that's what you mean."

"Right. That's what I meant."

She doesn't know, then. I decide in an instant that I won't tell her. There's no reason. The rain has stopped for now, and it would do no good to tell my sister that it looked like blood pouring from an open wound. If I said that, she wouldn't sleep a wink tonight.

We do not move out of the den. I fail in every attempt to separate Jill from the radio, even long after the special broadcast is over. In the end I join her in her burrow of fleece and cotton stuffing, and we remain there, bundled tight—Jill, her radio, and me.

April 3, 1976

Craig,

Art _is_ science, though. I'm not trying to argue
with you, only show you another perspective.
Art is science, but that doesn't mean science
saps the joy out of art. I think it only makes
it better, when you know all the complexities
behind a brush stroke or your favorite song.
Take music, for instance. There is a reason we
humans prefer thirds and octaves to seconds
and sevenths. It is about harmony and unison
versus dissonance and lack of resolution.
It's about how we are conditioned and what our
biology craves—_science_. That doesn't make a
song less beautiful, either, whether it is by
the Beach Boys or Rachmaninoff. It makes it
richer, I think, and deeper. It's just another
way of looking at it.

                              Your sister,
                                Stella

17

Galliard

WEDNESDAY, AUGUST 10

"What is it, acid?"

Archer hasn't stopped talking since I walked into our room.

I wasn't the only one caught outdoors when the downpour began, and by the time I got to Heather House's front doors, our residence leaders—Faith and Wes—had implemented a "procedure." All of us who had been touched by the rain were asked to strip down to our underwear on the covered porch and wait to be washed off with a garden hose. Faith saw to the girls and Wes to the guys, in separate lines, but the whole thing was still humiliating. Once deemed clean, we were handed scratchy bath towels and sent inside, ordered to stay in our rooms until further notice. Back in my room, I deposited my briefs in the trash, sealed the bag, and placed it outside my door—as instructed. Only then could I finally change into clean clothes and receive the full force of Archer's snickering. Tonight of all nights, he decided to stay in and play cards with some of the guys. The lucky bastard.

Archer and I have shared a room since we were ten and first assigned to each other in Sage House. Now, that's carried over to Heather House. For the most part, it's fine. Archer isn't messy, and we got along so well we became friends, which means the Council's pairing system wasn't an utter failure. Nights like this, though, I wish I slept alone.

"It's not acid," I say, not for the first time. "If it were acid, don't you think I'd be in the infirmary?"

"Well, I don't know, maybe it's *delayed* acid. Could take a few hours to sink in."

"That's not how acid works, man."

"Okay, well, it's raining *blood*, so I'd say the laws of nature are in question."

"It's not blood, either. The rain is just red."

"Oh right." Archer is trundling around the room, casting the occasional manic look toward our one window. "Sorry. The rain is just red! The sky is just green! The ground is just purple! Those are the fucking fundamentals of human existence, after all!"

I slump on my narrow bed and shove my pillow over my face. "Calm down," I say into the mattress.

I sure feel calm. I went Outside, without Archer's help, and tasted, quite literally, what it had to offer. I saw a different side of Slater, spent time with people who were worth spending time with. I felt *brave*. Maybe that's why I wasn't afraid to step out into the mystery rain and see for myself what it was: not dangerous, just different. I can take different. I can even *like* different. I wish Archer would get on that level with me, but it's hard to put into words the way I'm feeling. It's not something I can simply say. What's happened to me tonight requires more than words. It requires *music*.

While Archer squawks on, I get up from the bed and take out a sheet of lined notebook paper from my desk. I sharpen a pencil, peeling off its shavings, then put lead to paper. I write. I write and I don't stop. I write lyrics. I write a verse and then two. I write a chorus and a bridge. On a new sheet of paper, I draw out treble and bass clefs, and I hum riffs and pencil them in as possibilities.

I must be too quiet for too long, because Archer slams his hand on the desk, disrupting my work.

"Hey," he says. "You with me?"

"Not if you're still freaking out," I say.

"Yeah, you mark my words: The Council's gonna call a meeting about this. Not that they'll tell us anything important. They'll give us the usual 'We've got a fallout shelter, so every-thing's fine, blah, blah.'"

Archer thinks it's the end of the world. He thinks there's no logical explanation behind what's happening. I can see the logic, though. I see what my gods are up to. This rain, like the lightning, is a challenge. *Embrace it, Galliard,* they're telling me. *Do something new. Take risks. Take a chance, like we did.*

Tonight I listened to music made after the year 1970. And it was good. It was more than good—it was *inspiring*. The red rain outside isn't dampening the fire inside me; it's fueling it, asking it to rage on. I've never felt like this. I'm inspired, and I'm writing a new kind of song. It's not about love I've never known or about how great a place Red Sun is. I write about the rain. I write about a new kick in my heartbeat, set off by Stella's stories and Kim's music and Ferrell's hamburgers. I bat away Archer's hand and write and *write*, until there's nothing left I can do until I get to the Common House Yamaha and work it all out on the keys.

Now that the song is out of me, I feel purged. Exhausted.

". . . could be ending, and you think Rod would tell us? Not a chance. I bet they're reporting on television right now. I bet it's breaking news. Only we aren't going to hear anything, because—hey. Hey! Where do you think you're going?"

During Archer's ongoing tirade, I've risen from my desk and opened the door.

"You can't go out there," he says, like a whiny kid. "You heard what Wes said—no one goes out except to piss."

"Yeah, well. I have to piss."

I leave Archer to his raving and walk down the hall to the communal bathrooms. It feels as though I'm walking through a dream. Everything's murky and half-formed. What I did tonight. Where I went. The red rain, David Bowie, and Stella, Missouri. They're mashed up together, and I'm not sure I'm walking in a straight line, but I make it into the bathroom, and when I do, I see someone leaving one of the stalls.

It must be the murk, because it takes me longer than it should to realize who it is.

It's Phoenix.

It's just Phoenix and me, in the same room.

I clear my throat—once, twice, then a third and fourth time.

He doesn't pay me or my tics any attention. He goes straight for the sinks and washes his hands. We're playing that game where we don't acknowledge each other until I say something.

Only tonight I'm feeling risky. I'm feeling brave. So I say something.

"Hey. Phoenix?"

He cuts off the tap and looks up. For the first time I see the resemblance between him and Stella. The big eyes that look weird on her are what make his face babyish. Looking at him, my throat seizes up.

"Look," I choke out. "*Look.*"

Phoenix doesn't say anything. He dries his hands on his jeans.

What am I asking him to look at? What's there to say?

My throat tic rears its ugly head. I grind out a low, hard sound. Something flashes behind Phoenix's eyes—impatience, or maybe even annoyance. He pushes past me.

"*Craig.*"

It's out of me, and I can't take it back, but it gets the reaction I wanted: Phoenix freezes, one hand on the bathroom door.

He never told anyone here his old name. He'd already crafted his new identity by the time he showed up at Red Sun. He introduced himself to everyone as Phoenix. Just Phoenix. No one here knows who Craig Mercer is. No one should.

I've done it. I've pulled the element of surprise on him. And it's all I've got. I'm scrounging around for what to say next, but I've prepared nothing. I've got nothing.

"I know." Craig's voice is deep and measured. He stays facing the door. "I know you took her letter. I knew for sure when you asked for the painting. I knew you wrote her back."

My throat bursts with unwanted sound. Then, intentionally, I say, "It was because you wouldn't have."

"I told you, my family's dead to me. That part of my life is over."

"Damn it, Phoenix," I say. "She *loves* you. You mean a whole fucking lot to her. If you heard the way she talks about you—"

Phoenix turns around. "I don't want to hear it."

"Well, too fucking bad, man! Because she wants to see you. She just wants to *talk* to you. How hard is that? How hard is to meet with her once?"

"It isn't going to be *once*!" Phoenix shouts, slamming a hand on the door. "That's what you don't get. She doesn't want to talk. She wants me to leave. She wants me back with the family."

"You don't know what she wants."

"And you *do*? How long have you been writing her, huh? How long have you been pretending to be me? Because I could send her a letter tomorrow and end all of this."

I act like that doesn't affect me, that I don't understand what he's threatened: to expose me and hurt Stella. He could, though. He could do permanent damage, and he knows it.

"You'd do that," I say, "but you wouldn't send a letter two years ago? When she *needed* a letter? All she wanted was to know you were okay."

"No." Phoenix is messing up his baby face with very unba-byish fury. "She wanted to change my mind. She wanted to bring me back down. And I won't do that. I won't go back there. You think Stella cares that I'm happy here? No. She wants me back there for *her* sake. The world out there is self-ish. And I've left it and those toxic people behind. I told you that, Galliard. I *told* you."

"Yeah." My throat tic butts in, but I talk over it. "Yeah, you did. But *Stella* isn't toxic, and the Outside isn't half as bad as you made it out to be. And people on the inside can be selfish too. People who don't answer letters from the people who love them." My eyes narrow at him. "By the way, I hear our Moonglow customers are loving your art."

He leaves. He doesn't say another word. He punches open the door and walks away, while I watch him go.

Then, alone, I stay standing in the empty bathroom, listening to the angry slam of rain upon the roof.

November 21, 1976

Stella,

You make pacifism sound a lot bigger than
I think of it. The way you write, pacifism is
something made for countries and national
governments. I guess I can't make sense of it
when it's that big. For me it has to be small.
Personal. That's how Opal teaches it, anyway.
That pacifism is about respect for the person
standing across from you. You respect that
they are alive, like you, and they feel, like
you, and they deserve dignity. That is one of
the fundamental rules for behavior here at
Red Sun: We live in peace and unity and, above
all, respect.

 Not that there aren't fights. There
are. When they get noticeable, the Council
addresses them.

 But out there? It's a bad place. People are
filled with hate and bitterness and anger,
and that leads to violence. That's why Red
Sun exists. It's a place where no seeds of
bitterness will ever grow.

 Phoenix

18

Stella

THURSDAY, AUGUST 11

Kim was right about the news crews; they arrive early in the morning. I pass them on my way to the salon, walking along Vine Street. (In the excitement of last night, I forgot to get my bike off Kim's car, which meant leaving twenty minutes earlier to make the mile-long walk out.) From what I can tell, there are two stations—both local, from Wichita and Kansas City—gathered in front of town hall and the ever-present countdown, which now reads 07:16:54. Just over a week until the Unknown. I slow down as I pass them and pick up two fragments of conversation: "kid put food coloring in the fountain" and "slow news days."

So there are news crews, yes, but they certainly don't seem to be concerned about an impending doomsday. Everything looks much less terrifying in the new light of day. The sun is shining, and cars are working, and people are walking the streets as usual. The only indication that anything was amiss last night is a faint pink stain on the sidewalks. That and the countdown, its violet numbers as visible in the day as they are at night. It is a constant reminder, though of *what*, no one has a clue. Not that this prevents anyone from talking. *Everyone* in Vine Street Salon has something to say about last night—especially Connie.

"It's astrological," she tells Brenda Mae, her nine o'clock appointment. "It's all to do with the stars. We've entered a new age, and the heavens are *shifting, changing.* Aquarius brings with it modernization, but also rebellion and chaos. It's only natural that we're beginning to see these effects manifested in our daily lives."

"Connie," says Brenda Mae, gently chiding, "I'm not sure that's entirely in keeping with the church's teaching."

To which Connie replies, "If Jesus himself were alive today, he'd be told *he* wasn't entirely in keeping with the church's teaching."

Brenda Mae squirms but says nothing more as Connie skips scissors across her bangs in quick snips.

"Did you hear?" asks my third-grade teacher, Mrs. Byrd. "Mayor Branum is organizing another town meeting."

"Well, thank heavens for that," Connie says. "What we need is some rational discourse."

I agree with Connie, though I've a feeling the discourse will be less than rational. The town is scared. It's become clear through news reports and town gossip that Slater and only Slater has experienced the pink lightning and the blood rain and the mysterious ticking clock. It's enough to keep clients from surrounding towns at home, in fear of visiting us.

Three appointments cancel today, each citing the weather as their reason, even though it is eighty degrees and cloudless now. We're not experiencing our usual problems of overbooking and impatient clients, but I'm faced with a new dilemma: I have lots of downtime, and today of all days I forgot to bring along a book. This leaves me to swivel listlessly on my stool and spy out on Vine Street. Even though I am being *That Stella*, that doesn't mean I'm going to completely abandon *This Stella*'s job.

One of the news crews has packed up, and their van lumbers by. Frank's Deli across the road, which is usually open all day, is locked and unlit. Not *everything* has gone back to normal, then, and every so often I get a sense of unease. I feel especially uneasy when I think of what happened this morning.

Dad came home at dawn and found me and Jill asleep in the den. I was the only one to wake, and he asked me to join him in the kitchen. He fixed coffee, and I poured a bowl of Moonstones cereal. Neither of us mentioned the rain. Dad drank his coffee, and I ate my cereal, and as I was sipping away at the stained dregs of milk in my bowl, he said, "Gayle brought you up the other day."

I said nothing.

"She said you've got a mind for numbers. Something about these rocket plans you have in your room. I didn't know about those."

I washed my bowl in the sink. "It's not that big a deal," I said. "She was just trying to be nice, find something for us to talk about."

"She says you're very gifted in math."

"Yeah, well, I did take advanced calculus at school. Only girl in the room, that's me."

Dad was silent, because it was the only alternative to saying, "I didn't know that."

My father has never been one to ask about school. He never took a good look at my report cards, and he certainly did not take part in the PTA. Since I was a good student, he didn't have much cause to be involved in my school life. Anyway, he was too busy with work. I understood that.

"She says you'd benefit from a college education. Says you could study engineering."

I looked at my father. I couldn't read his face or tone. He seemed guarded and thoughtful, and almost sad. I wasn't sure why he was telling me these things. I'm not sure he knew either.

I set my bowl in the dish rack and wiped my sudsy hands on my jeans. "It's a nice thought, but the application deadlines have passed."

I said this as though application deadlines were the only obstacle that stood between me and college. I was tempted to tell him that *That Stella* had a perfectly charmed life and had been accepted into the mechanical engineering program at the University of Kansas, and that made everything all right.

"I'm tired," I told him. "Going to sleep a little more before work. If work is happening."

As I was about to leave the kitchen, I found myself saying, "The rain. It's not anything to do with the plant, is it?"

My dad's brows cinched in tight. "Slater Creek? No, of course not. Hon, I don't think there's any good explanation for the weather we've been having."

"Yes, there is," I said, though more to myself than him.

Yes, there is, I tell myself now. Though that reason is as veiled to me now as ever. Even if I knew the scientific explanation behind everything that's happened—the winds, the animals, the storms, the rain—that doesn't mean it *can't* be the apocalypse. Kim said so herself, voicing the thought that had only lived inside my mind before. I wonder if she was only joking, though. Maybe she feels silly about it now, in the daylight.

I don't think it's silly. My closet door won't let me. I checked on it after breakfast, only to find those same violet numbers, perfectly synchronized with the ones over town hall. That must *mean something.* Something for me, personally. Otherwise, wouldn't everyone else in town be talking about the numbers in *their* closets?

I seem to be the only one in that predicament.

According to the midday weather report, it is supposed to rain again tonight. The real question on everyone's mind is, naturally, if this rain will be of the regular or doomsday variety. Connie says there's no reason to fret, but the salon's clients do not share her confidence. The phone rings repeatedly with cancellations, and in the end, Connie closes up shop a full hour early. I've already checked in with Mr. Cavallo, who after grousing for upward of five minutes about how this weather is killing his business and how he has absolutely no retirement saved up, confirms my expectation that, no, the Dreamlight will not be open tonight.

I go home. The first thing I do is open my closet door and read the ongoing countdown there: *07:07:54.* Seven days, seven hours, and fifty-four minutes. I have a full week to do what I never dared before. Standing in the closet, I have a good view of my bed, and my thoughts fix on the project hidden beneath it. *This Stella* would want to work on her project more than anything, but *That Stella* would like to complete it too. The project, it would seem, is the intersection of my two lives, and I decide that this will be how I use the rest of today's precious time.

With my bedroom door locked, I haul the wicker bin out from under my bed and set its contents on my desk: four sets of walkie-talkies obtained from multiple visits to the army-surplus store, the finely sanded wooden frame, the as-yet-unopened package of nine-volt batteries. I set to work, and I do not stop. I pull myself away only to put TV dinners in the oven, and then to remove them. Tonight Jill and I break with our *Nightly News* tradition. I set Jill's dinner on the kitchen counter as she listens to a radio broadcast detailing more about the arrest of David Berkowitz. I take my dinner back to my room and shut the door. I work, eat a bite of lukewarm mashed potatoes, and work more. I don't answer Jill the first time she calls my name, an hour later. Only when she pounds on my door do I shove the project into its hiding place and let her in.

She doesn't say a thing, only runs to my window and tugs open my blinds. I had not noticed the sound of the rain until now.

It's back. It streams down my window in thick sluices.

And it is red. Red as blood.

Jill takes it well, considering. She does not scream or ask a lot of unanswerable questions. In fact, her overwhelming opinion on the rain is that it is "real neat."

"It's like the ten plagues!" she says, sprawled on my bed. "You know, from the Bible."

"Yes, Jill. I know what those are. I'm not sure that's the best comparison, though."

Jill says, "Who knows." Then: "Why isn't this national news?"

"Because it's not happening anywhere else," I tell her, tummy-crawling to where she lies on my bed.

I've put my project away for good tonight. It is clear that while Jill may not be in hysterics, she does not intend to leave my room anytime soon.

"*Nowhere* else?"

"No. None of our out-of-towners at the salon have talked about anything out of the ordinary—no downpours, no pink lightning, no blo—um, red rain. Just us."

"That's not how weather works," says Jill, frowning. "Weather doesn't happen to *one town*."

"It's fine," I say, as much to myself as to her. "As far as we know, no one's been hurt or killed. And I'm sure they're testing the rain as we speak. It seems harmless."

Jill takes one of my pillows and hugs it close to her chest. "So you think we're okay?"

"Yeah, Jill. I do."

I say so, even though I don't feel okay myself. That is what older sisters do.

"Does Dad?"

"He said not to worry; it's just something wacky in the atmosphere. It'll sort out."

"What if it doesn't?"

"It will."

"Promise?"

"Yes."

"And you'll be here. You won't leave me if it gets scary, right?"

"I'll be right here."

Jill falls asleep on my bed, and I do not have the heart to move her. I remain next to her, listening to the *tip-tap* of rain on the windows. Though I'm expecting sleep, it doesn't come. An overwhelming urge falls on me as I lie there. I sit up, quiet and careful not to jostle the bed. Slowly, carefully, I sneak from my room out to the hallway. Then, faster, I tiptoe down to Jill's bedroom.

I open the door, wincing at the unavoidable creak of its hinges, and push it only as far as I must to fit through. Then I make quick work, crossing to Jill's closet door.

I swallow a burning breath as I place my hand on the knob and, slowly, turn it. It's too long a wait, though. Impulse takes over me, and in one swift motion I throw the door open.

There is nothing there. No violet numbers.

I am not satisfied yet. With less care than before, I make a thorough inspection of Jill's room. I scan her walls, her ceiling. I open her bureau drawers and even the small, pearlescent jewelry box on her vanity. Again and again, I am disappointed. I find nothing. No countdown.

Of course. I knew this already. Jill would have told me. Unlike me, she would have shared. But I needed to be sure. I had to check, to see if it *isn't* just me.

It is, though.

Why is it only me?

The question drives into my head as I quietly return to my room and sit back on the bed. At the shift of the mattress, Jill mumbles and curls her knees closer to her chest.

I envy her sleep. I envy her peace. And yet, somehow, I'm filled with a greater feeling of freedom than I've had before, when I first discovered the numbers in my room.

I am the only one.

Good.

That Stella takes this as a sign to carry on.

The red rain continues to fall. For three days it comes down on us, spasmodic, in unpredictable intervals of calm and storm. We begin to make local news every night. Reporters confirm that the phenomenon appears to be concentrated solely over Slater. Meteorologists come into town, even researchers from KU. Reporters ask them questions, and they reply in ten-second sound bites. From what they can tell, there is nothing wrong with the rain other than its discoloration. They continue to run tests. They continue to hypothesize and speculate. Some cite similar cases in highly populated and polluted areas, though none of these documented incidents match what is now being called "the Slater Scenario."

On Saturday I stop watching television. I've lost interest in reiterated facts and confounded scientists. In the end, it doesn't matter *how* the end is coming, just that *it's coming*. Connie calls to say she's closing the salon for the weekend, due to far too many cancellations. The Dreamlight has been closed until further notice.

During pockets of reprieve, when the clouds clear with

alarming rapidity and the sun comes back out, townsfolk race to the grocery to stock up on bread and milk and jugs of water. Dad takes a trip out on Saturday afternoon and returns after a fresh downpour has started up, his clothes stained crimson, like he is a character from a Stephen King horror novel.

Outside, rivers of red rush down street gutters, as though our house is downstream of a massacre. There is nothing anyone can do about it, save skip town. And some people do. I overhear our neighbors talking one night, through the den's thin windows. The Metzes are going away to visit family in Missouri. They don't know when they'll be back, but according to Mr. Metz it won't be until "every last drop of wrath's been poured out." That isn't an option for us Mercers. We have no distant relatives to visit—both Mom's and Dad's parents are dead—and even if we had, Dad couldn't take off work, and we couldn't afford a trip out of town.

If I am honest, though, I wouldn't want to leave. I want to see how this apocalypse plays out. I want an excuse to be *That Stella* until the bitter end, whatever end that may be. If I am honest, I secretly think this red rain may be on my side. It's preventing me from working day and night, the way *This Stella* would. It's allowing me to be *That Stella*—a girl who doesn't have to work, a girl who can stay at home and do what she likes, even be lazy.

Jill and I play her *Happy Days* board game so often that even she grows tired of it. I read *The Cosmic Connection* through again, re-underlining my favorite passages. I bring the record player into the den, and I play my three Elton John records on repeat. I do these things because I couldn't before, and now I can.

I continue to work hard on my project, and I finish. I am *nearly* finished, anyway. I only need one more part from the surplus store, which I intend to visit once the rain lets up. *If* it lets up.

Jill is the first to notice a change. On Saturday night, she calls me and Dad to the den and points excitedly out the window. There is nothing to be seen . . . and that is the point. Together we look outside, expecting new showers to start any second. Minutes pass, and then hours. The rain holds off. The night sky is clear and starry.

Though none of us will say it out loud, the hope among us is palpable:

Maybe, just maybe, this part of our apocalypse is over.

Sunday morning, the sky continues to be clear. Not even a wisp of cloud mars the cerulean sky.

When my father wakes up, he and I debate whether to drive out to Ferrell's. In the end, we decide that not even the possibility of town-wide destruction should keep us from observing our Sunday tradition. Anyway, there cannot be town-wide destruction yet. The countdown on my closet door reads *04:16:12*.

Four more days.

Ferrell's is open, but there are only two employees on shift—one server and one cook. I'm surprised even they are around. The crowd is always sparse when we come here, since most of the town is in church. Today we are the only car in the lot. Our server comes out to tell us that the deep fryer is not working, so we order extra-large malts in place of tater tots. The radio is playing another Bay City Rollers song. It seems Dad cannot take any more of the lively chorus, because he clicks it off, and we eat the rest of our meal in silence.

We pass First Baptist on the way home. It's still steeple-less, but the parking lot is full. I suppose strange events and uncertainty bring people out. I wonder what Slater's preachers are telling their congregations. Is this a punishment from God, or is it, perhaps, discipline? Are we townspeople supposed to repent, or is someone else to blame? I know what Pastor Barkley must be saying in First Baptist; he is no doubt blaming the depraved pagans of Red Sun. The commune was a favorite topic of his even back when we attended services. He warned how its members exhibited the worst excesses of the fall of man. They rejected traditional forms of family and government, and they indulged in the pleasures of the flesh. They were a warning to us, the members of God's flock, about what dangers lay outside the fold. While I do not doubt that Pastor Barkley is casting blame on our resident hippies now, I know that not everyone in his congregation thinks the way he does. The Mrs. Humes of the church, who fought for my mother's burial, who maintain that neither life nor death is easily defined. Town meetings might be bad, but surely not everyone in Slater is that narrow-minded.

We turn onto Vine, and as we do, Jill draws our attention to a large, hand-painted sign outside town hall that reads COM-MUNITY MEETING, THIS WEDNESDAY, 6 PM.

I calculate how much time we will have left on Wednesday at six p.m.: one day, seven hours, and twenty-four minutes.

"Hey, what're those boys doing, trying to get a haircut?"

I startle at Jill's laughter. She's pointing at the storefront of Vine Street Salon, where two boys in Red Sun tunics stand outside. One of them leans, arms crossed, against the door. The other is peering inside the darkened salon, and though I cannot make out his face, I know who it is.

"Dad!" I shout. "Dad, stop the car!"

19

Galliard

SUNDAY, AUGUST 14

"Hey. Hey, man. That car's slowing down—should we beat it?"

We've been outside the salon for ten minutes, and most of that time's been spent figuring out what to do next. Archer told me it was a gamble to come out on a Sunday and that most businesses in town are closed for church. But I had to try.

It's the first day since Thursday that the red rain hasn't poured down, and this morning, the Council finally decided to allow us out of our residences. Which is fortunate, because I've come *this close* to wringing Archer's neck on nine different occasions, and I don't know that I would've resisted the urge on the tenth.

He and I have played every card game you can name. We even invented a few of our own. Last night we built a tower that reached the top shelf of our closet. The whole time, Phoenix's painted Stella looked down on us with brush-stroked eyes. This morning, I took the canvas off its nail and turned it paint down on my desk. It feels wrong to have that painting now that I've met her.

Then I told Archer, "I've got to see her."

"Oh man," said Archer. "Oh *man*."

He insisted on coming along, and I didn't feel I had the right to refuse. It's been Archer who's tried to get me to go out every summer, after all. And then there's the fact that, during the three days we were cooped inside, I finally cracked and told him about the letters. About Stella. About Phoenix, formerly known as Craig. Everything.

Well. Almost everything. Not the part about how I think these weird storms are the work of Holly, Hendrix, and Joplin, or how I've written my first song since being on the Outside and it's like nothing else I've composed.

"Okay," he said, when I laid it all out at three this morning. "I get why you did it, but it's fucked up."

"I don't know how to tell Stella the truth," I said. "Phoenix is being a dick, and I can't tell her he won't see her *and* I've been pretending this whole time. That'll be too much bad news at once. I can't tell her the whole truth until I convince Phoenix to speak to her."

"Yeah, well, Phoenix isn't gonna do that."

"I'll make him."

Archer cackled for a full minute at that. "With what army? Galliard, c'mon."

I glared at him for the cackling, but especially for being right.

"You gotta tell her everything," said Archer. "I'll be your backup. Make sure she doesn't kill you."

I never said I wanted that kind of backup, but Archer's taken it upon himself to provide it, should Stella Kay Mercer attempt to castrate, blind, or immolate me on the spot.

I've taken this morning's clear skies as a sign. My gods have heard my plan and approved it. The good weather is their blessing.

Things at Red Sun are stable in general. The rain hasn't killed the crops or the chickens; it's just keeping outsiders in their homes and away from the Moonglow. Like Archer predicted, the Council called a commune-wide meeting this morning, and its official opinion, announced by none other than Rod, is that pollution is to blame for the strange weather, which means it's the Outside's fault. I'm not about to tell them it's *mine*. All my actions line up perfectly with the freak weather events. To me, though, they're not bad. They're changing me. They're making me brave. They're the work of the Life Force.

And so, armed with that bravery and a new resolve, I biked to town with Archer, to the salon where Stella said she worked, and I prayed to Buddy for confidence and Janis for bravery and Jimi for cool. Then we arrived to find the windows dark and a sign flipped to CLOSED. And it's as we stand there, deciding what to do next—ride back to Red Sun or look for a place to eat—that Stella appears.

"It's her," I say, in answer to Archer's question. He's already mounted his bike, but I shake my head in disbelief. "No, that's *her*."

The car comes to a complete stop. A man looks out at me from the driver's seat with large, dark eyes. Stella's eyes. Phoenix's, too. Beside him sits Stella, who looks as bewildered to see me as I am to see her. She throws open her door and races around the car toward the two of us. Her hair is big, frizzier than usual. She's wearing a pink paisley top and matching shorts.

I tic, opening my mouth wide, then slamming it shut. Beside me, Archer snickers.

"What are you doing here?" Stella asks.

She comes close enough for me to smell the chocolate on her breath.

"He missed you real bad," says Archer. "He was moaning your name in his sleep."

My skin erupts with heat. I tic again, right when I'm trying to give Archer a menacing glare. He grins and shrugs.

"Uh-huh," says Stella, who seems unaffected by Archer's attempt at humiliation. She turns to the car, where her father is waiting, and motions for him to drive on.

"It's fine," she says. "I know them."

But he doesn't move the car. He's staring hard at me and Archer. From that distance there's no way he could've heard what Archer said. Even so, I feel under fire. This guy doesn't like me, doesn't trust me. One errant move, and he'll run me over, I have no doubt. I stay completely motionless, like a hunted animal. At least until my unstoppable tic betrays me.

"*Dad,*" says Stella. "It's fine. They're friends of Kim's."

A head pops into view next to Stella's father—a younger girl wearing long pigtails. This has to be the little sister Stella mentioned at Ferrell's.

"Who are they?" the girl shouts.

"They're friends, Jill," Stella repeats. "Dad, it's fine."

It sure doesn't look fine to Stella's dad. He's glowering at me and Archer.

Finally he says, "Be back before I leave for my shift."

Stella nods impatiently and motions again for him to drive off. This time he does.

"Okay," she says to us. "Why are you actually here?"

How to phrase this. *Oh yeah! Hey! I'm here to tell you I'm a liar. A fraud! And your brother is the worst person I know!*

Archer is bouncing his eyebrows at me. Why the hell did I let him come along?

"Did you talk to Craig?" Stella asks. "You said he wouldn't be out of his silence workshop until—"

"Yeah, no, I haven't talked to him." I don't look at Archer. I don't dare. "It's not that. It's—"

Nothing. I've got nothing.

"Did you want a haircut? Connie closed for the weekend. Anyway, we're not open on Sundays."

"Yeah, I see that now. But, uh . . . is the Exchange?"

Stella looks really confused.

"Kim wanted me to visit," I say. "And I'd like to listen to recent stuff. I'd like that a lot."

Stella still looks confused, but she's nodding a little. "Oh. Well, yeah, I think they open at noon on Sundays. It's just down the road."

"Right. Right, that's where we were headed. You know. Before."

"Even though you already passed it, coming from the commune?"

"Did we?" I look around, bewildered. "Oh wow. Oh shit."

"*Whoa,*" says Archer, deciding to play along. "How did we miss it?"

"We're so used to commune life," I say. "We have a bad sense of space. Direction. Time. You know."

It's a weird moment, because we all know I'm lying, and only Stella doesn't know *why*. She looks annoyed. Also kind of entertained.

"Okay," she says. "Let's head in the right direction. Down this sidewalk. Do you boys remember how to walk, at least?"

"Shhh," says Archer. "Shhh, I can't walk *and* talk. We were never taught that on the inside."

"You remember Archer, right?" I ask Stella, walking alongside her and pointing ahead at Archer, who's making a show of wobbling along the concrete path.

"I remember his condescension and bad British accent, yes."

I tic, my mouth forming a perfect oval.

"Yeah," I say. "Sorry, he can be kind of a pain. He's a good guy, though."

"Whatever you say."

"Shut up!" Archer turns on us in a rage. "I've *got* to *concentrate* on my *feet*."

Stella stifles a laugh.

The Exchange is only a few storefronts down from the salon. It's made of big glass windows, and a black-and-white sign is painted on the door in boxy lettering. When we walk inside, I'm hit by a stale, close-to-fetid smell. It's not a clean place, exactly. The signs are handwritten on bent and torn pieces of paper. Records sit in long wooden bins, and they're also piled in stacks on tables and in corners, and there's no apparent order to anything. Behind a fingerprint-clouded glass counter stands none other than Kim. She's dressed in black jeans and a torn red T-shirt, and she's got a pair of giant headphones on. Her eyes are closed, and she's nodding to an unheard beat. When I tap her on the shoulder, she shakes me off and puts one finger in the air. The message is clear: *I'll get to you when I get to you.*

The three of us wander the store, browsing. Archer lifts up an album, laughing, and shows it to me. A family—mother, father, and three full-grown children—are dressed in matching floral dresses and suits. In yellow lettering are the words "The Wilson Family Sings Gospel" and, beneath it, the album title, *I Am God's Child.*

"They've got *everything* here," he whispers.

Stella hangs back from us, tipping half-heartedly through the records, watching Kim. For the fiftieth time since leaving Red Sun, I ask myself, *What are you doing?*

I guess it was a nice save, coming up with the Exchange in the heat of the moment; it's a completely plausible reason to be out. But it's a save from *what*, exactly? Doing the right thing? Using my newfound bravery to tell the truth? And now Stella looks uncomfortable, out of place. Like she shouldn't be here. When I came into town specifically for her.

I'm such a little shit.

"Okay, what?" Kim removes the headphones. She doesn't look surprised to see us, or all that enthused, even though we're the only customers here. And even though she made a point to invite me more than once.

I approach the counter, my jaw twitching to one side. "Came for the tour."

Kim looks to Stella. "Sure you want to be hanging out with these two for the last days of your life?"

"Galliard wants your recommendations," Stella replies. "Just no punk."

"You can't say *no punk*. You can't say that to me, Stell."

Kim shuffles to a turntable behind the counter. She flips switches attached to boxes attached to speakers—a collection of contraptions I assume will give us sound. Then she drops out of sight, riffling through boxes beneath the counter. I'm guessing it's a collection of her favorites, there for easy access.

"Punk is the future," she says in a real serious voice. "It's the fucking *redemption* of rock and roll."

She slips a record from its sleeve and fits it on the turntable. After more fiddling, sound crackles through the store speakers, followed by the blast of an electric guitar. The drumbeat is persistent, and the chorus comes in quick, a chant of "I'm so bo-o-ored with the U.S.A." The singer sounds drunk.

I don't hate it, though. It's a song that makes me want to throw my head around.

"You know how much I shelled out for this?" Kim shouts to me. "An international import from fucking *England*."

"They're English?" I shout back, as my jaw jerks.

"They're the *Clash*!"

Archer is into it. He's slamming away at air drums and screaming along with the chorus. Stella looks unimpressed. She winces at the louder swells of the song. For her sake I tell Kim, "Okay, okay. What else?"

"Ramones, clearly."

249

She pops up the turntable needle and switches out records with a speed that honestly scares me.

"Hang on, hang on," she says, aligning the needle to the right track. "This should be your introduction. These boys are good ol' American stock."

A driving, frenetic beat bursts through the speakers. Archer hasn't stopped his dancing. He throws his fist into the air and, once he's picked up on yet another repetitive chorus, joins in with "Sheena is . . . a punk rocker! Sheeeena is . . . a punk rocker!"

"It's kind of like the Beach Boys," I shout.

Kim snorts. "Yeah, the Beach Boys with *balls*." She tips her thumb at Archer and says, "Sorry, who *is* that?"

"Archer!" screams Archer, saluting Kim.

Stella isn't having fun. She's taken a seat in a folding metal chair, behind the counter.

"*God*, Stell," Kim shouts. "You wouldn't know good music if it punched you in the eye."

"It's basic!" Stell shouts back. "It's the same chords over and over. They're not *talented*."

Kim rips up the needle. "Don't blaspheme."

"Play him something we both like," says Stella. "Play him Queen."

"Sure, sure. Can do."

Kim slips another LP from her bin and onto the turntable. Before she lowers the needle, she looks to me. "Ready for this, Sir Stuck-in-the-Sixties?"

"Yeah."

"Oh yeah?"

"I'm ready."

"Okay, but your cult leaders can't sue me if you drop dead."

The needle falls.

It's hard to explain what happens next. It's a thing that happens *to* me. I'm not listening so much as I'm being *sung into*. The music and the words and the harmonies—they push through my pores and into my bloodstream. They're in me. The singer's voice isn't close to anything I've heard before in the Back Room. It's dense and elastic, just the right amount of ragged on its edges. A chorus of harmonic voices backs him up as he hits notes I know are tough to nail. He makes it sound easy. Natural.

Kim can see the transformation under my skin. She looks less bored and more smug.

"Queen does gospel!" she shouts.

Behind the counter, Stella sits very still. Her eyes are shut and her head tilted up like they were Wednesday night, under the stars at Ferrell's.

"Let me tell you about my ideal man, Galliard," Kim shouts over the music. "Bowie's body. Strummer's attitude. Mercury's pipes. I like 'em androgynous and feisty and with massive powers of harmony. Oh wait, wait, here's the guitar solo."

The guitar wails out a line of ascending notes with precision, but what I've been listening to, beneath it all, is the piano.

I could play this. I could learn it.

The beat pulses in my chest. Layered, harmonized voices build in a crescendo, singing the same line, again and again: "Find me somebody to love."

Kim doesn't interrupt my rapture again. When the song

ends, she reverently ticks the needle up, throwing the store back into silence.

"Who plays the piano?" I ask.

Kim looks mildly surprised. "That's Freddie Mercury. He's the front man."

"He's the lead singer *and* the pianist?"

"Yeah." Kim taps the counter. "What, you play?"

"Shit, yeah." Archer slaps me on the back. "This man is Mozart. The commune's prodigy."

"I'm not a prodigy. I've just played for a long time."

Kim motions behind me. "Well, you can rattle away over there, if you want. My manager brought that thing in years ago. Used to be his brother's or something. Couldn't let it go, but his wife wouldn't let him keep it in their house."

I walk over to a small piano, set up in the back corner of the shop. It's painted in a swirling rainbow of psychedelic colors—pink and green and yellow and blue. Records sit piled atop its backboard, along with a thick coat of dust. The white keys are painted black, the black keys white. The keyboard spans only four octaves, and beside it are two buttons and five sliding levers. Like a machine.

"Never seen a combo organ before?" Kim comes up behind me, messes with the buttons and sliders, then points me to the keys. "Show us what you got, Wolfgang."

Feeling like an idiot, I tentatively hit my thumb on the highest C.

A bright, loud whistle sounds out.

"Wow," says Kim. "Yeah, man, you're a prodigy, for sure. Oh hey, Stella! I have your bike. *Stella!*"

Behind the counter, Stella's eyes flutter open. "What?"

"You left it on my car the other night, remember? We can go out and get it if you want."

"Oh." Stella looks as though she's been woken from a seven-year sleep. "Yeah, actually, that'd be great. I have an errand to run after this."

"Cool." Kim jerks her elbow into my shoulder, hard. "Don't let this store burn down."

The girls head out, and once they're gone, I fit my hands over the keys in earnest. I play a C-major arpeggio, then D and E, working my way upward. The sound from the organ is arresting, and I can't control its dynamics with the pressure of my fingers like I can the Red Sun Yamaha. I'm on the A scale when Archer throws his fist against the lower keys, disrupting everything in an electronic howl.

I look up. "What was that for?"

"Excuse me, sir," he says, in that fake accent of his. "I believe you may have lost this. I found it on the floor back there." He holds his empty hands before me. "It's your spine."

I push a ragged sound from my throat. Then I shove his hands away. "It's not the right time."

Archer scoffs.

He doesn't understand that I need this. I have to enjoy this precious remaining time on the Outside, because there are only two weeks left to cross, and after I set things right, it won't be the same. This won't be an Outside where Stella Kay Mercer likes me. It will be an Outside where I have a mortal enemy.

"I'm *going to tell her*," I say, around a throat clear. "Maybe I don't want to with you breathing down my neck."

"If I wasn't breathing down your neck, you'd *never* tell her."

"I would."

"Sure. Right. Uh-huh."

I put an end to the conversation with a two-handed G chord. Archer cusses and drifts away toward the record bins as I begin to play a song.

It's one of my favorites from the Back Room, taken from an album by a band called the Bee Gees. It's called "I Started a Joke," and it's the only song on the LP that I like, but I like it a whole lot. I can't improvise on the organ the way I can on the piano. Any stray notes are too loud and overpowering, so I stick with solid chords. After a few cycles through the verse, I start to sing.

I don't stop. I sing the song through. Three verses, two choruses. The energy crawling under my skin pushes back out, into the musty air around me. The organ keys are firm under my fingers, and their sound is hard and insistent. But my words are soft, because these lyrics are sad. If you listen closely, you'll understand: They're really fucking sad.

I finish, straightening from my bend over the keys.

I hear Archer say, "You *crying*?"

I turn. Stella is close by—closer than I thought. She's leaning against a record bin, and her eyes are brimming with tears. Rather than answer Archer, she wipes her knuckles under each eye and says, "I'm heading out."

"What about your very own Elton John?" shouts Kim, who's back behind the counter.

Stella smiles tightly at me. "It's this errand I've been waiting to run, and there's no telling if the rain will start up again. I'd better go now."

She heads for the door, and pain shoots through my arm. Archer has clenched his fingers into my elbow.

"Go on, man," he growls.

What he's saying is, *Here's your chance—no breathing down your neck.*

I know he's right: This is the moment. Maybe that's why it takes me a damn long time to get the words out. By the time I do, Stella's halfway out the door.

"Hey, Stella?"

She stops. Warm wind blows into the store, unsettling the must. She looks upset. Maybe even a little angry. I tic, blinking in her direction.

"Can I come with you?"

"Oh. It's . . . not that interesting."

"That's fine."

She seems to be struggling. Over at the counter Kim snorts. "Subtle, Galahad."

Stella blushes. I can see it from the other side of the store. I feel kind of hot myself. I blink harder.

"Um," she says. "If you want to come that bad."

I nod, blinking. But then I say, "Hang on."

I dig into my back pocket, retrieving the wad of paper money there.

"How much is that LP?" I ask Kim. "The one by Queen."

Kim snorts again. "You want to *buy* it?"

Archer gives me a look. "Hey, man," he says. "Forgetting something?"

I shake my head. "How much is it?"

"Just hold on." Kim is flipping through a bin labeled NEW

255

RELEASES. She pulls up a plastic-wrapped album. It's black, with a brightly colored illustration at its center. She inspects it, then says, "Six bucks. You got that much?"

I sort through my money, and the smallest number I can find is a ten. I set that bill on the counter.

"Well, what do you know," says Kim. "Still making sales at the end of the world."

She takes the money and hands over the record. I stare so long at the cover I don't realize she's trying to give me something else.

"Your change." She stuffs the green paper into my hand. "Want a bag for it?"

"No. Uh. No, actually. I wondered, could you hold this for me?"

Kim gives me a weird look. "Folks do that *before* they buy. What do you want to buy and then hold it for?"

"It's because he can't bring it back." I'm startled by Stella's words. She's been watching this whole time from the half-opened door. Her tears are all gone, and she speaks with confidence. "Remember? Nothing made before '70."

"Oh. Right," says Kim. "Then sure. I tell you what, I'll keep this one on hold till the last of days."

I nod weakly, thinking of Red Sun's gatekeeper, Charlie. There's no way I could sneak this LP past him. There was no reason to even *buy* it. I'm not sure why I did that. I just felt the overwhelming need to *have* the music for myself.

I only have days left on the Outside. I want a souvenir.

Maybe between now and the end of Crossing, I'll figure out some way to sneak it in. After all, I became a pro with letters; why not records, too?

Stella and I bike a half hour down Eisenhower. We pass the Dreamlight and even Red Sun. We keep pedaling, between walls of corn, straight out on the flat road, for mile after mile.

Stella rides a little ways ahead of me, her bike wheels *tick-tick-tick*ing with every one of their quick revolutions. It's the only sound, aside from the occasional car or truck passing by. I'm thinking about the red rain. The pink lightning. The Back Room. The combo organ. Stella's watering eyes. That's why I don't notice at first when she slows, matching her pace to mine.

"It's not much farther," she says.

"Huh? Oh. Where are we going, exactly?"

"Surplus store."

"What's that?"

"A store of . . . surplus things? From the base nearby."

"The base?"

"The army base."

"Oh."

"You're pacifists, aren't you?"

"Yeah."

"Me too."

I sneak a look at her. Her frizzy brown hair is blowing all around.

I could say, *I know you're a pacifist. You've written me long letters about it.*

That could set it off. If I'm looking for a segue, there's one. I could take it now.

I don't.

Not surprised, you're saying. *You're a damn coward, Galliard.*

Don't I know it.

We don't speak again until we reach a squat, concrete building lined by overgrown, thistly weeds. There's only one car in the lot.

"You don't have to come in if you don't want," says Stella, leaning her bike against the wall.

I do go in, though, following her up to the counter, where a middle-aged man sits in a lawn chair, listening to the radio. At the sight of Stella, he claps his hands and stands.

"Right, right. Got what you're after," he says.

Stella waits patiently, eyes big, as the man disappears into a dark doorway behind the counter. When he comes back out, he's got some kind of metal contraption in his hand. It's bigger than an ear of corn, and it looks heavy.

"I make a point of not asking what you do with these," says the man, ringing her up at the register. "But I'd appreciate some assurance you're not building a bomb."

Stella smiles. "If I were doing that, I'd need plenty of things you don't sell here."

"Well, now, who's to say you aren't going elsewhere?"

Stella slides her money across the counter. "I guess you can't say, Rick."

"Don't want the Feds sniffing around, is all."

"If they do, it won't be because of me."

Rick's been laughing with his eyes. Now he laughs for real. Then he points to me. "With this one hanging around, there's no knowing."

I start, clearing my throat.

Without looking at me, Stella says, "He's harmless."

"Maybe so, but cults ain't."

"He doesn't belong to a cult, Rick."

My damn throat clears continue. Rick squints at Stella, then at me. I feel hot around the neck, itching to say something, because Rick and Stella have been talking as though I'm not in the room. Only now Rick turns to me and says, "All the same, you'd best stay out of town, boy. Plenty of folk are saying it's you and yours who started this end-of-the-world business."

"Duly noted, Rick." Stella's voice is tight as she takes her purchase. Then she pushes past me, and I follow her outside, away from Rick's squinting stare.

I want to say something about what's happened. I feel as though I have been accused of something, made dirty in Stella's eyes. I want to scrub myself clean before her. The trouble is, I'm not clean. You could scrub me hard, and I'd still be filthy underneath. Rick is right: I *am* the one who started this. The lightning, the red rain, even the wind—they have to do with me. They were lessons from Holly, Hendrix, and Joplin. And for all the bravery my gods have taught me, I'm not brave enough to do the one thing that matters most.

Maybe Rod was right: Maybe I am weak. I'm weak enough to want to keep the Outside perfect a little bit longer. My gods can't begrudge me that, though, can they? I have so short a time left here. Surely they don't mind if I hold off the truth for a few more days. That's what I tell myself. And that's why, instead of telling Stella what matters, I ask her a pointless question.

"*Are* you building a bomb?"

"Maybe."

"What is that thing?"

"A walkie-talkie. I get them here because army walkie-talkies have the best range."

I clear my throat. "What's it for?"

"A project. Nothing important."

She's tense around the neck, the same way she was the other night, when she told me about the Voyager missions. She never wrote in her letters about a project, or about trips to the surplus store, or walkie-talkies. And I get now how rude it was for me to invite myself along. This is something private. It's something Stella won't even write her brother about.

But then, if she hadn't wanted me to come along, she wouldn't have let me.

Right?

"Do you work on a lot of projects?" I ask.

"No. Well, I do, but most of them are in my head. I don't have the things I need to work on *good* projects."

"How's that?"

"I'd need parts and a soldering gun and a work space. Those are expensive. So I just think about projects, mostly."

"You could go to school, though, couldn't you? A university? Can't you work on projects there?"

Stella tips her nose toward me. "How do *you* know so much about higher education?"

"We're not stupid. We know *about* the Outside."

"You just can't listen to new music."

"That was Rod's decision, really, not Opal's. It wasn't always that way."

"Who's Rod?"

"One of our leaders."

"And he's the one who says you can't listen to certain things?"

"He weeded out a lot of our library, too. We can't import any new books."

Stella's frowning hard. "That sounds suspect."

"What do you mean?"

"I mean, that's censorship."

"We're not a cult." I sound kind of mad, saying that. I guess I am.

It's not that I like Rod, but he *does* think I can be a leader. And sure, I don't enjoy the ban on new music, but the only alternative is leaving Red Sun for good.

"Didn't you hear me in there, with Rick?" Stella asks. "I never said you were a cult. I only said this Rod guy is suspect."

"Well . . . maybe. I dunno."

"Doesn't anyone challenge him?"

"No, that's not—you don't get it," I say, frustrated. My jaw shifts to the right. "At Red Sun we live in unison."

"Don't you care, though? Don't you care that you're going to live the rest of your life there? And that you won't have books or music or any connection to what's happening out here?"

My jaw jerks again. "I *care*. But there are . . . there's a lot of good things about the inside."

The kitchen. Archer. The chance to do something. Change something. To even be on the Council. I tell myself this, as well as Stella. There are plenty of good things in Red Sun. Reasons to stay.

Stella keeps jamming her thumb into the handlebar of her bike. "There are good things out here, too."

"Yeah, I get that."

Her gaze cuts to me. "You don't think it's depressing anymore?"

I smile. "I liked Ferrell's. I liked the music, too."

"See? Not all bad."

We're quiet, but I don't want the conversation to end, because I feel wrong. I feel like Stella thinks I'm wrong.

"I had a plan in there," I say. "I knew what I wanted. Then I didn't get it, and after that, everything felt . . . *off*."

"I'm sorry."

"Not your fault."

Your brother's.

"I want to play music," I say. "I want to make that my life. I guess I always thought I could in there. Now I'm not so sure."

Stella's putting it together. "That's why you came out. Because everything changed."

"Yeah. I guess."

"What are you thinking now?"

"I don't know. I'm still . . . figuring it out."

I'm figuring out what would happen if I stayed. Would everything go back to the way it was? Would I work ten or more years at the Moonglow, eventually become a Council member, and live the rest of my days in peace? Not music-filled peace, maybe, but *peace*?

I'm figuring out what would happen if I left. Would I make it? What if J. J. was right, and the Outside is too tough for me? Then again, what if I'm inspired to write a whole lot of new music, like the song I composed on the first night of the red rain? Would my gods support me, if I faced this new world? Would I have them on my side, at least?

Stella's looking at me funny. I can't read her face as she says, "Maybe it *would* be easier to shoot you into space."

Honestly? Sounds like the perfect solution to me.

"You could come too," I say. "You could work on all kinds of projects up there."

Stella nods, serious. "I'll call NASA and make arrangements. I get *Voyager 1*, you get *Voyager 2*."

"We're flying separately?"

"Well, you know. Weight distribution."

"Yeah, but . . . it might be better to be alone together. In case we start to go crazy. Or something goes wrong."

My face is burning. I can't help it.

Stella says, "I don't know if arrangements could be made on such short notice."

"Rocket scientists are smart, though. They could make anything work."

It happens in a flash—a bolt of lightning, a match strike.

She drops her bike against the concrete wall, and then, with the walkie-talkie still in one hand, she reaches up, and she kisses me. Her mouth grazes my chin first, then folds onto my lower lip. Her hands grab my tunic, and my hands grab her waist, and I'm kissing her back, and it's good, and it's awful, too, because my chest explodes with guilt and unexplainable sadness.

And then I tic. It's sudden. My head jerks hard, and Stella staggers back. I step away.

"Fuck," I say. "Fuck. Stella, I'm sorry."

263

She touches her lips, eyes wide.

"It's fine. It's fine—I need to go." It's more a wheeze than words. She fumbles for her bicycle, shoving the walkie-talkie into the bike basket. She mounts, and she pedals away from me, fast and hard, without looking back.

I don't shout after her. I just watch her go.

20

Stella

SUNDAY, AUGUST 14

I pedal. I don't stop. I think I am surprised. I think I am stunned.
I think I am startled. I am not sure if any of those words suffice.
I am not sure if every one of them is the same.

It was only a kiss, I know.

Only, it was a *kiss*.

It was my first, and I gave it, and it was returned.

And then . . .

I've left Galliard behind, and all that remains of him is in
the cracks of my lips.

It's not something *This Stella* would ever do. *That Stella*
stole my body, used it, and then released it to me with no explanation. No formula can reveal the why of it. Why I would kiss
him, with no warning and no direction.

It could've been the way his eyes lit up like a child's when
he heard "Somebody to Love," or the ravenous energy with
which he purchased that LP.

It could've been the song he played, and the way his voice
dove and rose with soft assurance, carrying on it such sad
words: *I finally died, which started the whole world living.*

It could've been what he said outside the surplus store—that he understands what it means to be alone together. He *understands*, and I never thought anyone but a Mercer would.

The world without has gone wild and unpredictable. Now my world within has done the same. The way *That Stella* lives is dangerous, confusing—so much so that my thoughts dim, and the only thing left to me is the muscle memory required to bike home.

When I get there, my father is on the front porch. He is sitting on the top step, smoking.

I don't remember the last time I saw my father sit on our porch. I do, however, remember the last time I saw him smoke: It was the day of my mother's funeral.

"Stella," he says, as I wheel my bike up the driveway.

I nod, continuing toward the garage.

"Leave that for a second," he says. "Come here. We need to talk."

It'll be difficult talking now, I want to say, *as I am existing on minimum brain function.*

I set the bike against the garage entrance, though, and I join my father on the steps. Before I reach him, he has jammed out the cigarette on the concrete.

Once I am seated, he says, "I want to know what's going on."

So do I.

"Who were those boys? The ones in Red Sun clothes. How do you know them?"

I could lie, but I don't have the energy. And if my world is ending in less than a week, I would rather it end with me on honest terms with my father.

"Their names are Galliard and Archer," I say. "I met them at the Dreamlight. I've been showing Galliard around town."

"Why?"

I know I need to tell him this. It is a truth I think he already suspects. That does not mean it's easy. I've kept this secret for two years, and every day I've kept it has made it harder to push from my mouth.

Eventually, I do.

"I've been writing Craig. I've been writing him for a while now. And I wanted to see him again, and Galliard said he could make that happen."

My father is silent. He does not look taken aback, exactly. He looks thoughtful, the way he does when Jill asks an "adult" question about politics.

"I'm almost eighteen," I say. "I know you gave us rules about Red Sun, and I know why you gave them, but I'm an adult now, Dad. Talking to Craig is something I need to do as an adult."

My father nods, but I am not reassured. I do not think it is a nod of approval.

"Have you?" he asks. "Met him? Talked to him?"

"Not yet."

"All right."

I look across the street, to a brown vinyl-sided split-level. The Metcalfes used to live there. They were the ones who owned Major, the collie we found dead two weeks ago. They moved away to Indianapolis. A new family moved in, and I've never learned their name.

"Stella," says my father. "Do you want to go to college?"

I have not been expecting this question, of all questions. There are so many unpleasant things I would rather talk about. I would rather tell him about my kiss with Galliard and the resulting confusion inside me. I would rather speculate on the red rain, and if the hippies of Red Sun are responsible or if it is God's wrath or if it is the work of alien life-forms.

What I don't want to talk about is college. It hurts inside, a burn around my throat. To talk about this means revealing the two Stellas and their disparate lives.

I glance back at the garage, where my recent purchase is resting in a bike basket.

I decide then that I won't speak; I will show.

"Hold on," I say, getting to my feet.

I go to the garage and remove the walkie-talkie from the basket. Then I go inside, to my room, and pull out the wicker bin from under my bed. I do not hesitate. If I do, I will reconsider.

I walk back outside and set the bin on the porch between me and my father.

"What's this?" he asks.

"It's something I've been working on. An invention for the salon."

I take out the pieces, one by one, and arrange them on the concrete, fitting them into their proper places beneath the wooden frame, ensuring that each wire is snug and in its proper slot. Then I set down the walkie-talkie I purchased today from the surplus store. I take out a Phillips screwdriver from the bin and set to twirling loose each of the screws on the back plate. Once it's off, I am in familiar territory—a small town, neatly mapped. I lift the circuit board for Dad to see.

"I'm not done," I say. "I have to fit this into one of the other walkie-talkies so the aesthetic is uniform. At first I thought I would have to desolder a transistor; that's what was faulty with the last usable one. Instead I can just switch out circuit boards. That makes it much easier."

"I . . ." He frowns, uncomprehending. "What's it for?"

I set the walkie-talkie down. Carefully, I grip my project's wooden frame by the edges and tip it over, revealing its presentable side. It is a lectern-like contraption fitted with buttons and labels, painted in the orange-sherbet trim of Vine Street Salon.

"The salon gets busy," I say. "A lot of women come from out of town and don't have time to spare. They want to get their errands *and* their hair done, without much downtime in between. Connie's scheduling doesn't allow for that, though. Which is why I came up with this."

I take out one of four intact walkie-talkies, which I've painted over in white acrylic paint and labeled with the number two.

"It's bulky, but it will fit in any woman's purse, antenna up." I pull the antenna to demonstrate. "This is how it works: A client checks in with me at the reception desk. I write down her name and assign that name to a number—in this case number two. Then I tell her she's free to browse anywhere on Vine Street; she'll be in range. When Connie is about finished with her most current client, I press this."

I press the button on the lectern labeled 2. In my other hand the corresponding walkie-talkie sounds a shrill, electronic beep.

"The client is notified and can make her way back to the salon. Meanwhile I can stay at the desk and tend to any other incoming or outgoing clients. No running around, no confusion. Order. And when the client arrives, she returns the walkie-talkie, and I can assign it to a new client. Like clock-work. It's a basic idea. Nothing complicated about the design or mechanics. It mainly requires collecting parts and arranging them to look pretty. But it'll save a lot of trouble at the salon."

I hand the walkie-talkie to Dad. He grips it, running his thumb over the label. "Where did you get the supplies?"

"Here and there. I've been saving up my Dreamlight tips for this specifically. I had them special-order a few things at Belmont and Mike's. Mostly it's from the surplus store. They have high-range walkie-talkies, and that's what I needed. I tried with toy sets at first, but they only reach thirteen hundred feet."

He raises his eyes to me, startled. "You've been biking to the surplus store alone?"

"Not always alone." My face turns hot at the thought of my trip with Galliard. "The paint is left over from when Connie redecorated the salon. I haven't told her what I'm doing. There's a chance she might hate it. Or not understand. But now that I'm working there full-time, I wanted to make things easier for everyone."

My father lifts the walkie-talkie, gives it a gentle shake. "Gayle told me she has a connection with a professor at KU— an old schoolmate. She says they have an excellent school of engineering. Wants to introduce you there, look into the possibility of applying for spring admission. Did she tell you any of that?"

I shake my head, mute.

"Is that what you want, Stell? Do you want to go to college?"

I am crying. I wipe at the tears streaking my cheeks, unable to form a response.

"You never told me that," he says. "You never said anything about it. I thought you were happy."

That is when the words break free.

"I thought I was too," I say, blotting at the tears with my first. "And I don't want to let you down. I don't want to leave you, and I don't want to leave Jill, but . . . I don't want to feel stifled here. I don't want to feel I *have* to stay, and grow bitter, and . . . and go mad from it. I don't want to be *Mom*. And I'm so scared I will."

It is a terrible thing to tell him, but it is what I need to say. I need him to hear it, and *I* need to hear it, out loud: I cannot become Diane Mercer. I cannot stay in this town and turn into someone's wife with two children and scribble on graph paper in my spare time. I cannot tend to a house and cook meals and also do what I'm best at. I cannot be *This Stella* and make it through alive. I must be *That Stella*, or I will die. And I'm not sure I knew that until now, in this very moment, on this porch, with the scent of cigarette lingering around me.

Dad is crying now too. "Did you feel I was forcing you to stay here? I never said you couldn't go to college."

I take the walkie-talkie from him and place it back in the bin. I drag the backs of my hands across my face.

"It's not that you said I couldn't. You just never said I *could*."

I stop my attempts to get rid of the tears. They come far faster than I can hope to make them disappear. I feel as though I am waking from a dream, only to realize I've shown my heart to Dad, shown my *project*. I don't know whether I am terrified or elated. Whatever the emotion is, it's strong. It wraps around my body and squeezes the breath out of me.

"I think you should talk to Gayle." My father stands. He slaps his hands together as though ridding them of dust—like my project has left residue there. "You should call Gayle, meet with this professor friend of hers."

I stare up at him. "I couldn't go spring semester. I don't know if I could go at all, Dad. Maybe I'm not good enough. And I'd have to quit my jobs here and take out loans, and I can't—"

"You should talk to her." His hands fall to his sides, clenched tight. "You're not the breadwinner of this family. You shouldn't be. You're an adult, as you say. You deserve to get away. And I'd rather send you off than have you run off like . . ."

Craig.

Craig, Craig, Craig.

His name crackles in the air around us, though I spoke it many minutes ago.

"Jill needs me," I whisper. "She's growing up. She needs me here."

"That's not a reason to stay, Stella."

"Are you serious?" I turn on him. "It's the *best* reason to stay. Family is what matters. We're all each other's got."

"We'll still be family if you're in Lawrence. You could visit on weekends, if you wanted."

I shake my head. "It's not the same."

I can't be my mother, but I can't be my brother, either. I can't be *This Stella*, but I can't be *That Stella*.

I don't know what's left to be.

I shut my eyes, and Dad goes back in the house. I think he is gone, but a moment later he returns to the stoop and places something on my knee, papery and featherlight. I take hold of it, but I do not open my eyes until he has left again, this time for good.

The paper in my hand is small and square, ripped from the kitchen grocery list. On it is a series of carefully printed numbers, and a single word: *Gayle*.

Dad told me to call her, and now he has given me the means.

I am in a daze when I go into the house, hauling the wicker bin to my room. I sit at my desk, staring at my project. All that effort, to be indispensable at a job I don't enjoy. It's funny, only I don't laugh. I look at Gayle's telephone number, written on paper now damp from my holding it so hard. My breaths turn short, my head light. I am suffocating here, in this room.

I make my escape. I walk, and I do not stop until I reach the kitchen phone. I set the paper before me, on the kitchen counter, and then, with a trembling index finger, I dial. The numbers spin out, one by one, each heavy stroke of the rotary drawing me closer to a connection.

Then the number is complete, and the phone rings. It continues to ring—three, four, five times. My heart falls. Gayle isn't there. She isn't going to answer. I am about to hang up when I hear, "Hello, this is Gayle Nelson."

"G-Gayle?" I sputter.

"I'm not available, but if you leave a message with a number where you can be reached, I'll be in touch soon."

Then there is a long, loud beep in my ear, followed by silence.

An answering machine. Gayle Nelson has an answering machine. Of course she does, I reflect. She's an important scientist, and if anyone needs that fancy piece of equipment, it's her. Only after that reflection do I realize that an answering machine means I am being recorded. I could hang up right now, and Gayle wouldn't know it was me. There would only be a few seconds of dead air. I imagine she gets a lot of that, since I don't know of anyone in Slater who has an answering machine, and those callers certainly wouldn't be expecting one on the other line.

This Stella would hang up.

That Stella doesn't. She speaks.

"Miss Nelson? Gayle. It's Stella Mercer. My dad told me you spoke with him about me, and I don't really appreciate that, but . . . but . . ." The remaining words burst out: "I want to know if you can help me. With college. If you think I can go, what I can do. I want to talk about that. All right. I'm sorry, I don't know if I—I'm—I'm sorry."

I slam the phone on the receiver, so hard the clang echoes through my skull.

Then I run, down the hallway and out the front door. I cannot stay still. I take to the sidewalk and circle around my street, once, then twice. When I reach my house the second time, I return to the door, but I don't go inside. I sit on the stoop with my head between my knees, gulping in long breaths. Slowly, very slowly, they even out.

I feel rather than see the sun lowering. My skin cools and dampens, and the birdcalls change. I am coming to terms with a new reality. By leaving that message with Gayle, I have done something wholly irretrievable. *That Stella* is no longer an experiment.

When I finally go inside, Jill is in the den, already watching the news, a TV dinner on her lap. I check my watch and find that it's a quarter till six.

"Oh my God. Jill. I'm sorry, I lost track of time."

She doesn't answer me, too absorbed in Cassie Mackin's report and her steaming mac and cheese. I leave it alone. I don't fix a meal for myself; I have no appetite. I go to my bedroom, ready for sleep and for this long, ravaging day to be over.

I don't notice the damage at first. It isn't until I've fallen back on the bed that I see the shreds of finely ripped paper scattered on my desk and the surrounding floor.

I sit up straight, dragging my eyes over the wreckage. The shuttle drawings, the escape-pod plans—they have been torn from their place, tacks scattered in a dangerous constellation on the floor. All that is left of the sketches and equations are long, thin strips of graph paper and the now-indecipherable markings of pen and pencil. And there, close by on the floor, is the wicker bin, overturned.

I know what I am going to find before I right the bin. Even so, the sight makes my heart thump hard against my ribs. The project has been destroyed. Wires have been ripped out, lights broken, walkie-talkies smashed apart. It is the work of angry hands and shoe heels and, most likely, a hammer.

I realize now how stupid I have been to assume Jill would know nothing. That she wouldn't eavesdrop on my adult conversations with Dad.

Of course Jill knows. She is always the first to notice everything, from the dead collie to the lightning-struck steeple to the two boys from Red Sun outside Vine Street Salon. She is the sleuth, just like her heroes.

And now I am her enemy: the culprit.

A letter from Diane Mercer, written July 20, 1969

Please believe, it is not your fault. Sometimes only life is to blame, not people. I don't blame any of you.

I wish I'd known, before I was a wife and before I was a mother, that I could not be a wife and could not be a mother. I cannot be enough for you, and you cannot be enough for me.

I need to use my mind for more than errands and your meals. I need more than what I can find in this town. I need a city, I need a job, I need an outlet for all the things I was before.

I can't have those without leaving you.

And I can't leave you and live with myself.

That is why I must leave in this way, for good. Please understand. I hope one day you will.

21

Galliard

TUESDAY, AUGUST 16

I don't know what the hell happened.

I mean, I do on the surface.

Stella kissed me.

I ticked.

She left.

And I haven't heard anything since.

That's on the surface, but it sure doesn't mean I know what's going on *below*. What actually *happened*.

Archer's been merciless.

"You had the chance," he railed on Sunday night, when we were closed up in our room. "You had *every* chance."

"I was going to tell her. I was building up to it. I didn't think she'd kiss me."

"She wouldn't have kissed you if you'd *told her first*. So stop whining about it. Stop. I don't want to hear you talk about it until you've fucking done something, for real."

Since then, Archer's been flinging all kinds of jabs in my direction. ("Hey, Galliard! Or wait, is that *really* your name? I hear there's some confusion." And "Will you tell Thunder—no, hang on, I'd better tell him myself; don't want him thinking it's coming from *you*.")

I don't fend them off. I deserve them.

There's one important detail I didn't tell Archer: how badly the kiss ended. It would be too humiliating. Especially after Cynthia.

Cynthia and I were friends growing up. Then one day we were holding hands on our way from morning prayer to Dining Hall. And then we were making out. And touching. Nothing more than that, though.

The Council doesn't condemn sex for us youth, but it does advocate safety. We got an earful about protected sex and how to be smart about it when we turned thirteen. It's this grand speech repeated annually by one of our residence leaders or by Saff herself, and accompanied by the talk on how we're allowed to take on friends and lovers, but we must never think of ourselves as individual family units; instead we're a part of the greater family of Red Sun, in which there is neither mother nor father, and the children are every member's responsibility. It's *particular familial bonds* that are discouraged, not procreation.

So it wasn't guilt or anything that kept me and Cynthia off each other. I guess it was that neither of us felt ready. I was fourteen, and she was fifteen, and we kept stopping at the part where it'd be pretty damn usual to take off each other's clothes. It was that way for a few months. And then she stopped kissing me. And then she stopped holding my hand. And then she started holding hands with Cal—the one who got hit by a car on Crossing. Cynthia and Cal have been together ever since.

And I was left like I am now, wondering what happened. Though I've got a big hunch.

Eventually, someway, somehow, I fuck everything up. Sometimes it's the tics that do it, and sometimes it's just me, but the fucking up? That part is a sure bet.

Even J. J. said it. He said I wouldn't make it on the Outside, the way I am. I can barely make it on the inside as is. I can't even get a girlfriend here, or the job I want. How much worse would it be in a world where people don't support one another the way we do at Red Sun? What kind of living hell would that be?

I thought my gods had a plan for me. I thought they wanted me to give this Outside thing a go, while I have the chance. I thought they wanted me to be daring, take risks the way they did. Maybe I got it all wrong, though. Maybe I misinterpreted the signs, and really the blood rain and the lightning and the raging winds have been warnings—or, worse, punishments. Maybe I was never supposed to have set foot out of Red Sun.

Sure, the idea of leaving Red Sun is a nice one, in theory. Life on the Outside would be different and new and even exciting. When I was with Stella, though, I forgot how ugly the Outside can be. It's also a place where people get hurt, and no one around them gives a fuck. Where they throw you against walls and talk about you like you're not even in the same room.

So Red Sun's music selection isn't extensive. I can make my own music.

So my assigned job isn't the best. It's not the worst, either.

So I couldn't bring back that Queen LP. It's a small price to pay for the community I've known my whole life.

And, as Opal reminds us during our monthly meetings, contentment is the key to happiness.

I remind myself of that now, and I tell myself to think of my gods' signs a different way. I decide to try my hand at being content. Contentedly, I attend morning prayer, and I pray to Jimi for cool about Stella Kay Mercer. I pray to Janis for the strength to not punch Phoenix in the face every time I see him around. I pray to Buddy for understanding about my situation, locked into cooking green beans every damn day.

Will they answer my prayers? Will they show mercy on their wayward son? It's too soon to say.

I've resumed my work at the Moonglow, which the Council reopened after a full day of clear skies. Life goes on, and as the days pass, it seems our strange weather has finally ended. The skies are clear, and at night I can see my gods shining down. The Life Force seems to be saying, *There's a good boy, Galliard. Stay here, and it'll be fine.*

Tuesday morning the Council calls a special meeting. We adult members leave our usual tasks and gather in Common House.

Opal speaks first. "We know the fear and concerns that have been circling Red Sun. There's been an excess of negative energy due to the strange events in past weeks. That is only natural. However, we on the Council believe it is time to now purge that negativity from among us and refocus on our callings."

Rod takes over from there. He tells us, not for the first time, that these frightening events are due to pollution and the misuse of precious resources by those on the Outside. He tells us we should mourn for this ignorance, but that we must focus on our community, asking ourselves what we can do to combat the damage outsiders wreak daily upon the earth.

None of this is new to me. I've heard the same explanations thrown around in whispers and dinner conversations. The outsiders are to blame for this, and we must be the better people. We must choose the higher path. That's what everyone says.

Today Rod adds to that sentiment with some practical steps. He tells us the Council will hold new weekly "unity" meetings, during which we will share our fears and lift one another toward the Life Force.

Then he tells us, "Due to various concerns, we've decided to indefinitely suspend Crossing. It's too volatile a situation outside our walls, and we cannot guarantee the full safety of our youth. For this reason, no one will be allowed out of our gates until we can be sure of stability in the town and surrounding area."

Thunder, one of Archer's usual Crossing crew, calls out, "But it's almost over anyway!"

"I'm aware of that," says Rod, raising his hands. "We understand your frustration. However, safety comes before special privileges. Remember, we *allow* you Crossing rights. This isn't a restriction on your freedom; it's a precaution for your well-being. We don't want any of you to be caught outside the safety of Red Sun, should a new anomaly visit us and a panic break out in town."

"Fuck that," Archer mutters beside me. "Like there won't be panic *here*."

Here's the thing: If I were truly content, the way I'm trying to be, I wouldn't be upset about Rod's announcement. Sure, I was putting off going out one last time to find Stella and tell her the truth. But for Rod to say I *can't*? Seeing her again would be uncomfortable. *Not* seeing her again isn't a possibility. I *have* to see her. I have to finally make this right. It's my final business on the Outside.

Now, instead of having two weeks left to cross, I have zero. No weeks, no days, no hours. My chance is over. No more considering, no more flirting with the Outside and its possibilities. Rod, fucking *Rod*, has made my decision for me. And even though I'm trying to be content, I'm not. I'm pissed.

Not that any of the crossers are happy. They're grumbling and shaking their heads, and Archer has scrunched his face in tight like he's a kid about to throw a tantrum.

Opal steps in front of Rod to address us. "Red Sun," she says, "has been and always will be about cultivating a supportive community. We ask that our younger members please understand, this order is only an attempt to do what we have always done: hold one another toward the light. And for those of you with remaining concerns about these unsettling events, we remind you that Red Sun has a clear safety protocol in place. We are equipped with a shelter large enough to accommodate this entire community. It was built for times like this. There is no need to fear. Let us instead concentrate on putting positive energy back into our surroundings."

Afterward, once everyone's gone, Archer and I sit on the back steps of Common House, near the wildflower garden.

"Rod's such a bastard," Archer says. "He needs a history lesson. Restrictions only lead to revolt. It's twisted logic. People tell us we can't do something, and then we want to do it more."

I clear my throat—a tic. Then I ask, "Is that how you feel? You want to go out?"

Archer is quiet. His eyes are on me. "Do you?"

Another harsh sound claws up my throat. "I . . . don't know."

"Yeah."

"This place is everything to me. It's everything I know."

"You and me both."

"Do you think they do that to us on purpose?" I ask.

Archer frowns into the sun. "Do what?"

"Make us this way—dependent on them. So that, even with Crossing, we don't want to leave. Even with Crossing, we choose to stay here."

"Shit. I . . . I don't know."

I never told Archer about my meeting with Rod. Didn't even hint at it. There was never a good time and no way of phrasing it that wouldn't make me sound like a kiss-ass prick, same as Phoenix. I think I need to say it now, though. It's been hanging around in my head, a piece of a puzzle that won't seem to fit.

I tell Archer what I can. What the Council told me on Assignment Day and what Rod said to me in his office, about training with him and the community respecting a guy who has labored with his own two hands. When I'm through, Archer whistles.

"Think that's true? You think the bastard meant it?"

I say, "Part of me thinks so. The other part thinks it was Rod trying to stop me from Crossing again. Because he thought I was in danger of—I don't know, abandoning ship. The Council never cared what I did before."

"It's about the PR," says Archer. "Think it through: You're the first Red Sun member who was born and raised in the commune. How good would it look if, after sixteen years on the inside, you up and left?"

I haven't thought of it that way, but maybe Archer's got a point. It *would* look pretty bad if the very first commune baby ran away to the Outside.

"Was Rod right?" he asks.

"What?"

Archer leans forward, looking me over with his mud-brown eyes. "You abandoning ship, Galliard?"

I clear my throat with gusto. "*What?* No."

"Haven't even thought about it?"

I look around. There is no one walking past. The door behind us is shut tight. Most people are at their jobs or indoors, hiding from the summer heat.

"Have you?" I ask.

"Sure." Archer stretches his arms lazily down his legs, wrapping his hands around his shins. "Loads of times. I'm thinking of it now."

I stare, and my blinking tic starts up. "Are you shitting me?"

"Honest to God, Galliard. Don't tell me you haven't."

"I haven't." A familiar indignation bubbles in me—something I've carried with me every Crossing summer until

285

this one. Something Phoenix set alight. "I mean . . . I hadn't. People made the Outside sound so wrong."

"Especially Phoenix."

"Yeah." I shake my head, blinking rapidly. "Why would you leave? You like it here, don't you? You wanted your job with J. J."

"Sure. But . . . I don't know, man. Some people can grow up in a place like this and go out in a place like that and be okay when it's said and done. Some people don't dig the parties, the rush. Plenty don't. Those kinds of people made Red Sun to begin with. Some people, though . . . they go to the Outside, and it ruins them. Fucks them up big time. Because they've seen it, and they can't forget it, and after that they feel they're always going to be missing out. I guess that's me. I guess I'm that kind. I'm the crosser who leaves."

"I thought you might be."

I say it quiet, and, as quiet as me, Archer replies, "There are plenty of kitchen jobs on the Outside."

I look straight at him, still blinking hard, but he won't look back. He just digs his thumbs into his calves.

It's true: I've been scared Archer would cross over to the Outside since his first summer in Slater. I shouldn't be surprised. I'm not, really. I don't even feel sad. I feel . . . jealous. Which isn't right. I have every reason in the world to stay here. I've been reciting those reasons to myself for days now.

I decide not to think about the jealousy. I decide to be helpful and ask, "You need anything from me? You can take my allowance. What's left of it."

Archer shakes his head. "I've got a plan. My uncle and

aunt live in Pasadena. That's in California. They tried to make contact with me a while back. Sent a letter, before the Council tightened the mail restrictions. Told me to get out, this place was a cult, they'd put me up. I've got an address. The plan is, I hitchhike to Kansas City, then use my allowance on a Grey-hound ticket. It's pricey, but I've done the research. I've been saving up since my first summer. I've worked out everything."

Since his first summer. He's been planning this all along. And again, I shouldn't be surprised, but again, there's envy lodged in my chest.

"I wish I could cross again," I say. "Do it one more time."

Then I clear my throat. I'm thinking of Stella, but I'm also thinking of myself. Of the music Kim played for us at the Exchange. Of my fingers on the keys of the combo organ. Of Ferrell's hamburgers and red rain, and the new song I composed.

Archer is quiet for a while before he says, in that bad accent of his, "You always could, old chap."

"I can't."

"Sure. Sure. Fair enough." He claps me on the back. "Anyway, don't you have work to get to?"

I do. We part ways there on the steps.

The Moonglow is nothing but rapid chops and sizzling oil. I don't want to think. I only want to work. I'm working until someone tells me to stop.

Then Mac swings into the kitchen, eyes big.

"It's crazy in there," he says. "Some people are *crying*."

This gets him a round of "What?" from the rest of us.

I can tell it's bad news, because Mac looks freaked.

I think it's about town. I think it's about the weather. I think it's about something that doesn't affect me.

So I'm not expecting it when, red in the face, he says, all excited, "Elvis Presley died."

22

Stella

TUESDAY, AUGUST 16

The sky remains cloudless. Slater is quieter than usual. It's waiting, ready for the worst though hoping for the best—that the unexplainable weather is over and, regardless of who or what is to blame, life has resumed its normal course. It's only a hope, because the countdown has not disappeared from town hall. The violet numbers keep ticking off on the inside of my closet door. I check each night and am greeted by the faint glow of the shifting right-hand minute:

03:03:24

03:03:23

03:03:22

On Monday, Kim called my house to say she'd set aside some records at the Exchange she thought will interest Galliard. I did not mention that I haven't seen Galliard since we kissed and I fled. I've told myself that, if Galliard wants to talk about it, he knows where to find me.

But I'm not sure if I can be found. I'm not sure of who I am anymore. The project is gone, and my plans for the salon—a better system, a better job—have been destroyed along with it.

I didn't do anything. I didn't yell at Jill or tell my father. I threw the strips of paper away, and I placed the parts of the project that could be salvaged back into the wicker bin. I haven't spoken to Jill since. Monday night I merely fixed her dinner, set it on the kitchen counter, and locked myself in my room. I cannot see her right now, cannot speak to her—not because of the damage she caused, but because she *knows*. She knows I've considered the possibility of leaving her, and my resulting guilt is all-consuming.

I don't know what I've been playing at for the past week. How did that countdown in my closet ever make me feel *free*? I should have felt terrified. Why did I think this weather gave me permission to lose control? I should have been more cautious than ever before. I realize now, I've been treating the possible end of the world like a game. I thought I was only make-believing *That Stella*'s life, and now I am facing very real consequences.

I am seeing something that I've been blind to for two long years. It is the answer to my biggest question. It is the reason why my brother left us.

Craig was *This Stella* first. He played the role of older sibling, parent, caretaker, confidant. Then, when he left, he surrendered the job to me. When Craig left, *I* made dinner, and *I* shopped for Jill. I did all the things that he'd been doing before.

I know now, though, what I didn't at age fifteen, when I first stepped into these worn work shoes. I see what he could only see after years in this role: There's no way out. You either accept your place in the family, or you abandon the post altogether. There can be no in-between. You must choose. And at eighteen, the age I'm about to be, Craig chose to abandon us. He chose what was worst for us and best for him. I think he felt he had to, as strongly as I feel that I must stay. Mom left the post first, and then Craig, and now it's down to me. I'm the only one Jill has left.

It's time for me to snap out of it. I'm returning to the skin of *This Stella*, a girl who knows her place and what is prudent. It's time to right my wrongs. And if that clock really is counting down to apocalypse, I only hope I can do what I need to before time runs out.

On Tuesday, Vine Street Salon has a full load of clients. Women who canceled last week are now bravely venturing out for their rescheduled (and overbooked) appointments. It would have been the perfect time to try out my project.

I try not to think that way. I take down names and brook the sighs of Connie's annoyed clients. It's what *This Stella* must do.

When work is over, I do not bike home straightaway. Instead I walk farther east down Vine to the town's one pay phone, located in front of Belmont Electronics. I take out a folded paper from my jeans pocket, along with a dime for the call.

I was wrong to consider Gayle's offer—that's clear now. Calling her Sunday night was an act of frenzied weakness. I'm not *That Stella* anymore, and the fact is, I should be angry at Gayle. Very angry.

Gayle Nelson does not know me. She does not know the life I live. She may think she is helping, may consider herself some savior come to rescue me from my blue-collar life so that one day I can be the first female astronaut and thank her profusely in a bestselling autobiography. She may think that, but she is wrong. She doesn't know that we Mercers cannot take another departure. She does not know how much Jill needs me. She doesn't even know if I could cut it in an engineering program. If anyone thought that, they would've told me by now. But none of my high school science or math teachers ever took me aside and told me what a good job I was doing. None of them told me I should consider a field in science or technology. They gave me As, and I left their classes, and that was that. Not even my guidance counselor put up a fight when I told him I planned to stay in town and work full-time at the salon. *They* are the people who would know if I am qualified to make it in college, and not a single one of them told me I could.

I pay the phone my dime and dial Gayle's number, praying that she will not answer.

She does, after two rings.

"Gayle Nelson, Slater Creek."

I am struck silent. I'd forgotten how Gayle speaks, confident and familiar, and like a chain-smoker. Something in her voice makes me want to cry.

"Hello?" says Gayle. "Hello?"

"It's Stella. Stella Mercer."

"Stella? Well, hey! How are you? I'm so sorry I haven't returned your call yet. See, I've been trying to work out some things with KU before I got back in touch."

"I didn't know this was your work phone. I don't want to bother—"

"Uh-uh, no bother. Happy to talk."

I am silent. I am trying to form the words. I need to tell her. I need to stop this—even the chance. It has to be dead. An impossible thing. Maybe once it is, I won't feel short of breath.

"Listen," Gayle says, "I want to apologize. I realize I overstepped my bounds by bringing this up to your father, but I truly believe—"

"No, *no*. I don't want you to apologize. I—I changed my mind. I can't do it."

"Oh."

I want her to say more. I want Gayle to tell me she understands, even if she is disappointed. I *need* her to understand. I feel the way I did the night she was over for dinner—as though I mustn't let her down.

I clutch the phone hard to my face, to keep my hand from trembling, and say, "I have to stay here, with my family."

"I respect that, Stella, but—"

"You won't convince me. I've thought it through, and I've made up my mind for good this time."

I turn my teary face toward the storefront windows and away from passing cars. That is when I see the color image flash up on the five display televisions of Belmont Electronics: David Brinkley of NBC news, solemn-faced, his words muted by the glass. To his left is the photograph of an all-too recognizable face, and beside that are the words *Elvis Presley, 1935–1977*.

I swallow. I swallow again.

"Stella?" says Gayle.

"I—sorry, I've got to go."

I hang up before she can reply.

"Oh my God," I say, gripping the phone where it rests on its cradle. "Oh my God."

I hear jingling bells, but I'm too absorbed in my attempt to lip-read David Brinkley's report. I do not see Tom Whalen, the manager at Belmont Electronics, until he is a mere two feet from me, saying my name.

I cry out and stumble back, but he does not apologize. There is urgency in his voice.

"What're you doing out, Stella? Didn't you hear there's a tornado warning?"

He must see that I am not processing his words, because he repeats them, slower. "There's a tornado warning out for Slater."

I look to the sky. It's grown cloudy, and I only now become aware that the world around me is blanketed under green haze, eerie and ominous. I've seen this several times before. It is a charged green stink discoloring earth and sky and everything in between. The times I've seen it, it's been April or May— tornado season, not late summer. The clouds have rolled in fast, eating up the blue sky. It is a storm from nowhere.

I step away from Tom Whalen. I grab my bike, mount, and begin to pedal. He is calling after me to come back, to take shelter right away, because the man on the radio says touch-down is imminent. I do not go back, though. I do not take shelter.

I have to get home to Jill.

Instinct carries me, leading me down Vine and left on Oak and past house after house. Dogs howl and whimper in yards; the birds are deathly quiet. My wheels rotate in loud, rapid *tickticktick*s. I pedal harder, and harder. From above, thunder claps across the sky.

Jill will be all right. Jill notices everything first. She will have heard the broadcast on the radio and already taken shelter. She will be all right, she will, she *will*, and I will get home to her and hug her close and be her safety. I will be *This Stella* for her. I will be the sister she needs me to be.

When I turn the corner onto our street, I look up. Congregated in the sky are a host of black clouds, and from them a slender funnel has emerged. I brake, going perfectly still, and watch as the funnel lengthens, forming a tether down to the earth. Wind roars around me, whipping my hair into my face. The twister cannot be more than a half mile away, in cornfield territory.

I push energy back into my legs and I pedal even harder than before, to my house. I abandon my bike in the driveway and run for the house, stumbling on the first of the porch steps, then lunging toward the door, throwing it open with enough force to crack the storm door. I keep running. I run into the hall, shouting Jill's name.

She answers me from the bathroom.

"Here! In here!"

She is sitting in the tub, radio clutched to her chest.

I slam the bathroom door shut behind me and crawl in beside her. Then I do what my arms have been itching to do this whole time and wrap them around her, tight. Jill is not crying or shaking. I am doing both.

"I'm fine," she tells me, straining her neck against my grip. "This is the safest place in the house."

I realize then that Jill is not listening to weather updates, but to jazz music.

"Elvis died," she whispers.

"I know," I say, dismissive, distracted by a thumping sound I hear overhead.

A train is speeding toward us. We are on the tracks, and the engine chugs on an inexorable path to where we sit.

"Just pass," I whisper into Jill's hair. "Just pass, just pass us by."

An image slices into my mind, white hot. It is of Galliard and Archer and their friends, huddled together at Red Sun. Craig once wrote that the commune had built a fallout shelter. He told me that, I think. I *think*, though my brain is pounding so hard I cannot be sure. Only what if Galliard does not even know about the tornado? What if no one is listening to their radio, or what if he is out in the fields? And does he know yet about Elvis? Does that death mean to Galliard what he claimed it would mean? How is he? Where is he? Will he be okay?

"It isn't fair," I say out loud. My voice echoes, accusatory, on the bathtub tiles. "It can't be now; there's time on the countdown. I still have time to make things right."

"What're you talking about?"

I don't answer Jill.

The chugging train is on top of us, and Jill turns tense in my arms. Her hand grabs for something and lands on my ankle. Our toothbrush holder rattles across the sink, then falls and crashes against the tile, breaking into a dozen pieces.

We do not scream. We only clutch tighter at each other as the thundering *clack-clack-clack* turns deafening.

I expect to faint, or to black out, or simply to cease being. But the tornado does not tear us from our hiding place.

It passes.

It thunders on, and the sound of the chugging engine grows fainter and fainter.

Jill exhales against my chest, and I hear the serenade of a bright saxophone coming from the radio.

Then Jill looks up at me.

"I have something to tell you," she says. "I guess you already know."

I start to laugh.

I laugh and laugh, and I cannot stop.

Though Jill's brow creases, she is undeterred. "I ripped them up. I ripped up your plans."

"I know."

"I did it. I broke everything."

"I know."

"I was angry. You should've told me."

I stop laughing. "I know."

"And I'm not a baby. I can take care of myself."

"Jill, I know."

My response is on instinct, but I realize right after I say it that it's not true.

I don't believe Jill can take care of herself. That is why I am staying here. That is why I will be *This Stella* until the end of the world.

Jill turns stiff in my embrace.

A real sleuth. She knows the truth too.

23

Galliard

TUESDAY, AUGUST 16

When it comes to negative energy, you can only handle so much before your body turns off. Goes numb. Won't let you feel a thing.

At least that's how it works for me.

Even as we sit huddled in the shelter, waiting for the tornado to pass, I'm not scared. And I'm not trying to be a jackass about it either. I'm not saying I am oh-so-brave or enlightened beyond the fear of death. It's just *too much* down here in the claustrophobic dark, and so I stop feeling. That's when I begin to see things with a new kind of clearness.

Elvis is dead. Another flame of energy snuffed out too soon. A new star to add to my collection.

A tornado is ripping through Slater—another strange and unexplainable event, right when we were ready to say the bad things were over. Right when I've been doing everything *right*. Or at least I thought I was.

And as I sit here, shoved between Archer and Mac on a bunk in the fallout shelter, I figure something out:

I could live here. I could make it work. I could be content, for the sake of the greater good. For the unity of the community and our fellowship with the Life Force.

I could live here.

But I don't want to die here.

I say it out loud:

"I don't want to die here."

"None of us do, man," says Archer.

He doesn't get it, though.

It's not that I don't want to *die* here.

I don't want to die *here*.

If I'm going to die early like my gods, I don't want it to be locked inside gates, where my music has to be a hobby. Where I can't hear and see and drink in the new sounds the Outside has to offer. I don't want it to be in here, with pricks like Phoenix, who care more about their own happiness than anyone else's existence. I want it to be out there, with people like Stella Kay Mercer, who have been hurt and tossed around by the Outside but still look at the sky. Who take risks—like kissing me.

I don't want to die *here*.

I won't.

Even if it means breaking rules.

Even if it means defying the Council itself.

When the storm passes and I find myself *not dead*, I know what I have to do. After the damage is accounted for—uprooted crops, but every resident safe thanks to our shelter—we are ordered into our rooms for the evening.

I break curfew.

I leave Heather House after midnight, through the bedroom window, while Archer is sleeping.

I make my way across the dark commune paths, feeling more ghost than human. Though the storm is over and the twister gone, a warm damp hangs in the air, and I push through it as though I'm pushing through wet gauze. I open the back door of Common House. I walk inside, take a seat on the piano bench. I lift the lid from the Yamaha's keys and I place a sheet of paper against the stand.

I play my new song, the one inspired by the Outside. Little by little, I work out the chord progressions for verse and chorus, making careful notes as I go, with a pencil. I take my time, searching the keys, playing past mistakes and miscalculations until an identifiable sound emerges. I don't speak the lyrics at first. I build the melody until it's strong, pumped full of lifeblood. And when the music takes me there, I hum at first, then sing softly, then let my voice swell with the chords.

I feel brave again, like that first night of the red rain. I know now, without a doubt, that *this* is what my gods have wanted from me. I'm no longer Galliard. The music transports me, transforms me. I'm not Galliard; I am the music. A song is never just a song.

It's as if dredging up his words has summoned him here, because when I open my eyes, I see him in my periphery. Rod is standing a yard off, watching me.

My hands jolt off the keys, as though they've been electrically zapped. I shrink back, staring at Rod's shadowy figure. It's dark in here; the only light comes from a half moon shining through Common House's windows, and the expression on Rod's face is obscured. My guess is he's not happy.

"What are you doing here, Galliard?" he asks.

His voice is low. And definitely, *definitely* not happy.

"Couldn't sleep," I say. "The twister . . . it freaked me out."

"That's no reason to disobey an order."

"Maybe not." Then, because I'm feeling fearless, I ask, "What are *you* doing here, Rod?"

He's quiet, and I'm half convinced he's going to punch me square in the jaw—so much so that when he steps closer, I flinch. He doesn't hit me, though. His arms are crossed. The moonlight catches more of his face, clean-shaven but grooved around the mouth and eyes. He seems to be suffering from his own brand of insomnia.

My flinch is followed by a tic, my jaw jolting to the right.

"What happened today was . . . unsettling," he says. "I understand."

"Yeah, I guess that tornado was the Outside's fault. Pretty crazy, huh? Turns out they can control the weather."

I'm shocking myself. I know I shouldn't say what I'm saying, but it's coming out of my mouth anyway. It's like the music has made me drunk.

The grooves around Rod's eyes get deeper. "No one controls the weather, but we humans *affect* it."

"Reckless living." I elaborate for him, my jaw still jerking. "Waste, excessive consumption. That's what you're saying."

"Yes." Rod's voice is hard as iron. "That's what I'm saying. And you act as though you don't believe it."

I shrug. My jaw jerks. I play middle C. Then E. Then G. My fingers rest on the chord.

"You know what I think, Rod?" I say. "I think they're not too different from us. You talk about how selfish everyone is out there. I dunno, though. Maybe we're selfish too. Maybe we're just as bad."

"That's not—"

"Think about it," I interrupt. "You blame them as much as they blame us. Seems neither side can throw their hands up and say they don't know why the hell any of this stuff is happening. Because someone's always got to be wrong, huh?"

"Galliard. You're not—"

"No, no." I butt in again. I am gloriously intoxicated on the C chord. My fingers shift down the keyboard to play A minor. "I've been thinking it through, Rod. About why you and Phoenix screwed me over. About why you said I'd make a good leader. And here's what I think: It's bullshit. All of it. I have what it takes to be resident artist. A song isn't just a song, and you know that. Songs are dangerous. They make you feel things. New things. They make you brave. And you don't like that, do you, Rod? That's why you stopped the new music. That's why you shut down the imports. That's why you chose Phoenix for resident artist: because he was a safe choice. A recent convert, someone who hates the Outside as much as you.

"And this bull about me making a good leader? You don't really think that. You never noticed me until I started Crossing. Galliard, the kid who was born in the commune, the kid who was so infatuated with Red Sun he didn't even have to *try* the Outside. And all of a sudden he's leaving, exploring. That wouldn't do, would it? You realized you'd pushed me too far.

That's why you came up with this leader bullshit to reel me back in. To hold it over my head, something to aspire to instead of Crossing. Because if I kept Crossing, if I *left*, that wouldn't be great for your image: born-and-bred Galliard ditching Red Sun for good."

My chest aches deep down. I feel I've been purged, like some clinging parasite has finally been expelled from my body. I feel weak, but in a good way—the way I do after taking a long walk in the sun. I'm staring at Rod, brazen. I don't even care that, in the wake of my long, loud speech, I am ticking. I clear my unclearable throat, then clear it again. I don't even care.

"I had no idea," Rod says, quiet and still. "No idea you'd been this corrupted. That the Outside would work on you this quickly. That you would be this malleable. I'm . . . disappointed in you, Galliard."

"What?" I say between throat clears. "What, am I *weak*? Is that what you're going to say, Rod? Because you know who I think's weak? People who hide inside here instead of facing the real world. I went out there. And yeah, parts of it are bad. Parts of it are absolutely shitty. But they have music and stories and futures we don't. That's worth the shitty parts. That's what I'm starting to think. And I don't give a damn if you call that weak."

"It's *ignorance*!" Rod shouts into the dark. "That's what it is, boy. It is *willful ignorance*. How do you think that music is made? How do you think those futures are achieved? By standing on the back of Mother Nature. By grinding down your fellow man so *you* come out on top. That is everything Red Sun was founded to combat. It is everything we are *against*. And you want that. You want to be one of them."

"Maybe I do!" I shout back. "At least out there I won't be forced into a fucking kitchen."

"You don't think *they* will force you? Look at yourself, Galliard. You're a young man with no experience on the Outside. No formal training. No connections, no money. You think this Outside of yours will welcome you with open arms? Especially with your condition."

Rod knows he's said the wrong thing. I see the regret on his moonlit face. Only I don't think it's regret for making me feel like shit. It's regret for pushing me a little too far. Because he has pushed me. My chest is fiery with shame . . . and also with anger. My throat produces sound, low and visceral.

"What the fuck do you know about my *condition*?" I'm on my feet, my chords forgotten. "I can handle myself fine, thanks. I know *good* people on the Outside. People better than me. People who wouldn't use my *condition* to win a fucking argument. Don't you talk to me about—"

"I only meant that the world can be unkind, Galliard. Unkind to *anyone*. Take your friend Phoenix, and what he experienced before he—"

"He's not my friend," I spit out. "And I don't know what happened to him before this place, because he won't talk about it. He won't even talk to his own sister, who's the best damn human alive."

I know I'm saying too much. I don't care. I'm drunk again. I'm rip-roaring, over-the-top, burn-the-bridges drunk on this moment.

"You can keep your Red Sun and your *positive consequences*. And Phoenix can keep his fucking resident-artist position. Me? I'm going someplace else. Somewhere I can breathe."

And I mean that in many ways, because I really do need to *breathe*. I need to be out of this room. I make for the door, and I clatter down the steps, and I don't let up. I run and run toward Heather House, past dark shadows and phantom lights. I climb through the window with less grace than before, toppling onto the floor so loud that I wake Archer.

My bones are burning with resolve. I know this fire will calm if I don't speak. It's better to say this now, forgetting everything else. Forgetting Rod and Phoenix and Ruby and J. J. and the reasons that will come pouring back into my head in the morning.

There's a new god in the sky. A king, recently arrived. He's calling to me, in his immortal voice. He's singing, *It's now or never*. He's saying, *You better run*.

Archer stares at me, half-asleep, disgruntled. "What the hell's going on, man?"

I don't hesitate. I ask the question.

"Think there's room on that Greyhound?"

24

Stella

There is a dark, thick line that rips across our roof. It is a testament to shingles torn from their places. It is the handprint of a twister.

I stand in the front yard with my father and Jill, surveying the damage.

Dad came home early last night, within an hour of the tornado's passing. He won't go back to work today. I don't think anyone in Slater intends to. Not after this. Some of our neighbors stand on their lawns too, taking in the sight of broken branches that litter our street.

We now know the details of what happened. There was one distinct tornado, which touched down on multiple occasions. It was relatively weak. Most of the damage was to farmland, resulting in uprooted cornstalks peppered on rooftops down Vine Street. There were a dozen moderate injuries— broken bones and one reported concussion—but no casualties. The system formed over and damaged only the town of Slater. Surrounding towns reported mild wind and thunder, nothing more.

Today the sky is clear and the sun bright. There is no indication that more foul weather will follow. Then again, we've been fooled before, and the countdown over town hall continues to run.

01:14:24.

One day until the unknown end.

That's why we won't be going to work. We'll be going to the town meeting tonight, and then, most likely, we will be barricading ourselves in our houses.

More people have fled town until further notice. Most of us, though, have chosen to remain. We will not abandon Slater. Not even us loner Mercers. This is the only home we know.

Dad keeps me and Jill at the house. Even when we head inside, sobered by the sight of our street and the knowledge that we have no money to pay for the damage, he won't let us out of his sight. Jill tunes in to 580 AM, where our tornado has actually been acknowledged. The announcer reports minimal damage, no deaths. Only I can't help wondering if that report includes Red Sun. If any town officials have checked on them. If everyone is all right there.

If *Galliard* is all right.

I want to know for myself. I want to pedal my bike out full force until I reach the Red Sun gate, and to climb it if need be. I can't leave my father's sight, though—can't even go to the bathroom without him asking about it. And I *wouldn't* leave Jill. Not now. I promised that when the bad things came, I'd be here. So I stay. And together we wait for the town meeting.

• • •

"Isn't this a job for the National Guard? Why are we paying our damned governor if he won't protect us?"

The auditorium of Slater's town hall is packed to overflow. I sit between my father and sister in a row of seats toward the back, which was the best we could manage, even after arriving an hour early. It seems that every single citizen of Slater, young and old, is crammed inside these walls.

People are frightened. They are terrified. After only fifteen minutes of what Mayor Branum calls an "open forum," the conversation has descended into a mess of shouting and finger-pointing. The question most people want answered is not what we should do in case of a more severe emergency, but rather who is to blame for what's already happened.

According to Lewis Tate, one of Slater's two dentists, this is the government's fault.

"It's their job to protect us!" He waves wildly at us with calloused hands. "They say they'll secure our life and liberty and pursuit of happiness, when that fool of a peanut farmer is in the Oval Office giving *us* lectures on how to use our petroleum. Why hasn't anyone from the FBI come to investigate is what I want to know. No one can explain those damned numbers!"

"Yes, thanks, Lewis. Thanks for that." Mayor Branum speaks into a thin microphone hooked up on the auditorium's raised platform. Even so, he has to shout to be heard. "Thanks, Lewis, but we're going to hear from someone else now! Uh, yes, John? John Barkley, I've seen your hand up for some time."

I crane my neck to see Pastor Barkley, who stands several rows ahead. He's placed his hand over his heart, as though readying to pledge allegiance. His voice booms through the room.

"I've said my piece to my own congregation, and I've said it before in this very room. So I will only take a minute more of you good folks' time. I think the Lord Almighty has made clear his displeasure at the sins of the libertines who reside among us."

I think of Galliard and grind my fingers into my palms.

"You've asked us to voice our concerns, Grant," he continues, facing the mayor. "You've also asked us to recommend a plan of action. My plan relies not on the strength of men but the power of God. We do not need the National Guard. We need broken and contrite spirits. We must examine ourselves, and we must repent, and above all else, we must expel the wicked from among us!"

"Aw, fuck that!" shouts a rough voice in the crowd. "It's the Reds who're responsible! This whole time we've been expecting 'em to drop nukes, they've been studying how to alter our air supply. And we're the first experiment, because no one cares about a town like Slater. We're the first to go, but mark my words: Next comes Chicago and Los Angeles and New York City!"

"That's enough now," Mayor Branum begins, when an awful blare of feedback shoots through the room, temporarily silencing him.

"It's aliens!" screams a woman behind me. Her face is

gaunt and bright scarlet from exertion. "We've disturbed their space with our rockets, and now they've come for retribution. They're coming for us!"

This is enough to send the crowd into an uproar. People start shouting for the woman to sit down and stop with the conspiracy theories, while others yell in agreement, claiming to have seen strange lights in the sky this month. Others call out about their dogs acting funny and sensing ghostly presences at night and how the government must be conducting experiments at the Slater Creek plant.

Mayor Branum keeps slamming his fists on the lectern, for lack of a gavel. Sheriff Allen runs onstage and grabs the microphone, yelling for everyone to calm down, and they will listen to everyone's concerns and proposals one at a time. It is clear, however, that this crowd is beyond calming.

What happens next is difficult to explain. It isn't that everything goes dark, more that everything goes *dim*. The overhead lights remain on, but the daylight that's been spilling through the auditorium windows suddenly vanishes. The glass panes turn black, as though it is three o'clock in the morning, not six o'clock on a summer night.

The sudden change turns everyone silent for one solitary moment.

Then a man screams, "It's happening! *They're here!*"

He does not specify who "they" are—aliens or Soviets or punishing angels or government agents or some other, unnameable monster. In the end it does not matter. What matters is that whoever "they" are, they are real and present, and they are sending the crowd into a frenzy.

Everyone around us is on their feet, pushing and jostling. Immediately I grab Jill's hand, and she grabs my father's, and we share a breathless, panicked look.

"Come on." Dad draws us both behind him. "Hang on to me, both of you."

He begins to push through the crowd, shouting above even the loudest shouts, "Get out of the way! *Get out of our way!*"

His voice cuts through my skin, down to my bone. I did not know my father could speak that loud, or with such confidence, and I wonder, even as I am fighting to stay upright and protect my sister from trampling feet and jabbing elbows, if he has picked up some of that confidence from Gayle.

There's a painful tug on my hand. Jill has stumbled and is trying to right herself. A man in overalls shoves into her, knocking her off balance again. The tension between my other hand and my father's grows taut. Then Jill is fully on her feet again and back in my keeping, and I see the reason why: Galliard stands beside her, a hand on her elbow, to be sure she is stable. His eyes catch mine.

"You okay?" he shouts.

Then Dad is at my side, asking me and Jill the same question, and it is more pushing and jostling and stumbling until we burst out of town hall's doors and into fresh air.

Though I cannot be sure it is fresh air. I cannot be sure of anything out here, because the sun, which should be out for another two hours, has vanished. The sky is tar black. There is no moon; there are no stars. Vine Street's lamps are on, shedding light on the shouting, running masses. Car engines rev to life, and headlights spill across the street. There are frantic footsteps all around us, beating into the pavement.

My father leads us toward the station wagon, parked farther down Vine, in front of the salon. He says nothing, only walks forward in determined strides. I look around for Galliard, but he's disappeared. Then a hand slips from mine.

"Jill!" I shout.

She's stopped in place and is pointing at the storefront of Belmont Electronics. The display televisions are broadcasting the news, live. A woman is interviewing people congregated outside Graceland, in mourning for Elvis Presley. They are not cast in darkness. The sun shines bright over Memphis, Tennessee.

I've been expecting this, I think. I already know there is no other town in the country under this cloud of darkness—only Slater. Still, the sight holds me in place. Even my father is motionless, eyes fixed on the screens.

The sound of shattering glass breaks our trance. I grip Jill's shoulder, and we watch as two men, no younger than my father, break through the door of Mike's Hardware.

"Come on, girls." My father tugs on Jill's hand. "Quickly."

When we reach the car, he opens the door and motions us inside in jerky waves. I'm pushing Jill ahead of me, into the back seat, when I hear my name.

"Stella!"

It's Galliard, emerged from the crowd. Lamplight hits his face in a hard-shadowed glow. Archer is right behind him, and they both look as scared as I feel.

"What're you—" I begin, as Galliard says, "I had to—" and both of us fall into silence.

Dad is in the driver's seat and shouts through his open window. "Stell, get in this car, damn it!"

"I'm sorry." Galliard looks suddenly resigned. He takes a step away from me and motions limply toward the idling car. "Sorry, I—"

"Shut up. Shut up—you're coming home with us. Both of you, get in." I turn to my father. I do not ask a question. I say, "They're coming home with us."

Whatever his response, it's lost in what happens next.

"*You!*"

Pastor Barkley is lumbering toward us, a finger flung at me in accusation. Only, I realize, it is not me he is yelling at, but Galliard and Archer.

"Get out of here! Get out! How *dare* you set foot in our town!"

"What the hell?" mutters Archer, shuffling away from the pastor's approach.

Pastor Barkley is close enough that I can see the spittle fly from his lips as he shouts, "Get back to your people, boy. Get back to where you belong. It's because of you degenerates—"

"Hey, I don't even *know* you, man!" Galliard shouts over him.

Pastor Barkley's eyes widen with outrage. He's clearly not a man used to interruption.

"What's wrong with you?" I shout, drawing his irate gaze to me. "Really, what is *wrong* with you? What kind of person yells at him"—I throw a finger toward Galliard—"and *him*"—another at Archer—"when they're as scared as you are? This isn't their fault. This is *no one's fault.*"

I don't wait for Pastor Barkley's response. I grab Galliard by the elbow and drag him to the station wagon, bringing him into the back seat after me. Archer throws open the passenger door, but before he can shut it behind him, Pastor Barkley grabs the handle and rips it back open.

"Expel the immoral man from among you!" he yells, then slams the door, knocking Archer in the knee.

"Fucking *fuck*!" howls Archer, as Dad hits the gas and drives us out of there, into the growing traffic on Vine Street.

"Girls," he says, "lock the doors back there."

"What's 'fuck'?" asks Jill.

Archer grimaces apologetically.

"No, it's okay," says Jill. "I've heard it before. I just want to know what it means."

"It means 'ow.'"

Jill frowns. She knows Archer isn't telling the truth. Crossing her arms, she presses her feet into the back of his seat.

"Who are these people?" she asks, throwing Galliard a sour look.

Galliard is jerking his jaw in a sharp, convulsive way that can only mean it's a tic.

"This is Galliard," I say. "And that's Archer. They're members of Red Sun. They're out for Crossing."

"Well," says Archer, "technically we're breakouts."

"What?"

"They stopped Crossing," says Galliard. "They said it was too dangerous."

"You should've listened to them." My father is gripping the steering wheel so tight I think it will shatter. His eyes are fixed on the road ahead as he makes the turn from Vine onto Lucille Street.

"I know, sir," Galliard says.

"But you were worried about my daughter?"

I sink deep into the middle seat. I close my eyes, and all I see is Pastor Barkley's rabid face.

"I—I was, sir."

"I wasn't," offers Archer.

My father drives on. Houses fly past. He must be going at least fifty miles per hour.

"Uh," said Archer. "We left our bikes back there. On Vine Street?"

"Did you chain them up?" Dad asks.

"Yeah."

"Then you can pray they won't be stolen. But we're not going back for them now."

"Why was Pastor Barkley yelling?" Jill asks me. "He looked crazy."

"He *is*."

"Really?"

"No," I say, after some more thought. "No, Jill. He isn't crazy; he's scared. He's a scared man."

Jill shoves her heels harder into Archer's back. He shifts to the seat's front edge, one hand on the dash to balance himself, but that doesn't do much good when Dad swings into our driveway, sending all of us in the back seat toppling onto one another. When I right myself, Dad is already out of the car and opening Jill's door.

"Out," he commands. "Into the house."

When I crawl out after Jill, starting to speak, my father shakes his head.

"Explain later. For now, I'm not leaving anyone out in . . . *this*."

I lead Galliard and Archer up the porch steps and into the house, where Jill has already turned on 580 AM. She sits on the den floor, legs crossed under the coffee table, listening in the dark. She shushes us when we enter the room, despite the fact that none of us are talking.

I switch on the floor lamp and sit beside her. Galliard and Archer take cautious seats on the sofa.

". . . reports of two vehicular accidents, one involving a tractor out on Old Pike Road. Again, if you're just now tuning in, this is Jim Goddard at 580 KZM, and we're using the station as a temporary emergency bulletin for the little town of Slater. That's right, city dwellers, you probably hadn't even heard of this blip of Kansan farmland until recently, when the town made local news after experiencing mysterious red rain showers. That's right, *red rain*. There have also been reports of unusual thunderstorms, and last night a tornado ripped through town, causing crop damage. Well, ladies and gentlemen, that's not all. We're getting reports there's been some kind of blackout in town. What? What's that? Sorry, I'm being told it's not your *average* blackout. It's—sorry, I'm being told that the electricity's working; it's the *sky* that's—what? Joe, the hell I will. This some kind of joke?"

"No!" Jill shouts at the radio. "It's not a joke!"

My father comes in from the garage, crank lantern in hand.

"Just in case," he says, setting it beside the sofa. "Did you lock up the front?"

I nod, but he's already left to double-check.

The skeptical Jim Goddard talks on. "We're being told that a kind of . . . uh, *black sky* has fallen over Slater. No reports yet as to how far this perpetual night has reached, but hey, folks, why don't you take off those sunglasses. Might not need 'em much longer. And for all you sci-fi freaks, you might wanna hitch a ride down to Slater, as there are some eyewitness accounts of UFOs. Beam me up, Scotty! What? Yes, I know what an emergency bulletin is, you bastard. I'm working with what I've got typed in front of me. If I find out you've been pranking me on air, I . . . fine, I'll read the damn thing. Yeah, if you're just now tuning in, this is Jim Goddard at 580 KZM, and we're using the station as a—"

"Some bulletin," says Jill. "How is that helpful? We *know* it's dark."

"Keep it on," I tell her. "They may get some useful information."

Jill turns down the volume until Jim Goddard's voice is a dull drone.

I look at Galliard. Only now am I feeling the weight of his presence here.

Galliard is sitting in my house. The last time I saw him, we were kissing. Only that doesn't matter much anymore. That memory seems so faint and silly compared to what is happening now.

His eyes catch mine, shining dark in the lamplight. Night

surrounds us, but the crickets do not chirp outside. Everything is serene, a calm before a storm. I know it is cliché to think this way. It's trite and highly irrational. Still, I cannot help believing that for all the bad luck that has befallen this town, we are lucky to be in this room together, safe with each other, even if we're hurtling toward danger.

The phone rings. Jill hops up and races toward the kitchen. I hurry in after her.

"Mercer residence! Yes? Oh. Oh, okay, here she is."

Jill thrusts the phone into my stomach and runs back to the den. My heart's beating fast. Who would be calling me now?

"Hello?"

"Stella? Stella, hello! This is Mr. Cavallo. Mr. Cavallo from the Dreamlight."

"Uh . . . Hi, Mr. Cavallo. Is everything okay?"

"What? Oh, sure. Sure, things are fine. Who turned out the lights, though?" Mr. Cavallo laughs here, like he is talking about an episode of *The Carol Burnett Show* and not the fate of Slater, Kansas. "Listen, kid, you may have seen my posters around town. Meant to call you about it earlier."

"Sorry, no. What posters?"

"About my end-of-the-world showing!" Mr. Cavallo laughs again, and I am starting to worry. "If those numbers over town hall are to be believed, we don't have much time left. That's why I'm planning a little shindig at the Dreamlight for zero hour. A last midnight showing of *Star Wars* tomorrow night. Was planning on it before this confounded blackout, but the show must go on, huh? At least we've got our electricity."

"Mr. Cavallo, I don't know if that's a good idea. . . ."

"What? No, no, it's the best idea I've had in my life, kid! See, if it *isn't* the end of the world, then I've got to recoup some money from these rainy-night losses. And if it *is* the end of the world, isn't it best to go out in style?"

I don't have an answer for that.

Mr. Cavallo goes on. "I need some folks to help out, though, as always. Wondered if you'd be willing to run concessions."

"I . . . Mr. Cavallo, it's nice of you to ask, but I don't think I can."

Mr. Cavallo sighs heavily into the receiver. "Well. *Well.* I figured you might say that. Parents concerned about safety and all. Rather be with the family. Thought I'd at least ask."

"I hope it goes well," I say, unsure of what else would be appropriate.

"It promises to be! I tell you what, Stella, we're living in a B movie here in Slater. It's something else."

"It sure is, Mr. Cavallo. It's something else."

"What did he want?" asks Jill, when I return to the den.

I tell them about Mr. Cavallo and the midnight showing. Jill says, "But that sounds fun! Why won't you go?"

"Because Dad wouldn't approve. And because I can't leave you, and I definitely wouldn't take you with me. It's not safe."

Jill grumbles and turns up Jim Goddard on the radio.

It is that little thing—Jill ticking up the radio volume—that stirs something inside me. I recognize the feeling. I know what it is: an inspiration.

I slip out of the den and into my bedroom, shutting the door behind me. Then I pull out the wicker bin from beneath my bed. It is a wreckage site—fragments of plastic and now-useless batteries, circuit boards exposed. Jill was thorough in her damage, taking care to smash the body of each walkie-talkie. Only maybe, *possibly*, she wasn't thorough enough.

I set the bin on my desk, turn on the lamp, and take a seat. It may not work. It's only an idea, and sometimes ideas don't get you anywhere. Even so, this is something to do. A way to be useful with my hands and mind alike. I pull out the parts and begin to work.

June 5, 1977

Craig,

I've graduated high school. I didn't go to
the ceremony, so I suppose that's something
you and I have in common. If I <u>had</u> gone, I
would've had to give a salutatorian speech.
Nothing long—less than a minute's worth of
inspiration. Even though I knew I wouldn't
give it, I wrote one anyway:

<u>Let every one of us stay curious and</u>
<u>ask questions, even now that school is over.</u>
<u>Because scientists are curious, always</u>
<u>asking questions, and we are all scientists at</u>
<u>heart.</u>

It's mawkish. I'm sure you hate it. Let me
put it this way, though: You've written before
that not everyone can be an artist; some
people simply have an artistic <u>gift</u>. I suppose
that's true, in the same way professional
scientists must have a gift with numbers
and facts and figures. But don't you think
that, deep down, we're all born artists and
scientists? When we're children, we are
curious, and we see the beauty in the world

321

around us, and we laugh about it and clap our
hands, and we toddle off to find more of it.
Then somewhere, somehow that gets stomped
out. People tell us no, stop gawking, stop
asking your questions. So most of us stop.

We just stop.

I hope Jill never does. She is always on
the search for something. She drinks in her
mystery books like water. I love that about
her. She asks questions, and she has no shame.
I hope that stays with her, don't you?

Now I have to ask you something. I'll
understand if you say no. It's been two years,
though, and I miss you the same as ever. I
know you want to stay in there, but can't we
at least meet? I only want to see you face-to-
face. I want to remind myself you're real. I
want to know how you look and how your voice
sounds, and how you're getting on. You never
write about that. Nothing about your daily
life. I want to know those things, because
you're my brother, and

What can I say?

I'm curious.

Your sister,

Stella Kay

25

Galliard

WEDNESDAY, AUGUST 17

We make camp in the den. There are pillows, blankets, books, and also a big pitcher of bright orange sweet stuff that Stella calls Tang. Jill brings up the fact that there's not a whole lot of food in the kitchen. Mr. Mercer says there's plenty and there's no way we're going out At a Time Like This. People steal At a Time Like This. They get violent, even in small-town Slater, Kansas. That's what he tells us, and I believe it. I still feel pretty shaky about that purple-faced pastor yelling at me.

But the humor of the incident isn't lost on me.

It's really funny. I should've expected it:

The Outside blames the inside as much as the inside blames them. Maybe, if they could get over hating each other, Rod and that pastor would be the best of friends. Who knows. Maybe we're all to blame.

Maybe none of us are, but we're horrible people anyway.

I think this through a lot. I think a whole bunch there, in our camp. We spend long hours sitting, listening to the radio and watching television.

Slater is on national news, which seems to be a big deal.

The governor of Kansas has declared a state of emergency, which seems to be a bigger deal, and he's sent in the National Guard, which seems to be the biggest deal. Posts have been set up on the edges of the darkness, which encompasses the drive-in and Red Sun and even the Slater Creek Generating Station. They're not allowing anyone to enter or leave town. They're calling it a quarantine, because so far the darkness is only over Slater, and no one can be sure if what's happening in here is spreadable. No one knows much of anything.

On 580 AM, Jim Goddard has been replaced by a television news anchor—this guy named Charlie Bridges, from Kansas City—who brings on guest speakers. He talks to experts like meteorologists and university professors. He even interviews people off the street in an end-of-the-hour segment he calls "A Word from the People."

"It's the end of times," says an elderly woman, "and it's beginning right here in Kansas. The chosen are gonna be raptured to the sky; we're gonna be taken out of wicked Babylon. Now's the time to repent, is what I say. Repent before the four horsemen come a-trottin' to your door."

"Charles," says a professional-sounding man. "I'll tell you what I've been telling everyone since '74: Nixon's to blame. I've no doubt what's happening in that town is the direct result of one of his undercover nuclear experiments gone wrong. And we should be worried. Not just us folks in Kansas City. This whole nation should be worried about what's to come. Who's next."

"These people are kooky," says Jill, and the kid couldn't be more right.

We keep on listening, though, because we've *got* to listen, and even if it's just more scientists saying they don't have an explanation, we keep on tuning in, trying to make sense of it all.

The only break in the Slater reports is the televised evening news. Elvis will be buried tomorrow. Cameras pan outside Graceland, where hundreds of people have gathered. If only they knew he's not in that coffin. Now he's in the sky, with the other gone-too-soon gods.

"Why go to all this trouble?" a reporter asks one of the mourners—a blond woman in big sunglasses.

"Because we love Elvis," she says, teared up. "We still do."

"You're not going to get in, you know," he says, the helpful asshole.

"Doesn't make any difference."

"Those people are kooky too," says Jill. "Everyone's kooky."

But I can't agree with her there.

It's my first time watching TV. The novelty of moving pictures on a screen has worn off fast, replaced by this awful ache in my chest. What's the point of moving pictures if all the pictures are sad?

I'm not numb the way I was during the tornado. I feel it now: It's a too-soon death of a too-talented musician who ended every one of my Back Room listening sessions. I'm not exactly surprised by Elvis's death; in a way, it feels like an inevitability. He was too big to live long, I guess, like Jimi, Janis, and Buddy. So it feels inevitable, but it still hurts like hell, and I'm relieved when the news report moves on to something called the Panama Canal. Eventually, Stella comes into the den (I don't know why she left it, or even *when*) and turns the TV off. Mr. Mercer, who's been watching with us on the sofa, stands up.

"I'm going out," he says. "To the plant."

"What!" Jill's on her feet. "You can't! Not At a Time Like This. *You* said so!"

"Gayle isn't answering her phone." Mr. Mercer says this to Stella. "I need to make sure she's all right."

"Okay. We'll be fine." That's what Stella says, even though she sure doesn't look fine.

Mr. Mercer kisses her on the head. He does the same to Jill.

"You better be back soon," she says, pouty. "Be back soon, okay?"

"As soon as I can."

Then Mr. Mercer gives us another lecture about staying in the house and how if there's an emergency we should take shelter in the bathroom, and how we're not to open the door for anyone.

When he leaves, Stella gets up and says, "Who's hungry?"

She fixes us a dinner of boxed, frozen foods that she heats inside an oven. The food looks bad, and it tastes even worse, but I'm not in any place to complain. Archer and I scarf down our meals with no comment save "thanks."

In case you're wondering at this point, Archer and I do have a plan. Or, more like Archer's plan, plus me. We're using our allowance money to buy tickets for that Greyhound bus, headed for Archer's aunt and uncle in Pasadena. He already called them from the pay phone on Vine Street, and they say they couldn't be happier that he's out of the commune. They say they'll help him start a new life.

We've got this plan, but Stella's part of it. Because I can't leave until I finally tell her everything. And *now* we can't leave because the government won't let us. It seems we're stuck waiting it out, eating from tinfoil trays. Waiting for California, or maybe waiting for the end.

The end of the world—that's what everyone's started calling it. And not just the kooks on the radio. I mean, come on, let's face the facts: There's a countdown over town hall telling everybody we're one day away from the unknown.

I don't have any explanations left.

I fall asleep, and when I wake, the phone is ringing. It's Mr. Mercer, who tells Stella he is at the plant with Gayle, but they've been put on lockdown until further notice, because of the darkness. When Stella tells us this, Jill tears up. Then the two of them don't talk about it again. I guess they're too upset. Or trying to be brave.

It's Thursday afternoon, not that you'd guess that from looking outside. It's as dark out as before. We keep listening to the radio, and we eat more tinfoil tray meals until there aren't any left.

Jill's been folding and unfolding a crumpled sheet of paper. It's this advertisement I saw posted on Vine Street yesterday, before the town meeting. It reads:

END OF WORLD SHOWING

MIDNIGHT, THURSDAY

DREAMLIGHT DRIVE-IN THEATRE

HELP USHER IN THE END OF TIMES WITH
A SPECIAL VIEWING OF *STAR WARS*

ADMISSION $5

"Why aren't you going?" Jill asks Stella, not for the first time. "It could be fun."

"It won't be fun," Stella says. "It'll be a bunch of loons, drunk and high and out of control. It won't be safe."

"You're *boring*," says Jill. "We're going to stay cooped in this house forever."

"Better to stay cooped in and stay alive."

"Nuh-*uh*. Better to have fun and get killed."

At which point Stella claims we can stay alive *and* have fun and asks if Jill wants to play one of her board games.

Like that, Jill forgets the end-of-the-world showing and runs to fetch a game called *Happy Days*, which is based on some fictional television show. She and Stella and Archer and I play three full rounds, and we make sure Jill wins every time.

The radio stays on. Time passes. Outside, it remains dark as midnight.

Jill falls asleep on the sofa, one arm draped around the radio. Archer falls asleep sitting upright in a rocking chair. Stella and I are awake, our backs to the coffee table, staring at the television's blank screen.

I nod toward Jill. "She's got strong opinions."

Stella smiles. "She's a detective-in-training. Craig used to call her Inspector Clouseau."

I don't know who Inspector Clouseau is, but I sure as hell know Craig. He's been the unspoken word between me and Stella this whole time. And this is it. We're alone, or as good as.

I've got to say it now.

"Stella. There's something I have to tell you."

"No. You don't." She shakes her head. "We can forget it happened. That kiss. I don't know why—"

"No, it's not—"

"And I already know about Craig."

Shit. She knows? I stare at her, petrified. Then I start to blink.

"You . . . do?"

"He told you he doesn't want to see me, right?"

Shit. She doesn't know. I blink, fast and hard.

"Stella," I say. "That's not—"

"Did he ever tell you why he left?"

"I . . . well, he said the Outside was a bad place. He said people here are selfish."

"That's it?"

I could tell her about Phoenix's rants. Rants about war and crime and financial depression, about double-dealing politicians and the uselessness of families and religion. But that's nothing Stella needs to hear. And anyway, I don't think it's what she's after.

So, blinking, I say, "Pretty much, yeah. That's it."

"He didn't tell you about Walt?"

I shake my head at the unfamiliar name.

Stella heaves out a sigh. She closes her eyes, and she doesn't open them again, even as she speaks. "He was our neighbor. Walt Metcalfe. He was older than Craig, so they didn't exactly hang out growing up. Walt got drafted in '69, and when he came back, he lived with his parents. He and Craig became friends then, when Craig was in high school. They hung out, started a lawn-care business together. Craig really looked up to him.

"A couple years back, in the spring, when the North Vietnamese took over Saigon—no one knew how much the news affected Walt. Craig went over to hang out, same as always. And they were in the Metcalfes' basement, talking, like nothing was wrong. And then Walt . . . He pulled out a shotgun from between the sofa cushions. And he shot himself. He shot himself right in the face."

I feel sick. I feel I might vomit on both my and Stella's shoes. She's crying, but she keeps on talking, pushing the words out like she doesn't have a choice. Meanwhile, I clear my throat, again and again.

"Craig passed out. I guess it was the shock. But the Metcalfes' collie, Major—he was there in the basement too. And he got upset and ran outside. The neighbors found him running in circles, going berserk. They caught up to him, and that's when they saw it all over his coat. There was blood and brain, and . . . and they called the cops and Mr. and Mrs. Metcalfe, and the whole street was full of police and firefighters. The lights were flashing the whole night long. And Craig left the next week."

"Stella. I'm—"

"So, I *know* why he left. And I know why he said the world is an awful place. I thought maybe he only needed time away, a year to heal, a chance to get his head straight. I thought he'd come back to us one day. He didn't, though, and it's clear to me now: From the very beginning, he meant to leave us for good. These two years, I've told myself that he left because of Walt, but that's not true. Walt was only a catalyst. Craig was unhappy before that. He was stuck here, in this family, in a role he didn't want. He didn't just leave; he left *me* to be what he couldn't. And I hate him for it. I hate what he did, and I need him to know that. I need him to say he's sorry for doing it wrong."

I want her to be okay. I want Stella to be okay, but I don't know how to help. I don't have the right to hug her or tell her it'll be fine. The only thing I can say is, "I'm sorry."

After what feels like minutes of silence—punctuated by my throat clears—she looks straight at me. Her face is wet and rumpled, shadow-cast in the dark den.

"The dog ran away," she says. "Major, the dog—after the neighbors called the police, they couldn't find him. He ran off, and they never tracked him down. The Metcalfes looked everywhere before they moved. People figured he got hit by a car out on a country road. That it was one more tragic thing to add to the list.

"But . . ." Stella grinds her knuckles into her jaw. She looks startled, almost wild. "*He came back*. I saw him, Galliard. I saw him dead, on the side of the road, almost three weeks ago. When the winds blew into town. When everything began. It was Major, I *know*. I just don't know what it *means*. I know it

331

can't be connected to the other strange things. That's absurd. It's completely unfounded. But . . . isn't life connected in weird ways? Like you and me, connected through Craig? Or how you and I were talking about Elvis a week ago, and now he's dead? And I know, I *know*, it's coincidence. It's not cause and effect. It's the same as horoscopes, how you start seeing the world a certain way, mystical and predictable, and that's ridiculous. But I can't get rid of the *feeling*. I've got this feeling deep down that if I see Craig now—just *see* him—it will all be over. The strangeness and the bad things, they'll finally stop."

"Stella." I say it slow, like a sentence, not a word. "I don't think that's how it works."

I want to tell her I understand, though. I've thought, like her, that this strange weather has had to do with what my gods want of me. But this isn't about me. It's about her, and her story, and I have no right to speak.

"I *know* that's not how it works. It's only a feeling; I told you."

She stands up suddenly and leaves the room. There's light from the kitchen, and rummaging, and the commotion wakes Archer, who sits up and blinks around.

"What's that?" he rasps. "What'd I miss?"

"Nothing." I stare at the light of the kitchen.

When Stella returns, she holds two glasses of water. "We need to stay hydrated," she says, setting the glasses down for me and for Archer, though it's clear she meant Archer's for herself. "We don't know what's going to happen next."

The Stella sitting here a minute ago is gone, and so is my chance.

The world outside is black, no stars in sight. Buddy isn't here to give me confidence. Jimi can't give me cool. And Janis can't give me the courage I desperately need.

Even so, I know what my gods want of me. I'll have to do it without them, on my own.

26

Stella

THURSDAY, AUGUST 18

Everyone in the den is sleeping. They've all dozed off except for me, and the room is filled with the soft drone of 98.5 and Archer's uneven snores. Quietly, I slip off to my bedroom, flick on the lights, and check my watch. It's ten thirty, and it's as dark out as it was at noon. The night hangs heavy, a kind of buildup with no release.

I haven't bothered to hide the wicker bin. It sits where I left it, atop my desk, alongside two walkie-talkies. I've finished one and am working on the other. They were the least damaged of the lot, by no means perfect, but salvageable. The first was the easiest to repair—plastic broken off on one corner, exposing some of the interior. It only required a bit of duct tape and some cereal-box cardboard I scavenged from the kitchen trash. The other walkie-talkie was more complicated—a frayed wire connecting battery to circuit board. That's where a third one came in handy. Using pliers and red electrical tape, I've performed a kind of organ transplant between the two. Now all that's left is to close up the back shell and test the efficacy of the surgery.

I do not touch the walkie-talkies yet. I sit at my desk and stare at the bare wall where my paper plans used to be.

I don't know how so much can change within the space of a month. How we Mercers, notorious loners for years, could bring new people like Gayle and Galliard into our lives. How my perfect plan for *This Stella* could be wholly derailed. How I could kiss a boy I only met two weeks ago. How college, only a pipe dream before, could seem attainable. How the town of Slater can fall apart while we watch and listen from the den.

For once, reasons and facts do nothing to help me. I can only wonder at it all.

My closet door is open, and from my desk I stare at the glowing violet numbers there. *00:05:24.*

It's nearly here, whatever end is coming for us. I wish it wouldn't, right when so many things are changing.

The knocking on my door is soft at first, then louder and more rapid. I'm quick to my feet, and I hurriedly slam the closet door shut, hiding away my personal doomsday clock. Then I return to my desk chair and assume an expression of nonchalance.

"Come in," I say, expecting it to be Jill.

It isn't.

"Am I bothering you?" Galliard asks.

I straighten in the chair, casting about for an excuse for my absence. The obvious answer is there, though, scattered on my desk.

"Making that bomb," I say.

Galliard doesn't laugh. He blinks rapidly. "I can leave you alone," he says, retreating.

"No, no! Galliard, I'm kidding. You're fine. Actually, I could use you for something."

He looks uncertain, still blinking, but I do not give him time to back out. I slip the plastic shell into place on the second of the walkie-talkies and hold it out to him.

"What's this?" he asks, taking it.

"See the button? The red one. Right, that one. I want you to go out there, to the bathroom. I'm going to try talking to you with this." I hold up my own, duct-taped talkie. "If you can hear me, after I say 'over,' you press the red button and *you* say something. Then we'll know if they work."

"Uh . . . okay." He looks upset, so I say, "I don't know what Red Sun told you about technology, but there's not a demon inside that thing."

He shakes his head. "No, I know." Then he steps out of my room and disappears from view. I wait fifteen seconds before pressing my button.

"Stella Kay Mercer to Galliard . . . I don't know your last name, Galliard. Over."

Now here it is. The moment of truth. I sit tensed, worrying my lip. A second passes, and then another. My heart tips from side to side, then begins to fall. I hear nothing from the speaker. I am about to give it up as a failure and call Galliard back to my room, when a crackle comes through.

"It's Lazzari," says Galliard's voice. "Galliard Lazzari. Um. Over."

I smile wide. "Excellent, Lazzari. Report back to the base. Over."

It's cheesy, I know, but I'm excited, and more than a little proud of myself. It's not the satisfaction I dreamed of feeling had I unveiled my project in Vine Street Salon. It is *something*, though. It's a victory, however small, that both *This* and *That Stella* can be proud of.

Galliard slips through the door and shuts it behind him. He hands me the walkie-talkie, and I set it beside its mate with satisfaction.

"Just in case," I say. "We don't know what's going to happen. It's nice to have some military-grade communication devices on hand, right?"

Galliard nods. "Sure."

"Everything okay in there?" I nod toward the den.

"Hmm? Oh, no, it's fine."

"It's funny, isn't it? The world could be ending, and we're eating TV dinners."

I smile at my own words. Only Galliard is not smiling back. His face is carved in hard, somber lines. He blinks several times.

"Something wrong?" I ask.

Galliard looks at me, then at the floor.

"There's something I need to tell you," he says. "I should've told you a while ago."

I'm thankful his back is turned to me, so he does not see my nervousness. I think through every possible explanation, but there is only one clear answer: *Craig.* This has something to do with Craig.

"He's never going to see me." I surprise myself with the strength of my voice. "I think I've known that for a long time. It's just, after some of the things he wrote . . . And now, with everything that's happening out there, I thought maybe—"

"He didn't write you those things."

"What?"

Galliard turns to me. "He didn't write you. He didn't write any of those letters. I did."

Since he entered the room, a suspicion has begun to take shape in my mind. Though it's been forming, growing, its details have remained vague. Now they sharpen into focus, too quick and too awful to behold. I shut my eyes, and I say, "What are you talking about?"

I don't want him to answer. I don't want to listen.

He speaks, though, and I hear every last word.

"I found your letter in Phoenix's wastebasket. He told me he'd moved on and didn't want anything to do with his old life. I respected that, because that's what we do at Red Sun: We respect each other's decisions. But . . . I don't know. I was younger then. I was curious. So I took your letter, and I read it, and I felt terrible."

"You felt terrible for reading my private correspondence?"

"No. Well, yeah, I did. But I felt terrible for—for *you*. I could tell how much you loved him, and I couldn't stand to think that you wouldn't hear back. *Ever*. I respected his decision, but I didn't think it was the right one. I didn't think it was fair to you. It bothered me for days. I tried forgetting about it, but I couldn't.

"Then finally, one night, I wrote you back. I used the typewriter so the handwriting wouldn't be an issue. I tried to write the way I heard him talk. I answered your questions the way I thought he would. I worked it out with Ronnie, in the mail room, to send and get your letters direct. See, the commune has this thing about particular familial bonds. Honestly, I don't know why they let your first letter through to Phoenix; probably some new guy on the job. But I told Ronnie it wasn't hurting anybody, that you were a potential member, and I was working on you. After a while, I knew he didn't believe me anymore, but he also didn't have the heart to stop it. I don't know what I was thinking. I guess part of me thought it wouldn't actually work. It did, though, and you kept writing, and I kept answering. The more I got to know Phoenix, the easier it was to write you back. Then . . . I don't know, something changed. I started to know *you*, and I wanted to know you better, and I wanted you to know some real part of *me*. That's when I started to write things Phoenix wouldn't say and things I would. I figured you'd chalk it up to the commune changing him."

The longer Galliard speaks, the faster his words become. He is sweating at the brow, and his eyes roam the room in a disoriented way. He pulls at the hem of his white tunic, shaking his head, and his wild eyes suddenly fix on me. "Fuck it, Stella, I don't know what I was *doing*. I never had an endgame. I just liked our letters, and hearing from you was the highlight of my damn *week*, and I knew I couldn't keep it up forever, but I didn't want to stop."

I am quiet. I have heard everything. I understand it on a basic, informational level. Only it is not sinking any deeper. It has not reached my heart. My voice is stone hard when I say, "Did you come to the Dreamlight on purpose?"

"No. What? *No*. I had no idea you'd be there. You never talked about the Dreamlight in your letters. I didn't know. I swear, I wasn't trying to meet you or fuck anything up. But then you caught me and Archer, and I recognized you from Phoenix's painting, and I couldn't help it. I was saying your name before I could stop myself. It was so stupidly improbable that you were there, of all places, on the first night I decided to leave Red Sun."

"It was," I whisper. "It was highly improbable."

He draws closer, and as he does, his jaw jerks hard to the right. The tic repeats seconds later, then again. He is only a couple of feet from where I sit, my arms crossed tight over my stomach.

"I know I should've told you when you came to Red Sun that first time. I should've admitted everything right then and been done with it. I was a coward. I told myself it was because I didn't want to hurt you. I think underneath that, though, I was scared. I was scared of you hating me, right when I was figuring out that I was . . . I was . . ."

"You were what?"

His words are sinking deeper, at last. They are entering my heart, filling its chambers, rushing through its valves. They make it beat faster, heavier. Tears fill my eyes and fall down my face. My heartbeat will not slow. I am feeling too much at once, too much for my body to contain, too much to ever, *ever* capture and write down in neat equations. I am hurt, and I am gratified, and I am astonished. More than that, more than anything else, I am *angry*.

"How could you do that?"

Galliard begins to answer, but I do not let him. I am not through.

"How could you ever think that was the right thing to do?

340

If Craig wanted to hurt me, then it was on *him* to hurt me. It wasn't on *you* to make things better. And you didn't make them better, Galliard. You've been lying to me. You've been lying to me for *two years*. Do you know how wrong that is? How *sick*?"

"I know, Stella. God, I know, I—"

"No, you *don't* know!" I shout. "Because *you've* known the truth this whole time. You've had the luxury of feeling however you want about me, because you've known that I'm *not your sister*. And what, did you think if you told me the truth we could just . . . be friends? Friendship is equal footing, Galliard. Friendship is *honesty*."

"I know that! Fuck, I *know*. That's why I'm telling you now. I wanted to make things right."

"You mean you want your conscience clear before Buddy Holly and the rest of your gods. You want to be at peace before the world ends and Elvis calls you home to some shining Graceland in the sky, is that it?"

"I'm telling you because I *know* it was twisted. And I know it I ever wanted a chance with you—"

"A chance with me?" I rise from my chair. "We are far beyond a chance with me. You had your chance when we first met. And even then, do you think there was ever going to be a *chance* with me?"

Galliard's face contorts. His jaw is jerking hard right every few seconds.

I realize then what my words could mean.

"It's not about *that*," I say, trembling. "Your tics are fine. They're completely *fine*, Galliard."

"They bother you, though. They bother everyone out here. How could I—"

"No!" I yell, throwing out my arms. "You want to know what bothers me? You pretending to be my brother. That's wrong. That's so *wrong*, Galliard. It has nothing to do with your tics. Don't tell yourself that so you don't have to confront the real issue here. That you purposefully stay cooped inside a tiny, fenced-in shelter that won't let you do what you love."

"Right!" Galliard shouts back in my face. "Right, because you don't have that same exact problem."

"But I can't do anything about it!" I scream. *"I can't leave!"*

My back is to the bedroom door, so I do not notice that it has opened or that Jill is standing there. I don't notice until Galliard's startled gaze flicks to her, and I turn and see.

"Jill," I say. "What's—"

Her expression is blank. She holds her hands behind her back.

"Dad called. He says the plant is still on lockdown. That means they can't leave." When I say nothing, she adds, "I *did* knock."

I nod limply. "I'm sure you did."

Her eyes flit from me to Galliard to the walkie-talkies on my desk. She backs away slowly, then heads down the hall and out of sight.

Galliard shifts behind me, clears his throat. Then he clears it again. I know it must be a tic, because there is no chance he would willingly draw attention to himself. Not now.

I do not look at him. I keep my eyes to the hallway and say, "I want you to leave."

He clears his throat.

"I don't care where you go. I don't care if aliens abduct you or fire and brimstone come down or the earth swallows you whole. Just get out."

His shoulder brushes mine as he steps into the hall. I do not wait to hear what reaction there will be in the den. I slam my bedroom door. Then I crawl onto my bed and keep my eyes shut against the world. Against Galliard and my brother and even my little sister. Against this entire month and every change it has brought into my life.

27

Galliard

THURSDAY, AUGUST 18

I feel like shit.

I feel like the worst possible outcome of the human race.

And it's what I deserve.

That's right, you're saying. *C'mon, Galliard, you had one hundred chances to tell Stella everything, and you chose now, at the end of the world.*

Which is what Archer is mind-screaming at me. I know he is, even if he doesn't say a word from the time we leave the house to the time we reclaim our miraculously not-stolen bikes on Vine Street to the time we're well down Eisenhower, pedaling through thick dark, with only streetlamps to light the way. He doesn't ask where we're going, which is just as well, because I don't know.

It's so quiet. I can't hear birds or crickets or traffic. Everyone's inside, as they should be. Everyone but us. If we keep biking out this way, past Red Sun, we'll run into the blockade. I know we've got to stop eventually, but I don't know where.

Where do you hide when you're trapped in an apocalypse?

Where the hell do you go to hide from yourself?

I hear noise. At first I think it's got to be in my head. Then it gets louder—the sound of talking and shouts and car engines running. I see something too, off the road and up on the left. It's a burst of light in a dark sea of cornfields.

The Dreamlight.

Not *everyone* is safe inside.

Some Slater residents are out for the Dreamlight's midnight showing.

Archer and I slow our bikes to a stop. We stand looking toward the glow of the concessions hut and the big, illuminated screen. There are two dozen cars in the lot.

"How long till the National Guard shuts it down, you think?" asks Archer.

"We could find out for ourselves."

Archer looks at me. I look at him.

"I never did get to see the movie," I say.

Archer grins. He shakes his head, long and slow. "Why not."

And really, why not?

I've already made the bravest and probably stupidest decision of my life. There's no turning back, no looking over my shoulder at a setting Red Sun. Call it weak. Call it ignorant. A song isn't just a song, though, and a movie isn't just a movie. I'm going to see *Star Wars* at the end of the world.

Why not.

July 30, 1977

Stella,

I'm not going to send this. I already know
I won't. I think that's best. It's what I
should've done at the start. I should've left
your letter unanswered.

It wasn't my place to interfere. It wasn't
my place to decide what would hurt you and
what would help.

I've been thinking about aliens again.
How you've been writing to one this whole time.
Someone different from you, from another place
and perspective. And you didn't even know.

Point is, I got the things you said. I
think you got the things I said too. Maybe we
disagreed on points, but we had a conversation.

So maybe I've changed my mind. Maybe it is
possible to make an alien connection. Maybe
they'd actually want to reach out and talk to
us. But only to the humans who could believe
it. The ones who had an open mind.

It's something to think about. And I wish
I could tell you that not as Craig, but as me.
Because it's really

Galliard

28

Stella

MIDNIGHT, FRIDAY, AUGUST 19

I wake, which comes as a surprise, because I do not remember growing tired.

There have been no knocks at my door, no shouts, no clamor. When I walk into the den, there is no one there. The radio is turned off. In fact, from what I can tell, the radio is gone. I peer into the kitchen, but Jill is not there either. She is not in her bedroom, or our father's.

My heart begins to thrum. Now, fresh from sleep, I can't believe what I've done. How could I shut my door without thinking that Jill might react to what she heard? That, like Galliard and Archer, she might *leave*?

"Jill?" I call.

There is no reply.

I check the garage. I check the bathrooms and even the linen closet.

Nothing.

The thrum of my heart grows louder. I hurry back to my bedroom and lace on my sneakers, ready to go outside, to search the yard and the street and every inch of Slater, if necessary.

That's when I see what is on my desk. Or, what is *not* there.

One of the walkie-talkies is missing.

No, I think. *She wouldn't.*

She would, though.

I grab the remaining walkie-talkie. Pressing the red button, I say, "Jill? Jill, it's Stella. Over."

I release the button and wait.

And wait.

My bones are burning with panic.

"Jill," I say. "*Answer* me. This isn't funny. Come back home. Over."

Release, and wait.

And wait.

"Jill, at least tell me where you are. Over."

Nothing.

I hate myself. I thought that by repairing the walkie-talkies, I was doing something useful, making us safer. Instead I've given Jill a reason to run away. A chance to be a real-live Nancy Drew, in action.

I'm crying as I hurry to the kitchen and fish a well-creased paper from my jeans pocket. I dial the number written there in rapid strokes.

The telephone rings and rings and rings.

Then: "Hello, this is Gayle Nelson. I'm not available, but if you leave a message with a number where you can be reached, I'll be in touch soon."

There's a long, loud beep in my ear, followed by silence. I

stutter for a moment, then push speech from my mouth.

"Gayle? Dad? Please call me. Please, *please*, if you're there. Jill's run away, I don't know where—"

I catch sight of something on the counter—a sheet of paper. I grab it and read, in Jill's careful cursive, *Going to investigate. I'm okay on my own.*

I flip the paper, looking for something, anything more. It is Mr. Cavallo's flyer about his end-of-the-world showing. I check my watch. It's nearly midnight.

"I think I know where she is," I say into the phone. "I'm going out to find her."

I slam the phone on its cradle and make quick work of gathering items into a rucksack, including two flashlights and the first-aid kit from the linen closet. Then, most important, though currently most useless, the walkie-talkie. I drop the bag into my bike basket and pedal out of the garage, not bothering to stop and close the door behind me.

There are sirens wailing in the distance, and a rumbling sound, like thunder. I look to the sky, but there are no storm clouds overhead—only blackness. As I speed down Vine, and as Vine turns to Eisenhower, the sirens grow louder. I know where they are coming from, but I do not want to think it. To think that means to entertain the idea that my father is not okay.

I keep pedaling, heading in the direction of the Dreamlight, and beyond that Red Sun, and beyond that the Slater Creek Generating Station.

A car speeds past me, heading toward town, horn blaring.

Then another passes, and another, and another. One passenger rolls down his window and shouts, "Get off the road! Get to shelter!"

Then they're gone, zipping off into the dark, and I do not have the chance to yell back that I will only get to shelter when my sister's hand is in mine.

The ground is trembling. At first I think it is only the rumble of passing cars. Then, as I pull off the road at the Dreamlight entrance and dismount, a crevice forms before my eyes, splitting through the road a mere yard from where I stand.

I turn toward the drive-in. Up on the large, lit screen, C-3PO stumbles fretfully along a corridor as though he, too, can feel the moving earth.

"Stella?"

I start at the sudden life fizzling from the walkie-talkie in my basket. I grab it, waiting for more.

"Stella, it's Jill. Over."

My sister's voice is distant and choppy, but it is her.

"Jill," I shout into the walkie-talkie, "where are you? I'm coming for you. Over."

"I'm looking for . . . sirens . . . know where . . ."

Jill's words cut out in longer and longer patches of static.

"Jill, I can't hear you!" I shout. "Try again, over."

She hasn't heard me, though. She hasn't broken her own transmission. She speaks on, her words growing more garbled by the second.

". . . problem with . . . don't . . . going to see . . ."

I shake my head, desperate, useless. I wait for the transmis-

350

sion to cut entirely before shouting, "Don't go anywhere! *Tell me where you* are. *Over.*"

I release the button and wait. The speaker crackles and sizzles. No words come through.

"Jill!" I shout. *"Jill!"*

Then it happens. There, right before my eyes. The ground rumbles around me, and the projection of a larger-than-life Darth Vader *sinks into the ground*. One moment the drive-in screen is there, and the next it is not. It has vanished, folding in on itself and disappearing into the earth. It is gone. Simply *gone*.

I don't know for how long I stand there, motionless, senseless to my breath and heartbeat. However long, it's enough for the chaos to begin. When I regain my senses, people are shrieking and shouting commands and running past me in unorganized swarms.

I grip my bike handles hard and mount, pedaling over uneven ground, through the long grass, toward the concessions hut. The fluorescents are on, but there is no sign of Kim or Mr. Cavallo. I skid to the back door and hoist up my bike, taking it in with me; I'm sure that if I leave it outside, it will disappear.

"Hello?" I shout. "Hell—"

I spot Kim. She's tucked under the sink cabinet, knees to her chest, hands over her head.

She smiles weakly at me. "Duck and cover, right? See, I remember something from school."

"Is it the plant?" I crouch beside her. "What's going on?"

I ask, even though I know. There is a word for what

happened out there: "sinkhole." I've seen pictures in physical-geography class. I want another answer, though. Any other answer.

"Hell if I know," says Kim. "The sirens at the plant started ten minutes ago. Some people left, but Mr. Cavallo said the show must go on."

"Why did—"

"Hey, I don't know anything. I only know I'd rather die from a nuclear blast than get trampled or knifed by one of the crazies out there."

What Kim's saying makes perfect sense. If I were her, I'd do the same thing. But I'm *This Stella*. I have a sister to find.

"I'm looking for Jill. Have you seen her?"

"Your *sister*? I've seen her maybe twice in my life."

"She's around four foot four, dirty-blond hair—"

"Yeah, sorry, Stella, I'm not going to be any help there."

"Okay. Okay."

I grab the rucksack from my bike, take out a flashlight, and shoulder the bag.

"What, you're heading out there again?" she demands.

"I have to find her."

"Okay, well at least take some kind of weapon. People out there are going *insane*."

I scan the room. We sell food, we don't prepare it, so there are no knives or heavy dishes around. I know of a trusty weapon, though. I throw open the cabinet beside Kim and lug out the bottle of Clorox.

"Seriously?" she asks.

I throw her a dirty look. "Unless you have a gun?"

She grimaces, shrugs.

I make for the back door, and as I'm leaving, Kim pipes up. "Hey! Hey, I hope you find her. And thanks for not being a shitty coworker. You made the job not half-bad."

Kim isn't crying; she's never struck me as a person who *can* cry. If she could, though, I think now would be the moment.

I say, "Thanks for sharing your punk music."

"Radio Birdman. Look them up."

"I will."

Neither of us believes I will.

Then I step out into the din. More people have fled the premises, and the darkened field is slowly clearing out. Where the thirty-foot movie screen should be, there is only uninterrupted darkness. Terror threatens to freeze me in place there, in the dark, amid shouts and crying and the ever-present wail of sirens. I don't let it. I push it back and focus on one thing: *I must find Jill.*

But I don't know where to begin. My walkie-talkie is now useless, a constant stream of static, and I don't know how to search for Jill in a shifting, panicked crowd. I don't know how she will ever hear my calls for her over dozens of other raised voices. But I have to do something. I search, and I call her name. I shout it again and again as I run toward, not away from, the sinkhole.

When I feel the grip on my arm, I react on instinct. I realize too late that the bleach bottle lid is screwed on tight, so I use it more primitively, swinging it up in a cramped arc toward my assailant's cheek.

"*Fuck!*" he shouts. "Jeez, Stella, it's only *me.*"

I shine my flashlight straight at his face, breathing hard, adrenaline skittering through my body.

"Archer?"

"You shouldn't be out here," he yells. "There's no telling if this whole field is going down or not!"

I shake my head. "It's Jill. I can't find Jill."

He starts to answer, but I hear nothing. I am falling, and I register hard pain in my chest and the sight of a man's elbow and the unforgiving slam of ground at my back. My vision swims. I fight against it.

I must find Jill.

I fight, but this time I am losing the battle.

The darkness swallows me up.

29

Galliard

"Stella."

She whimpers and blinks, dropping incoherent words from her mouth. Archer and I are crouched down, supporting her shoulders as, around us, people scream and run. The muscles in Stella's back shift under my fingers. Then she slumps again, weightier than ever.

"We have to get to shelter," I say.

It's not a question of where. Archer and I both know our best bet.

We swore we weren't going back.

Everything inside me rebels against the thought.

But now, it's not a matter of inside or Outside. It's a matter of living or dying.

We get to our feet, hauling Stella up with us. She's only half there, and as we walk, she takes labored steps alongside us.

Archer and I heave toward the cornfield, the shortest route to Red Sun's front gate. I use Stella's flashlight to guide our path through the dark, boxed in on both sides by thick rows of cornstalks. Panic keeps building and bursting inside me. My tics are in full force—constant throat clears and frequent jaw jerks. We're moving way too slow, and I'm getting these creepy flashes of what might be hiding in the corn around us: monsters and killers and alien creatures. Stella stumbles, mumbling more indiscernible words.

The front gate is open, abandoned. There's no sign of life in the Moonglow or the parking lot. Everyone here must've fled to the shelter a while ago.

Archer and I walk faster, and Stella moves with us, more in sync, more independent, as we make our way toward the back of Common House. There in the ground, bordered by rows of California poppies, is a large, two-door metal hatch.

One door is still thrown open.

Maybe, I think, my gods are looking out for me, even behind that veil of black.

Thank you, I pray. To them. To whoever is listening, and helping.

I recognize the man standing under the hatch, at the top of the stairs. It's Charlie, our front-gate keeper. He recognizes us, too. At the sight of us, his eyes bulge and he shouts down, "We got more!"

Archer and I kneel at the entrance, helping Stella down to where Charlie stands.

"Take her first," I say. "Someone needs to look at her; she could have a concuss—"

There's movement behind Charlie. Someone's coming up the stairs.

"She's not allowed down."

It's Rod. His eyes are reddened. His chin is littered with gray stubble. He's blocking Stella's path to the stairs.

"There's no room here for outsiders," he says, in as calm a way as he would give a community-meeting report. "Those boys chose to leave us. They've chosen to be outsiders too."

"Fuck *that*, Rod!" Archer shouts.

"There's room for us," I say, crouching close to the earth so that my eyes can meet his. My jaw twitches, and my throat produces a gritty sound. I carry on. "There's plenty of room, Rod. Just let us down."

"You've made your decision. Our shelter is for members of this community." Rod turns to the crowd of people below and out of sight. "I don't hear any of our members crying out for your inclusion. Do you?"

Between my throat clears, I listen. Below is only a noisy kind of silence—movement and coughs and children sniffling. No one speaks. Not Ruby, not J. J., not Thunder or any of the other crossers.

Not Phoenix.

Rod is the authority, and they will not contradict him. I don't belong to Ruby and J. J. any more than I do the rest of them. And no one should welcome us back in if we have willingly left. That's Red Sun regulation. I just didn't believe it until now. I didn't think those rules would hold true in this moment, when we're all screwed anyway.

There's a low, long thundering sound above our heads. The wind begins to howl, grabbing at my hair and smacking into my face like a solid thing.

"What do you want us to do?" I shout, pounding a fist into the grass. "You want us to die out here, Rod? For fuck's sake, *you want us to die*?"

The red in Rod's eyes spreads to his face. "You made your decision!" he roars, pointing a trembling finger at me and Archer. "You left our protection when tough times came. We raised and nurtured you both. We kept you from corrupting influences, and you abandoned your home for *outsiders*." He lowers the accusing finger on Stella, who's sunk on the metal stairwell, weak and confused. "Outsiders brought this on us, with their wars and hate and misuse of Earth. And I will be damned if I allow them to survive the destruction they've brought on their own heads! I'll be damned if—"

Rod's eyes go wide, his face slack. Then, without warning, he crumples forward, onto the stairs. Stella cries out and scrambles away. Where Rod once was, Opal now stands, with an electric lantern held aloft in both hands. Her pale eyes cut quick across me and Archer.

"Get down here, the three of you," she says. "Charlie, close that door. We can't risk it any longer."

It takes me longer than it should to move. I'm too stunned, because *Opal just took out Rod*. She broke the commune rule of nonviolence and knocked him out cold for *us*.

Two other members are on the stairs, moving Rod's unconscious body down below. Archer climbs in ahead of me and helps Stella to her feet. I drop down after, and immediately Charlie lunges for the hatch door, slamming it hard behind me.

Then I descend into the shelter.

There are no frills here, only rows of bunks and hard,

earthy floor. Kids sit on the top bunks. The three closest to me are playing a game of cards. On a bottom bunk two down, I see Thunder and some other crossers. Some others who said nothing when Rod refused to let us down. And then I spot Ruby and J. J. They're standing against the wall on the far end of the room, opposite me. Ruby's arms are wrapped around J. J.'s middle, and I can imagine what she's been whispering in his ear:

"We were right. We were right. This is why we came."

She meets my gaze for only a second before shaking it off again.

Because I'm not a kid to be coddled anymore. I'm sixteen, and I've made my own choice.

Another throat clear bursts out of me.

"Jill. Where's Jill? She's not down here."

Stella's now fully alert, and frantic. Though her hair hangs tangled in front of her eyes, she doesn't make an effort to push it free. She is scanning the faces around us, not lighting on the one she wants to see.

"Galliard," she says, turning to me. "She's up there. She was going to the movie. She's still up there."

"What? I thought she was at your house."

"*No.* Why would I leave her alone? Why would I . . . Get me out of here. *She's up there.* I've got to get—I've got to—"

"Okay," I say, nodding, then clearing my demanding throat. "Okay, okay. We'll find her. I'll go. Let me."

She shakes her head hard. "She was talking to me. She was *talking* to me, and then the screen went down, and she could be . . . in trouble. Galliard, she's . . ."

Stella doesn't see Phoenix push through the crowd behind her. She doesn't see his look of bewilderment, of recognition.

I don't know what he's after. I glare at him, warding him off, but he keeps advancing until he's right behind her, and he places a hand on her shoulder.

Stella jolts, spins around.

Silence fills my ears like cotton the moment Stella and Phoenix stand face-to-face. And it stays there as I watch her tense her right hand into a fist and swing it up, into his jaw.

30
Stella

FRIDAY, AUGUST 19

It is the first time I have seen my brother's face in two years. It has changed. It is older.

It is beneath my fists.

They make contact with the soft of his cheek and the bone of his jaw, again and again and again.

I know now. I know the meaning of my countdown. Even if those numbers mean nothing, even if they're only a fluke, I know what they mean to *me*. My brother stands before me. After all this time, I am seeing him. And I am fighting him with everything that is in me.

He does not fight back. He does not cry out. Or it may be that I am insensible to touch and sound until fingers dig deep into my arms and pull me away, thrashing. I wrench around to see who has done the pulling. It is an older woman, in her sixties, at least. She is yelling something at me, and like her grip, her voice is surprisingly strong.

"That's enough!" she says. "We'll have none of this here. If you wish to stay in the shelter, you must act *peaceably*."

Stares drive into my back. Everyone in the shelter is silent, looking at me and Craig.

I glare at my brother, chest heaving, pulse thumping loud in my ears. I've drawn blood at the left corner of his lip. It's not the blood that captures my attention, though. It is the look in Craig's pale blue eyes—a look of unspeakable sadness.

I don't understand. Craig isn't supposed to be sad; he's not *allowed*. He's supposed to be awful in this moment. He's supposed to look at me with utter disinterest and dismiss me as dead to him, forevermore. He's supposed to be the Craig who left me, who never answered a single one of my letters. And he *is* that Craig, but he is another Craig I didn't expect. A Craig I don't understand. A Craig with sad eyes.

"Why are you looking at me that way?" I demand.

"I thought it was you." My brother's voice is soft as he speaks through bloodstained lips. "I had to be sure."

"*Why?*" I ask, still hot with rage. "Why'd you have to be sure? You clearly haven't wanted to see me the last two years."

"That's not true," Craig says, still soft. "It not that I didn't want to see you. I *couldn't*. If I saw you, I'd go back out there. And I can't do that, Stell. It will kill me."

I flinch at the use of his nickname for me. It feels wrong, coming from the mouth of this man in a Red Sun tunic.

I want to yell. I want to hit him again. I want to spew out two years' worth of hurt. I find that I can't, though, now that I'm looking into my brother's eyes. They contain not only sadness, but pain, and fear, too. There is so much fear swimming in all that blue.

I cannot hurt him anymore. I can only say the words that have been burning in my heart.

"You're selfish," I tell him. "You left the wrong way, and I'm mad at you for that."

"I know," he replies simply. He makes no excuse.

Instead I make the excuse for him.

"That's how you had to be, isn't it?" I say slowly. "You were selfish because you were afraid. Because you weren't strong enough. Maybe you'll never be."

Craig doesn't answer. He only looks at me with those pained, pale eyes. There is something in that expression I recognize. I have seen it before, painted on canvas. I've seen it in one of Craig's portraits—the one of my mother, on her wedding day.

I know that what I've said is true as surely as I know what I have to say next:

"You were a good brother to me, for a very long time. I'll remember you that way. I'll remember our backyard Olympics."

Around us, people have begun to shift and talk. Though the older woman has softened her grip on my arm, I'm aware that I only have a little more time.

"Good-bye, Craig," I say, looking straight into those eyes. "Good-bye for good."

Then, without hesitation, I turn away.

The older woman strengthens her hold on me once more. "You listen, young lady," she says into my ear. "These people are panicked enough, and I will not take any more excitement.

Either you behave yourself, or you take your chances on the Outside."

This is not a decision that requires thought. I cannot stay in this place with *him* and not do violence. I did not know that until now, but it is suddenly fact, as sure and intractable as Newton's laws. I tell the old woman, "I understand."

She lets go of me, and immediately I start up the metal stairwell leading to the surface. I ascend, and I do not look back. The man guarding the door gives me a hard look. "What do you think you're doing?"

"I'm going back out."

I feel calm. I feel fine. This is the only thing to be done.

"You crazy, girl?"

"I'm leaving. Let me out."

"Go on, Charlie," the woman says from below. "She's full grown. It's her decision."

Charlie shakes his head at me as though I've lost my wits. In the end, though, he unlatches the iron door he is guarding, and I climb outside.

The wind is strong. It forms a wall I push past, walk against. I am vaguely aware of Galliard shouting my name from below. I am aware of the thud of metal and heavy footsteps. I pay them no mind. I walk on into the dry, cold darkness.

I can see very little, so I take out the remaining flashlight from my rucksack, and I turn it on. There are small squares of light in the distance that I take to be windows of a commune building. Beyond that are the streetlights leading east to Slater and west to Slater Creek. I find comfort in this. If the lights are working, nothing very bad can befall me. Though the world may be dark and the earth may be crumbling, these lights can guide me to my family. I have no family here, at Red Sun. He disowned me long ago, and now I have disowned him.

In my other hand I hold the walkie-talkie. It's silent, no transmission, but there's a chance I can find Jill, and as long as there is a chance, I must try. I place one foot in front of the other. I am walking on soft grass. The wind is strong. It howls in my ears, a desperate, dying animal.

There is a shout behind me. Pressure at my back.

I turn, and Galliard is there, panting, blinking so quickly.

I say, "You should go back."

He says, "Not a chance."

"I'm still mad at you," I shout over the wind.

"Okay."

"I'm not going back down there. I can't look at him. I can't—I'll kill him."

Galliard squints against the iron press of wind. "Then where are you going?"

"Jill. The drive-in. I have to find her."

"All right. I'm coming too."

I don't argue. I hurry on, speeding into a jog. The rucksack thuds against my back, and the walkie-talkie grows sweaty in my hand. I keep running, past the Moonglow Café, deep into the cornfields, toward the Dreamlight, or what remains of it. The wind howls, blowing so hard into my lungs that I can barely breathe. The plant sirens wail on.

Then the corn clears, and we are in a place familiar to me, but changed, too. Desolate. There are no more screams or racing bodies. They've cleared out. What's left are abandoned blankets, cups, and popcorn containers; ruts and depressions in the ground; and ahead, a gaping black hole where the movie screen once stood.

I head toward the hole. There is a feeling in my gut, deep and unshakable. I tell myself it isn't dread. I tell myself it isn't fear. I run on, and Galliard runs alongside me, until he's reaching out, blocking my chest with his arm, and pointing at the ground.

"It's not stable," he says. "Look."

Earth and grass crumble a few feet ahead of us, into a pit of nothingness. The sinkhole. Large enough to take down the screen, as well as any moviegoers sitting close by. Mr. Cavallo did a good job of roping off the perimeter, though. He wouldn't have allowed anyone this near the screen; they wouldn't have *wanted* to be this near, where the picture would be too close. Unless they weren't here to watch the picture.

Unless they were here to investigate.

I slap Galliard's arm away and get to my knees, waving my flashlight in slow, searching arcs.

"Jill!" I shout. "Jill, where are you? Can you hear me? Jill!"

"Stella," Galliard says at my back. "I don't think—"

"Shut up!" I scream, extending the range of my searchlight. The bulb is flickering, sputtering out like a last, gasped breath.

"Jill, I'm here! Where are you?"

The light goes out. I yell, hitting hard at it with the heel of my hand. It's no use, though. The batteries are dead.

"*Jill!*" I'm sobbing, fumbling with the walkie-talkie. I jam the button and speak into it. "Jill, please, *please*. Tell me you're okay. Tell me where you are."

I don't bother to release. I'm bent over, stitches in my sides, crying into the cold ground. Then there's movement at my side. Galliard is sitting across from me in the dark.

"You can't do it!" I shout at him. "You can't make plans for yourself—you, or any of your versions. The universe doesn't care what we want to be. It doesn't care if we live or die."

He doesn't answer. I grab his tunic and drag him close to me. I put my lips to his ears so that he cannot misunderstand. I ask, "What happens now? Do we become stars?"

"Stella, I . . . don't know."

"Then *what*?" I demand. "Just the cold space in between?"

I hear his mouth open and close, but no answer comes out.

"Well, you better be praying. You better be praying to Buddy Holly, or whoever else can save us."

I am sobbing hard. Galliard's arms enfold me. It is not meant to be romantic. I can feel that in the press of his hands on my shoulders: This is not a romancing; it is a comforting. A human and a human—a connection.

We sit in the dark, on the edge of a gaping hole in the earth, the wind snarling around us in a deathly swirl. My flashlight is pressed between our bodies, and suddenly, defiantly, it bursts back to life, shooting up a column of blinding light. I cannot see Galliard's face. I can only press my eyes shut against his shoulder and hold on to this one solid thing.

Though I cannot see the numbers on my closet door or over town hall, I know they are close to a full count of zeros.

And I know you cannot make any plans with certainty. I know I would probably never have become an engineer for NASA, and Galliard would probably never have played his music before a crowd. I would've liked to have tried, though. I think Galliard would have too.

"I'm scared," I say. "I'm scared this is it."

My words are absorbed by his tunic. Not even I can hear them. The wind roars in a deafening swell. My hair blows from my face, tugged so hard it stings at the roots. I struggle to stay upright, clinging harder to Galliard's back.

Another tornado, I think. Or something far worse. The extraterrestrial abduction. The nuclear blast. Or, as Pastor Barkley would have us believe, the hand of God come down to punish. Light bursts behind my shut eyelids. I open them to see the sky rent by pink lightning. There is no storm to accompany it, no thunder. The spindling fingers of light tear through the sky in bolt after bolt after bolt.

"Stella."

I shut my eyes. I hold Galliard. I wait for the end. For darkness. Or light. Or heat. Or cold. Or oblivion. Nothingness.

I wait.

"*Stella,*" Galliard says, louder than before.

I can hear his voice. I can hear it just fine, because the wind is no longer clogging my ears.

There is no more wind. Everything is still.

I open my eyes. The lightning has ceased. The sirens no longer sound.

It is dark. Quiet. Like before.

Only not like before.

There is more light.

I can see the stars.

•   •   •

I push out of Galliard's arms. Scrambling to my feet, I turn a slow circle, head craned toward the sky. The world breathes around us, and the night proceeds as though nothing has been or ever will be amiss.

"What's happening?" I ask.

Galliard shakes his head.

"Hey! Stella? Stella! Over."

I whip around. It isn't Galliard speaking. It's my sister's voice, coming from the walkie-talkie. It's Jill.

I grab the walkie-talkie from the ground, hands shaking.

"Jill! Jill, where are you? Over."

There is silence—agonizing silence—as I wait for a reply. Galliard comes close, arms crossed, and we stand stooped, breathing hard.

"On Eisenhower. We're coming home. Over."

"Jill! Who's—what're you—who do you—"

My sputtering is interrupted by a shrill, static screech. The walkie-talkie turns hot in my hand, too hot to hold, and I drop it to the earth, where it bursts into orange flames.

"What the . . ." says Galliard, but I'm grabbing his hand and wrenching him after me as I run toward the road. Toward Eisenhower.

On Eisenhower. Coming home.

My sneakers hit hard, cracked asphalt. Towering cornstalks flit by, waving us on with leafy hands. My calves are burning, and my throat is too. I stop and turn, looking in every direction.

For a moment, everything is still and dark.

Then lights blind me. A car has swung onto the road,

headlights blazing. It is speeding toward me and Galliard, swerving over the lane line.

"Watch out!" I shout to Galliard.

The car decelerates, then slams to a full stop yards ahead of us. Almost instantly, the driver's door swings open.

"Stella! *Stella!*"

It is my father.

All the muscles inside me turn weak. I run to him, straight into his arms.

"Jill," I choke into his chest. He smells of cigarettes. "Dad, Jill's—"

"She's fine, Stell. She's here."

And she is. I look past my father's shoulder to see Jill scrambling out of the passenger seat. She stumbles toward me, encumbered by an overlarge piece of clothing—my father's jacket. Then she crowds in on us and throws her arms around my waist.

"I'm old enough," she cries against me. "You don't have to stay for me. I'm old enough."

I kneel to meet her eyes, pushing back sweaty hair from her brow.

"Jill, you don't have to be old enough."

"I know. But I *am*."

I look up at my father. There are a dozen questions in my face, and he sees at least a few.

"She biked out to the plant," he says. "Of course security made a to-do about it, and then the sirens—"

"What happened?" I ask, even though I know he's trying to tell me just that.

"There was a misreading; we went into emergency shut-down. The engineers have confirmed that the reactors are stable. Gayle overrode the lockdown protocol so I could drive Jill out. So we could find you."

"Dad."

It is all I can say.

"Galliard?" he says, and the rest of the world rushes back into my hollowed chest. I turn to find Galliard standing on the road. He looks unsure of himself, as though he is contemplating running away.

"Come on, son," my father says. "You get in the car. We're clearing out of here."

Galliard does not move. "Where to?"

"Home. Our home."

I know, with conviction, what I will find there. The violet numbers that have been on my closet door for seventeen days will be gone, as though they never existed. As though they were a hallucination.

And perhaps they were.

Perhaps all this was a shared hallucination. A mass hysteria. Stranger things have happened.

Or it could be aliens. Aliens who don't intend to make an appearance. Aliens who would alter the lives of an inconsequential Kansan town, and that of a seventeen-year-old girl living there.

I wonder what Carl Sagan would postulate. I wonder, if the question were put to every higher-up at NASA, what explanation they would provide.

Only, for now at least, I do not need an explanation. The

countdown has counted down, and the time has passed, and we are still breathing. We are alive.

The stars are back in the sky, Galliard's gods all in their place.

From where I stand in the road, I hear a whip-poor-will's call.

31

Galliard

FRIDAY, SEPTEMBER 2

Two weeks ago Slater, Kansas, came to an end.

At least the Slater, Kansas, I knew.

The work in the kitchen. The morning prayer. The Back Room. The Red Sun Yamaha. The nights spent talking to Archer in Sage House. The people I'd known my whole life. All of it gone.

For me.

I left it behind.

Two weeks ago, the countdown reached zero. The strange things stopped. The darkness lifted, and everyone came out of their homes.

Some people were pretty busted up. There were bones broken and muscles pulled, contusions and internal injuries, but the strange things didn't kill a single one of us. They simply started one day, and then they stopped.

Slater got visits from the FBI and from nationally known scientists. When the blockades were lifted, tourists came to gawk. They took pictures of the sinkhole at the Dreamlight, and they gathered around town hall, even though the mysterious purple numbers weren't there anymore. What these people really gawked at, though, was that, aside from the sinkhole and the wind damage, Slater, according to them, looked like any other Midwestern town. Just an ordinary place, visited by the extraordinary, and for no apparent reason.

"But then," said the philosophical tourists, "do extraordinary things *ever* happen for a reason?"

I guess it's only natural that people try to come up with explanations. They want answers to every question. Me? I don't need to listen to any of the pastors or conspiracy theorists or scientists or even the Red Sun Council itself. I've already got my answer to everything:

Get the hell out of Slater.

Two weeks ago, the strange things stopped. A day later, on August 20, America shot a probe into the sky: *Voyager 2*, destined for the planets and beyond. I thought of Stella when I saw the newspaper headline. I took a second to wonder if *Voyager 2* would ever fly far enough to see my gods close up.

I guess it's possible. If I can leave Red Sun, anything's possible.

I can't be entirely sure what they think of my decision— Holly and Hendrix, Joplin and the King himself. They've been silent for a while. No strange changes in the weather.

Maybe they were never speaking to me. Maybe their stars are just gas, burning in an eternal sky. Even if that's the case, though, I don't mind. In the end, for the time that it mattered, they were real to me. Buddy gave me confidence. Janis gave me strength. Jimi gave me cool. And Elvis? He gave me what I needed most, through a song. He told me it was now or never. He told me to run.

Archer emerged from that Red Sun shelter, and he left the commune behind for good. He and I headed out yesterday morning, a day after the blockades were lifted. We hitched a ride with a tobacco farmer heading east on Eisenhower. We bought our Greyhound tickets at the Kansas City station last night, using our pooled allowances. We didn't bring much with us, just a shared bag with money, food, paper, and a pen.

Stella met me on the outskirts of town before we caught our ride. Kim came along too, to give me a certain LP, on hold no longer. She told me that Queen is going to change my life.

Stella told me to write.

She said, "You can if you sign it *Galliard* this time."

Then she turned and headed back to town—to her father and Jill and the woman named Gayle.

She sent me on my way and went on her own.

I haven't decided about writing Stella yet. Archer says it's a bad idea, and once we get to Pasadena, I'll have other things on my mind.

But when we stop in Albuquerque to change buses, we have an hour layover.

I walk to the post office next door, and I buy a dozen long envelopes and a book of stamps.

"Mom," says this kid in line. "Why's he moving like that?"

This little boy, this outsider, is talking about my tics.

"Shhh, honey," says his mom.

But I turn with my purchases in hand. I smile at the kid, through the jerk of my jaw.

"It's fine," I say. "It's nothing to be scared of."

And I step out into the hot, terrifying, beautiful Outside.

32

Stella

"Is she here?"

"No, Jill. Twenty more minutes. You don't have to roll out the welcome wagon yet."

I smile at what, to me, is a private joke. The end of Slater has come and gone, and the mysterious numbers have disappeared, both from town hall and my closet door. Now here I am, in the aftermath, creating brand-new countdowns of my own.

Twenty minutes.

Twenty minutes until Gayle Nelson arrives to take me away to Lawrence, Kansas, for a campus tour of KU and an interview with her professor friend.

Twenty minutes until my future begins.

"Stop looking out the window," Jill pouts from over her Nancy Drew book, *The Crooked Banister*. "You're making me nervous, standing there like that."

Jill has a point. I packed my suitcase early this afternoon in a bundle of nerves and excitement, and since then I've had nothing to do but wait. Wait, and watch, looking for a sign of

Gayle's tan Karmann Ghia on our street, even though there are twenty more minutes to go.

Once she picks me up, a new countdown will begin, and more waiting along with it. I don't have appointments on campus until tomorrow morning, but both Gayle and Dad deemed it best for me to spend the night before at a nearby motel. I'm looking forward to the time alone with Gayle, talking about her work and her own story. I will have the chance to ask her questions I didn't dare before. Because my new future is a daring one.

I figured out something on Eisenhower Road, in that early dawn, after so long a night. To be *That Stella* is selfish, and to be *This Stella* is misery. That much I knew. What I figured out was this: Maybe it is possible to be a new Stella altogether. Maybe both Craig and my mother were wrong, and there are not just two options. I can be brave *and* loving, happy *and* giving. It is possible, and Dad and Gayle and even Jill are on my side. It's an experiment, another project, only this time it's my *life*. And it will begin when Gayle shows up at my door in—I check my watch—eighteen minutes.

I step away from the window, per Jill's request, and head to the kitchen to pour a glass of lemonade. I'm not thirsty, only in need of an outlet for nervous energy, and when some of the liquid plashes out from the pitcher, onto the counter, I'm grateful for yet another task. It's as I'm running the tap over a washrag that I hear my father enter the room.

"Hey," I say, turning around with a grin.

Dad is hardly grinning back. There's a heavy crease in his brow and a troubled expression set deep in his eyes.

"What's wrong?" I ask.

I'm letting the washrag drip on the tile. Coming forward, Dad takes it from me and gently sets it on the kitchen counter.

"I want to talk to you, Stella."

My skin buzzes with apprehension. I find that I *do* need that lemonade after all; my throat has gone dry.

"O-okay," I manage.

He motions toward a stool at the kitchen bar, and I take it, realizing as I do what a smart move that was for my very weak legs. Dad remains standing, arms crossed.

"I want to apologize," he says, and after noting my uncomprehending stare, he continues. "It's long overdue, and that deserves its own apology. We should've had this talk two years ago."

I know, with certainty now, we are talking about Craig.

"There was nothing to say," I tell him quietly.

"No, there was. There was plenty to say, same as there was plenty to say when your mother passed away."

I lift my eyes to his, feeling a rush of blood to my heart.

"Stella." My father lifts a trembling hand to his cheek and presses it there, as though to reassure himself of his realness. "It's not easy for me to say these things. The way I was raised, we didn't talk about feelings, or about tragedy. You simply pulled yourself up by your bootstraps and carried on. But I'm seeing now—Gayle's helped me to see—that wasn't the way I should've raised my own children. We should have talked. You deserved that."

"Dad." My voice catches, and I'm too overwhelmed by the unexpectedness of this to go on.

"Your mother was unhappy here. I saw that and pretended I didn't, the same as I saw that your brother was unhappy too. After what happened to Walt, I should've . . . I simply should've done more. And when Craig left, Stella, I saw how that affected you. You were forced to be a new person, to do so much more than any fifteen-year-old ought to. I knew, when you skipped your graduation, that something was wrong again. I was too afraid, though. Too afraid to say or do anything. I almost let you slip away too. I—" My father breaks off in a muted sob and covers his tear-filled eyes with his shaking hand.

I am off the kitchen stool in an instant, and by his side. Then I'm hugging my father, holding him close.

"It's all right, Dad," I tell him. "I forgive you."

I pull away slightly, tugging down his hands to look him in the eye. "You were doing the best you could. I've always thought that: You were doing the very best you could."

"You didn't have the chance," he cracks out, "to be a normal teenager."

At that I cannot help myself. I laugh. "Come on, Dad," I say, squeezing his hands in mine. "There was never any chance of that. Anyway, what does 'normal' even mean?"

Dad pulls me into another hug, and for many moments we stand there, swaying slightly, as I take in the scent of fabric softener in his cardigan.

Then, from out in the hallway, there's a commotion.

"*She's here!* Stella, you liar, you said that—" Jill stops her shouting when she swings through the kitchen door. "Oh. Um."

I smile at her through glistening tears and say, "C'mon, Jill. Family hug."

She doesn't need to be told twice. Jill gallops happily toward us, throwing her hands around my waist and Dad's and squeezing tight. That's when I know for certain that this is my new favorite memory of our family: three Mercers coming together, in spite of all the hard times that came before.

It only lasts a second before Jill backs away from us, hands on her hips. "You lied," she says to me. "Gayle's outside."

I glance at the kitchen clock to confirm that, yes, Gayle is a whole ten minutes early.

"That happens sometimes, Jill," I say. "Life surprises you."

I think, in that moment before the start of my future, about Galliard Lazzari and his friend Archer, about blood-red rain and pink-veined lightning. I think about two years of letters, and I think about Kim rocking out to the Ramones. I think of a Ferrell's malt and of the buttery scent in the Dreamlight concessions hut. I think of walkie-talkies and a border collie named Major, and of a matinee showing of *Marooned*. I think of *This Stella* and *That Stella* and everything in between. It's a giddy, cacophonous swirl of visons and scents and every sensation felt in my eighteen years. It's almost enough to knock me off my feet.

Life does surprise you, and not just sometimes. More often than not.

The trick, I'm beginning to see, is welcoming the surprise in all its unexpected, unknowable glory. That's how this *New Stella* will live her life.

The doorbell rings. The countdown ends.

My future begins now.

Stella Kay Mercer
Kansas Cosmosphere and Space Center
Hutchinson, Kansas

September 5, 1977

Craig,

You won't read this. You will throw it in the
wastebasket the same as you did my first
letter. Or perhaps it won't even reach your
hands. Either way, that is all right, because
this letter is not for you. It's for me.

When Mom died, some people blamed it on the
moon. I see now that, in a way, they were right.
What she wanted was as good as the moon. It was
unattainable, and that drove her to despair.
So I understand why you left us. You had to
attain what you did, or else despair like our
mother.

I understand, but that doesn't make it
better.

You should have explained. You should
have left the right way. If you had, maybe I
wouldn't have believed that I could never be
both happy and a good daughter and sister.
You made me believe I had to choose. Because
you chose to be happy, and your happiness
hurt us.

I am sorry I punched you, but I am not
sorry to have left you behind. I will always
love you, Craig, but I don't like you. I'm not
sure I ever will.

Now I know. And now I will not waste
another moment waiting for your next letter,
or hoping you will choose to see me. That is
over. <u>That Stella</u> is gone.

The <u>New Stella</u> paid a visit to the
University of Kansas today. She went on a road
trip with a wonderful person named Gayle. She
met with three professors of engineering—
one mechanical and two aerospace. <u>New Stella</u>
will get a college education, and with hard
work and luck, she will help design parts of
airplanes and perhaps a space shuttle or two.

<u>New Stella</u> will not abandon her family.
She will not forget them. She will study, and
she will learn more than she ever thought she
could possibly understand. Then she will come
home. On weekends she will visit a town that
is recovering but on the mend. On Sundays,
she will go to Ferrell's with her father and
sister. She will order a chocolate malt and
a Coney dog and a large order of tater tots,
and she and her family will sit in the station
wagon listening to the latest hits on 580 AM.

<u>New Stella</u> is finally paying a visit to
the Kansas Cosmosphere—a surprise stop

on our way home. (That's what Gayle called it, even though it wasn't really on the way.) There are artifacts here from Soviet and American space travel, including actual metal that's flown beyond the Earth's atmosphere. It is a strange sight to behold in a small city in Kansas, but I have seen much, much stranger things this summer.

New Stella woke up today and looked out her motel window at the blue sky, knowing that Voyager 1 was launched into space. It will visit the asteroid belt and Jupiter and Saturn, and it will fly far beyond. Perhaps when you and I are going gray, it will even pass into interstellar space. This mere composition of wires and metal that we humans made is flying out ahead of us, beyond our quarrels and wars and petty problems, into unexplored territory. Into the unknown. New Stella cannot wait to watch it all unfold.

New Stella does not need to hear from you again. She is writing someone else. Another Voyager, like herself—traveling on another trajectory, but with his own worthy mission.

This New Stella is

Your sister,
Stella Kay Mercer

ACKNOWLEDGMENTS

Thank you to Beth Phelan for being this novel's champion from the very first day I shared my cult obsession with you. Without your sage advice, *Unknowable* would've been called *August*-something-or-other, and thanks to you, I now know that was a mistake. Also, a heartfelt thank-you to the marvelous folks at both the Bent Agency and Gallt & Zacker.

Endless gratitude to my editor, Zareen Jaffery, for your enthusiasm and insight throughout the publication process. Thank you for rooting for Stella and Galliard and for guiding me through this great, (sometimes) unknowable process. Many thanks to both Mckisha Telfer and Alexa Pastor for your super-human assistance. Hugs to Aubrey Churchward for everything you did for my little ol' novels. SSDGM, girl. Thanks to Karen Sherman and Jenica Nasworthy for keeping me thoroughly situated in 1977 through their copyedits. All my thanks to Chloë Foglia for the beautiful cover design, to Carolina Rodriguez Fuenmayor for the breathtaking art, and to Danielle Davis for the magnificent lettering. You brought my vision to life!

I owe a massive debt of gratitude to the folks at the Tourette Association of America for providing resources as I wrote this book. I also heavily consulted the following works: *The World's Strongest Librarian* by Josh Hanagarne and *Front of the Class* by Brad Cohen with Lisa Wysocky. Many thanks to these authors for telling their stories. My sincerest thanks to Ellen Rozek, who provided me with invaluable insight and feedback as I portrayed Galliard's TS.

Thank you to my ever-awesome, ever-supportive friends. Mai, we may now be hundreds of miles apart, but I always look forward to our FaceTime book clubs for two. Thank you, Nicole, for cheering for this book at an early stage and making excellent use of the alien emoji. Destiny, I'm so glad we're authors-in-arms together. Katie, thank you for reading my stories and allowing me to be a part of yours. Shelly, thank you for lighting up my life with your Double Ginger Wonder.

Thank you, dear Alli, for all your love and support. You and I are soup snakes.

Thank you upon thank you to the amazing librarians, educators, and bloggers who have shared my books with others and who do unimaginably valuable work on a daily basis. Special thanks to the folks at YA Interrobang, to the talented Jenna Clare, and to the fabulous Jen at Pop! Goes the Reader.

My undying gratitude to Rod Serling and Carl Sagan for the many life-changing works they created. I wrote *The Great Unknowable End* with lots of sounds blasting in my eardrums, including the *Close Encounters of the Third Kind* soundtrack by John Williams and the songs of David Bowie, Stevie Wonder, Donna Summer, Fleetwood Mac, Elton John, and the Rolling Stones. Thanks for the tunes, you all. And thank you to Jenny Lewis for her album *The Voyager*, which served as a musical touchstone during my drafting process.

Thank you to my extended family for their ongoing love and support. Matt and Annie, thank you for being the best siblings, most epic hosts, and coolest people around. Mom and

Dad, thank you for never once placing a limit on my dreams. Also, thank you for being my ever-helpful '77 consultants.

And to you, dear reader—thank you for going on this journey with me.